Frank Delaney

Novelist, broadcaster and journalist Frank Delaney was born in Tipperary, Ireland. His non-fiction works embrace James Joyce, John Betjeman, Boswell and Johnson, the European Middle Ages and the Celtic civilizations. He has lived in Britain for twenty years, where he broadcasts frequently. *Pearl*, his seventh novel, features Nicholas Newman, who first appeared in the highly acclaimed *The Amethysts*.

PEARL

'A gripping story that links a terrible atrocity during the last war with organised football hooliganism and neo-Nazis today. The pace gathers to high-speed express . . . satisfyingly complex. Delaney scores with the reader to win a definite result.'

Irish Times

'Stylish Delaney has produced a wonderfully appealing book that deals with the devastation the loss of a loved one can wreak . . . perfectly judged. The inexorable rolling out of psychological discovery has a precision and power that echoes Delaney's beloved James Joyce. But Delaney's language is never opaque, and this is storytelling of a rare order.'   *Good Book Guide*

THE AMETHYSTS

'The fusillade of shocks, and the crescendo of menace and confusion are contrived brilliantly. Inescapably gripping and sinisterly erotic . . . the pace rarely flags. *The Amethysts* is taut, tense and full of threatening emotional power.'   *Daily Telegraph*

'Delaney effortlessly hooks the reader . . . This mix of John Fowles-cum-Ian McEwan turns flammable.'   *Guardian*

'A compelling novel written with pace, verve and imagination.'
Mail on Sunday

'A psychological thriller as harrowing as it is absorbing . . . powerful, almost poetic prose style . . . always intense, emotional and uninhibited. This novel may prove unforgettable.'

Sunday Telegraph

FRANK DELANEY

PEARL

HarperCollins*Publishers*

Apart from certain historical facts,
this novel is entirely a work of fiction.
The names, characters and incidents portrayed in it are
the work of the author's imagination. Any resemblance to
actual persons, living or dead, events or localities is
entirely coincidental.

HarperCollins*Publishers*
77-85 Fulham Palace Road,
Hammersmith, London W6 8JB

www.**fire**and**water**.com

This paperback edition 2000
1 3 5 7 9 8 6 4 2

First published in Great Britain by
HarperCollins*Publishers* 1999

ISBN 0 00 651324 7

Typeset in Meridien by
Palimpsest Book Production Limited, Polmont, Stirlingshire

Printed and bound in Great Britain by
Caledonian International Book Manufacturing Ltd, Glasgow

In memoriam
Duncan Edwards
1936–1958

The deep pain that is felt at the death of every friendly soul arises from the feeling that there is in every individual something which is inexpressible, peculiar to him alone, and is, therefore, absolutely and irretrievably lost.

Arthur Schopenhauer, 1851

1

When he was late for our lunch I knew I would never see him again. I knew it by the fear that caught my breath. Fear is a clever emotion: it knows whom to choose. It knows when, where and how to strike, and with what weapons.

Such as humiliation; I waited for him in a restaurant that reeks of power. People stared. One can't save face amid those ruthless tables.

No course of action helped. I looked thoughtfully into the distance. I pretended to write a note to myself. I used the menu as a shield, chose my starter and my main course. And chose them again. Meat, to fish, to meat – I changed my mind three times, something I loathe doing. And anyway, I thought, when it eventually comes to the actual moment of choice I shall have forgotten.

The wine list gave me some pleasure. I tried to recall the names of the châteaux in the upper Médoc, from the Pointe de Grave down to Pauillac. He would chuckle and argue for Margaux, and I for St-Estèphe. Yes, he probably will drink, it's Friday. But I never ordered the wine.

No notebook with me, no file, nothing to doodle on; left my writing case at the cloakroom.

A spicy tomato juice.

A glass of water.

And, to hell with it, a glass of champagne.

Now what? Eat alone? To be covered with confusion when he arrives? 'Oh, God! Antony, I'm so sorry, I've started.'

I never ordered food either.

The *maître* brought an *amuse-gueule*. I sent to the foyer for a newspaper. My breathing didn't settle: every so often I made little gasps – and then I felt the lurch spread to my stomach. Why was he late? Why was I frightened? Because he was late? Because Antony was never late? No, it was more than that, as I now know.

Dull newspaper; my daily check of the stock market showed nothing dramatic in any of my holdings since yesterday. Read the letters column, including one from another architect decrying 'the craze for cleaning our old public buildings'. He used the arguments of those who oppose the restoration of paintings: 'We are also, after all, the sum of what we accumulate.'

Indeed we are. In my life I have accumulated at least anxiety. But this was fear and it grew.

By choice, the office driver dropped me at the river entrance so that I could walk that pretty labyrinth of Savoy panels.

Antony is never late.

What's the traffic like?

Did he confirm?

Yes. He rang yesterday.

'My treat,' he cajoled.

'No, no,' I said. 'You paid last time.'

'Let me pay, Nicholas. I have good reason.'

'Antony, you always have good reason.'

'I truly have this time,' he said. 'Two reasons, in fact. There is a surprise I have for you. And I want a favour.'

I defied him and made the booking.

They gave me a table I had long desired, in a straight line from the door, on the far wall, with a full view of the room. I shall be able to see Antony the moment he arrives, the heavy, white hair, the quick but measured step of a man who knows he's old but feels young. He'll come in at the Strand entrance, the only street in Britain where traffic drives on the right-hand side. Those were my thoughts at ten minutes to one.

I liked our Savoy lunches; I always arrived early, no matter who was paying. This gave me a breather, time to come to terms with the room, time to check around in case I met someone I knew. Nobody today, only some uneasy two-somes, one grinding lunch meeting, some excited Japanese women, an American family complete with baseball caps on the children, and a nervous young politician with an elderly woman.

For Antony, our Fridays meant not hurrying afterwards. We talked and talked. He liked being a mentor and he shared his knowledge generously. On fine days we walked by the river afterwards, he taking my arm when feeling his age. He lamented again, and I teased him again, that he had never bought up those river-front properties from which – 'Before my eyes, Nicholas' – everybody else was making fortunes. At Waterloo Bridge we could see as far as my cone, cube and sphere on the City skyline. He called it 'Newman's Folly', and I laughed every time he said it.

Half past one. Antony put dependability first among all virtues. His place setting grew cold; the glass, the cutlery, the linen felt harder, hostile. My mood switched, regret, chagrin, annoyance – and then the clamp on my stomach reached for my bowels.

I owed much of my success, my status, to Antony. He persuaded me there was no conflict of interest in being both his architect and an investor in his developments. I made a lot of money from his brilliance and kindness.

Also, I felt educated by him and I knew he wanted me to think of him like that. He read more widely than I did, tried to get me to broaden my focus. I liked his frivolity too; every time I wore a new shirt or suit he demanded details.

Now I understand how he used his great urbanity and charm to deflect attention from himself. If I had ever thought about it I should have realized how superficially I knew him. I saw things less clearly then.

3

A quarter past two. I had fixed it beautifully; my next appointment fell due in an hour, at a quarter past three in a suite upstairs to meet a new client.

I tried to focus on that meeting, and failed. My mind wouldn't do it. It was the memories, I think, the sum of experiences – they told me that I knew something awful. I looked around me and watched the postures of those who move and those whom they shake, and my friend Antony Safft never came to lunch.

A concierge appeared and the *maître* pointed me out. At last – the explanation.

Wrong. The young concierge was carrying a package.

'Mr Newman?'

'Yes.'

I signed the courier documents for a long, small box, heavy. Puzzling, I opened it. Inside lay a brand-new, silver-coloured knife – with a note: 'For you'; a workman's knife, a Stanley.

Slightly angry, I said – to nobody – 'This isn't for me,' then checked all the paperwork; yes, clearly intended for me: 'Mr Nicholas Newman lunching with Mr Safft at the Savoy Grill. Table for two, one o'clock.'

I pushed the ratchet on the knife's spine and out slid the blade. Now Fear lay in my hand, cold and deadly as a little shark. I put the knife back in its box, paid my bill for water, tomato juice and champagne and left the Grill.

An hour to go until the upstairs appointment. Down at the river entrance, rain had begun, fine at first, then slanting fast, and I couldn't walk in that. The package in my hand felt heavy and sinister. I took out the knife and looked at it again; too hard to the touch, much colder than steel, a hardness and coldness that I know and dread.

My secretary, Lemon, said there had been no call cancelling lunch. She rang Antony Safft's office, then called me back to say he'd been travelling from home. I didn't have his home number with me.

In the river the tide was filling. As I stood and watched it I felt an undefined sadness. Craving some warmer emotion, I hurled the knife and its box into the brown waters. Rain stung my ears and stomach cramps forced me indoors. Later, as I washed my hands, I had the disturbing impression that my face in the mirror was a great distance away.

2

From his shaven black skull down to his famous toes, Johan Pearl, short and blocky, gleamed like a star should gleam.

'I'm afraid,' I said, 'you've met the one man in England who knows nothing about football. Not even on television. I mean I've seen glimpses . . .'

'What I am is a winger.' His handshake nearly broke my fingers.

'I probably just about know what a winger is.'

He laughed. 'What they say is I can run at a defender without looking at the ball.' He wore a white tee-shirt from Angelo Caroli's health club in Milan.

'The defender he sees me looking at his eyes, not at the ball. When he goes on looking at my eyes I have him. Then he backs away from me and I know I really have him. See? Defenders should never retreat. If they only knew. Every step they take backwards they widen my angle. See? All sportsmen have different eyesight to that which is normal people's. Some don't blink much, some have wide-wide vision. I have for me both.'

He strolled around the carpet as he talked, in a pair of baggy black sharkskin trousers and bare feet.

'They's only two kinds of defender, the ones who look at the ball or the ones who look at my legs. What'll I call you? Will I call you "Nicholas"? But you're English and we have only met.' Another large laugh.

The suite looked out on the river. My unease from lunch retreated. His warmth gave me back a little perspective. The garrulousness and laughter suggested nerves or at least

6

shyness. He spoke such good English – and in England we speak no Dutch. Now he said with surprise, 'You're alone?'

My turn to smile; 'Did you want to meet more than one architect?'

He looked puzzled but laughed it off.

'So, I want you to design for me what I will call for you "a Dutch farmhouse". Your secretary has a nice name, Lemon.'

I asked, 'Did she say to you, "That's my real name"? She says it to everyone.'

Small talk. He had provided tea and coffee.

'She speaks with a funny accent,' he said. 'See?'

'She's white Jamaican. Pronounces it "Jam-aiya-ka".'

He laughed. 'White? Oh, you don't say.' Johan Pearl laughed again. 'You some man.'

'Why?' I asked. Now I found myself quite short with him. He was, I thought, about to say something edgy. Had I been racist? I didn't think so. Lemon *is* white and Jamaicans mostly aren't. Pearl changed in mid-thought.

'You never asked me how I found you. They is a thousand architects in London. They is maybe five thousand architects in Britain. Why did I select you, Nicholas?'

'Where do your family come from?' I asked, staving off discomfort at his uninvited leap across the 'Nicholas' boundary. He also seemed about to pay me a compliment; I hoped he wouldn't.

My office forced me to take this job. You're all star-struck, I told them. I argued we don't need another residential project and we don't need something with absolutely no innovation. No use; and no point in palming it off on one of the others – the client had asked for me.

'Think positive,' they gibed. I admit I was truculent; that same morning another client had just told us he didn't want the four marble ramps we had flown like lovely geometry through his atrium – he wanted steps.

Hal Callaghan, who runs the practice for me, flooded a newspaper across my desk; 'Johan Pearl. Profile. By Henry Winter. Worth reading. Gets the guy right. You do know he's a superstar, don't you?'

Why does Brahms's violin concerto sound like 'Don't Cry For Me, Argentina'? Why, for that matter, does one of Mozart's horn concertos sound like Glenn Miller's 'American Patrol'? That's all the wrong way round. I've got a window in the Holborn Foundation that's a straight quote from the Gulbenkian Foundation in Lisbon that's a straight quote from King's College in Cambridge. Or is it? I looked at Johan Pearl. Something's the wrong way round here. I shouldn't be taking on this project.

'My great-grandfather's Dutch Guyanese. That's the black bit.'

'And the sporting gene?'

'I do not know. I could have been a chef,' Johan Pearl said. 'My father's an excellent cook.' Innocent young man. Cheerful. And bright as a button. He asked, 'Where do you stand on Le Corbusier?'

My amazement showed.

'You haven't done your research on me, have you?' he said. 'But why should you? I'm paying.'

I remembered, in that *Daily Telegraph* profile. 'Oh, yes, I have. Only footballer in the Premiership to have graduated from the Sorbonne. One of only two or three to have been to university.'

'We had a lecturer very keen on "Le Corb" he called him.'

'I never call him that.'

'You wrote a piece criticizing him, Nicholas.'

I said defensively, 'I didn't criticize his use of space.'

'Hey, man, not to trouble. Did you enjoy Cambridge, Nicholas?'

I laughed. '*Your* research. Not particularly. Since you ask.'

8

'What did you do at Cambridge?'

He was a merry young man. Unusually soft hands. Fitness glowed in his skin as if from some inner nucleus. An interesting vein of something else ran through him too, something over and above his quick responses. Something I couldn't pin yet.

I said, 'What you should know about me isn't about Cambridge. In case you wish to change your mind, I know nothing about football, as I told you.'

'It's an accident to me.' He waved his hand. 'I found out I was good at it. But I am good at all sport. My life as the footballer will be short, which is good, it is not what I wish.'

He sat cross-legged on the couch opposite me, completely self-assured.

'Is that a Calabrese watch?' I asked.

He laughed like a child. 'You know things, man.'

I said, 'I've always wanted one.'

He took it from his wrist. For one dreadful moment I thought he would insist I take it, as the Arabs do.

'Beautiful.'

'Isn't it?' he said. 'I think to afford it.'

'Why do you like it?'

'Because, look –'

He came to my side and pointed to the mechanism that seemed to float within the turquoise-tinted case. 'That's what I try to do, I try to move through the air, like I could run just above the top of the ground.' He skimmed the carpet with his hand. 'They pay me so much I should do it.'

'Does it spoil you?' I asked. 'All the money and the adulation.'

'Add-You-Lay-Shun.' He toyed with the distracting word, then answered my question. 'I read a lot. The others – they don't interest me.'

'What are footballers like?' I asked.

9

He grinned. 'I don't even ask myself that question – in case I answer it. Naw,' he said, divining my prejudice, 'there's plenty bright players, see?'

'My office is looping the loop about you.'

'I must give them autographs. Can I come in and meet them, Nicholas? I like seeing what other people do. Not all other people.'

His eyes spread wide apart and he seemed to have perfect skin, neither matt nor shiny; he never stopped smiling. All his being had a superb sheen of quality – his teeth, his feet, his biceps under the tee-shirt's short sleeves; and when he moved he seemed never to waste a movement – rather like the mechanism of the watch.

'I gather football's the new world power,' I said.

'Did you play sport?'

'Swam. Quite well. For my school. Not for my university.'

'I had a bad time last weekend, Nicholas,' he said. 'The boss told me out for laziness. Things he called me! Man!'

And more laughter.

My resistance to him fell a little. I looked at him indulgently, thinking how lovely he must have been to hug when he was a small boy. My resistance fell some more.

'And were you lazy?'

He curved thumb and forefinger into a tiny arc. 'A little. They pay me so much that a little lazy was probably a lot.'

Twin qualities merged in him – stillness and perpetual motion. I had often heard it said that great sportsmen seem to have unlimited time in their actions. When this young man made a gesture the shape of the movement remained in the air.

'Down to business,' I said. 'You're paying for this meeting.'

He asked the questions. I told him the rules of engagement – percentages, builders' penalties, planning applications.

10

'Try not to change your mind when we're actually building.'

I told him about scale models. 'Do you want one?'

He asked about schedule, materials, landscaping. Then he said to me rather shyly, as if fearing he might offend, 'This isn't, anyway, the most original job you ever had, is it?'

I laughed, a touch embarrassed, and made a palms-out gesture.

Then he smiled again. 'But I think you'll like it. You will see in my childhood house why I want another like it, see?'

I stayed longer than I intended. He told me of his life – the team journeys, the treatment room, the drudge of training, the thrill of scoring, the attentions of the media.

'I don't mind it too much. They is mostly kind to me. I don't play cards with them as much as I should.' The Dutchness in his accent grew more guttural the more he relaxed. 'The challenge is good, I like the winning. They all tell the fact that when I score I go and kick the ball in the net again, only very harder. And I like recovering from the defeats because the feeling to win is better the next time.'

'Do you ever get tired, I mean exhausted?'

'Not from football, it is the other things that does that, the exhausting. The advertising, I has all the cheese from Dutch television I can ever eat for ever. And the millions of photographs they all has to take.' His English also grew more careless with comfort. 'But it is so nice too, I am so lucky, that is what I say to the boys with bad tempers.'

'The others, your team-mates, are they bad-tempered?'

'Oh, man, they is like girls, some of them. See?' He pouted and he preened; I laughed.

He said he had no thought to his future because he didn't need to – he had already created enough wealth to support his entire lifetime.

'I has some property – a house on the Herengracht in Amsterdam, an embassy rents my flat here at Green Park,

11

I has a house on one of the Virgin Islands. Now I has this awful flat near the training ground. Yaah! But there are many things why I must not complain. Now it is time for you to drink, see?'

I still held his watch: it said half past five and I jumped to my feet.

'No, heavens. I've taken up your whole afternoon.'

'No troubles, it was for you.'

'Where are you playing next?'

'Man, you do know nothing about football. We playing in London, that's why I'm here. I have special permission to stay in this hotel last night, now I have to join the team hotel, yaah!' and he mimed strangling himself.

I gave him his watch back and confirmed the second half of the appointment – made for me by my eager colleagues. On Monday I was to meet Johan Pearl in Holland and see his family home.

3

No driver waited outside. I telephoned the office and I telephoned the car. No reply. Everyone gone home.

When the cat's away . . . There are times when I know just how important and wealthy I am, oh yeah?

The cab driver maintained silence, probably because of my mood. More likely because of his. Roadworks still closed Sloane Street and I walked from the corner. My lights switch on in all the rooms when I enter my hallway. On days like that I know why. My unease had returned.

Somebody answered his telephone, 'Yes.'

'Is, ah'm, Antony Safft there?'

'Who wants him?'

For some bizarre reason I refused to say. I replaced the receiver and sat down once more. The telephone rang and a voice said, 'You just called the number of Mr Saaaaafft.' He elongated the *a*.

I almost said, 'Safft, not Saaaaaaafft,' but in my astonishment said nothing, pressed the cradle and left the telephone off the hook. An hour later I rang again. The same voice said, 'Yes?'

It was an uneasy, unsettled evening; I cooked indifferently, got nothing done, forgot to put on any music. My mood moved between worry over Antony and anger at the delivery – clearly mistaken – of that Stanley knife. I decided to stroll a little before supper, and then I decided against it. I rang Antony once more, and now his phone rang and rang and rang.

Finally, I managed to dictate some meeting notes on Pearl

and his house, then prepared for bed, listening to some Thelonious Monk. The shower hurt my skin; I should have had a bath. I think I dreamed, but all I can remember is vagueness, the colour yellow and some unidentified animals running in the open.

Next morning, my driver, Sean, still didn't answer his mobile. I tried to reach Hal and he didn't answer either. At the garage where my car was being serviced they couldn't spare a driver to bring my car to me – but 'we're open all day.' I spilled coffee on my shoes and socks, had to change. My anguish about yesterday's aborted lunch nagged. I decided to drive from the garage to Antony's house in Hampstead.

It rained in the busy London streets, therefore no taxis; I waited half an hour. Time was when London on a Saturday enjoyed being empty, like Paris in August. With great reluctance I headed for Sloane Square Tube station; I hadn't used the Tube for years.

At the bottom of Sloane Street a hurricane of alarm roared into my mind. Directly behind me I heard the hard unison of marching boots. They slammed up close on my heels. I never look over my shoulder; I do now. The boots rang in step with me and never tried to overtake.

I should have known the marchers were ominous. Pedestrians coming towards me focused wary glances at those behind me.

When I stopped to buy a ticket the boots stopped too. I could hear the breathing, and some garish cackles. Their footsteps hammered hard after me down the stairs to the trains. I heard them next to me on the platform. When I stopped they stopped. People drifted away.

There was also an arrogance in my never looking back; it's not there any more. I boarded the train and heard no more footsteps.

Does everybody hate everybody else down here? Humans without contact, yet strangers' armpits inches away; that

14

intimacy makes it a circle of Hell. The London Underground punishes our reserve. Everything causes difficulty. Take the etiquette. What do you do when space becomes available all round, yet you still sit as you set out – in this case beside a burly old man, shoulder to shoulder? Is it rude to move to the empty row opposite? Deep in such thoughts, I came late to the frightened silence in the carriage.

By which time it was too late. My own eyes followed the other passengers' glances. Through the glass panel of the next carriage door leered a bunch of heads. They looked like those joke photographs taken in booths – several trying to get in the frame and some joker hanging upside down. But these faces were all glaring at me. I looked around. And I looked back. Yes, at me. No doubt of it.

I turned away again, looked straight across. Nobody sat opposite me, just the black wall whizzing by. In my peripheral vision I could see the taunting features. They were young men, shaven-headed, blubber-lipped, leering vilely and silently mouthing. One wore an Afro wig and a pair of joke eye-glasses.

I don't believe I carry the spoor of the victim. I've thought about it. It did happen in school; I was singled out for bullying (not for too long) but my work has always enjoyed notable critical success. Ask *Modern Architecture*. Ask the Prince's Trust. Ask *Vogue* or *Tatler* or *Harpers*. Their view of me reflects what I see too – I mean to live the life I have grown.

For example, here I am on my way to pick up my car from the garage where it's had its first service. This evening I shall, back in my apartment, decide whether to get a single theatre ticket and dine out afterwards. Alone. By choice. Or cook at home having chipped away at some drawing – perhaps a sketch for Pearl. An architect's profession, as I am known for saying every chance I get, is solving problems. I solve my problems by doing the next thing.

So, Nicholas – solve this one. Why should a bunch of thugs wearing football scarves single me out? I searched my conscience. No reason. I wish I knew the laws governing the word 'random'. To my horror and my surprise my urine began to slip from me onto my thighs; my body is a better forecaster of danger than my mind.

I looked back at them, directly this time. The eye contact seemed to drive them amok – violent teeth-baring, savage throat-cutting gestures in the soundless frame of the carriage window. In the film *Shoah*, Polish workers talked in the fields near Auschwitz. A half-articulate farmhand told how he made throat-cutting gestures to the wealthy, fur-coated trainloads of Jews who waved so gaily at them. 'We tried to warn them,' he said. I shuddered – and now shuddered again, as though keeping time with the train's halting movements.

Massive relief at the station – the faces vanished *en bloc*. One or two passengers glared at me. Not my fault. Everyone else exhaled and the metallic voice clattered its dead-slow warning, 'MIND. THE-GAP.' The doors began to hiss closed. I checked the angry window again. My eyes bathed in the relief of its emptiness.

But – 'EH-HAY!' roared a voice in my face.

Jesus!

They piled to where I sat. All my continence faltered. They had waited to give the impression they had left the train.

Their leader knelt down and placed his elbows on my knees. His Afro wig tilted and his mock-spectacles mask shone.

Straight to my eyes he said, 'Well, fuck me! Eh?'

I looked at him. My head fought my fear. 'Keep neutral,' the streetfighters say. I looked away – difficult to do if someone's breathing up your nose.

His accent had a wild London chirp to it. 'Yeah. Fuck me.'

Again I looked at him, and again I looked away. Who knows what to do in such fright?

He said, 'I'm speakin' to you. Hey!'

I looked back at his face and said, 'Me?'

I tried for ordinariness and some vague air of puzzlement.

He laughed and led the others in chorus.

'Me?' they mimicked. 'Meeeeeeeeeeeee-eeeeee? Ooooh?!'

Their leader put up a hand and stroked the side of my cheek. 'Shaved, did we? Nice. Nice one. Goin' anywhere nice?' Still focusing at me, he called, 'Fellas, come and look at 'im, i'n'e nice?'

They squatted closer and stared at me. I drew back; what else could I do? They poked me like tribesmen. One stroked my knee and leg. Another tapped the other knee, looking for reflexes.

'Noddy, you shoulda brought your little 'ammer, doctors have little 'ammers for doin' that, don' they?' said Afro to him. I felt he exaggerated his accent.

Then they subsided and, still looking unblinkingly at me, began to hum, a drawn-out and ghastly sound, caricaturing the noise one makes at something sweet.

'Mmmmmmmmmmmmmmmmmmmmmmmmmmmmmmm!'

Afro sat a little straighter. He switched from taunting to command.

'Juicy! Name yer trade.'

Juicy had a bloodshot eye. A ridge of fat on his neck wobbled with his mirth.

'Cutter and finisher!' – and all laughed.

'By royal fucking appointment.' This was Juicy speaking. 'Cutter and finisher. That's me. Mister fucking Cutter and Mister fucking Finisher.' He wore a tee-shirt with a furious bulldog cartoon.

Retching rose at the back of my throat. Sweat gathered in my hair. And all I could do was sit still.

'Nice bit of cloth,' hailed Afro. I was wearing a black, double-breasted Hector Janolo jacket with a slightly open weave.

'Juicy, nice bit of stuff, eh?'

Afro's girlish fingers rubbed my lapel hard, as if he'd found glue there. Like a nuzzling dog he tilted his head and rubbed his Afro wig into my face; it smelt of musty beer; I wanted to kill him.

Now Afro leaned back and gestured to Juicy, 'Get his tits out for the lads.'

The bulldog tee-shirt wrinkled as Juicy produced a Stanley knife. My mind went red. Stanley knife. But I couldn't address the connection. Think of the river. Knife in the water. Where's Antony? Antony's a big football fan. My thoughts had no sequence. Like a broken necklace. Beads all over the floor.

Juicy pushed forward the ratcheted button and the blade slid out like a shining fang. He leaned over and simply cut away my right-hand lapel down to the waist. I watched. That is the extraordinary thing about being in the grip of dread – you watch it happen to you.

'Yeh,' Juicy said, 'fucking nice bit of stuff.' And elaborately wiped his nostrils on the hacked cloth.

Bubbles gurgled somewhere between my throat and my nose. I looked around for help. Nobody had pressed the alarm signal. Because it would stop the train. Could I sit there and take this? Irony. Is irony a weapon? I wanted to say, This won't bring out the best in me. Practicality intervened: what will he cut next? Juicy fingered my ear. Van Gogh. Oh, shit. And after my ear? The other ear? Van Gogh walks into a bar. Barman says would you like a drink. Van Gogh says I've got one 'ere. Jesus. Might as well die. Condensation from my own breath fogged my spectacles. Can't wear contacts, my eyeballs too close to eyelids. Inside I began to weep with fear. Will my lip tremble? Stiff upper lip.

18

Beseechingly, I looked around once more. Everybody turned away. They stared straight ahead of them. Some people had risen to their feet, anticipating the next station. I had the irrelevant thought, Bet it won't be the stop they actually planned to get off at . . . They swayed with the train.

I half-rose to my feet. 'Look here, I can't put up with –'

'Now-now!' called the leader in friendly indignation.

Without rising from his squat, he pushed me in the stomach with a hand as large as a shovel and I was forced back onto the seat. He squatted closer; now he was between my knees where only a lover goes.

'Oi,' he said to the others, and on their hunkers they crowded ever closer to him. I could feel cold wind in my nostrils. All six crouched there in the narrow space between the rows of seats.

Then they fell silent and this was the most terrifying moment of all. It hit everybody. The young woman handling her child and its awkward, folded pushchair looked around because she felt the silence on her back. Two schoolboys turned firmly but fearfully away and huddled together. A lanky man stared and never thought of doing a thing. Juicy cut the second lapel, and then cut through the cloth into the inside breast pocket, from which he removed my wallet and handed it to Afro. We travelled and travelled.

The old Indian gentleman beside me attempted to leave his seat, but Afro wagged a warning finger at him and the man sat back.

'You are disgraceful,' the old man said. 'You are a disgrace.'

I gasped. Not for myself. Never gasped for myself. Gasped for the man. Survival rule: with dangerous animals – never draw attention to yourself. Something had to happen. The gang looked at each other and smiled and slowly they turned to look at the man. Extra light flooded the carriages – the

19

approach to a station. Every station in the London Underground is built on a little hill so the trains can slow down up the slope as they arrive and get a little start down the slope as they leave.

Did any other useless information come into my head at that moment? I don't know because Afro commanded, 'Juicy! Queen and country.'

Fear moves at the speed of light, not sound. In one movement Juicy reached across my face, grabbed the old man's hair and jerked his face towards me. With his Stanley knife he drew a hard and violent line down the centre of the old man's nose. When the blade reached the soft part, it went deeper until the nose was opened out to the nostrils.

Somebody screamed. It wasn't me. And it wasn't the old gentleman. He sat there with blood spurting everywhere, on his white shirt, on his grey anorak, on his hands, on me, my face, the collar of my white buttondown, on my shoes, where I saw the blood drop like berries. Juicy pried apart the split skin; the nose was spatchcocked. The train stopped. They had cut him in, I should think, three seconds.

'Right,' said Afro to me. 'Out.'

In all this time I never truly saw Afro's eyes; the Perspex of the joke eyeglasses distorted them.

I rose – out of terror but there was a time when I would have tried to persuade myself that I did so from a wish to keep further violence from the old Indian man. My thighs were warm and wet. Over my shoulder I saw the other passengers begin attending to the blood.

The ghastly phalanx walked me fast from the train. They surrounded me and made it look, laughing and joking, as though we were a bunch of friends travelling together. On the crowded platform they kept close to me and we brushed people aside with our speed.

At the escalator, one of the thugs, Noddy, stood directly in front of me; another, Juicy, immediately behind; he made

20

sure his body leaned against mine. Noddy faced backwards at me and breathed into my eyes. Once, he absent-mindedly wagged his lager can against my head with a little clang. All the gang looked at me all of the time. One, I don't know which, took a soft part of my thigh's flesh between his thumb and forefinger and pinched. That, as every schoolboy knows, is the sorest pinch in the world.

Outside the station we joined a football crowd, scant at this stage because there must have been some hours to go before kick-off. Marching like soldiers, my escort sidestepped this relaxed mainstream and took me down a side street.

Fifty yards on, 'Stand there,' said Afro, patting the low brick wall of somebody's garden.

I obeyed and they all stood back.

'Jemima!' called the leader. 'Name yer trade!'

'I'm bleedin' David Bailey,' said the thinnest, tallest and most dangerous-looking.

'Hey, Ringo,' said Noddy to Afro, and he pointed down, and I knew they had seen I had wet myself. The sun shone. I had the thought, It'll dry my trousers.

'Aw, poor baby,' called Juicy.

'He needs some attention,' said Jemima. 'Shine him up.'

Afro/Ringo stepped forward and began to pat my hair into place. He took off my spectacles; 'Cutler and Gross,' he read from the tab. 'Fucking gross I call it.' He spat on the lenses, polished his scarf across them, then put them back on my nose. I began to fear they would hear me whimpering. No chance to run – I had checked that. And nobody, not one person, not man, woman nor child, passed by.

'All yours, Jemima,' and Afro/Ringo stepped back.

Jemima stood in front of me, gazing at every part of my face and head. I cast my eyes down, not knowing what dreadfulness was about to follow. Should I faint? Feign a faint? Feint a faint? Why does the mind play word-games at such terrible moments? Jemima reached in his pocket, and fumbled for long moments. Then he took out one of those small disposable cameras and began to click at me from various angles and distances. Into each ear. Up my nose. An inch from my eyes. He finished the last frame and leaned forward and kissed me on the mouth, tried to put his tongue between my lips. It occurred to me to bite his tongue.

'Know what I think? I think he's a virgin,' said Jemima, stepping back, and then, stepping forward again, he fondled my testicles. At which I had two fears – that he would squeeze savagely, or that my tissues would respond involuntarily. Instead he gave a kind of appreciative pat, as a whore does when she's got her money.

They lined up in front of me, one foot away. Each looked at me in silence. No one else saw them and me.

A large white van swung around the corner. Afro/Ringo hit me hard in the stomach. The six sprinted to the van, leapt inside and it drove away.

I doubled up, folded back against the wall – Oonnhhh! – Jesus Christ! Then I leaned over the wall and was violently sick and a window opened somewhere and a voice cried, 'Get out of it! Scum!'

On the streets no cab. I was dazed. Two policemen came over and I said, 'I need to get home. I've had my wallet taken.'

They looked at me suspiciously and one asked, 'Where's home?'

I said, 'Chelsea. Knightsbridge sort of.'

A cab came and I took it and they made no effort to stop me.

'Wooo! Late night, mate?!' hooted the driver. 'Been in the wars? Hope you've got an understanding at home!'

I realized what he meant – my jacket front hung like a remnant. I leaned back and closed my eyes and let out some tears.

The streets jarred my back. My watch was gone; I'd forgotten they'd taken it. They never touched the cash in my trouser pocket.

My apartment is Fort Knox. I slammed the door behind me – a French, triple-bar locking system, I discovered them for a Gulf client last year and got some for myself. Fearing collapse, I made it to the bathroom and heaved and heaved, then reached for the phone above the bath – nineninenine, I think I pressed it twice.

4

No idea what to do now. Do I change? Or will they need the sight of me as evidence? Take photographs? DNA? On my jacket? The crotch of my trousers where he put his hand? I doubt the police will take such interest.

My head spins. Shall I wash? No. Touch nothing. Isn't that what they say? Must ring Antony again. Must calm down first. I have to be in Holland on Monday. Do I need a doctor? Look in the bathroom mirror, the entire room such a contrast to the vileness from which I have come. Mahogany. Chrome. Glass. Tile. Stainless steel.

My door buzzer screamed. That was quick. A uniformed constable in a van. He came in, looking at me and asking, 'You all right, sir?'

'I don't know.'

'D'you need a doctor?'

'I've just been mugged on the Tube.'

'D'you know where, sir?'

'I was on the Underground. No landmarks.' My face wouldn't stop sweating. Heroics I might have tried coursed through my mind.

He turned away and began to speak into his lapel walkie-talkie. The door buzzer screamed again – two detectives.

Said to me, 'We tried to ring you, sir.'

Said, 'We needed to let you know it was us.'

Said, 'But your line was engaged.'

They must have been well trained – I felt guilty already.

'I know. I left the phone off the hook.'

'Shouldn't do that, sir, not if we're trying to help you.'

They wore almost identical, double-breasted suits of – what else – gunmetal grey. The junior one strolled around the room, picking up this, looking at that. His partner stood in the doorway of the kitchen as I made them all coffee.

'No rush, sir, you've had a shock. Take it easy.' The uniformed man stood kindly in front of me, inspecting my shattered jacket. 'Is this what they did to you, sir?'

My apartment is full of police, screamed my mind.

'I didn't change my clothes. I mean, I wanted to, but I thought you might need to see –' I believed all three were looking at my stained trouser legs. 'It's just that – well, I mean – one doesn't know what to do. So I did nothing.'

The first detective said, 'That shows presence of mind, sir.'

The younger one gave crassness new strength.

'I suppose you saw the reports of that case recently, sir? That gang which targeted country houses. Which was successfully caught, sir. D'you think they know where you live?'

Squawk-box: the uniformed man identified himself and I could hear – everyone stopped talking – the news coming over of an incident with a passenger on the Northern Line and of a man being attacked with a knife, ambulance called.

'Were you injured, sir?'

'No, not me, another passenger, they cut his face open. They've got my wallet.'

Taking out a folder, the uniformed policeman said, 'I'd better take some details, sir. Shouldn't you sit down, sir?'

The older detective offered, 'We can help – with credit cards and that. Make sure you check your locking systems, sir.'

'Name, sir, if you would, and the full address, and your date of birth.' The uniformed one had a pad.

When adrenaline departs, things blur.

'Look,' I said. 'You'll have to tell me your names again. The shock. I didn't hear you properly.'

Now my hands had begun to shake but at least I didn't spill the coffee. Hopeless. I answered all questions.

'This you?' said the younger one, holding up a photograph of me with the Prince of Wales outside the new Allied building. 'Yeah, it is you.' He looked impressed.

The younger said, as if with a new thought, 'But if it was football scum, I mean, that'll go 'bove our heads.'

I gave them a full description, from the first footsteps on Sloane Street.

'Blue-and-white. Oh, yes. Without question. Blue-and-white scarves.'

This made them all look one to the other.

On several occasions I thought my voice would crack and begin to sound like the little black squawk-box, which kept speaking.

When I had finished my say to the man in uniform, the older detective said, 'I think it's best, sir, if you come in and we'll go through your details.'

'When?'

'When's your car coming back?'

'Oh, my god, my car! Will you excuse me?'

I rang the garage, got a sympathetic man, told my story.

'He says, within an hour.'

I returned to my chair. I discovered this about myself before – a compulsion to tell everything to a policeman.

'What d'you drive then?' asked the younger. 'Roller? Jag?'

'I have a Saab,' I said.

'Mm. Good design and that.' He was evidently the one who knew about cars.

I asked them all, 'I'm going to be sitting here terrified. What do I do if they're there when I go out? I mean – will I be able to go out? I mean – safe?'

I thought, Ah. So I am an hysteric, after all. Then I thought, No, but I sound hysterical.

'Given the football element,' said the older one slowly – I liked him; he had an intelligent face – 'you're probably okay. It's most likely random. Bad luck sort of thing.'

'Whooooo! You'll be lucky!' squirted the younger one. 'They've got your address.'

The uniformed man said, 'I'll mention the risk, sir, get a few extra drives past.'

I looked at the bloodstains on my shoes, at the flitters of my jacket.

'Yeah, keep them all,' said the detectives. 'Bring them in with you.'

'Why don't you take them?' I wanted to rid myself of the day's smear.

'Whoo, no, no, can't do that, might not be on the case,' said the second.

They all left together.

At the door I asked, 'Can somebody possibly ring me? About making a statement?'

The younger one said to the older detective, 'Whoo-ooo, no way, José,' and to me, 'It don't work like that.'

'Sorry, sir,' the older one said. 'I'm sure something can be arranged. Get some sleep, I should advise.'

For a long time I sat in silence, numb and dumbfounded. The garage man came, the managing director himself.

'Mr Newman. I'm so sorry. I do hope you're all right.'

He actually patted me on the shoulder – probably worried that I'd sue him.

When he left I continued to sit in my silence. Eventually I undressed, put all my outer clothes carefully in a plastic bag as the police suggested and had a long, long bath.

In the bath I recollected my wallet's contents. Only one credit card gone. Using Directory Enquiries I telephoned from the bath. The card emergency line checked and so far nobody had attempted anything. Good. I never carry

27

more than one at a time unless I'm going abroad, so no other problem.

What else did they get? Mobile phone company list of handy numbers. My Harvey Nichols card. Rang them too, no problem so far, that card also cancelled. British Airways Executive Club card – useless anyway, unless I fly three hundred and seventy-five thousand miles a month with BA, Tuesdays only and provided it's raining. Loyalty, indeed. Cancel it.

'Need a new one, sir?' asked BA.

'Don't bother.'

Good to have some target to lash out at. Some relief arose: my wallet didn't have my address. I rang again each of the companies I had alerted and told them on no account to give any information to anyone.

The violence began to play in my head like some upfront film. A self-disgust surfaced when I found myself aroused at the recall of their aggression. Then I fell unaccountably asleep.

5

The cold awakened me, the cold of the bath water on my shoulders. In theory, could I have drowned? Well, I told myself, I didn't. I found my warmest dressing gown and turned up the central heating.

The only food I had that night was toast. Comfort food. No television. Why? Because I might see some violence in some drama or film. And, Saturday night, bound to be football. Perhaps even the game those thugs attended.

Two hours later I took another bath. Called nobody. Once I kept a string of girlfriends. Some were the wives of friends; all clandestine, of course, and none knew about any other. Then I jettisoned them all, merely stopped calling. I thought for a wistful moment if I could have called one of them now . . .

Shall I call Elizabeth? No. She's been getting tiresome. And anyway I've arranged to see her next week on my way back from Holland. Since Elizabeth retired from the practice we seem to see more of each other.

Mystery of life. Why is it the case that, if the original bath is not well run, that is, drawn to the right proportions of water temperature, the adding-in of all the hot or cold water in the world will not work? Discuss.

Must remember Elizabeth's birthday. She won't say which one.

Mogadon. Melatonin. Whatever. All useless. I never take them any more. Either I sleep or I don't. I think she's seventy-five. *Who's Who* doesn't give a date.

I didn't sleep, or, rather, I did and I didn't, so I rose at seven and thought I might as well go half a day early to Holland, feel safer there.

Careful packing helps me to keep my life in order. I have three sizes of overnight bag; I chose the middle one; hung an extra jacket in the car. Bright morning and, thank God, nobody outside the flat – except a police car parked rather obviously at the end of the street. The police never rang me last night. Yet I told the detectives I was going to Holland to see a client.

My ignorance of football fazed them.

'Whose ground was it, sir? I mean, d'you know what fixture it was?'

'Fixture?' To me a fixture is a detail on a specification. Fixtures and fittings. At the office they talk football all the time. Football, football. In the car I leant my head against the glass of the window. It cooled me and brought the outside world into focus.

What am I? When my morale is assaulted I try to measure myself. Not that I do it successfully – but at least, as I tell myself, I do it. Not terrifically well, but better than most of the people I know. They all live unexamined lives. I know they envy me; they say it to me. What they see is a man growing wealthier all the time and with no family responsibilities. They chirp – 'Name in the lists again, Nicholas, I see?' Most Eligible This. One of the Richest That. Among the Influential Other.

What can I say? I smile. It's not like that inside me.

Along the Brompton Road I saw in my rearview mirror a white car some distance behind me. Still there when I climbed onto the M4. Will it still be there when I hit the M25 past Heathrow? Am I getting paranoid? I settled back and endeavoured to think calmly about myself. But I kept my eye on all three mirrors.

So long as I work every day – I survive. So long as I draw every day, or look at a drawing every day. So long as I do, I can afford the rest. I can afford the solitude. I can afford the raiding threat of that sudden 'alone' feeling. I can afford the boredom, getting bogged down in the mundane – services, infrastructures, regulations, planning permissions. They help define my inner life as well as my outer; I use them as headlines and benchmarks.

Services? I employ a range of services – handmade shoes to food supply to specifics of hairdressing to cleaning. The white car's still there. If I slow down a little?

My infrastructure – car, flat, communications – has the shape I want. Regulations, local ordinances? I live from one law to the next; private legislation; prohibitions: never drink alone, no sexual relationship now for some time, never get drunk in front of someone else, no nostril stuff, no white powders, tablets, nothing, never did. Okay, so I'm uptight.

The white car disappeared. Or did it follow me? Or take another route to get ahead of me? Planning permissions? I know exactly what I shall be doing and exactly where I shall be one calendar year ahead. Always. If I kept a diary I might call it *The Anals of Nicholas Newman*. But so long as I know I'm anal.

On the M25 another white car overtook me, swung in ahead. Following me from in front? CALM DOWN, calm down. My hand touched my nose. That poor Indian gentleman. Or Pakistani. He was in his late sixties perhaps, with quiet dignity.

Sunlight gleamed in the white air of Folkestone. The Chunnel was packed. In line behind me waiting to embark sat three white cars. Ridiculous. Calm down.

Those high lands north of Calais always feel open and welcoming. I saw a television programme once in which three historians were asked for their version of Dunkirk. One, learned in military strategy, saw it as a well-managed military retreat. One, a socialist, saw it as the private soldier providing war's fodder – again. And the most political of the three saw it as Hitler's lost opportunity. Adolf was going to make Oxford his capital.

That's when I thought, Revenge, that's what I need, revenge. If those thugs are caught and arrested I'll ask the police for a few minutes alone with the one who cut my jacket, or the one who took photographs of me, or the leader with his Afro. Or. Or. Which one? Any of them will do.

The car telephone rang. Answer the bloody phone. They never do it in suspense movies, always let it ring for several rings.

'Are you Nicholas Newman?' asked a man with a heavy nasal breath.

'Yep.'

Clunk. The caller replaced his receiver. Oh, Jesus.

I'm in Belgium. South-west of Ostend a little, coast road, heading for Bruges and the Dutch border. The telephone rings again and this time I snatch it, the element of surprise. Same voice, same breathing.

'Oh, Mr Newman, this is Battersea police station.'

'Did you ring a moment ago?'

'Yes, sir. This must be a mobile number, is it?'

'I'm abroad actually.'

'Yes, sir. Somebody said you're going into Holland?'

'Into' Holland? Nice touch, the 'into'.

'Yes. Place called Noordwijk aan Zee. North of the Hague.' There I go again, telling a policeman everything. 'Via Antwerp.'

'Yes. When you back, sir?'

'Does someone need to see me?'

'Yes, sir, perhaps. Just to tell you, sir, we may need your help. That gentleman on the Tube, sir, he died last night, his heart gave out.' He paused. 'Bad luck it all is, sir, but you're suffering no damage?'

I winced. 'Shock.' My nose hummed.

'Yes, sir, you've got to be careful.'

'I think I'm back in London Thursday morning.'

He sucked hard. 'No sooner?'

'I will be back in England, but I have a site visit on Wednesday. In Wiltshire. I'm losing you,' I said. 'Must be a dodgy reception area.'

'Can you hear me now, sir? Haaaa-lo? Haaaa-lo . . . ?'

I lost him. The beep-beep-beep of the mobile cut us off.

Spatchcocked nose. The new dead. A depressed friend of mine once described how he drives through San Francisco betting with himself how long he dare keep his eyes closed behind the wheel. Shall I try it now? Dead. His blood on my shoes. Not on my hands. Pull yourself together, Nicholas. The poor man. The poor, poor man.

Sparkling afternoon. I want to kill them. Stamp on their shaven heads. Reef their skin with knives. I hurt my gums grinding my teeth. Signs for The Hague and then Noordwijk. I am alone. I drive alone. The oil-painting landscapes, these immaculate roads with their cycle lanes and the scrubbed Dutch families out now for their Sunday spin, they will heal me, these pleasant sights, and soon the sand dunes shine in the October sunlight.

I stopped at a holiday car park, climbed the wooden steps to the dunes and gazed out at the North Sea. People lay sunbathing, some naked; the landmass of the continent must keep Holland warm. I walked to the sea. On the sand at my left sat a large girl with big peasant nipples. She watched me walk towards her across the sands and she raised her arms to fix her hair.

The sea spreads before me. I wish it would offer me a metaphor or image for my life. Perhaps it does. No, that's too fanciful, calm on top etc. Rubbish, Nicholas. My life has been largely a life of control and determination – and emotional solitude.

From the top of the dunes I can see the writing on the roof tiles of the hotel where I am to stay – De Witte Raaf. Johan Pearl will meet me tomorrow in that hotel: 'You will call it the White Raven,' he said. The sea sparkles and my mood swings between the peace of that light and the troubles I am seeing. Antony Safft didn't answer his phone. A man died on the Tube.

I checked in and slept until six o'clock, went for a long walk in the dunes paths until seven. For half an hour I tried to telephone all the associates of Antony Safft's I knew, but got only answering machines and left no messages. If I'd been able to contact anybody I'd have felt foolish. Shall I ring Antony's number again? I shirked it.

At eight I had dinner, found a wonderful hock to drink with North Sea salmon-trout and slept the sleep of the drunken – or the shocked.

6

Monday morning: I started ringing the office early but, cat's still away, nobody in the office until nine, ten o'clock Dutch time. I told Hal Callaghan about the Tube.

'But keep it quiet.'

'Bastards! I mean, they're not supporters, Chief, not of the game that I love. How was the Black Pearl?'

'I've done a report. Has Antony Safft rung?'

'No.'

'He never showed on Friday.'

Hal clucked his tongue. 'Yeah, Lemon said. I think I'll ask. Call you back?' My apprehension had spread.

'Use the mobile. I want to see if it works here.'

A few minutes later Hal rang and said, 'Chief – it's bizarre. Rang his office. Got an evasive answer. Some woman I'd never spoken to before.'

We both paused to consider this.

Hal said, 'Could be anyone, I s'pose. But that office, I mean, he runs it like a machine. You okay, Chief?'

I muttered some answer.

For the next two hours I worked in my room; interiors for the Duchess Group refurb. Hal always calls me 'Chief'. Awkward, that distance between us. I don't like 'Boss' and he's not comfortable with 'Nicholas', although all the others are. Hal always gives me too much information, too quick to tell me a problem. He has no power over me. So why do I always get the feeling he is trying to acquire some?

At half past twelve I went and sat by the sun-lounge windows to wait for Pearl. Ten minutes later the red Z3 snorted down the sandy avenue. Word had got out. Or perhaps superstars radiate light beams. Two boys sought autographs from him as he walked from the car park. As did the young hall porter. A receptionist pranced up and asked for a kiss.

I watched him. Equable with everyone. Impossible not to notice his physical poise. He greeted me as though he loved me. Two weeks ago I had never heard of him. He didn't get that jacket for less than two thousand pounds.

'Was your journey good? You have rested? First, lunch, then the house? So nice to see you, Nicholas.' Sincere enthusiasm, and we shook hands a second time.

Shock is like toothache. It recurs. Apprehension, not what I wanted to feel, came at me like a ghost. In the split of a second I saw the blood of my past life flowing down the walls of the foyer. I could cut their throats. Feel the spurt. I could hammer their shaven heads blue. Now stoppit, Nicholas, stop IT!

Pearl considered the tables on the terrace.

'It's warm enough to eat out.'

'Not for me,' I said. 'I'm rather cold-blooded.'

If only. Then shock wouldn't affect me. Nor absent friends. I looked around again. Were I only having lunch, I wished, with someone I could tell about the appalling events on the Tube. Or my worry about Antony. The dining room panels were genuine ash, not veneer. Antony's face suddenly filled my eyes like an apparition. Pearl's voice sounded distant. I shook myself.

'I hope you do not expect too much *haute cuisine*, Nicholas. This is only a seaside resort. Have you been to this hotel in Los Angeles they're all talking about, the Bellagio?'

'You mean Las Vegas. I know one of the architects,' I replied. 'I'm going over soon. But have you been to the original Bellagio? On Lake Como?'

'Should I?'

'You might hear a soprano rehearsing on her balcony,' I said. 'The divas from Milan, they all stay there. No, thank you, I don't drink if I'm driving.'

'Is your room comfortable?'

'Yes. Yes, thank you.'

I looked more closely. Again I was surprised by his elegance. I tried to stop my hand from shaking.

'You've had a busy time,' I ventured, nodding towards the contusion above his left eye. Difficult to see against the black skin.

'A clash in the air.' He smiled. 'Marcel Desailly, he has a hard head. But he is nice.'

'Have you made friends?' I asked. 'Among your colleagues, I mean? In England?'

'Yes and no. I need to settle down. The Italians at Chelsea, they're fun. I like Roberto di Matteo. He has the best English.'

'And do they all want to bring their houses with them?' I asked.

This gave me a comfortable way into the topic of business.

He laughed, taking the point pleasantly. 'I need a house. I need this house. Not this yaah! neo-apartment. You will see why, Nicholas, oh, yes, you will see why. I am going to capture you.'

'Do you mean "captivate"?' I asked, and he laughed again. I felt he bridled a little at my implication that he lacked originality. 'You didn't mention a wife. In domestic architecture I find . . .'

He cut across. 'Girlfriend. Nicola. She is English. But she – she – she is not interested in houses . . .'

'You talked to me of your "vision". For the house, I mean. How would you sum up your need?'

'I like feeling very secure.'

He began to tell me of growing up in the farmsteads inland.

'We had vegetable and flower contracts to supply hotels and grocers. Mainly Haarlem. Leiden, the university. One or two in Amsterdam. But that was sometime difficult. My father felt his produce was never good enough for the bigger cities and this was hard for him because his grandfather once supplied all Amsterdam. Until the war. But then it was a different place.' For a moment Pearl grew awkward, and then swung out of it. 'We did well. That is true. We have a sea-house near here in Scheveningen. And the farm has grown, we have bought more land and my brothers now deliver to hotels in Amsterdam. We even have a contract for the diplomats in The Hague.' He pronounced it 'Haag' and his Dutch accent had begun to roll.

'It is an unusual background, yours,' I said.

He smiled. 'Not to me, of course.' Food arrived. 'And my house?' he asked. 'How is it?'

I said, 'Seeing the site on my way back. I've got all the maps. Want to see them? The survey's up and running.'

'How long will it all take, Nicholas?'

'On the fast track you asked for – that you're paying for – about four months. It's mostly wood. Which helps.'

'That is what your friend at your office, Hal, is his name? He said four months. Also I liked him, he was very friendly.'

'Big fan of yours.'

'You must come and see me play. Let us see if we can make a fan of you. See?'

Only twenty-three? Surely not.

'What is it you like?' I asked him. 'I mean, in life?' One of those meaningless but sometimes useful questions to a client – it can start an idea.

'Friends,' he said. 'I want a very comfortable place so that I can have my friends around me.'

Lunch came to somewhere between adequate and quite

good: excellent vegetables. We generated a pleasant atmosphere – although we did have a disturbance, which gave me pause.

His telephone rang and he apologized as he answered. He listened and then spoke. 'No. I cannot, man. I cannot.'

With a flinch he put the phone away, trying to fight off anger, or was it distress?

'A journalist,' he said.

Do the stars shiver when a journalist rings? Perhaps. It certainly took him a moment or two to compose himself.

'Am I your first black client?' was his next question.

'Why do you ask that?'

'Hey, no worries, Nicholas. I thought maybe you don't do –'

'Would I be taking you on?'

My coldness rose to my face, the blush of ice I know so well.

'Oh, dunno, footballer, prestige, all that. You know – the house's gonna be in the papers, and on television, big publicity anyway. Have you many black people in your office?'

I hesitated. 'It isn't like that –'

Normally I would have flinched but I steeled myself.

'Do you like me?' he asked, his big eyes on me.

'I've only just met you,' I said formally. 'Nobody asks people whether they like them.'

Has this young man no boundaries?

'Why not? Is a perfectly okay question, see?'

'I'm English.'

'You got two eyes. You got two balls. You're alive.'

I bristled further. 'Do people ever ask you whether you like them?'

'No. People's too uptight, Nicholas. But if they did I'd tell them.'

He patted my arm and his warmth thawed me. I turned

our thoughts back to the business in hand; lunch came to a relaxed end.

When I begin any residential project my first question to myself addresses the pitch of the roof. Who was the actor who famously studied all roles by the kind of shoes the character wears? Alec Guinness? Was it Ralph Richardson? It may even be Harrison Ford. It's a cliché now. For me the pitch of the roof does it. Driving through foreign countries absorbs me. A day's motoring from Calais to the Midi brings me through six different roof pitches. Start with the needle-sharp of the north coast, to the fullness of Picardy, ever softening into the timbers of Normandy, graduating downwards to the eventual and gentle full-Romans of Provence. As for a Dutch barn-house? 'High and square' were my first thoughts.

My heart ambushed me when I saw Pearl's family home. Huge, that was my first reaction; this was a house fifty feet tall, white-clapboarded all round with a low brick foundation and long splays and friezes of Delft tiles. The roof was pitched high, hipped, square-gabled, a warm, fatherly roof. Yes – high and square.

The greatest charm lay inside; this house had been built, essentially, inside a barn. Cattle and horses poked their heads on winter nights over stable doors into the warm and large kitchen. Imagine, then, climbing the stairs to sleep in long, timbered rooms above the gentle snuffling sounds of the beasts in their stables a floor below. The less wintry part of me wanted it for myself.

I was taken completely by surprise. Pearl's house stirred feelings that distressed me, feelings of loss, feelings of warmth never found, and I tried to close them down.

He looked at me carefully, measuring my reaction. Then he patted my arm.

'Ah! So you got emotions after all!' He seemed thrilled. 'I tell you things about this house,' he said. 'Nice things.'

My skin tingled. I loved the blue-and-white Delft tiles everywhere, even in the stables. I loved the sensible way the doors worked – outer stable doors opening outwards as stable doors must, and those on the inside opening back into the residential area, the kitchen principally, so that even a small child could shoo back into its pen a pushy cow and close the door on it. I loved the glimpse of hay from the chairs by the wide, handsome tiled fireplace. Did I laugh with delight? No, I tend not to – but I might have done.

Frau, Signora, Madame, I didn't know which – Mrs Pearl, his mother, greeted us. The young man's kiss for his mother seemed to land on cold flesh; she all but turned her face away. She led us to the table on which stood a large blue jug of the most wonderful and bitter drinking chocolate. Her body had some of the Dutch squareness.

'She powders it herself,' Johan explained. 'I do not know what she adds to stop it congealing when the hot milk hits it. This is my brother, Sebastiaan. My father is gone to Amsterdam. He is sorry to not see you.'

His mother excused herself and Sebastiaan took over. He was not as black-skinned as Johan. I tried to puzzle out the genetics – their mother was blonde. A girl, a housemaid perhaps, came in and served fat gooseberry pie.

Mrs Pearl returned. She had changed her hair a little, wore a little blusher on her cheekbones. The top button of her blouse had come undone. She checked my name again and asked me to call her 'Elma'.

Johan showed her great tenderness, but she had difficulty with him. As did Sebastiaan; I above all know when people are holding themselves back. A family row going on? 'Ah, money,' I thought, looking around. But no, this family did not need anyone's financial support. Their comfort was evident and deep and old.

'My house in England will be exactly like this house, Mother,' Johan Pearl said. 'Exactly.'

She showed no enthusiasm. Nor did Sebastiaan.

I asked, because I felt embarrassment rising all round, and perhaps sensed resentment, 'How long has the family lived here?'

'We were away for a hundred years or so,' said his mother. 'We lost it in a wartime marriage, a difficult marriage alliance. But we got it back again.' She looked more at my eyes than my mouth.

As I was about to ask, 'Hitler?' she said quickly, 'In eighteen hundred and eleven.'

I subtracted out loud. 'So if the family lost it in seventeen-eleven –'

She corrected me. 'Seventeen-ten. It was a bad quarrel, and there were military things too.'

'That means it was a well-established house in seventeen-ten?'

Sebastiaan and Johan said nothing. Their mother continued, 'It is said that Vermeer stayed here. More than once.'

'But it looks so – so fresh?'

Elma Pearl said, 'There is a painting by Pieter de Hooch, it is called *The Mother*, it was painted here, look, this is the door and this is where the little girl looks out into the sunlight, see, the black-and white tiles on the floor, the same tiles?'

Pearl said, 'The painting is in a gallery in Berlin. We have postcards of it.'

Sebastiaan interjected, 'We repair the house a little every year.'

I looked at the three of them, all at different removes from each other. Elma looked back at me with a sharp directness; perhaps Johan got his freeness with other people's boundaries from his mother. I broadened the conversation.

'Do you have many farmhands, I mean employees?'

Sebastiaan answered, 'Today, fifty. It goes up and down with seasons. Soon, in the full winter, it will be thirty,

42

soon after that it will be eighty for a time, then a hundred.'

Their English had more guttural sounds than Johan's, and they showed exquisite manners by never speaking to each other in Dutch while I was with them.

'You need to see all the building,' Johan stated.

'If that's not an intrusion,' I said hesitantly, looking to his mother.

Ignoring Johan, she said, 'You must first see the big bathroom. It is very traditional.'

I rose and moved towards the staircase that had echoes of a ladder in it.

'No-no,' she said. 'It is downstairs,' and she led the way. Behind me the brothers entered into some exchange I didn't hear.

Through a low wooden door which had four tiles as a panel, I followed her into a huge room, as big as the kitchen we had been sitting in. Three long and tall baths stood along one wall, as they had for centuries. Modern plumbing reached to them from the tiles. The open drains, lined with blue-and-white ceramics, had remained undisturbed.

'Delightful!' I said and meant it.

'When we were growing up,' called Johan, 'we all together took the bath in here.'

He looked to the others for their shared approval and pleasure – in vain. Within his family his sentences ended in question marks; I wondered if they felt envy towards him.

On the other wall spread a row of six huge ceramic blue-and-white basins with broad, flat rims. All along the panelled and tiled walls ranged rows and rows of shelves and wooden pegs from which hung bathrobes. A fireplace opened wide on the third wall.

Sebastiaan and Johan talked by the door.

'But this is lovely,' I said.

Elma stood in front of me and very quickly and softly murmured, 'Johan needs help. He will not listen to us.'

The complaint of any mother? Who has a son in his twenties and whose life is lived farther into the fast lane than anyone could ever have planned? Or something more?

'Will you take an interest in him?' she asked, not looking at her sons.

I didn't have to answer because Sebastiaan left, stooping through the low door, and Johan bounded over.

'My bathroom must be exactly the same, Nicholas.'

Now his mother responded to him with sudden warmth. I couldn't figure the change in her – then I realized: Sebastiaan's absence.

We left the bathroom and climbed to the upper floors. In Johan's room a large stuffed black-and-white cow grazed on the bed.

'That is Sonja.' He grinned.

'Do the media know?' I said and they saw the joke.

The master bedroom was laden with the atmosphere of sex. Elma walked me all through it and the adjoining dressing room where flagrant underclothes lay on chairs. We stood, all three of us, gazing at the beams. Johan heard Sebastiaan call and went to the door. Elma led me to the deep bay of the window and stood very close to me – as she had done throughout my visit. Outside, across the dunes, the North Sea became a coral fire as the sun descended.

7

Next day, I drove home through that little neck of France. Slowly and if not peacefully, uneventfully. In an *antiquités* near Malo-les-Bains I found an old Quimper bowl but it had a crack. From the car I tried Antony's office and got the answering machine; 'For the moment the offices of Safft Development will be closed.'

My morbid and sinister thoughts felt confirmed. Antony had had an accident or a heart attack. I had no knowledge of his health. Now that I looked closely I saw that Antony had, overall, an air of mystery about him. My knowledge of his private life consisted of impression – I knew almost nothing concrete. His house gave little away – the books on his shelves could have been the books on anybody's shelves. No family photographs, only trophies, like mine: Antony pictured with the great and the starry. The most powerful individual item he owned hung in the study – a wooden board with the weathered word 'SOUVIENS-TOI' cut into it.

'One day I will tell you,' he told me.

I played on the meaning.

'Is it a souvenir, or must I remember to ask you?' I said. He didn't smile. I didn't remember. And he never told me.

An unexpected ache hurt my neck where the thugs had jerked my face on Saturday. The fantasies of revenge had not so much calmed as set – from the red of rage to the blue of ice. I telephoned the police again.

'What do you mean "Nobody has been questioned"? I understand that all football hooligans are known to you.'

'Scotland Yard is dealing with it, sir.'

45

'Who at Scotland Yard?'

'I'm afraid I can't tell you that, sir, but if they want you they'll contact you.'

'When am I to make my statement?'

'Can't say, sir.'

The driving began to ease me, as driving always does. I had to resist slamming down the pedal when I thought of kicking their faces, their ribcages.

That lovely house. But – that maternal concern. Elma Pearl. Not my business. I am unaware of any parental instincts in myself. A sense of her lingered. In the past she might have developed into an opportunity. 'Tell your husband you're visiting a friend in Amsterdam.' But I berated myself for this desecrating thought; with such indiscipline I had derailed myself in the past.

To haul myself onwards I began to dwell upon Elizabeth. No, she can't be seventy-five. Yes, she can. Is she feeling her age? For some months now she had shown me bizarre moods. She went even faster from warm to cool to skittish, often within the space of a dinner. My experience told me she either harboured a grudge or was planning something. I knew not which, and cared little. This thought also deserved some chiding – selfish of me to dismiss her so lightly now that she could no longer make a contribution to my ambition. Tonight I would behave beautifully to her. I should do. How long have we known each other? I recall two major birthday parties, ten years apart. Dear Elizabeth. Faircombe in all its welcoming splendour. If she had modified it, you would never know.

'Dear Nicholas, how lovely to see you.'

And as ever, the evening promised well.

Fires blazed in Faircombe's rooms. Do I never learn? Elizabeth is at her most welcoming when she most wants something. But Della beamed her usual house-keeperly mother-of-all beam. Della, to everyone's amazement, had married last year at sixty. Far from retiring as Elizabeth had dreaded, Della had brought her new husband to work as a male factotum. Hence the fires.

'He's costing me a fortune,' lied Elizabeth, one of the richest women in the south of England. Faircombe, with three hundred Home Counties acres, had been in her family since 1710. 'Della ordered him to light these fires when she heard you were coming down.'

'What's he like?' I whispered, although we were miles away from anyone.

'Oh, didn't I tell you?' Elizabeth had taken my arm as we stood in front of the fire. 'He's dumb, he can't speak. A mute.'

'Good God!'

'Mmmm. Perfect for Della. He can't argue. He can't query. He can't answer back. He reminds me of that old joke about the perfect wife – a deaf-and-dumb nymphomaniac living above a pub!'

'Elizabeth, you can't tell jokes like that any more.'

'I know! Isn't it awful?! Between PC for computers and PC for political-what's-it I can't tell where I am. Dearest boy, how are you? The office said you were travelling.'

'What did you ring for?' I have always handled Elizabeth best by being direct. She, as ever, evaded.

'How do you come to be here, you goose?!'

Elizabeth's games are deep and long.

'You're the goose,' I said. 'You invited me.' I pressed on. 'You've been gardening. Your face is glowing.'

'Paradise. Bliss. Gardening is the new sexual intercourse.'

She poured a glass of frightful wine. Probably Bulgarian, if not New World. Luckily, she pours little of it, too mean.

We settled in our chairs.

'Business good?' she asked – but she always asks that.

'Expanding,' I said with a gloomy air. 'More people, more trouble.'

She wore her usual evening colours – black trousers and white shirt, huge lapels; her bony frame enhances everything she wears.

'You've had your hair cut, Elizabeth.'

'Oh, do you like it?'

'Very much.'

'A "Bastille" they call it, we used to call it a "French crop". They simply must rename everything these days.'

'I like it very much. Makes you years younger.'

'I feel fifty,' she declared. 'That's the trouble. I don't feel like a woman my age. It's very depressing.'

I've known Elizabeth almost twenty years. She hired me. She launched me. She made me. Twice in that time she made serious errors of professional judgement that nearly cost us the practice. A third error – personal rather than architectural – almost cost my life.

After it she resigned and gave me as a gift – or as an atonement – her shares in the practice, lock, stock and barrel. Technically speaking, I bought it. But she offered it to me for one pound and fifty pence, pointing out that in old sterling this was thirty shillings, thirty pieces of silver. She believed she had betrayed me. A crime of such magnitude – whether it had truly happened – was something Elizabeth Naomi Mackinnon Bentley could not bear to have committed.

I looked around the room. Two Matisses, one large, one small; a Rouault; a Rousseau and an early Chagall, oil on board, delightful. A Lavery. An Orpen. A Roderic O'Conor. On one wall hung a blank space.

'Where's the Braque, Elizabeth?'

No answer came. She is the most controlling human being I have ever known. Then I, too, gazed into the fire. Some ten or twelve minutes later, from down the flagged passageway, Della called us to supper in the gloomy dining room.

48

As we rose Elizabeth suddenly said, 'I hear you've got a black client. You've changed your tune.'

She took my arm as we walked along to the dining room. Lights from the passageway windows floodlit the lawns.

I ignored her, halted her to look out at the night.

'Elizabeth, do you still get that vixen in the garden? I remember the cubs.'

The same wine persisted but we had glorious food. I drank a lot of water. Twice she looked hard at me during the first course – creamy carrot soup with coconut. She drummed the table with her fingers and once I caught her scrutinizing me when my eyes had been elsewhere. What was biting her?

Then her mood changed again, to merry sharing.

'Did you hear about Elise Banchory?'

'No.'

'Some servant or other, somebody from her past, I think there was some kind of low-life fling or something – he took naked photographs of her. They're going to appear in the papers.'

'Oh, God!' I said. 'How dreadful.'

'Not a bit. She's thrilled. She said to me on the phone, "At least my bitch of a sister will be reminded what a wonderful figure I had." The newspaper apparently rang asking her to confirm and she told them, well, she couldn't very well confirm anything she hadn't seen, and then she asked them could she keep a set, that she'd never seen them and would love to have them. They'd expected her to be furious. I shouldn't be at all surprised if she hasn't killed the whole thing.'

'Shrewd ploy,' I said.

'You are staying the night, aren't you?'

I nodded.

'What have you been up to in general?' I asked her. 'You can't garden all the time. Or perhaps you do. I thought you might write a memoir.'

'No. Too many of them. Every little jack who ever did anything he didn't expect to is writing his memoirs. I have a nice new neighbour. Did I mention Commander Lloyd to you?'

'Are you being wooed, Elizabeth?'

She laughed. The icebergs began to drift away.

'Only in the sense that I'm doing some drawings for him. He needs a fairly large ground-floor modification. Big Edwardian house. He's a gardener, too. Poor man, his wife has arteriosclerosis.'

'Elizabeth!' I laughed. 'I never thought I'd see the day,' I teased her. She had railed against all domestic work while senior partner. All our government work came through her.

'At least,' she said, 'he's not a footballer. I haven't sunk that low.'

'Does he fancy you?' I also needed to draw a little blood.

'No, Nicholas. It's simply that I find I can't stop myself drawing. Or thinking about drawing.' She changed gear. 'Why do you mention wooing? You haven't fallen in love or anything, have you?'

'No, Elizabeth.'

'Don't people ever wonder if you're queer? That's what everyone thinks of the unmarried these days. Male or female.'

She subsided. I sensed her anger. This meant she felt she had been finessed.

'Wonderful cooking,' I praised. Which it was; grilled lamb and baked red cabbage with mint potatoes.

'Was that a Hollandaise sauce?' I asked Della as she took the main-course dishes away.

'Why not?' Della said – and brought back the chocolate cake, Elizabeth David's recipe.

'D'you remember that time we went to Arezzo?' I said.

'Piero's *Madonna*. Like a poem, isn't it? A red gown in Sansepolcro.' Elizabeth smiled. 'Shame the *Resurrection* was under wraps.'

Silence again. I wanted to remind her of other journeys together – Delhi, Jerusalem, Budapest – but her ice closed over my thoughts.

And so the evening proceeded, through cheese and then a brandy and then bed. Elizabeth's guest room has a television set. It being at the far end of the house, distant from anyone, I watched a late movie from somewhere until I fell asleep.

I awoke exhausted, went to breakfast in the sun room. Her new friend arrived – the Commander, a brisk and slightly pompous man, perhaps shy. He took some coffee and they talked gardening; he was smitten with Elizabeth. She behaved kittenishly; I never like her when she's like that. Della's new husband, Dick, brought the newspapers – a man at least fifteen years younger than Della.

I murmured to Elizabeth, 'You never said he was younger than her.'

'Nothing wrong with that,' she replied. 'And you don't have to mutter, he can't hear you.'

The Commander said nothing – and if he did I never heard him because Elizabeth, shaking out the newspaper, cried, 'Ooh, look! I always knew it, I never liked him. See – I told you so, Nicholas.' Women cannot manage newspapers: genuine fact.

'What did you tell me, Elizabeth?'

'That friend of yours, the slimy one. At least I found him slimy.'

'You found most of my friends slimy,' I said.

'This one's now formerly slimy, you could say.'

She brandished the *Daily Mail* at me. I saw the word 'Slain', and thought, Ah, yes, 'Murdered' is too long a word for a tabloid page, and this was a defence mechanism to help me cope with the photograph of Antony Safft. My hands moved so slowly to take that newspaper.

'Oh,' she said, 'he was older than I am. Well preserved, wasn't he?'

51

When? *When?* That question leapt ahead of all others. When was he killed? I scanned like a savage.

'Police have released few details, other than to say it had been a particularly gruesome killing with no clues.' I scanned on. '. . . at the weekend. His office became worried on Monday afternoon when he had missed a second consecutive lunch date . . .'

Elizabeth rattled on but I only heard distant words.

'He dressed too well . . . Bit foppish . . . Never saw what you saw in him . . . I never like men with that kind of concertina wavy hair . . .'

The coffee in the cup beneath my nose smelled rancid. I held on to my feelings and conveyed not much more than strong surprise. The Commander opened a conversation about murder – 'When times were more decent we had decent murders.'

Elizabeth gave a theatrical shudder. 'I've always hated it if murder comes anywhere close. My mother hated it. It was quite a fear in my family.'

I thought, Thanks, Elizabeth. Soon the talk took another turn – towards Winston Churchill, as I feel sure it often did. I stood; I had to get away. For privacy.

'Ooh, you have a new overnight bag,' she said in the hall. Elizabeth makes intrusive remarks to her friends in front of others. 'Nicholas is a luggage freak,' she said to the Commander.

'Good luck with your extension,' I had planned to say to him and stare at his hairpiece as I said it. But I didn't trust my voice not to crack.

8

To deal with shock, find something that demands concentration. That's what they told me in school. From Faircombe to Andover is either an awkward but attractive cross-country drive, or straight lines of connecting motorways. I chose the awkward route, knowing that finding the way would concentrate me. An hour out I stopped to speak to the office.

Lemon had the news. 'D'you want me to keep all the papers?'

'Is Hal there?'

'Jee-zuz, Chief! What about that?'

'What do we know, Hal?'

'The papers. Nothing else. I've been trying his office but they're on the answering machine.'

I thought for a moment. 'Have you got the newspapers there in front of you?'

'What d'you need to know?'

'Time of death.' I said it casually; nevertheless he caught the thought.

'Yes. Of course. Christ, Chief, I never thought of that. Not a time to joke, I suppose, about alibis.'

My voice froze him. 'Do the reports mention a police station in charge? Or an incident room?'

'Yeh. It's Hampstead. Incident room.'

I took the details and rang immediately.

A police voice said, 'Not until later. It's Inspector Hurst in charge. Do you want to leave a message?'

'Yes. It's about the Safft murder. No – Safft, yes, that's right. I was to have lunch with him on Friday but he never

53

showed up. The Savoy. Yes, the Savoy Hotel, the Grill. One o'clock. No, not a word from him, most unlike him.'

In which case, she said, the Inspector would almost certainly want to speak to me. I held back the details of the mystery voice answering Antony's phone. Putting the phone on hands-free I drove like a hearse along the high-hedged roads towards the Ridgeway.

A small van drove away from the raw, greenfield site of Johan Pearl's new house. The surveyors, I expected; the two occupants had mapped out an area with red-and-white tape. By now everything jangled. Again I tried to concentrate. My stiff neck clawed at me.

The Black Pearl said he had chosen the site for 'Its vibes. Good vibes there, I like all that stuff, Camelot and that.'

So far as I knew – but I didn't tell him – there had never been any history to link King Arthur with Stonehenge. I looked down from the slope across one of the best views in England; the stones in the distance will be visible from his windows and his terrace.

My mobile rang and Hal asked, 'Where are you?'

'Stonehenge. On the Pearl site.'

'Bloody genius,' he said. 'Scored on Saturday, I still don't know how he did it, I was there. Ten-, fifteen-degree angle maybe, past three men, turned on the byline. I hate the little bugger.' And he laughed, then asked, 'Did the police get hold of you? An Inspector Hurst?'

'No. I tried to get him.'

'He'll ring you in a minute, just thought I'd warn you.'

Keep working. Concentrate. *Keep working!*

For me the pleasure of a site derives from its problems. South-western aspect – fine. Elevation? The surveyor said the existing levels were workable. Keep them and build to them. Sudden ennui hit me, something I associate with emotional stress. My concentration slips. The boredom usually attacks me in those areas of my work I most enjoy. Now it said to me, Never again accept a brief where the client knows exactly what he wants and especially where he has a model he wants copied. Why didn't he get a simple bloody draughtsman?

Shake my head to clear my brain. Concentrate. Pace the distance. Three hundred yards – this will be the terrace. To the copse at the rear. Yards. Three hundred, write it down. Pearl wants to keep the copse. Beech. Some birch. Do the trees have preservation orders? He wants some panelling made from these trees. Not in four months he won't. Four months? Well, he's paying the extra. I propped my little pad against one of our brochures. Written by me after Elizabeth's departure. She never had a brochure.

'Bentley Newman sees itself as essentially modernist but with a strong Renaissance sensibility.' What the flock does that mean? Hal, who (sometimes) tries not to swear, has a saying, 'Let's get the flock out of here.' What does it mean, 'strong Renaissance sensibility'? Anything from Mantegna in Mantua to – to whom? Helmut Jahn in Chicago? I made a note – 'Cherry'. He's got cherry trees in this copse, this must have been an old cherry orchard. They're chopping down the Cherry Orchard. One, two, three. Three more. Twelve cherries in all. Chekhov. Or Tchekhov. Suzy's lost her cherry. Shall I tell him? Will he not simply want to chop them all down? Perhaps I won't tell him about his bloody trees. Or tell him there's a preservation order. Antony, what happened? What happened to you? Dear man, what did they do to you?

'Previous commissions have included a railway terminal where we commissioned tapestries on railway history for the interior walls, and a City of London church inspired by Wren and Hawksmoor but with chrome minimalist interiors.' So why did I take this on? Good question.

'You must meet my girlfriend,' said Johan Pearl as we drove back to the White Raven.

Over here – nice plateau; yes, we've covered that. York

stone flags, reclaimed. A pedestal terrace. 'Display something,' he said. He can afford an Anthony Caro, make him buy one. Patronize the arts with the client's money. I do it all the time.

The telephone rang out. Stonehenge stood distant and friendly in the low sunshine. Isn't he too young to appreciate this view? Will his fans come here and vandalize the stones? Or his friends?

I try to jot down a word or two on a pad after I've met a client for the first time. A summary word, like 'bully', or 'shit', or 'stingy', or 'flamboyant', or 'invasive'. For Johan Pearl I wrote 'sparky'.

'Hallo?'

'Mr Newman?'

'Yes.'

'Hurst.'

'Yes. Inspector Hurst, I take it.'

'I'd like to talk to you, sir.'

'Of course. I'll help in any way I can.'

'Bit more than routine, sir. To prepare you, I'll be asking what you know of his friends, his business associates, that sort of thing.' A toneless but cultivated voice.

'I'm down in Wiltshire at the moment, Inspector, but I'm on my way back to London.'

'As you can imagine, sir, things are a bit busy this end, but if you could ring me, say, tomorrow?'

'If that's all right . . . ?'

'We'll be a bit more organized then. I'm sorry if he was a friend of yours, sir,' he said and just as I was thinking, Curious form of words, he corrected himself. 'What I mean is, I'm sorry you've lost a friend.'

'Yes, he was a very nice man.'

'So I gather, sir.'

'Inspector, could you help me with something?'

'If I can, sir.'

'The time of death. How precise are they about that these days?'

'Very, sir. Pathologist says he didn't survive the attack more than a few minutes, there's heart failure too. Puts time of death at between one fifteen and one thirty last Friday.'

'So he was attacked at – what?'

'Probably –' he spoke from thought rather than fact – 'I should think one o'clock. One ten. You were already at your table, sir.' They had checked already! That gave me a shiver. 'So, as I say, sir, I'm sorry.'

I rang the office. Hal, with his short attention span, had moved on. 'Seen the sports pages?'

'Of course not.'

'Our boy's in the news. Juventus and Inter Milan. Both of them. Offering the sun, moon and a few planets –'

'– a Pearl without price, you might say?' Hal didn't get it. I asked, 'But I think he said he'd been with, what did you call them, Milan?'

'Inter. Yes, and they want him back. If he goes it'll be the highest transfer fee in history. They're talking moonbeams.'

'That's obscene. Where are we on his survey?'

'Doing good, Chief. Heritage have no problems. That's the biggest hurdle cleared.'

I closed my eyes. Not again, no more, please. Whoever You are, wherever You are, please send no more violence into my life. Antony, I miss you already. Strange feeling. Both parents dead. And an only sibling dead. But I miss this man more – I think.

'What about the front pages?' I asked.

'*Evening Standard*'s just come out. All Antony Soft, two pages, we're even mentioned, or rather you are, Chief. Bad bloody business. Mutilation and that. Pathologist said it took a real sicko. Tough on a skinny old bloke like that.'

On the A303 traffic builds up around Stonehenge. I lose count of the ancient earthworks. This place must be one huge prehistoric burial ground. Tunnelling soon for a bypass. Cut and cover? Not a great solution but the best available. And I don't think those stones were raised as free-standing religious symbols. I think that was a roofed building, a temple.

'Safft,' I said. 'Hal, it's "Safft", not "Soft",' and my mind screamed, Why in the name of Christ could you never get his bloody name right?

All the way to London the pain endured.

'You called Mr Antony Saaaafft.' But not Antony's voice? A sicko. Mutilation. I can describe how panic hits. Every organ of the body has its own life, its own faculties, its own memory, hearing, feeling. The inside person in us all has them too, and the inside person in me was unable now to breathe. A sicko. Did he mean 'psycho'?

Traffic is never dense when you need it to be. I wanted to be slowed down; I reached Cadogan Gardens too quickly for my own good. When driving I have to control myself. My face and neck still hurt. Revenge burns. Revenge for Antony too? Oh, God.

What will console me? Rachmaninov's Vespers. A help, but not much. Nothing. Nothing. I am gasping and whining inside me. I go to the bathroom mirror to look in my own eyes to see if I can find some sort of clue there, some remote wandering truth that will help my shaken life. No. Some comfort? Dutch drinking chocolate from a tall, slim, red tin. Not as good as – as – as. Pearl's mother. The chocolate makes me want to throw up. What was her name? Elma, that's it. When I go to the fridge to get some water the food there nauseates me further.

The telephone rang and it was Johan Pearl, still in Noordwijk. Now in tears.

'What can I say? The best man to me I could have wished

for.' His accent was thick again. 'Oh, if you knew his kind-ness.'

I was staggered. 'But I didn't know you knew him?'

'Remember me asking if you were alone? When we met at the Savoy on Friday? I was expecting him too, he wanted to introduce us personally, see? I knew about your lunch. And that is why I was surprised, but I didn't want to tell you, that Antony sent me to you, because he wanted to tell you himself. If you knew what he said about you, how high he thought of you and you never knew what he thought of me, and I won't know now, he was the loveliest man.'

Grief defines the age of the grieving – this bright, brilliant star was only a boy.

'He was more loving than my father to me, oh, man what'm I gonna do? They's nobody I can say this to, what'm I gonna do . . .'

Antony Safft was crazy about football. That, at least, made sense, so I let Johan Pearl talk for a long, long time. He wanted details from me, he wanted to share our knowledge. This conversation became our wake for Antony.

'I met him through a property development,' I said. 'We got on well immediately and the next morning he rang and said to me, "I know you can draw because I've seen your buildings, and now I want you to do all my work." He was the best client – in every way – I ever had.'

'If he was at a game where I scored,' said the Black Pearl, 'which I have done quite often, he waited for me afterwards if he knew I was free – that's how we met, in the executive suite – and then at dinner he would tell me about all the other games in which the club had scored in the thirty-second minute or whatever time it was I scored. Oh, man, he was the grandfather I always wanted, Nicholas.'

'I never knew anyone with such a grasp of detail,' I said.

We recalled Antony's generosity, his taste – especially in shoes, Pearl remembered; his anxiety; his capacity to

59

schmooze a room: he taught me how to overcome – or pretend to overcome – my diffidence. The talking calmed us both, although Pearl disquieted me as we finished by saying, 'My life, man, it's bad right now and I don't know why. It should be so good.'

My own life didn't feel so wonderful.

The day had long grown dark. I wanted no food, I wanted nothing but stillness and silence. I undressed, and without taking my usual slow bath, climbed into my bed and then, I didn't mean to, I must have drifted off to sleep knowing that my feelings in the morning would hurt and hurt . . . and hurt . . . .

9

And so next morning, electric with jitters and my soul haunted and my body and heart aching, I returned to the office. My eyes were sore after fitful sleep. I woke to the ringings of several dreams and remembered them piecemeal. In one a bus drove by, a green-and-cream double-decker with an open top; the passengers were people I knew but didn't know. In another, a bright silver aircraft flew very low but didn't threaten me; moments later I was somehow inside it looking out.

My face felt sore and I used an electric razor. I couldn't tie my tie, I tried three times, so I changed my shirt and wore a long-sleeved knitted polo, three buttons.

I had been away only three days but it felt funerals longer. Re-entry's always difficult – it explains why I never take long holidays. Correspondence piles up; people get bad-tempered; I am their focus and when I am not there they perform less well.

On my return I'm always irritated that someone's used my drawing board. No matter how I say it, no matter how clear I make my displeasure, every time I return it's plain someone's been there. What's worse is, I feel I can say little. If there's pressure on space and facilities, and I'm not prepared to spend money on expansion or new offices – how can I complain? At least they have the courtesy not to work at it as I'm walking through the door. That was what I thought.

At half past eight a woman I had never seen before stood at my drawing board. She had one of my pens and, head bent, light switched on, was figuring something. I stopped and watched. She still wore her street clothes, a large grey coat, a silver herringbone scarf. Exquisite shoes – French? Italian? – high block heel and a strap over the instep. I walked forward. Did she see me? She affected not to.

'May I help you?' I asked.

'You may.' She never lifted her head.

'How may I help you? Did you know, by the way, that is my drawing board?'

'You ask two questions, therefore I give you two answers,' she replied. 'One. You may help me by giving me the job you've advertised. Two. I know it's your drawing board.' Only then did she lift her head and look at me.

A smart-arse? Maybe. Maybe not.

Then I remembered. Interviews today, one architect, one draughtsman (not 'draughtsperson' as one or two of the younger staff tried to call it).

'How did you get in?' I asked.

'I have an appointment for nine and a cleaner let me in.'

This annoyed me. 'But you're very early.'

'By an hour at least. I have a pathological fear of being late.'

Had she read a profile of me somewhere? Did the headhunters tell her I hated unpunctual people? I put my bag down and glanced at what she had been drawing on my board. 'What's that?'

'Something I did in my last job. I got it wrong and it still irritates me.'

Another bonus point. I had said in some interview that I always review my errors more than my successes. If you can't think of anything to say use a cliché. And go on doing it.

'Success is ninety-five per cent failure. Where was your last job?'

'California. Santa Monica.'

'Oh?' I asked, meaning, 'Why did you leave?'

'The sun got monotonous. I like variety in my weather.'

'Some good architects out there' – meaning, 'Who were you with?'

'Gehry. I also spent some time at Moore, Ruble, Yudell.'

'I know Charles Moore. And I've met Frank Gehry. But I can't say I know him.'

'Frank O. Gehry.' She smiled as she emphasised the 'O.' 'The Americans are more particular than we are. This was a house,' she indicated the drawing, 'for a computer wizard.'

I didn't ask her what the error had been.

'This is your celebrated democracy?' She waved a hand to indicate the fact that my main drawing board stands in the general office with everyone else.

Others began to arrive.

'Would you like some coffee?' I asked. 'I think we should go into my office.'

The cleaners had filled the Alessi with fresh water.

I said, 'I am at a loss. Because I've been out of the office for the last few days. And I don't know whether other interviewees have been called.'

'Two others,' she said.

'How d'you know that?'

'The headhunters told me.'

I frowned, wishing I hadn't. 'They're not supposed to tell you such things.'

'They're very sweet,' she said.

'You've obviously gathered who I am, so perhaps you'll tell me who you are.'

'My name is Mary Strait. Born here. Kensington. For school, Cheltenham Ladies. Then Cambridge at seventeen. Then a year's postgrad at the London School of Economics. Then another at the Massachusetts Institute of Technology. Then work. I brought a spare CV.'

'Just the two practices?'

'Just the two.'

'Have you had breakfast?' I asked, opening the fridge and taking out my fruit salad and the rye bread.

'Never do.'

My desk had, as ever, been prepared like a table, with small cloth, napkin and cutlery.

'Do you mind?'

'No, of course not,' she said and drew up a chair opposite me. She seemed not at all nervous.

We talked for an hour until Lemon buzzed me and said, 'Westminster. Client meeting at half past ten. Onsite, okay?'

'Is Hal there?'

He came in. 'Hal, this is Mary Strait.'

I nodded in a way he knew, meaning the decision had been taken. My instincts are good.

Hal hid his discomfiture well. I remembered too late that I had promised never to hire anyone again without consulting him and the others.

'Great references,' he said to her, shaking her hand. 'Best references I've seen in years, actually.'

'Does that mean – ?' she began to ask.

'Would you like a coffee?' he asked her, twigging that I had forgotten to pour one for her.

'I'm sorry,' I said.

She waved a hand; she liked being the focus of men.

'When do you want to start?' I said, trying not to be brusque. 'I mean – are you free now?' I looked at Hal. 'I need some immediate back-up on the Horseferry job.'

'We don't hang around here,' Hal said to her, which was his rebuke to me for the *fait accompli*.

'Has it stopped raining?' I asked.

Lemon came in and I made the introductions.

'The car's outside.' Lemon didn't like her.

Mary Strait asked, 'Where's the lavatory?' and Lemon showed her.

Hal said to me, 'Well, at least you won't get smitten by her.'

I looked at him askance.

'Come on,' he said, obviously still miffed. 'Big tits but she's no looker.'

I must have reacted – because he said, 'Oops?'

By way of recovery I said, 'Look, why don't you get even? You hire the draughtsman. I bounced you, I'm sorry.'

'No prob. She's the best of the bunch – on paper anyway. I s'pose I'd better cancel the others.'

'Yeh, good idea.' And when Mary Strait came back along the corridor I found myself smiling at her. 'Can you give us a minute?' I said.

Hal closed the door behind her, turned and said, 'Nicholas, [which he very rarely calls me] 'Antony Safft. Dreadful. I know how much you liked him.' He took care with 'Safft'.

I agreed. 'Dreadful.'

Hal's unaccustomed solemnity made me realize how upset I was.

'I've rung the office,' he said, 'no reply. So we've sent some flowers, asked on the card that we be posted on memorial services, and that.'

'Is there a funeral?'

'I can't find out, Chief. I suppose there's –' he halted, searching for a word. 'I suppose – an inquest?'

'The papers go big on it?'

'Most front pages. All the news bulletins.'

I said, 'Why would anyone kill Antony? Bastards.'

'Or bastard singular? What'd the police say?'

'It happened right at the moment he was supposed to be meeting me for lunch.'

'Aw, Jesus Christ!' He made another sympathetic grimace and turned the conversation. 'You know Pearl was Safft's introduction? He said we weren't to tell you, he wanted to tell you himself.'

'I know – but I didn't know.'

In the car I asked Mary Strait whether she had ever been hired so swiftly before and she said, 'Yes. Both times, actually.'

'What do you know about us?' I asked her.

'Have I actually got the job?'

'Oh, sorry! Did it feel like I was still interviewing you? Welcome to Bentley Newman.' She didn't feel that much younger than me.

'I think I know more about you than about the practice.'

I laughed. 'You don't have to flatter me now.'

'Four of us came over from California to see the Macedonia Trust building. The cone and cube and that. What was the client like?'

'We called him the Killionaire. He seemed to take no interest. Then when we topped out he appeared and told me he had visited the site most weeks during the build.'

She sat self-possessed in the back of the car, half of one thigh revealed.

'What other projects of ours do you know?'

The coat – Donna Karan, I saw the label as she opened it. Eyes lined lightly with black. Hair gives problems, I bet, too much of it. No earrings, no rings on her fingers.

'Most of the big ones. The Brussels glassworks. The Claude Arro stores.'

'And?'

'And what? Do I like them? Well, I'm here.' Yes, very self-possessed.

'Who else do you like?'

'Very few. Here, Denis Sloan. John Outram. Foster, obviously. And, I suppose, Richard Rogers. At least he makes a noise on behalf of all of us. There's an interesting guy in Tucson – Riley. Thought of getting a job with him. I almost applied to Giorgio Grassi.'

I was tempted to ask her why she liked us, but resisted.

'Did you work on Bill Gates's house?'

'No.'

'Bilbao?'

'No.'

'Oh? I thought everybody did.'

She uncrossed her knees and sat with her thighs side by side and a little apart.

I did something foolish. 'Are you free for lunch?' I tried to recover it. 'I can brief you better. On what's waiting for you.'

'Okay.'

At the meeting I introduced her as 'our new architect'. Nobody took any notice until she made two interventions. The meeting began irritably. I was annoyed that the Planning Officer hadn't done me the courtesy of showing up, had sent the more junior of his two deputies. They were annoyed that I was annoyed. But her interventions calmed things; she spoke fluidly and gave the impression she considered their position.

I don't know precisely what it was that impressed them. The even flow of her long sentences? Or the surprising authority in her voice, the cool tone? I think it was the way she said 'quite simply' three or four times.

If her first intervention softened them, her second stung.

'I've just been looking at the decision delays and I find to my horror they're four times longer on average than the American norm, which says a great deal about the length of time public money is allowed to run in Britain as opposed to in the States.'

Every poem has an effective line, my English teacher said. I find every argument has an effective phrase. In that instance, 'to my horror'. As, earlier, 'quite simply'. And, thereby, she intimidated them.

There was something of Elizabeth in her, I thought – a forthrightness, a directness, though she lacked Elizabeth's sexy verve.

We took lunch early. I decided on Shepherd's, perhaps to measure her; Shepherd's is always good for a VIP sighting – sometimes a Secretary of State, or at least a few lively backbenchers.

'I haven't been here for years,' she said.

'Oh?' I had thought to treat and challenge her all at once.

'A boyfriend.' She said it dismissively.

'Past tense?'

'Very.' She paused, as though deciding to tell me something. 'MP. And rapist,' she said softly. 'Now a Minister.'

I moved to help. 'If you have arrangements to make, furniture, family, any of that,' I said, 'the practice – we help.'

We talked of many things. From time to time, when she volunteered some information or opinion, she looked straight in my eye. Untypically for lunch I ordered wine – a simple white Mercurey; she drank more than half of it; I put that down to nerves. She seemed both steadied and loosened. Both her nipples emerged; not unpleasant to look at.

She asked questions. I answered them. I asked questions. She answered them. Her education must have been excellent. Every line of thought opened was followed through without undue digression; her summaries had conciseness and accuracy.

We got back to the office at half past two and Lemon said, 'That was a long meeting.'

'We had lunch,' and I asked her to show Mary Strait where she would work and to give her the tour of the building.

'Hal's seeing draughtsmen,' said Lemon, who was wearing a man's shirt and a tie with Wile E. Coyote on it. All afternoon that tie seemed to dance in front of my eyes.

'Look. Again. I'm sorry about Antony Safft,' Hal said. 'I mean, if I'm shocked, what must you feel? Pam and I spent

68

ages talking about it last night, she got all the newspapers when I told her. If you want to see them . . . ?'

I said, 'Now I've got to go and tell the police all I ever knew about him. Did we keep a file?'

On some clients we keep a cuttings file, with anything that might be relevant. To Antony's Hal had added the new cuttings.

I gasped to Hal, 'Did you know Antony was gay? I didn't!'

Jesus! How did I miss the fact? He didn't advertise it – but he didn't conceal it.

'As gay as a paper hat,' said Hal and I disliked him for it.

10

Inspector Hurst said Savile Row station: I had offered to go to Hampstead. In the car I looked through the file but the news cuttings distressed me. This was a man whose company I had sought and enjoyed without any thought to the thirty-year age difference between us. He had brought thoughtfulness and experience to me, made me take longer views. Antony was the only man in whom I perceived a tenderness I found valuable. The first pangs of true mourning surfaced. Plus rage at my own self-absorption in not thinking through Antony's lifestyle. No. I lie. I think that now. Back then, I didn't have the emotional machinery.

On the street I saw with a start somebody who resembled him; same walk, same massed white hair. Antony never spoke of relatives or family. My throat grew dry; I keep pastilles in the office car – someone had finished and not replaced them, how irritating.

My hands shook. Shock? My own uncertainty? My loss of a father figure? No, I am a natural suspect – or that's what I feel – and I wondered whether, all their assurances notwithstanding, the police still included me in their thinking over Antony's death. 'In the frame', as they would say. A Stanley knife. Antony dead. Pearl in tears. The Tube attack. Get me off this angry carousel.

A metallic voice blared at us, 'Don't park there!'

I looked out, could see no one.

The voice blared again. 'If you park there you will be arrested. You are impeding police vehicles.'

I thought to say, 'But I'm only being dropped off to come

70

into your bloody station –' There was no one to hear me, just a small Tannoy speaker high up on the wall blaring at me. Tannoy-annoy.

'Repeat! Do not park there.'

'Okay-Okay!'

I jumped from the car and waved it away. Ahead of me at the door stood a young policewoman.

I pointed to the loudspeaker. 'Is this the new touchy-feely police service?' I asked.

She said in a voice of cordite, 'If you have a complaint against the police you may ask for a form at the desk.'

'How d'you spell that?' asked the desk officer.

'N-E-W-M-A-N.'

'First name?'

'Nicholas.'

'Spell?'

'N-I-C-H-O-L-A-S.'

'Who're you here to see?'

'Inspector Hurst.'

A door opened on a buzzer. 'Second on the right.'

Inspector Hurst stood alone at a bare desk with a folder and a crisp handshake.

'Hallo. Thank you for coming along.'

I watched him. Not an inch was I prepared to give him.

'Hallo.'

'We've spoken on the phone. Your friend, Mr Antony Safft. I offer you my sympathies.'

'Indeed.'

'Do sit down. Would you like some coffee?'

Civilized at least, thirties; graduate intake – difficult not to ask whether he had enough experience.

At certain times I have no resolve. Far from reticence, my mouth opened and I began to speak unstoppably.

'Antony Safft. Originally French. Legal background. Lived in London since the war. Developed properties that had been bombed. Started in Plymouth. Always complained the big cartels kept him out of London. Did a lot of work in Liverpool and Coventry. Always war sites. Always. Then got astride the new drift towards shopping malls. Started those in Canada on account of his French speaking. Lost Canary Wharf. To, ironically, Canadians. Hated them. Still felt sore. Bought half of Leeds-Bradford, some of Chester. We did four shopping malls for him in the North and Midlands. And other things. Three residentials down below Tower Bridge. An industrial and shopping park in Hounslow. The Hyde Park complex – that's also a Safft development.'

'Why were you telephoning him on Friday evening? I presume it was to enquire why he hadn't shown for lunch?'

'Was it you who answered his phone?' I looked at him. 'No, it wasn't your voice. I suppose you checked the phone records to find me?'

'What do you mean it wasn't my voice?'

'Somebody answered.'

'What time was that, sir?'

'The telephone record will tell you. I suppose, about quarter past, half past six – and again later.'

'What kind of a voice?'

'A man's. He rang me back.'

'He what, sir?'

'Inspector.' I tried to keep the impatience – or was it patience? – out of my voice. 'I rang Antony Safft, as you say, to ask why he hadn't shown. It was most unlike him and I was worried. A man answered. I put the phone down, I don't know why. He rang me back immediately, I presume Antony's phone has one of those displays that tells you who's calling. Or he could just have dialled 1471.'

Inspector Hurst made rapid notes.

'And you say you rang again?'

'I rang twice more. About half past seven – and again he answered and again I put the phone down and then at about half past ten. No one answered then.'

'D'you remember anything about the voice?'

'No. It was just a voice. Slight mispronunciation – but people were always mispronouncing Antony's name.'

The Inspector finished writing, then looked through his file. More an executive than a policeman.

'How did you get on with him, sir?'

'Very well.'

'Brace yourself, Mr Newman.' He said it kindly. 'This was an unpleasant crime.'

Suddenly I was screaming inside my head. Oh, come on! Look! I don't want any details! Shut up, will you?! As ever, it never showed in my face. My file had been unsafely parked on the desk and now it fell to the floor.

He never moved; he waited until I was sitting upright again, my face bursting a little with blood to the head.

'I have to tell you, sir. They cut his throat. Ear to ear.' He resisted the temptation to gesture. 'They cut his male member off. And they carved a large triangle into his buttocks.'

I must have grunted, or moaned. In my head if not my voice.

'What's that?' I hadn't heard his next question and he repeated it.

'How close were you?'

'He was – he was an exceptionally nice man,' I said. 'I mean, if you're asking am I gay, no, I'm not.'

'I need to know whether there was any circle of friends – where he might have had enemies.'

I said, my face as open as a child's because that is how I felt, 'I don't know. My first thought is – anyone who knew Antony wouldn't kill him so viciously.'

The Inspector said, 'Yes, that's a good point,' and he wrote something down. When he looked up at me he said, 'I read your statement, your mugging on the Tube. Sounds awful.'

'I'm getting nowhere with that. Can I speak to somebody about it?'

'They'll get to you. You know the old gentleman died?'

'The triangle,' I thought out loud. 'Hitler did that to gays. Made them wear a triangle. The Stanley knife, was it done with a Stanley knife?'

I thought immediately of the thug groping between my legs on Saturday. Hurst saw me wince, saw my knees slam together reflexively.

'A Stanley knife. You mean – like carpet-fitters use?'

'Yes. A workman's knife.' I described it and told him about my mysterious gift. 'What do you make of that?'

He sat back and looked out of the window. The coffee he ordered had not arrived. He buzzed for it, saying to me he couldn't think without coffee.

'Any reason,' said the Inspector, 'that you know of, why anyone should wish to intimidate you or your friends?'

'Are you talking about the Tube incident?' I asked.

The Inspector said, 'You're suggesting, sir – there has to be a connection? A reason for all this?'

'Am I?'

He fell silent and I followed suit.

Eventually he asked me, 'I have to ask, sir. Do you take drugs?'

'No. Never have.'

'Do you owe any money? I mean serious money?'

'No. You can speak to my bank if you wish.'

'No need,' he said. 'Any unusual clients?'

'Not any that matter. Oil companies don't threaten their architects. Nor do banks, airport terminals, supermarket groups, bookstores, fashion houses.'

He smiled at the irony.

I carry inside my little pocket notepad a list of all current clients. Even in my tiny handwriting, the list covers both sides of the graph-squared, twelve-fifty-mill. record cards.

74

Should I read the names aloud? Yes; impress him. He listened impassively.

'Blue-chip, I suppose you'd call them all,' suggested Inspector Hurst when I'd finished. 'Thirty-two, you've read, sir.' He tapped his desk. 'The personal ones. That's where we should look. Although nowadays –' and he stopped. 'D'you have industrial espionage in your business?'

'A bit,' I said. 'But it doesn't hit us the way it bites into, say, a computer company. Or the components industry.'

'The personal clients, sir. Would you give me a little more on them?'

'Antonia Spey. House extension, Highgate. Woman in her sixties. Wealthy. Good works. Charities. Widow of a diplomat. Private income, too. Big spender.'

The list had always grown chronologically rather than alphabetically and I wrote a new, updated card every month or so.

'Billy and Bredy Cleland. Art gallery,' I explained. 'Bond Street, but they live above it. Amazing. Almost nobody does nowadays.'

The Inspector waited.

'George Pennant. St Tropez. Well, Le Lavandou. New house. Insurance millionaire. Out of the game now, sold to, I think, Direct Call.'

'I've got my car with them,' muttered Hurst.

'Johan Pearl. Footballer. Foreigner. Premiership. Makes forty thousand a week plus a percentage of his many transfer fees. Not that I understand how it works. Bought land in Wiltshire.'

He didn't so much as lick that bait.

'And two more – both residential. Gerry Nolan, the hotelier. Bought a big house in Bournemouth, wanted it gutted, exterior preserved with minimalist interior, we're knocking walls down everywhere. And Olivia Mossley, City high-flyer, married to a man who wants to be a house-husband, he was an actor apparently. She's spending three-quarters of a million for him on a warehouse complex by the canal in Camden. They have a barge there and they want it all to "interface" – so they say.'

I laid the little leather notepad on the table in front of me.

'They all you? Or your office?' asked the Inspector.

'They want me. But they get the office too, I mean others do the drawings, I'm mostly what we call "present-and-correct" – meaning, I take a look at the drawings before the next meeting, correct the things I think are going to be hard to sell to the client and then when the drawings are fully ready I present them.'

'This footballer?'

'Pearl. Johan Pearl. Dutch. Black extraction.'

'Yeah, I know him. Wonderful player. Winger, sometimes midfielder. Very fast. The Black Pearl.' The Inspector had found a brief light; 'The Black Pearl,' savouring the nickname. 'What's he like? How much do you know about him?'

'Only the house he wants.'

'Dutch international. Those football boys can have bad habits. And you were attacked by football hooligans.'

'Ye-es.'

'Coincidence, sir. Who knows? We had an instructor said, "Coincidence is the copper's natural enemy." So – there we are.'

I said, 'I gather he's a rarity – he's educated, cultured –'

'A cultured pearl?' He couldn't resist it.

I continued: 'He's a graduate. Which, I gather, puts him way above most footballers.'

'You mean like graduate policemen?' said Inspector Hurst, but it was a joke – while meaning to tell me about himself. 'He gay – Pearl?' he asked.

'He's got a girlfriend.' I smiled thinly. 'Does that make him not gay? I haven't got a girlfriend. That why you asked if I was gay? Are you gay, Inspector?'

Inspector Hurst had his revenge. 'You didn't tell me Pearl was sent to you by Mr Safft.'

Did I blush? 'Yes – yes, he was.'

'But you didn't say that, sir, did you?'

'I'm sure I'd have got round to it.'

'I hope so, sir.'

Inspector Hurst became a little more formal and moved on to – for him – the meat, Antony's death. We went back to the beginning. Not that it came to much when I opened it out. I added a few details – the studio/conservatory in his Hampstead garden, the fabulous hospitality, the fact that he never took his hugely rich company to the Stock Exchange.

'How much do you know about his family?'

'Didn't know he had one,' I said.

'There's a nephew.'

Antony never said. How odd.

'He's a young French lawyer. Called Philippe Safft. He specializes in tracking down war criminals. Been threatened many times. As was his uncle.'

Revelation upon revelation. 'Threatened? But Antony was harmless.'

'Nevertheless.' Hurst shrugged. 'He reported telephone threats. Two last month.'

'War criminals? You mean old Nazis?'

'I suppose so, sir.'

I said, 'Think again of the triangle.'

'Somebody will, sir. If it's necessary.'

My volubility slowed down. In answer to questions, as distinct from volunteering, I helped Hurst some more: details of Antony's life; people I had met at parties in his house, in his offices; men who might have been his partners by virtue of how often I had met them with him, or heard Antony speak well of them.

Then suddenly I felt like weeping. I repressed it, of course.

'Inspector, I don't feel I've been of much use.'

Hurst had nothing to say yet seemed reluctant to let me go. He rose to his feet.

'I wanted to meet you, sir, to sort of get a feel of the dead man's life, you know – I mean, was he a man who could have made enemies?'

'We all make enemies,' I said.

'I'd like you to give some thought, sir, as to where he got his money.'

'He made it. I told you. Property.'

'Yes, sir, but we all have to start somewhere. And I may want to speak to you again, if that's all right?'

'I don't know what I can add.'

'About his financial background, sir.'

'I know almost nothing about it, Inspector.'

I remember now – he gave me a curious look.

11

The car came round again, as it had been doing for the previous half-hour. From it I rang Hal.

'It's me.'

'How'd it go?'

'Brilliantly incisive. Solved in one go. Sherlock Einstein.'

'So – business as usual?' he said. 'Jesus, Chief, they are the pits.'

'They're majoring on Antony's finances. Hal, how much did we do with Safft Construction? All told?'

'I'd have to look it up. But – a lot. In fees alone over the past five years – I'd say twelve, fifteen mill. Ten major properties . . . So it could be even more . . .'

'Ten? As many as that?'

'Don't forget Shrewsbury. And Ludlow. Count it out, Chief, if we're on our own sliding scale, then you have to reckon he was doing four to six hundred mill in the same period.'

'That's my figure, too.'

'Learn anything?'

'Yes. None of it pleasant. But there's a nephew.'

'By the way – Lemon has a message for you. Quite urgent. Some lawyer.'

Lemon said, 'A Mister Lewison rang.'

'What is he?'

'A firm of solicitors, he said it was most important, he wants to speak to you today.'

'Where?'

'They're in Bruton Street.'

'That's where I am now.'

Mr Lewison took my call immediately. 'Mr Newman, I represent the estate of the late Antony Safft. May we meet?'

'When?'

'Sooner rather than later?'

'I'm outside your door almost.'

Get it all over with inside one day. Give me time to think of Antony. The least I could do.

Mr Lewison had tall red hair and a great deal, I should imagine, of bad temper.

'This may seem unorthodox, Mr Newman. But the police have asked for discretion. In fact they're forcing it.'

'Forcing it. What's that got to with me?' Mr Lewison had a large mirror on the wall adjacent to his desk. He looked at it often.

'Here you are.' He handed me a sheet of paper. 'This was written last Thursday, sent last Friday morning. This is all I can show you for the moment.'

Dear Mr Lewison

I enclose my will, as we discussed. Thank you for clearing up the point that a witness to a will may not be a beneficiary but an executor may.

Should anything untoward or premature cause my death, I believe it important that the two executors I am appointing, my nephew Philippe and my friend and architect Nicholas Newman, should meet each other as quickly as possible. Neither man knows he has been named by me; I intend to tell Mr Newman this week and I hope to see my nephew next week.

Yours sincerely
Antony Safft

'I don't know what to say.'

'Good piece of lawyers' advice, Mr Newman. For court

usually, but I find it applies across the board. When you don't know what to say say nothing.'

'I suppose we must do as he asks. Have you been in touch with his nephew?'

'He's very upset. As you must be. I see from the newspapers you were expecting to lunch –'

I interrupted him. 'Antony had said to me that he had something to tell me.'

Mr Lewison took back Antony's letter and, looking at his mirror, said, 'His nephew's arriving tonight. Staying at Brown's. He's going to call me in the morning. He has to go to the house. And there's the formal identification.'

I said, 'I'll leave a message for him at Brown's. I'd be grateful if you'd tell him to check messages.'

'Of course,' said Mr Lewison; lawyers always like to be helpful, especially to someone who's handling big money – as Antony's will was sure to be. 'By the way,' he continued, 'we have a chap here who's awfully good on securities – and I expect you know the scope of our conveyancing department?' He reached to a table behind him and handed me a glossy brochure advertising the partnership.

'Oh. Thank you,' I said. 'What happens now?'

'In a murder inquiry the police hold on to everything. I have the will here but I can't disclose it to anyone.'

Back at the office on this heaving, swirling day, Lemon met me.

'Miss Bentley's here.'

'Elizabeth? Where?'

'She's talking with the new architect. Do they know each other?'

'I don't think so. Why do you ask?'

'They're very chummy.' Lemon has useful antennae.

'Thank you,' I said, feeling more than irritated by this development.

Hal overheard and looked puzzled – and then I called him back.

'Close the door.'

He came in.

'Listen,' I said. 'I'm going to be involved a bit with Antony Safft's nephew.'

I had brought Hal from junior draughtsman to fully qualified architect almost against his own wishes. He hated studying for it, was perfectly happy being a draughtsman, had Pam and the boys and football, but he was a genius with services and the best negotiator with planners. Elizabeth never liked him.

'Miss Bentley's in the building,' I said.

'Lemon told me. With our newest star.' Hal sniggered.

'Break that up, Hal, would you? I mean – come on – we only hired her a few hours ago.'

'I've tried twice, Chief. No go.'

'Okay. Send "Miz" Strait in to see me.'

When she arrived, instead of acting upon my instinct and enquiring what Elizabeth wanted, and how Elizabeth had made her acquaintance, I asked her the lethal and inexplicably motivated question: 'Are you free for dinner tomorrow night? I believe it'll be Friday by then – not that I believe anything any more.'

She had a way of standing with her legs slightly apart.

'Yes,' she said, as though accepting some natural outcome.

Hal came back later: 'Miss Bentley's gone.'

'Gone?'

'Yup.'

'Is that good or bad? I mean – that she went without speaking to me?'

All offices have politics. Some architectural practices suffer hugely from them. I eliminated them by being the majority shareholder. Life is difficult enough.

Hal gave me a new problem.

'That cash advance, Chief – that's done,' he said. 'I rang the bank myself.'

I looked puzzled. 'Too much is happening, Hal. What cash advance?'

'Miz Strait's. She told me you okayed it.'

I fenced myself in on neutral ground. 'How much?'

'Two grand.'

'Have you adjusted the payroll? Or do we do this every day?'

Mary Strait had never discussed money. No need to – she knew the salary; the headhunters published it. Nor had she asked for a cash advance. Or was I now so bemused that my head could only think cryptically, couldn't deal with simple facts? I had yet to digest the implications of Antony's letter.

Sweating hard. Jacket off. My stomach had forgotten the lunch it ate. I got unaccountably hungry. Lemon found a sandwich and a grapefruit, heated a fresh towel on the radiator and gave it to me to rub my face and neck.

Calls came in, including Mr Lewison's secretary. Philippe Safft would meet me at Brown's tomorrow, Friday, at six; he needed to leave for the airport by seven. After all of which I had to turn again to Johan Pearl's drawings; he also had an appointment tomorrow.

By five o'clock shock wore off and fatigue set in. I countered by listing all that had happened and all that had to be done. Then I tore up the piece of paper. The evening ahead might help – Hal had arranged agency tickets to see the Black Pearl play. Why can he never tell me he has done such a thing without seeming to seek praise for it?

12

The car got us to within a hundred yards of the Executive Gate. First impressions: dense throngs of vertical, mobile human beings, all shoulders and legs and heads. Every few minutes another wave of crowd washed in. Everybody was going somewhere. Many of them sang or bantered. If a passable female came by they chanted, 'We're Gonna See Yer Tits Today!'

Mostly men, they strode, walked, swaggered and swore, they shouted, ate, drank, shoved fiercely to the lavatories or the aisles. We travelled along open corridors eighty feet above ground level, in concrete dense enough for the coastal defences. The broad, fast-moving, rough flow was fervid and relaxed and tight and loose all at once.

Brave was the man who stopped, forcing the waves to flow all around him. Children, with scarves and rosettes and favours and numbered, named shirts, ran and scampered and argued, faces roast-red with thrill.

The event had the compulsion of Picasso. From rowdy to friendly to deadly serious; from merry to aloof to aggressive; from boisterous and companionable to considered, even thoughtful – an anthropologist's dream.

I felt intrusive; I didn't know the codes. The crowd gave off a unity, a feeling of belonging to the place and the event in ways no outsider could ever crack. And yet I loved it. It almost blew away my general distress.

'We'll go straight to the seats,' said Hal. 'If you walk in front of people after kick-off you get shit in your face.' I wish he wouldn't pick his teeth with that eternal triangle of postcard.

Two new and powerful impressions now hit me – how small and green the pitch far below, and how steep the rake of the stand, steep enough for me to think about my balance. The seats were jointed together in a way nobody calling himself an architect would allow today. Hal ushered me ahead. On my right sat two men, all knitted hats and hamburgers. 'Cheers, mate,' said one as I apologized for brushing against his leg. A man in the row behind us snarled at me, 'Sit-fucking-down!'

I sat down.

'Wanker,' he said contentedly. The fantasy of revenge for the Tube blared again in my head. I had to grip my knees to calm down.

A huge television screen bridged one corner. Cheerleader girls sashayed across the pitch. A matey announcer yelled.

'Are you taking it in?' half-shouted Hal. He had assumed the argot of the fans, chippy, forceful, brash.

The mood of the crowd heated up. As the announcer roared on, the footballers chugged out – amazingly young, amazingly shiny, a cinematic gleam.

'Gladiators,' I thought, but kept it to myself.

They quickened when the crowd saw them. I looked for the Black Pearl. Near the end of his team, he shuffled and jigged, chatting and smiling over his shoulder. His face looked as though he had greased it; he must have oiled his head – it shone like an ebony shell. He did some jerks and stretches, ran a quick burst from a standing start; he looked like a small black machine.

For several minutes I focused on him. Was this the boy I saw looking for his mother's approval? Who poured out his incoherent heart to me on the phone, weeping at the death of our friend?

The players aired and exercised. A squad of squatting photographers roiled them into team photographs. They soon broke away and began to distribute footballs.

The Black Pearl flicked and foot-juggled. He looked heavier in strip and immensely fit; some of the others were actually shorter than him but even a football virgin such as I could see his power, and his command of the ball. He and another player did tricks – one's knee to the other's head, back to the head, returned to the knee. They did this three times and then the Pearl turned away and languidly drove the ball towards the goal.

'Physics,' I thought – because the ball hit the crossbar with such force it bounced twenty yards back.

I could hear some bizarre sounds – they came from the terrace near which the Black Pearl did his struts.

I asked Hal, 'That noise? What is it?'

'The sweet and gentle nature of the English football fan. They're making monkey sounds. They used to chuck bananas.'

'Why?'

'The *Black* Pearl.'

'But there are –' I counted – 'one, two – eight black players on the playing field.'

'Yeh, but he's foreign,' said Hal. 'Park, by the way.'

'Park?'

'Yeh. Playing field's Eton. This is the park.'

'Oh?'

Formalities occurred. Referee, linesmen, small silk pennants, handshakes. The toss, though I never expected it, was something I recognized from school cricket – my last experience of any team game in any form. Sport is too naked for me. If you aren't good at it everybody can see. I need thinking time to get good at anything.

The Black Pearl, numbered 16 on his back and shorts, broke away to the far side, playing along the touchline.

'Here we go,' said Hal. The crowd cleared its throat.

Some player stroked the ball from the dot in the huge circle that marked the middle of the field. Another drove it out towards Pearl, who raced after it. Without steadying he sent it high across the rectangle in front of the goal.

'One touch,' said Hal. 'I hate the little sod. That's the skill, Chief – make the ball go where you want with one touch.'

The play swung back in our direction and then began to flow here, there and everywhere. I leaned forward, absorbed.

After five or six minutes of watching I asked Hal's ear, 'Isn't it all about space?' I could hardly hear myself for the noise. 'I mean – it seems all about winning advantage by using space. Get space and you get advantage. Advantage becomes power. So space becomes power?'

I almost said, 'Like architecture,' but in my mind's early-warning system I heard Hal's word 'poncy' and held my tongue.

Hal nodded and said, 'Yeh – well, yeh.'

I found it completely engrossing. The floodlights heightened the sense of theatre. Part of me expected knife-fights along every row of seats. It didn't happen.

Then I had a new thought. With a game of such skill and exhibiting such superb diversity, why the violence from spectators? Because they can't do it themselves? No, surely not. But – shouldn't they all be as absorbed as I was? Even more so, given their knowledge and passionate allegiance?

And I had another thought – about the relationship between elegance and violence. Into the elegance I had fought for in my life had come inexplicable and terrible violence. And Antony, who had more natural elegance than most men I have known, died violently. How I missed him now; he adored football, often invited me; I never went.

The lights made the green playing surface luminous. Pearl got rapid attention every time he moved. He had a crucial ancillary skill – avoiding injury. Once or twice players came at him and I winced.

'Is that part of it?' I asked Hal. 'Avoiding injury?'

'Yeh. You should take lessons from him.' He laughed with his irritating wheeze.

Diagonal kicks, 'crosses', that travelled thirty, forty, fifty yards – they changed the pattern in an instant. Holding the ball from the opposing side as long as possible: 'possession', I learned to call it. When not actually on the ball moving into a position that anticipates the next move: 'Running off the ball,' said Hal, 'hallmark of a great player. You should see some of the Brazilians.'

This game was a matter of style, these were elegant patterns of movement. Lovely long lines, squares, loops. My thought continued; I don't see anything here to suggest why so glorious a sport attracts such savagery.

'But they all seem so bright,' I called out to Hal. 'And I know Pearl is bright.'

'Naw. They're bright in their boots,' he said. 'Pearl's unusual. None of them's usually that educated. The others'd piss on that. What they are's innocent. I mean, yeah, you get the messers, the coke-heads and that, or the big gargle customers. But the greater percent's just worrying about the usual things – like where the next Ferrari's coming from.'

'Who's he?' I pointed to a man in a suit and a camel coat chewing his hands on the sidelines.

'Manager. Most interesting man on the park. Hard as a jockey's bollocks.'

Suddenly Hal was up on his legs like a cat. The crowd beside and in front of me roared and jumped.

'What's happened?'

The man on my right answered. 'Usual fucking thugs you get here when this crowd's the visitors.'

The man beside him pointed, 'Keeper. See?'

A goalkeeper in his satin green suit trotted towards the middle of the field holding his head.

'Coin, I expect,' said the more reasonable man.

'Fucking animals,' said the other. 'They don't know how

to fucking behave. They have no fucking principles. They're fucking obscene, that's what they are. I'd cut their fucking balls off.'

'You mean someone in the crowd threw a coin and hit the goalkeeper on the head?' I asked, trying to get it absolutely clear.

The rougher one turned to me. 'Are you trying to climb up my arse?' He said it so aggressively I recoiled. His neighbour asked, 'Been to football before, mate?'

Honesty felt the best policy. 'No,' I said. And dishonesty. 'I've been abroad since I was a child.'

Why didn't Hal bail me out?

'Then fuck off back abroad, you prat,' said the nearer one. 'You're taking up a valuable seat.'

Hooligans in the stands too? A reasonable thought given my immediate neighbour. The language appalled me and I'm not squeamish. So much for the theory of obscenity as a barometer of self-disgust.

The crowd upheaval got no worse. Uniformed police frog-marched a fan to the exit. The referee stood at a safe distance, waiting to restart. Two minutes later Johan Pearl scored a goal so beautiful even I could tell. I have replayed it in my mind many times.

He exchanged the ball twice with a near team-mate – a 'one-two', Hal called it – then slipped it between a defender's opening legs – a 'nutmeg', apparently. He kicked it hard and low from a sharp angle and a distance of about twenty yards out. It bounced at precisely the most difficult spot for the goalkeeper to grab it. The net bulged and I loved it.

Pearl followed the ball into the net and thumped the ball again, as if trademarking his goal. Then he wrapped the net to his face like a lady with a veil making a joke. My neighbour swore a rope of oaths. Someone else threw a missile and it hit the ground yards away from Pearl. The crowd booed. After that every time he touched the ball three or four opponents moved on him. This distraction freed others; his team scored three more times.

Of that tally Pearl caused at least one. He ran the ball out on his wing, from a throw by his goalkeeper. Two men raced to confront him. He flipped the ball from foot to foot, rolled a boot over it and back again, feinted with his body like a boxer, shimmied to right, then left, then right again and broke away from them. Then he ran twenty yards with the ball as though tied to his boot with string. He chipped it over the head of another opponent straight to the other black player in his team, who headed it with the force of a kick past the opposing goalkeeper.

'And that's why they call it "The Beautiful Game",' said Hal in my ear. The players kissed each other and danced a cryptic jig, which the fans loved.

We never moved at half-time. Halfway into the second half my foul-mouthed neighbour wandered off. The game fell in tempo and interest. Near the end, I saw Hal yawn.

As we walked out Hal said to me, 'What d'you think?'

'Well, I had been puzzling as to why it's such a huge craze –'

He interrupted. 'Easy. Everyone's depressed and footie's brilliant. I mean, I've seen afternoons when the breath was taken out of my lungs. I saw a goalkeeper once from Atletico Madrid against Chelsea, I saw him fly through the air like a bird, I mean did he fucking fly? High ball, thirty yards out, Jimmy Greaves at his best, on the turn, outside of the boot and the dago keeper takes off like a falcon. Poetry.'

'Yes,' I said. 'Did it cheer you up?' He leaned forward, anxious to know.

'I saw its point,' I said.

'Whatcha think of our boy? The Pearl?'

'He seems like a superb player. I mean, I don't know enough but there's a style there, isn't there?'

'You bet. Little sod!'

When I reached home I was thinking about Mary Strait. And the Tube train. And Antony. Where is his body? Some chilly morgue. I still chastised myself for not having perceived him fully. The plastic bag containing my raddled Tube clothes stood by the door. Fatigue moved in again.

The buzzer went. At this hour?

A neighbour announced himself; 'I took in a package.'

Flowers – amid a huge bunch of roses sat an unsigned note; 'Get well soon.'

I dropped them on the floor as if infected. Knives and flowers.

Directory enquiries gave me the number of Hampstead police station, but it was a centralized number and someone told me I couldn't speak to Inspector Hurst until the morning.

In any case, what could he answer to my question, 'Why me?'

13

Next day I rose at six and – concentration again – hammered myself into long, driven hours. Trying to keep things at bay. Taking the usual escape route of work. Manic pace always has some meaning. I told Lemon to say I was abroad and I spoke to nobody unless essential.

Such as Inspector Hurst. He told me of the progress to date. Meaning – nothing. I asked him too what news of the Tube. Another nothing. We had inconclusive exchanges and gloom descended. Gloom accompanied by fright – not good.

I told him about the flowers. Not interested.

'Usually an error, sir.'

'But flowers *and* a knife, Inspector?'

He said, 'The world's more full of cock-up than conspiracy.'

Checked all my own jobs. Asked Lemon, 'What's the status on the Wiltshire planning permission?'

Lemon came back. 'One query. Re the National Rivers Authority. They want to know if the stream has ever flooded those fields. If the answer is no, full planning permission's okay.'

'Has Hal spoken to the builders?'

'I believe so.'

'Tight penalties, tell him.'

Now, enter my old enemy, my old friend – enter full-blown Depression. Capital *D*. I sat in the office, morose and withdrawn. Door closed. No lunch. Didn't draw, didn't read, didn't listen to music. Around three o'clock I walked over to Knightsbridge. The Friday exodus had begun. Went to an

92

empty Harvey Nichols, saw nothing I liked, thought about buying another pair of Oliver Sweeney shoes, hadn't enough energy. Went back to work, lecturing myself, reminding myself of the past I must continue escaping. Hadn't noticed Antony was gay. Too out of touch with others. Or too depressed to look, too inert. Wake up. Now I wobbled. Fractured feelings loomed. I fought.

I thought of seeking help. But I am reluctant. I help myself. Only me. Or do I? What's happening to me? I mean – inside. Here's the bind I'm in. If I look beyond my own threshold I have to cope with what I see. If I don't look – I get hit by events. What's the choice? No choice. Such a bind often drove me into a pattern where I always caused damage.

The endless beds. The games. The false emotion. I liked being the prey of women who wanted money and status – but I liked it only so that I could see the disappointment in their faces when I turned them down. At that sadistic thought a touch of the old panic returned. Perhaps – perhaps – the Beautiful Game? Is that what Hal meant? Fight off Depression.

In the office Hal and Lemon had put together a mass of football print. We do that with significant clients, show them we're thinking of them. The coverage amazed me – football played over acres of newsprint.

I strode willingly into this foreign country. Hairdressing, advertising endorsements, girlfriends, the cars they drive, the food they eat – football's razzle hits every sense. Approval and disapproval. 'On forty thousand a week he shouldn't miss chances like that.' The density surprised me. I, whose job it is to feel for the *Zeitgeist*, had let this gleaming force swerve past, hadn't checked into it. I kept up with music, with galleries, with cinema, with writing trends – how did I miss this? Snobbery, I expect. My mother called it 'a gentleman's game played by rowdies'. (And rugger 'a rowdies' game played by gentlemen'; for years I thought she had coined the phrase.)

I got interested fast. Pearl gave me a reason. In scanning the print a runway opened up – I could glide in on the middle-class ticket. The press coverage included anthropologists looking at this 'tribal substitute' and social historians discussing a replacement for war, smart women expressing sexual excitement, academics intellectualizing the hero factor. I'd join the 'soccerati', as I saw them called – those who followed for fashion, not passion. If the aristocracy were drinking in the taproom – it all added up to a conclusion that would let me in, too. Football had become a cultural appendage, glitzy and cool and political.

Perfect for architects. My job, too, is about using space elegantly and to practical advantage. And I read football managers, talking about their players 'expressing themselves'. Add esoteric skill to elitism and you get pretentiousness – fine, I like a bit of pretension as well as the next designer. There was always Hal. If I ever put it to Hal like this he'd say, 'Yeh, well, bollocks.' But pretensions aside, while I read that football coverage some of the game's compulsiveness drifted towards me on the wind.

14

Pearl came in fifteen minutes early, less assured on a strange patch. Lemon asked for his autograph.

He was quieter when shy. Then Hal arrived, his opening gambit as awkward and crass as only Hal can be.

'How old were you in July 1982?'

'About nine, I think. Or eight.'

'Brazil vee Italy? In Barcelona?'

'Oh, right!'

'Paolo Rossi, yeah? That's why I asked. Anybody said that to you before? They musta said "Paolo Rossi" to you.'

'Yeah, some guy in an Italian newspaper or maybe French. My father told me.'

'You've the same style as Rossi,' said Hal. 'He useta hit the net too when he scored, useta run and kick the net three, four times, saw him do it against Celtic. D'ja ever play against Celtic?'

'No, Rangers,' said Pearl.

'Same difference. Betchya felt the pain.'

'I always feel the pain,' said Pearl.

'How d'you stand all that team-bus stuff?' asked Hal. 'Why won't they let you travel under your own steam?'

'Steam?' asked the Pearl.

I said to him, 'You can talk about football all you like, so long as you know the meter's running.'

We spent an hour and more going through the plans. I allowed myself to be impressed by the clarity of his mind.

'D'you want to have actual livestock looking into your kitchen? That'd mean you'd have to farm.'

Pearl said, 'I want the stable doors opening in, see? I thought you could commission stuffed or carved animals. Or cartoons.' He waxed with delight. 'I can sit there with all doors closed. And then open them. Surprise everyone.'

I studied him again. Not yet mature. Clearly very fit. Self-contained in the smallest movement. Even-tempered. Sunny. Intellectually sharp. Nothing macho. Will probably become a businessman in something interesting when he finishes football. Such as? Such as – a gallery, or advertising, or the music industry.

'And the tiles?' he said.

'Your actual Delft.' I showed him the letter from the supplier. 'Samples within the week.'

At half past five I poured him a beer. He said, 'Can I have a favour?'

'Certainly.'

'Is it all right if I don't meet the rest of your staff today? I'm still shaken. Because of Antony.'

'Of course. We'll use the staircase when you're leaving.' My turn then to ask the questions. 'Is it difficult? Being so in the public eye?'

'It is. It is not in Europe, but here it is very –' He paused; he didn't want to seem critical.

'Aggressive?'

'People here take their football very directly.'

I broached the bigger subject. 'Have the police spoken to you? I had to go and see them.'

'They telephoned.' I guessed he might have tears in his eyes. 'Antony was so good to me. Man!'

Hal arrived, halting further such exchange. Pearl whistled when he saw the bundles of drawings.

I said, 'I'm working on this at home.'

Hal said to Pearl, 'Wish you'd seen George Best at his best.'

'Great name he had,' said Pearl. His smile returned. 'But

I was nearly "Pele" wasn't I? "Pearl" in some languages is spelled P-E-R-L-E and I could've dropped the *R* – see?'

Exit Hal, captivated.

At the street door, we shook hands and he said, 'Nicholas, you're going to have to call me "Johan", I'm too young to be "Mister".'

'I agree,' I said. 'I watched you last night.'

'You were there? Oh, right!' He laughed. 'It was comfortable.'

Already passers-by had begun to glance at him.

15

I looked at my watch – quarter to six: three-quarters of an hour to go before meeting Philippe Safft at Brown's. Hal buzzed, reminding me of a partners' meeting cancelled for next morning – too many out at site visits. I checked several state-of-plays on the computer – on eleven projects, nine of the builders looked set to hit penalties. Sitting back from the keyboard, I held my hands out like a priest – to stop them shaking.

The streets, clear and cold, gave me an open run to Brown's. When I got there, no sign of Philippe Safft. I thought, Poor man – certain to be late. Identifying the body – ghastly. I paced the hallway of Brown's. Eventually I enquired, in case Philippe Safft had decided to stay over.

The hall porter said, 'There's a message for you, sir. From the French gentleman.'

'Where is he?'

'He left at seven, sir, or thereabouts, said he had a plane to catch.'

'About *seven*? What d'you mean?' I looked at my watch – twenty-five minutes to seven. 'What time is it now?'

'Now, sir,' said he with a hall porter's international elaborateness, 'it – is, seven twenty-three.'

'Oh, shhhooooott!!'

Distraught but contained I found the message: *'This is my number. Please telephone me in this bad tragedy. Philippe Safft.'* The signature had more flourishes than a parade.

From behind me a voice said, 'They say it's the new fashion to keep a lady waiting.'

Oh, my God! Dinner with Mary Strait! Had I forgotten? I had.

'I am so sorry,' I said. 'My bloody watch let me down.'

'I nearly didn't wait,' she said. 'A dishy man left a message for you. I almost approached him to say I was meeting you here.'

'Drink?'

She said, 'You need one. You look – I don't know you well enough to say how you look . . .'

'Shattered? Bemused? Disappointed? Frustrated? Needing a drink? Was Sean at the office when you were leaving?'

'Who's Sean?'

'The driver.'

'He brought me here.'

I didn't raise an eyebrow; I resisted the thought, The car's not for you, it's for me.

'Is he on the mobile? He must be, mustn't he?'

I rang him, called him back to Brown's, gave him my keys, told him to take my car to my apartment. As I made the call I wondered what to say to her; then I said it.

'Sean, the car – they're not actually used as freely as that.'

She took the reprimand. 'Sorry. It's just that I thought, well, as it was you and I didn't want to be late – I thought it would be all right.'

'Okay, I didn't mean to sound tyrannical.'

The waiter hovered.

'Gin and tonic,' she said.

She drank it within five minutes.

Sean came; car sorted.

She leaned forward and pressed the tab of my shirt collar back under my jacket. 'Now,' she said. 'Which is it?'

'Which what?' I could hardly keep my voice civil; I loathe being pawed and some women paw one too much.

'Shattered? Bemused? Disappointed? Frustrated? Needing a drink?'

'My brain's lost all its pinions,' I said. 'Excuse me.'

I must get hold of myself. Everything's too much. Ran downstairs to 'Gentlemen'. I looked at myself in the mirrors above the brown marble. She was right; I did look torn apart.

Stood at the urinals; knew my bladder was full; nothing happened. Stood at the basins; sprayed water all over my trousers; looks as though I've wet myself. I began to swear aloud.

'Help you, sir?' I hadn't seen the attendant.

'Nobody can help me,' I snapped at him and gave him a pound coin to ease my conscience.

And that was true. To whom could I speak of all this? Ironically, Antony would have listened. He would have had an idea. Now I had to go back upstairs and brace myself for this evening I had so foolishly instigated.

'Your glass is empty,' I said and called the waiter.

'And you'll need another.' She handed me mine.

'Well, what do you think of our caseload?' I asked.

'Busy.'

'D'you think so?' Switch on the automatic pilot – if it'll work.

'Don't you really want,' she said shrewdly, 'to find out what I think of the practice?'

Automatic pilot not working tonight. 'Oh, fuck the shop,' I said.

'The shop. Of course. California knocks the irony out of one.'

She subsided, a little awry.

'Sorry,' I grunted. 'If I seem testy it's because I am.'

This made her laugh, then frown.

'Is something up?' she asked. 'I mean, if it's none of my business say so. But you're different from the man who hired me yesterday.'

'Yesterday?'

'Yes. Yesterday.'

'Jesus! It feels like –'

She was wearing a green Dévorée scarf, wide and lightly tasselled, beautiful. I got hold of myself, complimented her on the scarf and apologized.

'Something horrible happened. Maybe Hal told you.'

'The client? Property man. But – won't you keep the account? I mean, you've been very successful for them?'

'But he was also a friend. And he's made me his executor.'

'Any strings attached.'

'Strings?'

'Do you have to do anything? That's very common these days in American legacies – you have to build a museum in Arizona or something.'

'I don't know yet. The other executor's the man you saw here. His nephew. He's a French lawyer.'

'The dishy guy in the striped shirt?'

I said, 'It's only a week! A week ago today he was killed!'

Walking to Wheeler's I counted my soundtracks. On one, I thought about Philippe Safft. How dreadful to be late for him. Another soundtrack considered Johan Pearl and football. The excitement. The hunger to see more. A third soundtrack rued being Antony's executor. And then chided me for ingratitude. Another soundtrack considered the practice. Things were never better. Now is the time to be still. Finish the Pearl contract. Take a good holiday. Go to the West Indies. Or the Seychelles. Or the coast of Mexico. Or somewhere. Take a palazzo in Venice. If only for a weekend. With whom? Consider your loneliness, Nicholas, isn't it at the root of all your problems? So murmured the soundtrack I most dread. Shut up!

Another soundtrack asked me to consider Mary Strait, to give an opinion of her. What did I think of her? Did I like her? Why was I ready to confide in her? And the same soundtrack

101

warned me not to confide in her too much and above all else to say goodnight to her outside the restaurant after dinner, see her into a cab.

The thought made me ask her suddenly, 'Where exactly are you living?'

She made a mouth. 'Out of town.'

I said, 'Out of town?' and sounded as though I meant, 'Outer space?'

'Until I get my own place,' she said apologetically. 'My aunt's there. Home Counties.'

We climbed the narrow stairs. She hid her hips well under a full skirt.

My soundtrack asked me the question: Why do you want to confide in her? She's an employee. Why are you doing this?

I asked her, 'You like fish?'

'Not much.' She sat down.

'Jesus, I wish I'd known,' I answered, and I asked myself another question: Why am I swearing in front of this woman? I never swear.

'I was going to say so when you said "Wheeler's", but let me look at the menu. I like lobster. Does that count as fish?'

'Isn't it supposed to make you pregnant?' I said, again crossing one of my own boundaries.

'I never heard that – but what a nice way of doing things.'

She rolled her eyes in a way that irritated me – as did the slight Americanism in her expression. Now what do I do? Take up "nice way of doing things" and walk straight into a conversation about sex? Or ignore it and sound a bit of a prune? No matter which way I turned I lost that round.

If I said, 'Oh, there are nicer ways' – that had an element of the *risqué* in it, and *risqué* is invitation.

If I asked, 'Are other ways not nice?' it would sound whatever the male equivalent of 'coquettish' is.

And if I did neither and said nothing I would come across as a man disappointed in his sex life, and in any case I bet she had discussed my single status with the other women in the office, and anyway hadn't she indicated at our lunch that she knew a great deal about me?

I said nothing. Instead I looked very carefully at her under the picture of the horse called 'Leader'.

Not as plain as I first thought. This didn't cut any of the ice surrounding one view of her – which was that she could well be an irritating and probably smart-arse feminist, full of Californian political correctness. And who would now probably try and worm her way into my affections.

The large green menus arrived. 'May I have the lobster?' she said. 'Is it very expensive?'

Well – that stopped me. I believe she was the first woman in a decade who had ever considered the price of anything on any menu I had ever shared.

'I think you should have it too,' she said. 'You probably need a treat after all you've been going through. I'm sure they wouldn't mind if you took off your jacket.'

'No, I like my jacket on,' I said grudgingly. And, still grudging, added, 'Yes, I might have the lobster too.'

I sat back, waiting for the evening to begin.

She looked around. 'I like places that have these old-fashioned values,' she said. 'They make me feel the old world isn't slipping away too fast.'

'You won't be copying too many Edwardian faiences at Bentley Newman,' I said. She was making me dislike myself. I tried to become more amenable. 'Tell me about your life. Living "out of town". Is that good?'

'My life is chaotic,' she said. 'I don't seem to be able to organize anything, money, accommodation, transport, nothing. And I owe you an apology.'

'For what?'

'For a lie I told.'

And we hadn't even unfolded our napkins!

'Ah, yes.'

'You know?' She blushed.

'The cash advance?'

I noticed she made me say the words. Plus, she had disarmed me on one, two, three counts – not liking fish, the old values and the prices on the menu.

But there I go. I see all such things but I never seem able to do anything about them. Instead of defending I succumb.

'It was cowardly of me. It's just that I didn't clear out my checking account in Santa Monica. I had to leave some money in it for the winding-up of some bills there.'

'It's okay. How are you fixed now?'

'I'm okay, thanks. That was a huge help.'

I tasted the Meursault. She looked at the label.

'The best,' she said. 'So nice to drink French wine again.'

Had somebody told her of my near-violent opposition to so-called 'New-World' drinking? Or was she shrewder than a town cat? Or was she sincere?

'Are you looking for a place in London?'

'In theory. I saw something in Belsize Park. Something else in Primrose Hill.'

'It takes time.'

This was the territory of the disadvantaged. I had been so blitzed over the past ten days I had no time to concentrate on anything other than dominant events. Being late for Philippe Safft represented a kind of last straw. I drank a glass of wine so quickly I felt it in my nose; then I drank another. And Mary Strait kept pace with me.

The waitress proved over-solicitous. Of me. I muttered something.

Mary Strait smiled and said, 'Oh, come on! You must know why she's doing it.'

I blushed; again she suggested I take off my jacket; I didn't.

The fish cakes arrived. I don't know what they tasted like. Halfway through them came the next bottle of Meursault. Then the lobster. By now I had told her of the attack on the Tube, and of Antony, the Stanley knife, the anonymous flowers.

'They must be connected,' she said. 'There's no such thing as coincidence.' She had a fleck in one iris.

'Nobody's yet tied them together.'

Then, as I do, I fell instantly tired of talking about myself and quizzed her. She proved unexpectedly candid.

'I spend more than I earn. My clothes are everywhere, I don't have a pair of knickers I can lay my hands on at short notice. The worst thing of all is I don't even know what's in fashion at the moment.'

If a woman fancies me I find she gets some sexual reference into the conversation within ten minutes of talking. So – 'knickers' – yes, about eight minutes in, I reckoned.

'Grey,' I said. 'Grey is the new black. Or so they're saying.'

'How did you come to be so fantastically well organized?' she asked.

'Am I?'

'I look at your office and there's not a thing out of place and Lemon tells me that she's afraid to go inside the door in case she *un*tidies something – as she put it.'

Bad mark against Lemon, whispered the sneaky part of my mind; speaking about me like that.

'Either I'm completely anal,' I said, 'or it's something I've worked at. I suspect it's a bit of both. What I find is that it speeds me up. I always know where everything is. But it has taken me ages.'

More Meursault. For her and me. Excellent lobster; I love this restaurant.

'I know you have no wife,' she said, 'so I'm not going to play silly pretend games. But d'you think it'd be less easy to be so organized if you had a wife?'

105

'Yeah, well,' I said languidly. 'Who can say?'

'That's very noncommittal of you.'

'I am noncommittal. Isn't that why I'm not married?'

'Why do you attract such difficulty into your life?' she asked. 'I remember all the newspaper stuff a few years back.'

'Oh, you mean – "He hasn't married because a girlfriend of his was murdered." Wrong tree to bark up,' I said.

No, I'm not discussing my past life. Not even with myself.

'But it's an interesting question, isn't it?' she pressed. 'How tall are you?'

'That's an interesting question, too.'

'Six four, I'd guess.'

'Six three and a bit. And I suppose that means something. Especially the bit. If you've just come back from California and they're all talking *echt* or Est or whatever it is – I presume Freud's out by now – and there are things that can be stitched together into any pattern you like?' I lapsed into a satirical chime. 'So the guy's six foot three and a bit, and he may be self-conscious about his height, therefore he's making himself into a target.'

'You're too defensive,' she said.

Her tone turned gentle. But I wasn't used to being inter-rogated, and it didn't feel so kindly. More Meursault. I kept looking at her mouth and she at mine.

'You say "too defensive". Why bring "too" into it?'

'Too defensive to suggest that you haven't asked yourself the same question. By any standards what's happened to you in the last week is extraordinary. Hollywood stuff. A close friend doesn't arrive for lunch with you because he's been brutally murdered.'

'Oh, no, not murdered. "Slain",' I interrupted, trying to throw her. 'Isn't that what Hollywood would say – "Brutally slain"?'

She wasn't deflected. 'But here you are trying to take it

in your stride. Next afternoon, you are mugged by football hooligans. Somebody's sending you anonymous unpleasant-nesses. You sit here shrugging it away. How can a mind so organized as yours not join up all the pictures?'

Suddenly, to my amazement and my chagrin, she started to weep.

She held her hands before her and said, 'I've gone too far. I've done what I always do, I've said too much. I'm sorry, it must be the wine.'

If there are two things in life I hate it's women cry-ing – and women crying in public places when they're with me. Loathsome. I don't know any man who can cope with it.

'Back shortly,' I said, heading for the lavatory. I almost took the tablecloth with me in my rush.

When I returned she had sorted out her eyes.

'I'm sorry,' she said. 'I find all of that so frightening. Those things happening to you, they're not the sort of things that ever happen in any part of my life.'

'It isn't hilarious,' I agreed.

'I find – even at this remove – I find being touched by the finger of murder – it's dreadfully frightening. I know of nothing so unsettling. It was my mother's greatest dread.'

We calmed down. The rest of the meal became animated and warm, with me telling stories of clients and she anec-dotes of her Californian experiences. Only one other cloud passed over.

'Elizabeth Bentley was in,' I said.

'She's coming in again on Monday. I asked her advice on the Horseferry job.'

My hackles rose. 'Elizabeth doesn't work in the practice any more,' I said. 'She's retired. She sold me her part-nership.'

'I know, I know.' She produced emollient from some-where.

So did I. 'Which would you prefer – Armagnac, Calvados or Cognac?' I asked a touch rudely.

She shrank a little.

I awoke in my bed at four in the morning. Three bottles of wine. Five Armagnacs each. Mary Strait lay beside me, stertorous, white-naked and domed. The night gives and the night takes away. Around me the maelstrom swirled faster.

16

It takes such a short time to weaken one's position. I can argue extraordinary circumstances. Emotional stress? A need to restore my faith in my body? What good would excuses do? The only way back is up – try and climb to decency.

So, on Saturday morning, with coffee and good manners, I put Mary Strait in a taxi for the office where she said she had left her things. Out of my weak position with her, my guilt at falling back into old ways, I told her to come back if she felt like it: she did.

I also telephoned Philippe Safft to apologize.

'What can I say? I am most dreadfully sorry.' I claimed shock. 'And other difficulties.'

He would like to see me, he needed to see me, but he had no plans to come to London. And out of my weakened position with him I offered to go to France.

'In which case,' he said in his excellent English, 'is it any problem if you fly to Bordeaux?'

'Preferable, I expect.'

'I want you to meet me where Antoine would have wanted us to meet.'

'Of course.'

'Do you know of Oradour-sur-Glane?'

'No-oo.' A family root, I supposed.

'Ah, I see.'

He gave me directions. I remember wishing it could have been Montpellier or Marseilles, on which all small international airports should be modelled.

I made the intervening days a time of intensive concentration – and brought about moments when life almost sprang back to normal.

Nothing came of the Tube investigations, I wasn't asked to give any further statements; silence too from the Antony Safft investigations. The Pearl plans roared ahead. Three surveyors went to Holland to bring back precise dimensions. On each night from Monday to Thursday I had longstanding engagements; they kept me out until late and made me tired enough to sleep deeply. I didn't see Mary Strait all week nor did I make any such effort.

On Friday morning, I rented a car at Bordeaux airport and followed Philippe Safft's directions. As I pulled north-east out of Libourne, beyond Mussidan, beyond Sourzac, an extraordinary incident halted me. Were I superstitious, I might have taken it as an omen. A motorcyclist, flying down a steep hill into one of the long villages, lost control and hit a kerbside bollard. In front of my eyes he was pitched into the air and, fifteen feet up, he hurtled like a human cannonball for a distance of maybe thirty yards. He fetched up in a tree.

A lorry and two cars ahead of me saw what happened. So did a local police car sitting stationary on the village street. We all stopped and climbed out, went to help. When I reached the tree, a policeman was standing beneath it, speaking up to the motorcyclist. The officer half-climbed the tree, did some hauling and tugging on the branches and dropped down again – to be followed with relative agility by the biker.

He seemed completely unhurt. A doctor appeared. The police made the young biker remove his helmet, his tunic, his leathers; underneath he was wearing a tracksuit.

Not a mark did they find on him; not a bruise, nor a scratch, nor a blemish. The drivers alongside me went, *Merveilleux!* and *Merde!*

Accompanied by the police, the young man walked to his destroyed bike. I asked one officer whether they were going to charge him. He shook his head, saying the biker had learned a lesson.

The day lifted and brightened. This part of France is a land of wonderful clouds. They drifted away, leaving only high white gauze as I drove up towards Périgueux into profounder France. At Sarliac sur l'Isle I parted company with the river and jousted with the freight trucks on the N21. Somewhere between Thiviers and Châlus I stopped for a sandwich and had my second bizarre encounter of a bizarre day.

The *patronne* of the bar, a small woman in her forties, asked me conversationally whether I was German.

'*Non. Anglais.*'

She caught that the question irritated me and made peace by asking my route.

'*Village près de Limoges. Oradour-sur-Glane.*'

She stood and looked at me. 'My father took me to Oradour.'

Trying to match the ornateness of her courteous French, I said, 'A very dear friend – from France – he died tragically a month ago. I am going there to meet his family.'

She said, 'What makes me sad is that it was a holy place. For pilgrims to rest and pray. An oratory.' Ah – *oradour*.

Her lips turned down in regret.

Mystified now, to add to the apprehension I already felt, I set out on the last leg. I defeated Limoges's *périphérique*. How many towns in France have the name 'Beauvais'? The green hills of Limousin unfolded.

Mary Strait entered my mind powerfully. She had stayed in my flat on Saturday night too, when we had dinner in l'Arlesienne beneath the gold putti and the blue ceiling. A police convoy hurtled past me at Chamberet, a prison van at their core. Therefore, add it up, what – four, no, five times,

111

including on the floor on Saturday afternoon? I am confused by her.

A sign for Oradour also said *Village Martyr*. Why is Philippe Safft asking to meet me at some sort of Joan-of-Arc-ish shrine? 'After signs for Verneuil,' he said, 'leave the *route nationale* and take the D9.'

She knows where I am now, she knows why I am here. I should never have told her. So why did I switch on my mobile and ring her at that very moment? The sky was blue everywhere; any excuse will do.

Our new switchboard system let me dial her extension directly.

'Bentley Newman,' she said.

'It's me.'

'Oh, hi.'

'Can you talk?' Ludicrous; this is my own office and my own employee I am calling.

'Hold on.' I heard her tidy someone away.

'Hi, there.' She returned, warmer and looser, then whispered, 'Where are you?'

Had she forgotten?

'Near Limoges.'

'It's raining in London.'

'It's two thirty here.' Then, to stop her getting close, I asked, 'Why aren't you at lunch?'

'I have been,' she said.

Is she one of those people whose voice always sounds nervous on the phone?

'How's everything there?' I said, staying breezy.

'More to the point – how are you? I've been concerned.'

Oh, Gawd!

'I shall be on time,' I said. 'My appointment's three o'clock.' I could hear my own hesitancy.

Guilt is why I rang her, guilt at not having spoken to her all week.

'You still there?' she asked.

'Yes. Yes, I am.'

She pressed on. 'Are you in a position to take down the number of my proud new mobile?'

'Not really.'

'I didn't get a chance to say. I enjoyed the weekend.'

I hedged. 'It seems a long time ago.'

'You're a wonderful –' I hoped she wouldn't say it, but she did – 'lover.'

'Lovely day here. People are eating out. The home of that well-known character Al Fresco.'

She said, 'You sound apprehensive.'

Is there no way of keeping this woman at bay? She moaned under me. The welcome in her body took away some of the cruelty in me. When I held her, my lack of feeling – for anybody – hurt me. And, I expect, hurt her.

Without quite hearing what I was saying, I asked, 'I don't suppose you could come out tomorrow. There's an Air France in the morning. I can leave a ticket for you. It's Terminal One. Heathrow, that is. I'll meet you.'

'Yes,' she said.

I ended the call, booked her a flight – and didn't like that I felt fortified.

Now my heart is utterly disturbed as I drive down a road of lakes and scattered birches and beautiful farms. The other signs say 'Veyrac' and 'Nieul', 'Cieux' and 'St Junien' but one says, 'Oradour-sur-Glane. *Village Martyr.*'

I drive past a service station, through a crossroads and my road forks acutely to the right while the highway carries on towards some distant hill. Beneath trees dark with atmosphere I reach a gate with a sign: *'Souviens-toi.'* As though I have come to the very home of Fear, I know immediately that not only shall I remember – I shall never forget. It is exactly three o'clock. I park the car. Philippe Safft walks towards me.

He resembled his uncle Antony, small, elegant and power-ful; he was beautifully dressed, as for a funeral. His bearing conveyed that he wished to like me.

After our greeting – both his hands held one of mine – I apologized again.

'It was so stupid of me. My watch – it simply went wrong that day.'

'Not a' tall. I know how Antoine spoke of you. Now we are to do his bidding.'

'I shall miss your uncle. Rotten business.'

He said, 'I have brought my lovely Claire with me. She is English. Sometimes when I am distressed my English fails and I must speak in French. She will join us shortly.'

We stood a moment outside the gates. I dared not yet look farther. An impression reached me of ruined gables, jagged walls. What is this place? I looked at the sign, and said, '*Souviens-toi.*'

'*Ah, oui.* "*Souviens-toi*". Have you ever seen those words before?'

I shuffled the insides of my mind.

'Yes.' I didn't wish to tell him that the phrase rolled around my soundtrack once or twice since Antony's death.

'Antoine's house? Of course.'

'He had a replica,' I said.

'No. He had the original. He paid a large sum of money for it and they were happy to replace it. It was his way of making a donation.'

'A donation,' I echoed and didn't make the word a ques-tion – but the way I spoke invited some response.

Nobody came or went while we stood there. A car or two had parked nearby. I inhaled the warm-cold air and felt like someone entering a huge cemetery. My greatest wish was to get away.

Philippe looked at me closely. 'And you said you have never heard of Oradour-sur-Glane?'

'No.'

'Antoine never mentioned it?'

'Not at all.'

'So you know nothing? You do not know what to expect?'

'What is there to expect?' I didn't like any of this.

'Come. Before we journey through the whole village I will take you to the single place in it that Antoine spoke of most often.'

We walked through the gates. A bird flew by. Another hopped along the ground. I didn't hear them sing. Neither to right nor to left did I look as I walked beside Philippe. All around me I sensed blackness and devastation. Not my style to be here.

Philippe, now a stride ahead of me, turned left and stopped.

'I cannot say why this one location moved him most. Because, as you will learn, how can you choose? But this ground, here, was special to him.'

On the street corner he pointed to a sign.

ICI. Lieu de supplice où un groupe d'hommes fut Massacré et Brûlé par les Nazis. Recueillez-vous.

Again I followed instructions. *Recueillez-vous.* I stood in recollection.

'Massacred and burned,' I murmured. 'They don't mince their words. "By the Nazis." At home some military euphemism would be inscribed.'

'This is no place for euphemisms,' said Philippe. 'Let me show you two things.'

He stepped back to a spot behind where we'd stood, and he hunkered down.

'The machine gun must have been here. Look. You can see the arc of the bullets.'

He pointed to a series of large-small holes in the wall; they curved upwards to a highest point of about one and a half metres.

'Here, my friend.' He watched me recoil, then walked

115

over and took my hand and made me put my forefinger in each bullet hole. 'Do not doubt anything here. *Recueillez-vous,*' he said softly but passionately, and followed it with, '*Souviens-toi.*'

My poise wilted. To recover I wanted to say something about the French having the emotional courage of their convictions, whereas we would merely stiffen the old upper lip. But Philippe put his hands on my shoulders, turned me around and said, 'And now look.'

On the wall behind us, that is, opposite where the *groupe d'hommes* died, climbed a vine, in its autumn-winter bareness.

'Every year,' he said, 'it flourishes here.' He made me touch its stems.

A tall woman walked down the street.

'This is Claire,' Philippe said.

17

In a sense I was ambushed. I tried to recover, tried to open a file in my mind into which I could put Oradour-sur-Glane. File it with Roman towns, or a drowned graveyard beneath the sea that I saw in Ireland.

No chance; the French mean Oradour to become part of all who go there. They have documented it stone by stone. More crucially they have documented it hour by hour, minute by minute.

Why us?

They have mapped and measured across their undulating, fertile countryside the march of those vilest of German troops, the Waffen-SS.

Why Oradour?

They have racked their consciences for a reason and found none that finally amounts to anything other than Fate at her most random.

Why us, why our village, why so many of us and so cruelly? they ask. Six hundred and forty-two. Men, women and children.

To manage my incompetent emotions I depend upon facts. If someone sobs to me of a beloved's sudden death, I ask for the cause of death. Philippe spoke the facts of Oradour abundantly as we went to the top of the village to begin the frightful tour. As he spoke I condensed and memorized, sealing myself off.

In June 1944 an armoured SS regiment known as das Reich, a veteran of the Russian front and now quartered at Valence d'Agen on the River Garonne in southern France, was ordered to Normandy to help repel the Allied landings. Progress proved slow and frightful; the news from the D-Day beaches had re-energized the French Resistance. For instance, one division of das Reich, the Hermann Goering, had been pinned to one small locality for a fortnight.

Near Limoges, the Maquis abducted a Major Kampffe of das Reich. He escaped but was recaptured and shot. In reprisal, the regiment rampaged brutally – hangings, burnings, casual shootings of passers-by. They opened fire on men and women working in the fields; they shot people inside their own houses, at their front doors; they hanged the French in their village squares.

Major Kampffe belonged to the division of das Reich called der Führer. Commanded by a General von Lammerding, it reached the fabric town called Tulle, a hundred kilometres south of Oradour, on 7 June. Tulle had been liberated by the local Maquis and von Lammerding had orders to take it back. His soldiers arrested three hundred and more hostages. Of these, he culled ninety-nine and hanged them in the streets. All the rest he put on trains for the death camps.

That night von Lammerding and the officer commanding his first battalion, Major Dickmann, and two other officers, a lieutenant and a captain, headed for the *hôtel de ville* at St Junien, fifteen kilometres from Oradour. The locals told them two thousand armed Maquisards surrounded the town – therefore the Germans behaved in St Junien.

As dinner ended, the rank-and-file soldiers knew a significant operation would happen 'somewhere along the Panzer route' on the following day, Saturday 10 June. All the German officers were ordered to sleep together in a large classroom of the local school – except the four still in their planning meeting.

Some time the following morning they chose Oradour-sur-Glane. The villagers believe the Nazis knew of Oradour's peacefulness. By noon the 3rd company of der Führer under

Captain Otto Kahn was drawn up in St Junien. They had two tanks and several trucks carrying between one and two hundred troops.

'The average age of the soldiery,' emphasized Philippe, 'was about nineteen or twenty. The oldest officer was twenty-five.'

'The age of a football team,' I ventured.

Philippe took the remark in his stride. 'This was the point that most distressed my uncle.'

Their weaponry included heavy, belt-fed machine guns, light machine guns, pistols and an unusually large amount of grenades, with slabs of explosive.

Philippe's cadences grew more French. 'The column sat waiting in silence. Nobody had told them what was happening, where they were going. Until Major Dickmann and Lieutenant Barth appeared in a staff car, shouting repeatedly as it drove alongside them, "Today you will see blood. Today you will see blood." The column left St Junien.'

Philippe knew this story like a hymn. I have since discovered that he had memorized the official account.

'Where are those men now? Where is Dickmann?' I asked.

Claire picked up my outrage. 'The bastard died,' she said. 'Killed in action later.' She had so far not spoken beyond 'Hello.'

Philippe led us up the street, to a different gate, another commencement point. He murmured to himself and walked too fast for us.

Claire turned to me. 'I apologize in advance.'

Very tall. Who does that voice remind me of? Has she broken her nose at some point? Yet – profile clear and uncluttered.

'Apologize?'

She said, 'I will probably swear a great deal. When Philippe first brought me here I couldn't bear it. Now I swear out loud; it is the only way I can deal with it.'

I can't place who she speaks like – but in her enunciation every word has its own ring. A young Judi Dench, perhaps? Philippe, who seemed so confident, so groomed and commanding, deferred to this clipped, warm woman.

Claire said, 'Dear Antony. This is very difficult for both of us. I expect Philippe has told you how we met.'

'There hasn't been time,' I said. 'My fault, I missed our London appointment.'

She hesitated, then said, 'We loved Antony.'

The hesitation stuck to my mind. Philippe looked back at her and they clasped hands. I found nothing to say. 'From here, I will talk you through all of Oradour,' said Philippe.

'I may walk a little behind,' said Claire. 'Even though I have heard it all before I am still – I am always . . .'

She didn't finish her sentence. Nor did she walk out of earshot. Three fingers of each hand wore rings – coral, garnet, wide and narrow plain silver, emerald, a diamond. I thought, Which does she wear for pleasure and which for allegiance?

Philippe gestured to indicate the landscape ahead of us. We had turned around and were facing back down towards the way we had walked.

'It was a sunny afternoon. The young men were preparing in their talk for a football match next day. Against another village near here, very fierce rivals naturally enough. In Oradour, the Saturday, it was a day for inoculations. And it was a day when rations were given out. Especially the tobacco ration.'

Now I swallow hard, and I look around and what I can see is a sea of destroyed houses, charred timbers, black walls. The wires hung in the streets where the Germans cut Oradour off from the world. My back hurts like fury; poor ergonomics in the rented car.

Philippe pointed to a fence in the near distance.

'Here was found the body of a man spreadeagled. After

they shot him and he sprawled across the fence they tethered the reins of a horse to his arm. In a joke.'

'A Nazi joke. For which of course they were so famous,' said Claire. 'Very witty, the SS.'

A deaf man would have caught the irony. She looked at me and I remember that I registered her lips.

Philippe continued: 'They took an hour and a half to round everybody up. Soldiers harried old people from beds, men from workbenches. When they had collected them they divided them all up again. And so, at exactly four o'clock, with a grenade as the signal, the Germans began to kill everyone. They did not shoot them outright. Where possible they aimed at the legs, so that they could then put them through the torture of burning them to death. Because that is what they did; they heaped firewood and brushwood and other combustible materials on top of them where they lay, and set fire to them with kerosene and matches.'

On a wall as we passed by I saw a small lingering row of blue-and-white tiles. Were they from Delft?

'And when that was done they set fire to every building in the village, a total of three hundred and twenty-eight buildings, of which a hundred and twenty-three were dwelling houses, and forty were barns, and four were schools.

'And when that was done they looted and took away from the shops and houses what they could, and shot as many of the small domestic animals as they could find. All the cats fled to one house. The first people to filter back found them waiting to be fed.'

Claire joined in. 'And when that was done the Nazis hadn't finished.' She could spit in a murmur. 'They came back to try and bury all the bodies in communal graves. That plan didn't work – because the poor bodies fell apart. So they left, rounding up all the poultry and other edible livestock they could find. That was what happened to Oradour-sur-Glane.'

She held her hands out before her, out of words. Her fingernails had impeccable rose varnish.

We reached the post office. Already I'd seen the ruins of kitchens, bedrooms, parlours. Already my eye had measured the good strength of these old builders. Already I had taken in the fact that their gables remained sound – even when all the roof timbers of the village had blazed so fiercely that in the church (as I would find) the bell melted. Melted in the heat. The bell was silent in the air. Whose poem is that?

'Stop,' says Philippe, and I stopped.

'Look,' he says, and I looked.

I cannot bear it. There is – there was – a sweet and orderly post office on the rue des Desourteaux with twin letter boxes neatly organized in the wall beneath the windows. Gentle Art-Deco scrolls climbed to their own little *belle époque*. What are the trees? Scotch pine, I guess, and I have to guess something because I am looking away. Why am I looking away? I am looking away because I cannot bear where Philippe Safft's forefinger is pointing – to a plaque on the wall which says, '*Léon Faure. Architecte.*'

Was he the man who designed the post office? Did Léon Faure die in the flames? Claire has in her hand a list of all the victims but I'm afraid to ask.

I know what he felt, Leon Faure, when he designed those sweet climbing scrolls. He said to himself, 'Now the walls are going to seem a little plain. And the post-office authorities will not permit money to be spent on anything fancy. Nor would they like it if they knew about it. But façade walls, they need a little something, a little life. So what about these scrolls, and I will sell the idea to them as an afterthought. I will tell them they will not cost much, such little mouldings. Then everyone will be proud of them and the post-office officials will take the credit but I will not mind.'

Perhaps he doodled it at home on a Sunday afternoon, or at night with Mme Faure nearby at her needlework? What did Léon Faure think when he heard of, or perhaps even saw, what they did to his post office in Oradour on the little River Glane?

'Only good thing de Gaulle ever did in the war,' said Claire. 'He came here in 1945 and decreed that not a stone should be improved. It must stay like this for ever, he said. Oh, and you'll be interested in this. All the buildings in the new village of Oradour – over there – they had to have paintwork of grey. For mourning.'

Incongruously, my mobile phone rang.

'There's also a flight to Bordeaux tonight,' said the voice. 'I can change the ticket.'

'Oh, yes please,' I said – too eagerly; all my defences were down.

18

If you are depressed – go at once to Oradour. You will never have reason enough to be depressed again – after the bent stoves, the tangled bicycles, the charred and rusted sewing machines, the ovens, the tiles on the overmantels, the cars in the street (from which the SS took the tyres), the beds, the shelves, the doorways, the windows where Philippe showed me the marks of the incendiary bombs, the rusting vases, the impact and patina of inhumanity.

We stand in the middle of the street. Philippe says, 'See.' He points to a firmly built house. 'The home of M'sieu Dupic. That was the last house to be burned. Why?'

He nods to Claire and she reads from a falling-apart paperback with a blood-red phoenix on the cover, the authorized history.

In the village was a house especially well furnished with food and which also, as they say, had a nice wine store. It was the house of Monsieur Dupic, the draper, and so contained a large amount of fabric. The SS spared it in the main fire and it was only the morning after it was set alight. The delay was due to their desire for more time to empty it, as well as to provide a comfortable guard post in which to spend the night. A group of German soldiers did in effect remain on the site until the following day and only left on Sunday about eleven a.m. Was it not necessary indeed to destroy some excessively damning evidence of their crime? After the war responsibility must be allocated, consequently precautions had to be taken.

She flips over the page, pursuing another paragraph and – *'Without doubt . . .'* she stumbles on the opening words; on her cheeks appear red spots as she reads.

Without doubt during the night the most atrocious orgies occurred in this house. Monsieur Moreau, the mayor-delegate, found in the ashes of this building the remains of twenty to twenty-five champagne bottles.

Claire's voice snarls a little. I don't know where to look. I look up, and I look down, and I look at the roof of M. Dupic's house. No roof pitch to enjoy. She sees me gazing at the hulks, walks to where I stand and says, 'The first locals to venture in here next day – they came from other villages, from the farms up there. There was one man, with his countryman's eye, he saw the air was full of swallows. They were flying everywhere, not knowing where to go. All their nests, in the eaves, had been burned.'

Slowly, we begin to walk. I've discovered a means, a device, for dealing with things I can't cope with. It's as if I draw down, between my heart and the world, between my brain and what I'm taking in, a curtain of thick grey soft felt. Everything still reaches me but each awful fact must wait until I choose to part the curtain and admit it. Grey felt. Thick, grey felt. Sombre. But soft and comforting.

'There were six places where they killed groups of men,' said Philippe. 'Here on our right as we have seen before –' he spoke like a tour guide – 'was the wine store of M'sieu Denis. Over there is M'sieu Beaulieu's shed. M'sieu Beaulieu was what you call the blacksmith. M'sieu Denis obviously was the town wine merchant. In each place there were about thirty people shot, mostly men, sometimes twice that number. The men were separated from the women and children, whose fate we will come to later. There were also mass killings in the baker's barn, the hotel sheds, a garage.'

125

I parted my grey felt curtain a chink. 'The ages of the soldiers – were they really so young?'

Philippe shrugged. 'Weber – eighteen. Hohninger – seventeen. Hermann Frenzel – seventeen. Boos, the sergeant, was nineteen. Joined the Hitler Youth at thirteen. There was a trial in Bordeaux after the war and others of the accused actually testified against Boos, they said they saw him shoot two women. Antoine was a volunteer observer at the trial. Boos denied everything until it came to the part of his evidence about that building over there.'

'Which building?' I ask.

We stop, mid-street, mid-town. Philippe points.

'Sergeant Boos was asked questions. That was the bakery. Boos denied all knowledge of having anything to do with it. Then a court official – Antoine told me he saw this moment – brought in an exhibit for the trial. It was a firebox from the bakery, used for placing coals to make the bread bake. An eight-week-old baby had been placed in it and burned alive. Sergeant Boos went pale when he saw the firebox.'

Claire looked at me and murmured, 'You don't have to say anything. You don't even have to think anything.'

Philippe can't be stopped. 'And another of the accused, a young man from Alsace called Daul, he said he saw Boos participate in the shooting of thirty people. Then he said this dreadful thing, he said, "They took care of the dying with pistol shots." My uncle picked up on his language.'

Claire and I repeat the words; 'Took care of.'

I fold my grey felt curtain closed, and taking Claire's advice I say nothing, because I have nothing to say and I don't know what I feel. My view of things leaves me and soars into the air and from up there on some high invisible gantry I look down on us, two men and a woman somewhere in France beneath a cloudless autumn sky. What do we look like? Three friends out for an afternoon, dropping in on an historical site.

But in a moment I ground myself with my original point, the one that fazes me.

'It's the age of the soldiers. That's what gets me.'

Philippe says, 'Like Antoine always said. Same age as footballers.'

Could Pearl kill? Or were the Waffen-SS just like the louts on the Tube?

Claire says, 'They killed the village football team.'

This stuns me again. We walk on slowly. One other small group and a distant couple are also walking through Oradour-sur-Glane. The October sun will soon sink in the west.

Philippe has already pointed out the *hôtel de ville*, the tram terminus for Limoges, the schools. Claire points out '*Madame Reignier, Dentiste*', and we see the remains of the chair and the machine by which Mme Reignier worked her dentist's drill. Gaping doors and windows – my mind makes a terrible joke: 'Open wide, please.' Is that the best I can do?

Another school. A milliner's and a restaurant and a hairdresser and a . . .

At that moment, I start to list in my mind the number of shops a small town needs. I am familiar with such a detail, because I too, like so many children of my generation, had received one Christmas a toy town with all its little shops and buildings. Such a toy may well have owed its popularity to the rebuilding after the war and it is to this toy that I always secretly trace my interest in architecture.

It was called Mytown and came in a box made of cardboard painted to look like bricks. There was a high street, with a pub, The King's Head, and a butcher, Mr Lamb, and a baker and a candlestick maker. There were houses, and trees, and little figurines I could place walking here and there. Mytown could be added to like a train set, and for some years it was added to (by parents and pocket money) until eventually in the attic of the stables in Herefordshire I had Mytown laid out quite extensively.

After the age of embarrassment I was ashamed to be seen playing with it – but I often sneaked up there and rearranged the houses and the shops and the pedestrians and the tiny cars and the bus. The church was my pride and joy.

Ahead I can see the tower of the church of Oradour-sur-Glane. Beside me I hear a voice. It is Claire and she is reading – simply reading.

Desourteaux, Paul; shopkeeper, aged 39.
Desourteaux, Jacques; doctor, aged 38.
Desourteaux, Anne-Marie, aged 12.
Desourteaux, Genevieve, aged 9.
Madame Bichaud, née Deserces, Maria; glover, aged 43.
Doire, Jean-Baptiste; well-digger, aged 69.

My thoughts interrupt my hearing: a well-digger? The Romans employed local well-diggers and treated them decently, never made them bondsmen.

Doire, Marcelle; dressmaker, aged 17.
Doutre, Martial; carpenter, aged 51.
Doutre, Charles; carpenter, aged 18.

Doutre, père et fils. Carpenters. The word once meant chariot-maker. Claire looks at me, sees I can take little more, closes the official account with its fathers and sons and daughters and mothers and spinsters and golden lads and girls all must, as chimney-sweepers, come to dust – and we all three fall silent.

I walk across the street on my own, a displacement activity, to look at something. There stands a ruined petrol pump and it was supplied before the war by BP. Ahead of me I see a car, an old Citroën; every French detective who ever worked the cinema screen drove one.

Philippe will have something to say about it. Sure enough he strolls over.

'This is – was – Doctor Desourteaux's car. His father was the mayor. The doctor came back into Oradour from a house call and found the entire village population in the market square, watched over by six SS machine guns. He saw his father, the mayor, in interpreted conversation with a German officer. He saw the baker, as usual naked to the waist and as usual covered in flour. The baker approached the officer and asked if he could go back to the bakery as he had some pastry in the oven. Those fine soldiers of the Waffen-SS laughed and assured him it would be all right.'

I stroke Dr Desourteaux's car – for what? For luck? Strange kind of luck? Or perhaps I stroke the metal for fear – fear it will all happen again. My conscience gets at me.

'Will you excuse me for a moment?'

I walk away, fighting off images and I can't switch to a sweeter channel as I do when Bosnia or Chechnya or Albania appear in my home at night.

But the problem is this: even though it is right that I accuse myself of not wishing to know, I can never sustain such a thought beyond the next piece of comfort or affluence or success. Yet my attitude is the gateway through which these horrors will again pour. I see the six young men on their hunkers before me in the Tube train. I see the splayed, bloody nose of the old Indian gentleman. I see the young German soldiers on their hunkers with their machine guns . . .

A distance away across open ground stands a curious building. I climb the steps, then find an entrance to a world below, a recent mausoleum full of the debris of that frightful day. Identity cards, little photographs, toys, rings, the football team – items salvaged from the embers. I look at each display case for a moment and I escape again, up those dense stairs, my face turned up to the sun like the blind man I wish to be.

Ahead I see the village graveyard but I can't face it. On the roadway outside the cemetery gate I hear angry voices; a cyclist and a halted van quarrel in fierce allegation. The cyclist's bony, muscled legs quiver in anger. He receives no satisfaction and leaves, gesturing.

I return to Dr Desourteaux's car. Philippe and Claire are conferring, a serious conversation. At three o'clock in the afternoon the Germans ordered the men on this open sward to turn and face the walls behind them. The women and children were then removed, walked to the church; many, including their menfolk, thought they were being escorted out of the village.

Philippe walks forward and stands in front of me and looks up at me. How much taller than him is Claire – four, five inches? She is nearer my height, rangy with the long legs of a horsewoman.

'My friend, I see you are moved.' Philippe touches my arm.

'The petrol pump. Did you know it was British Petroleum?'

He ignores me. 'What is to come is worse. Now we go to the church.' He looks at his watch. 'It is almost four o'clock. The time itself.'

Philippe recites that about two hundred men were left behind and about four hundred women and children taken to the church. The men were divided into six groups and quick-marched to the six locations he had already pointed out. There they were shot and the barns and sheds in which they were crowded set on fire.

Somewhere there is a village, I think it is in Northern Ireland, which lost all its menfolk on the Somme.

We stand outside the church. I ask whether the crucifixion is some kind of memorial and I am told it was untouched by the horror. At exactly four o'clock Philippe leads us through the door.

I smell soot. That is the first detail I register – a smell of soot, soot that is more than fifty years old. Then I register three more details. Beside us to the right is a shapeless mass of grey metal – the bell that melted and fell. Silent in the air. Time was away and somewhere else. I try to do a quick recollection of physics – what is the temperature of foundry heat, smelting heat? I cannot remember. MacNeice. It is Louis MacNeice's poem. Time was away and she was here. Meeting Point.

Next I see another shapeless object – then I see it is not shapeless; it is a pram, or what remains of it, and whatever baby was in that pram on the afternoon of Saturday, 10 June 1944, hadn't a chance. Should I say, Hadn't a prayer?

Souviens-toi.

And I see again something that could be a symbol of Oradour. In the wicked irony of survival my mind seeks a German word, leitmotif – the arc of heavy machine-gun bullets as they left the muzzle and sprayed upwards. The walls of the church are pocked with their leitmotif. I want to put my fingers in the holes but I don't.

Philippe paces away from us to a spot not far from the altar.

'To this place,' he says, 'two German soldiers brought a large box. It had cords trailing from it. Two others stood down there –' he pointed to the door – 'guns across their chests like this [he gestures] and legs apart like this [he stands in straddle] and one of the soldiers up here lit the cords coming from the box, they were fuses. The box exploded and thick smoke came out of it. People ran frantic in all directions trying to escape from this. The soldiers opened fire from inside and outside the church. All the bodies were felled. One or two rose from the pile and they were either clubbed to death with gun-butts or shot with pistols.'

Claire asked me, 'You, Nicholas, you know space and buildings. How many people will fit in here?'

I look and try to assess. First time she used my name.

'As a congregation? With pews? Two hundred and eighty seated. Maybe three hundred. Maximum. Pretty crowded, though.'

'Four hundred,' Philippe says. 'Four hundred innocent people. Next the Germans, after many long fusillades, brought in firewood and they kicked down the confessionals here and over here to make more firewood. Then they brought kerosene and they spread it everywhere, all over the women and little children who, remember, were mostly not dead but shot in the legs. When they covered them with kindling and kerosene they threw some matches and some grenades. Some last volleys of guns fired loudly and then they withdrew and locked the blazing church. That was Oradour.'

Now I have finally had too much.

I close and fasten the grey felt curtain first across my heart and then across the eyes of my mind.

But as I do so, and I turn to leave the church, I see one last detail. The face of the Christ on the façade of the altar table has been blown away by a Nazi bullet.

19

There are not many things you can with equanimity do, not many things you can with equanimity say, after an afternoon such as that.

Philippe and Claire went to their car and I to mine. In convoy we drove towards Limoges. They turned left into wooded country, the Forêt de Veyrac, and then another left. A few more minutes and we arrived at one of the most charming hamlets I have seen, deep in the trees.

The inn, Le Chanticleer Rouge, had a courtyard with a clock – instant reminder of Herefordshire and childhood. Instant reminder of some man, a strange man in a uniform, coming to meet Mother joyously and then driving away with her for an afternoon. Instant reminder of my father returning and asking in an empty voice, 'Seen Mother lately?' and Kim thumping me afterwards because I described her visitor.

Five o'clock. Philippe and Claire waited for me as I parked and we trooped into Le Chanticleer Rouge. The bar had a fire and the *patron* called Claude knew Philippe and deferred. Drinks appeared; no choice offered; it was a *marc de Bourgogne*, as smooth as an almond.

'Well, now,' I began, making a noise like a plump man exhaling.

'You must eat,' Claire said to Philippe. 'He is a diabetic,' she explained to me.

'Is that difficult?' I asked.

I had been, if not churlish, abrupt in Oradour, but I felt more cheerful now because I had questions to ask. The answers might explain and even help to remove the violence in my recent life. When I got back to London I would help as much as I could with the police inquiry, take part fully in any memorial service, see through my Johan Pearl contract, tidy up all of that Safft connection, and then open some kind of new chapter.

With Mary Strait? Oh, God. With someone? No, not merely 'someone', not simply 'anyone'; been there, done that, isn't that what they say?

As I knew I would, I now regretted that I had invited Mary Strait to come to Bordeaux. Quick look at my watch. Could I still cancel her? Excused myself, went outside; because of the woods could get no signal on the mobile phone. I returned, not without chagrin.

'Is it too soon,' enquired Philippe, 'to ask for your impressions?'

'I doubt "impressions" can be an adequate word.'

'There are no adequate words, my friend,' and I defined what had been irritating me since I met them – his calling me 'my friend' like some continental stereotype. Will he soon say 'zis' for 'this'? And 'zaire' for 'there'?

Claire said, 'Astonishment, perhaps. That was my first reaction. And it remains more or less the same. The scale of it is astonishing.'

She had superb lips, just the right thickness in the centre.

I agreed. 'The scale.'

'The viciousness of it is astonishing,' she said. 'The overall savagery of it – astonishing. The pitilessness, the ruthlessness – astonishing. See how inadequate even the word "astonishing" can be?'

She drew her fingers down along her arched throat. My mother had that gesture, too. The *marc* massaged my thorax – but I slipped on its smoothness.

'Did they feel nothing, those soldiers?' I asked. 'Has any one of them ever come back to Oradour? I mean now, as tourists?'

Shouldn't have used the word: knew it as I said it. But somewhere in Oradour I let go of something. Something in me, some good system, lost a bolt or a ball-bearing.

Claire recoiled from the word and Philippe looked into his drink.

'Tourists?' he said.

I felt my embarrassment growing. He saw the advantage and took it.

'I believe you may be more accurate than you intended, my friend Nicholas. Twenty-one men went on trial in Bordeaux. All admitted to having been in the action at Oradour. Antoine told me that the President of the Court asked any of them who felt any remorse or guilt or pain to stand up. Do you know, my friend, how many did?' He held up three splayed fingers. 'That is all. Three. One for every two hundred slaughtered people. So perhaps the good word *is* "tourists".'

I cringed. He warmed up.

'Perhaps on summer days a car with a German number plate draws up here for lunch, and after lunch consults the map and the old gentleman in the car – and he will not be so old, will he? Hermann Frenzel will be only seventy. But he will say, "I was a soldier here during the war. That was a tough operation, we were faced by thousands of terrorists. But we won." And he will show his friends what a military success Oradour was. Yes, "tourists" – there is possibility for the word.'

In his anger he slurred; he said 'zaire'; I felt mortal embarrassment.

Claire raised an eyebrow towards me in the way that only English people can communicate. I retreated, and in my abjectness had to give something, but had to be careful not to give too much.

'Did everyone finally get off scot-free?'

Philippe took my offer. 'Effectively. The higher they were the freer they went. That was Antoine's crusade. He attempted

135

for years to have the general, von Lammerding, tried for war crimes. But the man lived out a successful life. Düsseldorf, prosperous businessman, died not too long ago. Untouched.'

At a gesture from Claire, the *patron*, Claude, arrived. Philippe explained that although we all wanted to dine here later we were hungry now too, and one of us had to go to Bordeaux to meet someone.

'Why not stay here tonight?' Claire said to me. 'The rooms are all right.'

Fine. We ate fat and wonderful sandwiches of *foie gras* and had another *marc*. So far we hadn't discussed our joint responsibility of Antony's will. It required attention; the estate must be enormous.

However, the balance between us had changed. I felt Philippe was putting me on hold. He was regrouping, rethinking his strategy. I sensed he knew nothing of what had been happening to me but he intuited something.

'Tell me,' I asked, 'how did Antony become interested in Oradour?'

'My family come from here,' Philippe said. 'We are old Limousin stock.'

'Hence Antony's interest,' I said understandingly. 'I presume he was – and you are – Jewish.'

Claire said quickly, 'He always claimed the war taught him not to be "anything". Being something cost people their lives.'

'Were the family all here when Oradour happened?'

'No. My mother was. Antoine was in London.'

'He heard about it,' said Claire, 'on the BBC.'

Philippe said, 'Oradour is only one such village. There is Putten in Holland and there are others in Byelorussia. Whole towns in Poland, Czechoslovakia. You must have heard of Lidice.'

'No, I'm afraid I haven't.'

'But Oradour is special. Antoine used to say, "Oradour is

awfully special." He called it the only joke he could make about Oradour.'

'That sounds like Antony,' I said.

'How well did you know him?' enquired Claire.

'How well does one know anyone? I saw a good deal of him. Most of it professional, although we became friends beyond that. I liked him a lot.'

For all my warmth, I found myself thinking of ways to get out of all this. May one refuse to be an executor? All my defence mechanisms began to activate. 'Boredom' does not precisely describe my rising feelings – that familiar ennui again, born of a wish to be clear of all this, to be back in the peace and ease of my well-ordered life. Followed by guilt at that feeling.

I fought myself. No. Give Antony at least this piece of respect. But another thought, from a region within me that I trust, suggested Philippe Safft had some unstated motive for bringing me to Oradour, something larger than the commemoration of his uncle. My ennui also arrives when I am asked to commit to something I do not desire.

Over the years – but I have not become proficient at it – I have tried to learn the gift of silence. It has many uses. I found some now. Then, drawing a deep breath, I asked slowly, 'How long – at night – will it take? The drive to Bordeaux?'

Claude was consulted. A hundred and seventy kilometres. But there is a fast way. We all pledged to meet for dinner. Before I left, Claude checked me into a large, soft room. Carnations crowded the wallpaper and the sofa and the counterpane.

20

Night roads delight me, especially in France. Napoleon's trees, when one finds a church of them, parade more formally in the dark. Once or twice I saw an old van, Renault or Citroën or Peugeot, parked in among the tree trunks, listing slightly towards the fields.

I like, too, the way they whiten the boles of the trees, friendly beacons. What are they – birch, aspen, poplar?

That pleasant drive proved the last success of the evening. Mary Strait's flight arrived on time, but she couldn't identify her overnight bag.

'That's it,' she said once, but a Frenchwoman claimed it out of my hand.

We waited – we had to – until all the baggage was off and two identical bags remained, unlike anything else I had seen on the carousel. I recognized them as Pullers, excellent American luggage.

'Yours?' I said.

'Yes.'

'Both?'

'Yes.'

She'd flung her arms around me when we met and I didn't like that. I knew she sensed my recoil – and she didn't like that.

I found Claude's route back again, but didn't find it an easy drive. Three things went wrong. First she said to me, rather in a burst, 'I've discovered that I'm to get shares in the practice. Or whatever they're called, are they called shares?'

'We call them "an interest", giving people an interest,' I said less coldly than I felt. Business being a useful distance-keeper, I warmed to the topic.

'Anyone who leaves has to hand in their "interest" and they get nothing back. You only get to keep it after ten years. It's a kind of long-service reward. But it has a practical use in that it gives you a vote in office policy.' And then I said firmly, 'I hold fifty-five per cent.'

'Much use the vote is,' she said tartly.

'I never go against any truly strong general feelings,' I said.

'But it doesn't stop you sacking people?'

I tried not to feel defensive. 'Companies have to be flexible. We don't sack people easily.'

Why is she opening this line of questioning? Then came the second annoyance.

'Anyway,' I asked, 'who told you all this?'

'Elizabeth.'

Sirens and klaxons in my head. 'When did you see her?'

'I had lunch with her today.'

Jesus! Bloody Elizabeth. Keep it calm, Nicholas.

'How nice. How did that happen?' My thought said, That's twice in one week they've met.

A hamlet called les Moulins came. And went.

'She was in the office. Said a lunch appointment had fallen through. We just went to the *trat* around the corner.'

I wanted to ask, Did she ask you anything about me? but I said, 'I'm devoted to Elizabeth.'

In my peripheral vision I saw Mary Strait's profile in the light of the instrument panels. Nose too big, jaw too long. I nearly crashed the car because –

'She asked if I'd slept with you.'

Oh, Christ! 'Dear Elizabeth. She is a minx.' I laughed, or tried to.

'I said I had.'

Couldn't cover my face with my hands; I was driving. This was about the worst news I could have had.

You – said – you – had? My mind spat each word slowly as my mouth said, 'Oh dear.'

'Well, I had, hadn't I?'

I needed to get a grip on myself. Although I wanted to yell, You stupid, big-mouthed bitch! You bragging cow!, I said instead, 'Elizabeth's a little, I don't know, indiscreet perhaps?'

I said it softly and she replied, 'I didn't know it was to be a secret. You should have told me.'

I wanted to scream, I thought you'd understand, but I said, 'It's not important.'

As I said it I knew I was caught whichever way I turned, and she caught me first turn.

'Are you ashamed of it?' she said.

'Heavens, no,' I said, changing like a racing gearshift through the ramifications. 'It's just – I'm careful. Office politics and that.'

'You mean, "Don't sleep with the hired help," don't you?'

'No. It's not like that.'

My head is shouting at Mary Strait, Get out of the car and go away! For ever!!

'What else did Elizabeth ask?'

'Was it serious? How many times? When was I seeing you again?'

I said, 'I must ring her,' but desperate to ask, Does she know you're here for the weekend?

'It was she who was with me when you rang. She sends you her love. Oh, and she wants us to bring her back some *marrons glacés*.'

My brain groaned. This got worse and worse. 'She loves France,' I said, 'and possibly me, that's why she talks about me so much.'

'She certainly does that.'

'I was her *protégé*,' meaning, What else did she say?

'She asked me not to tell you.'

I bet she did. 'We've known each other for – well, over half my life.'

Signs for Limoges. Heavier traffic these last few miles. Police. An accident – white cars and an ambulance and white faces by the roadside and saffron-coloured bright lights.

'She told me not to get hurt.'

'Oh? Of course Elizabeth's very caring,' – meaning, What did she say that for, spiteful old bitch?

'She said you had a track record.'

'Oh, Elizabeth!' Another false laugh. 'A track record?'

'Her words. Not mine. I notice you didn't ask what she meant.'

'Is this neighbour of hers – is Elizabeth being wooed? I asked her but she wouldn't say.' To get off a subject, first point it in a different direction.

'No, I think he's just a neighbour.' Mary Strait tried to curl her legs under her on the passenger seat but couldn't manage it.

By the time we reached Le Chanticleer Rouge we'd had a long silence. I was seething, because I could see how Elizabeth would use this. Then came another annoyance.

'Ah,' remarked Mary Strait as we saw the inn, '"*Le Chanticleer Rouge*" – the red cock. That at least is promising.'

I know she was only trying to brighten things up but I felt the remark too coarse for the kind of day I'd had. And too coarse from any woman I wanted to be with. But I am sufficiently well educated, and also sufficiently bourgeois, not to wash my dirty linen in public, and by the time we walked into the restaurant and I performed the introductions to Philippe and Claire we were all smiling like dear friends.

21

By the large round table near the fire, Claude kissed Mary Strait's hand and we smiled. The other diners had already reached the depths of their evening.

Philippe flexed his good manners. He attended fussily to the newcomer and she loved it. Claire and he also pretended not to have studied the menu. In the ice-breaking selection I chose the *potage aux legumes* and what proved a dry and perfect *confit de canard*. Graves for both wines; the red, a commonplace and excellent Château de Fieuzal. Philippe took over.

'I am sure, Mary,' he began, 'that Nicholas has told you all about Oradour.'

'No, he hasn't,' she said. 'We haven't known each other very long.'

Claire registered this and I watched her sense my discomfort. I wanted to kick Mary Strait, who said, 'I love these old nooks of France!'

Philippe said tactfully to Claire, 'I am sure Nicholas was sparing Mary's feelings by bringing her to Le Chanticleer first.' To Mary Strait he said, 'But you understand about my uncle?'

'I understand that he, that he – has died.'

'My uncle was murdered some weeks ago. We are here to think of him. Near here there was a Nazi atrocity and my uncle became very involved with its history. That is Oradour. Oradour-sur-Glane. It is a little river, the Glane.'

Philippe stopped. His lawyer's skill gave the impression he had told the whole story while inviting inquiry. It manipulated Mary Strait.

'When you say "very involved" – I mean, what could he do? It was all over.'

Claire, with her still face, watched. Did she feel distaste that Mary Strait was being led? Or did I alone sense a motive in Philippe?

'By "very involved" I mean my uncle took part in the trial of those accused. The German soldiers who were arrested after the war. He also tried to work in a war-crimes trial that was brought in Berlin. But they would not give him permission.'

There it was again – the finality of his remark, yet the gate left open. In Mary Strait walked.

'What could he have done? What did he want to do?'

'He believed – correctly – there were perpetrators who were never brought to justice. I know that for years he pursued the general who mounted the operation, von Lammerding. They even met. But von Lammerding died before Antoine could make international pressures work. It was different twenty years ago. Now it is better. When I spoke to him last he was still on the trail of one officer. He said he hoped he would not die before it happened.'

On Mary Strait went, rolling out the carpet for him.

'Can't you take up where he left off?'

'In this,' said Philippe, 'I need an ally.'

He didn't even look at me. Nor did he need to – Mary Strait did it for him and asked me, 'Couldn't you help?'

'No. I'm an architect, I'm not a –'

She said, 'But what a brilliant thing it would be?!'

'But – it's not something I know anything about –'

'Don't you think it would be a wonderful service to your dead friend?'

I hemmed.

'Don't you think you've been given a great gift – the privilege of getting involved in an important story of humankind? Of history?'

143

I hawed.

'Don't you think there's a question of honour here?'

'Don't you think it's something to give back?'

Her subtext said, You do all right, I work in your offices, I've seen your apartment, it's well known how wealthy you are, no other responsibilities.

And finally, 'Don't you think it would be so fulfilling?'

My mind said, Don't you think you should shut up? but my mouth uselessly said, 'I wouldn't be any good at it.'

She attacked. 'Perhaps that's what he was saying by making you both his executors? To continue his work?'

'We haven't seen the will,' I said.

Philippe said nothing; Claire hid discomfort.

Mary Strait raced on. 'How much is known about him? But how exciting! He might be a German politician for all we know! Remember all that fuss about what was his name? In Austria?'

'Waldheim,' said Philippe. 'But we do not even know this man's name. Not where he lives. Nothing. When you think of what he did' – Philippe in full flight.

'Maybe his name is in the will?' she said.

Philippe replied, 'It won't be.'

How did he know? I didn't ask – I had to keep my end up and enquired, 'Has anyone come close to him?'

Philippe shrugged. 'Antoine.'

'Oh, Christ,' said Mary Strait, 'that must be why he was killed.'

'He was killed –' I spoke with a surly and final air – 'by a neo-Nazi savage. It had all the hallmarks.'

Mary Strait jumped to the uptake.

'What hallmarks?'

She had drunk sparingly. Philippe had taken to her somewhat. Have her, I whispered to him in the silent surgery of my brain.

'The way he was killed,' I said. 'The violence to the body.'

Claire stiffened.

'Oh, Jesus!' I thought. She didn't know.

Philippe grew flustered. Mary Strait intensified.

'What violence?'

I was feeling angry. I should never have said it. Anyway, how was I to know Philippe hadn't told Claire?

He took over again. As with the 'tourists' remark (which I still regretted) he reproached me by not meeting my eyes.

'Antoine was mutilated. His assassin – or assassins – carved a symbol into his skin.'

Claire dropped her cutlery to her plate and threw her hands to her eyes. Mary Strait looked at each of us.

'A symbol?'

I said, 'A triangle.'

Philippe said, 'The Nazi symbol for homosexuals.'

She said, 'How awful.'

'The police think it's some gay shindig,' I lied. 'A *crime passionnel.*'

My emotions rode a bad surge that night. I had little control over myself. That isn't an excuse, it's a fact. Claire left the table.

Philippe rose to follow her, but Mary Strait said, 'I'll go.'

22

That pattern repeats. When under pressure I cause damage. If I have any control left I'm usually able to make a generous apology.

'Philippe, I'm truly sorry. Forgive me.'

He held out his hand and enabled me to show feelings I usually hide.

'You are not all right, are you, my friend?'

'No,' I said.

'Not a' tall. It is Oradour.'

'One cannot be unaffected by it,' I said, trying to reach a matter-of-fact voice. 'But it is other things too.'

'What are they, my friend?'

'Antony is one. I didn't realize how much I liked him. How much I'm horrified.'

We paused – the rare comfort of a shared bereavement.

'There is something else,' I said. 'I'm terrified. With good reason.'

He looked at me like a fire. 'Terrified? Of what, my friend?'

'But I must ask you not to tell anyone. Not even Claire. I need your opinion.'

I listed my hideous litany – knife, gang, flowers. Up to then I had forced my mind to deny them any link. I think I feared they made sense and how could I cope with that? Lastly I told him about Johan Pearl.

As I listened to myself, my dread felt confirmed – I ramified all across the murder of Antony Safft. No wonder my values had taken a dive. In recent times celibacy had been for me a standard. The likely reason I had kept Mary Strait with me that weekend became plain – I feared I was going to be killed.

In the days following Antony's death, amid the sinister happenings to me, I shut off some part of my mind. If I had a thought it was, Make the wish the reality. Believe there is no danger and no danger can occur.

My avoidance got worse. I came to Oradour principally because it took me out of London. How dishonest can one man get?

I told Philippe, 'Look, I'm even here on false pretences. The main reason I came to Oradour has nothing to do with Antony. Or my guilt at being late for you. I came here because I've been terrified at home.'

At which point tears came to my eyes.

I rose from the table and walked out under the night. The sky was as clear as reason and every bit as deep. No moon, only the hard and lovely dust of a zillion stars.

He followed me.

'It merits being terrified,' he said, and said no more. No further reaction.

I walked to and fro. In old movies, I thought, the hero now lights a cigarette. Way up in the night, the hard red blips of an aircraft flashed placidly. The flight path suggested Italy at least; the height, Venice or beyond, perhaps Athens, Istanbul. I wished to be on it.

Inside, the women had returned. I went to the lavatory, checked my face and eyes. In the passageway I asked Claude-le-patron whether he had a separate room for Mary Strait. His face and shoulders regretted. Presumably he reckoned we'd had a row. Even if he'd had the extra room, I thought, he'd have said no through some misguided wish to help. My paranoia ran that high that night.

Our meal continued differently. We talked of paintings and cinema and music and Europe. Then, as happens, we split. Philippe and Mary Strait conversed; he told her about his law practice in Rouen, the house on the Seine at Jumièges. Claire and I discovered a number of mutual acquaintances; we caught up on their lives and reminisced of them.

I had difficulty listening to her because I was looking at her face. Like my mother's, it had phases rather than expressions; she never looked the same one moment to the next. When she put her hand to her throat in that gesture I could see the complete outline of her left breast.

We began to disband.

Philippe said to me, 'If we meet for breakfast, perhaps? Half past eight?' He explained to Claire, 'We have, you know, to talk.'

Soon Mary Strait and I stood once more alone in a bedroom. She was out of her clothes and all over me like gossip. I pleaded the bathroom. Her overnight bags foamed shoes, underwear, cosmetics all over the floor. I had to step over this flotsam to reach the lavatory. She had left the basin half-full of water. Beside it lay soggy dabs of cotton wool – make-up, nail varnish, some such treatment. As I stood at the lavatory I heard her try the locked door.

'I'm on the loo,' I called.

No 'sorry' or any such word. When I returned to the bedroom she was beachcombing the debris.

'Bloody contact lenses,' she muttered.

Kneeling naked, she looked vulnerable as a child.

When she eventually went to the bathroom she – appallingly – didn't close the door fully. I grabbed the opportunity and raced into bed. Fortunately I had packed one of my Longjohn American sleeping shirts. By the time she returned I had turned out my light.

She whispered, 'Are you awake?'

I gave a false sleepy grunt. Soon she switched off her own light and hurled an arm in search of me. I heard her snore.

It's to my shame that I didn't resist Mary Strait from Day

One. I've never been good about shame. It's one of those emotions I tend to address with a swerve. After that first night with her – two days after I first met her, for God's sake! – I sat in my own bathroom trying to control my chagrin. I found only one benefit. My wild and loose departure from my norms confirmed the pressure I felt.

This calmed me. I was able to bring her a cup of coffee while she woke up. But I couldn't, however, join in tender conversation. She wished to discuss the night and its emotions – in some detail. I approached her body again, to stop her talking about 'us'.

What did I do then? I encouraged her to stay for the weekend. As the Black Pearl would say, 'Oh, man!'

The room never fully darkened. Somewhere the inn had a red rooster neon sign. I lay in the glow, which also lit Mary Strait's naked shoulders. Had the knot tightening around me loosened a little? I thought so. The articulation of my fear to Philippe had brought some relief. He understood such circumstances; a criminal lawyer passionate in the pursuit of justice who knew horror from all sides; he pursued its agents and now saw his own family charred by it again.

I also had the thought that Oradour objectified what had been happening. The place defines perspective, proportion. It confirmed the worst – that vile forces were trying to land on me. Perhaps I should fight them.

In my selfishness I hadn't asked whether Philippe had received threats. But I thought, Is it selfishness? Or is something holding me back? I sensed he kept information from me. Out of considerateness or manipulation? I'll ask him.

Anxiety's mill ground on. I thought, I have nothing in my gift or my power. Something has gripped me that won't let me go. But – how could *it* or its agents know it was all right to let me go? How could this violence know I was no threat to its source? Nor did I wish to be.

How could I tell it?

That thought made me try to give it all a name. What is this I have got myself into? A conspiracy? A complex? My old friend, Dr Pankratikos, once explained to me what, in psychological terms, constitutes a complex.

'It is a set of feelings, Nicholas, centred usually on one person. Most commonly a parent. And I liken it to a cube. A cube made up of many coloured parts. Like Rubik. Each part is its own shape. But each part is yet a part of the cube, yet may have nothing of the cube in itself. If you, Nicholas, have, say, a father complex, it might mean that you are, all at once, a poor and harsh employer, a man dependent on the good opinion of older men, yet a man who rebels against authority. If you have a mother complex, you may be a man who hates women but cannot do without them. Who idealizes them but likes to beat them, be cruel, sadistic. Who pursues them avidly and then drops them when he has captured their affections. Who thinks he loves them but cannot understand why they always disappoint him. So, the colours on the cube become very mixed up.'

I never asked Dr Pankratikos the obvious question – because I feared he would say, 'You, Nicholas, have both father and mother complexes.'

Now some lethal, impersonal 'complex' had caught me. All the analysis in the world wouldn't dissolve it. The violence towards me felt dedicated and precise. I feared – and sensed – a central power.

When I have more questions than answers I stall until I can get help. In a few hours I'll have breakfast with Philippe and perhaps some things will clarify. As to this predicament lying beside me . . . ?

Close your eyes, Nicholas. The blackened gables of Oradour. When I think of the trouble I take so that my clients may live in style and comfort . . . There's something particularly awful about the rape of a home . . . Go to sleep, Nicholas.

Europeans know nothing of the double bed. They push

two single beds together; or, their best effort, two single mattresses fill a large frame. I thanked their divisiveness; it kept the snoring Mary Strait at a distance.

As I began to drowse I worked out what I wanted to ask her about. Elizabeth. And then I had to consider the ramifications of having gone to bed with Mary Strait. Of Elizabeth knowing it. Of Elizabeth knowing of France this weekend.

Elizabeth would do two things. She'd use it to show she still had a significant knowledge of my life. And she might retaliate out of jealousy. Her age, and the nonexistence ever of any sexual relationship between Elizabeth and me would calm nothing.

I got no sleep at all.

23

Lovely morning; lemon sunbeams through hazy clouds. From the window I could see the condensation on the parked cars below. One dark rectangular space existed where an early car had left. No frost last night.

A small, intent brown dog walked very fast along the road. Across by the entrance to a long avenue, a woman, dressed and ready for the day, opened her door and smelled the morning. She went to her shed, peered into it and returned to her house. The brown dog looked at her, wagged his tail a little and walked on. By the long roof of a farmhouse at the end of the avenue, birds floated around the sky.

A car rode down the distant hill. Near Le Chanticleer Rouge it slowed down, some shrewd traveller breakfasting here. The two men in it, one in a check shirt, looked for a parking slot – or did they? No, they've changed their minds.

The car left the car park. At the exit it stopped and reversed, inspecting each parked car. It halted for a moment by the vacant slot between my car and Philippe's, changed its mind and drove away. I saw a Le Routier up the road yesterday. Perhaps they want a cheaper breakfast.

Quiet bath, slipped out of the room, took the air. How restoring is the smell of rural France: bread and farmyards and coffee and drains.

Philippe arrived as I opened *Le Monde*. We shook hands.

'Did you sleep, Nicholas?'

'No. You?'

'Not a' tall.'

I plunged into the talk I desperately needed. Wishing to show good behaviour, I led by asking about his own safety.

'I have been threatened, Nicholas. I have been followed. A knife was thrown at me twice. A bomb has been defused in my hallway. From time to time I have slept in many different places. It is always the same pattern. When the trail gets hot so does the enemy.'

'In my case – are you convinced that all this is connected?'

'Yes,' he said. 'But I do not know how. I mean I do not know where the links join. If Antoine disturbed something . . .' He looked shifty – but perhaps it was discomfort.

I asked the question I had been dreading to ask.

'Do I have to be careful?'

He gave it much thought. 'There are always three answers to this question. No. Yes. And – Maybe. We must rule out the "No" because it is clear that already you have been in difficulty. Therefore we must also rule out the "Maybe". Which leaves us only with the "Yes". That is how I see it.'

'Which leaves me with a very difficult problem.'

'I can see that, my friend.'

'But do you see the same problem I see?'

He had a quick mind. 'If Antoine stumbled on something – that you have no way of telling such people you are not interested in them?' He nodded. 'I have thought of that. If you were to take the front page of *Le Monde* and *The Times* of London – they might not choose to believe you. Not if they have the capacity to do the things they have done.'

'Do you know who they are?'

He hesitated. 'As I said last night. I believe there was an officer at Oradour. Who is still alive. But I do not know his identity.'

'Do you have a clue? Is he the one?'

'I do not know. Perhaps there are several. Did you know

they held an annual commemoration – the SS who were at Oradour?'

'How ghastly. But it doesn't surprise me.'

We were silent and we ate. Our conversation felt unsatisfying – like a conjuror's box where the bottom falls open. And I wasn't the conjuror. Philippe broke the silence by saying, 'Do you know how the croissant came to be created?'

'You are so like your uncle. That is exactly the sort of thing he used to come out with.'

Pleased, he continued. 'During the siege of Vienna it was the bakers who alerted the city defences to the fact that the Turks were about to make the surprise attack. The attack was repelled, the Turkish morale broken and the siege was lifted. As a reward the bakers were commissioned to create a pastry in the shape of the Turkish crescent. Or *croissant*.'

Delicious coffee.

Philippe said, 'There is something I must tell you. It kept me awake, thinking I should not tell you.'

Instantly I wished he wouldn't.

'Those deliveries. Hitler always sent gifts to those he was about to execute,' said Philippe. 'He learned it from Mussolini.'

'So?'

'An old Tuscan trick, I believe. And always the gift had some meaning towards the forthcoming execution.'

'Is there a point to this?' I asked rather rudely, fear again biting my heart.

'The police told me Antoine had received a knife in the post. And some flowers.'

I thought, At some point I'm going to have to learn how to freeze my fear buds.

Philippe's eyes looked darker and darker; I spilled my coffee all over my croissant.

We finished breakfast. 'Are you going back to Oradour?' he asked.

'I don't think I can face it.'

'I understand. But your – your companion, Mary? What will she want?'

Rather grimly I replied, 'She will want to go to Oradour.'

Philippe smiled. 'Affairs of the heart. Uh-oh.'

I said, 'I fear this is probably an affair of the wallet.'

He looked grave.

I pressed on. 'My wallet.'

He looked even more grave and then I sensed his political correctness. Oh, dear! It is possible to apologize for one thing by apologizing for another so I said, 'I am so sorry for upsetting Claire last night.'

'It is all right, my friend. She was a little angry at me for not telling her everything. It was not a good idea that I tried to shield her.'

Genuinely chivalrous? Some national stereotypes seem to be true.

'Very noble of you,' I said.

'It is something I believe in,' Philippe replied.

I had to get off the subject so I said the first thing that came into my head and was surprised at the words that came out of my mouth.

'I saw a car drive in here this morning early.' I pointed. 'It looked at your car and mine.'

'Who was in it?'

'I thought they were two men looking for breakfast.'

'I should have told you, Nicholas. Those will be associates of mine. Just seeing that everything is all right. It is a precaution I take.'

'Wish I had a precaution I could take.'

He paused – a lawyer's pause, guaranteeing full attention.

'There is one way.'

'Is there?'

'You could relinquish being an executor. Is not that the common bond in all of this perhaps?'

It should have felt like a beam of light in a dark pit. So why didn't it reach me like that?

'Would it make a difference?'

'Let me bear the burden. It is my family, after all.'

'But that would leave you – exposed?'

'I have a system to protect me. And I feel bad that my family has put you in this danger.'

At that moment Claire appeared. We stood to greet her. She walked around the table and gave me an unexpected embrace.

'I was such a baby last night.' She still had sleep written on her face.

'But I was such a churl,' I said.

'What is that word?' asked Philippe, and we digressed into a discussion of language. An hour later we rose to greet Mary Strait who said little.

All breakfasts taken and the day opened up, arrangements were made. Philippe and Claire would take Mary Strait to Oradour and return to the Chanticleer for a late lunch.

'Will you be all right?' asked Claire. 'On your own?'

I felt invaded by the fact that Mary Strait was going to Oradour.

Philippe said, 'About twenty minutes from here there is a very famous little church. It was part of a monastery. It is called St Gilles. Go *direction* Limoges. I think you will like it, Nicholas. In fact you should not miss it.'

They left soon afterwards. Mary Strait, reproach in her eyes, made a meal of a goodbye kiss. I had the bliss of a coffee alone and another croissant.

Glad to leave the chaotic room, I booked us all in for lunch, put my things in the car and set off for St Gilles. Plenty to think about. The thought about Antony having been sent a knife and flowers refused to activate. Avoidance? Denial, more like.

I switched to Mary Strait and how to extricate myself.

Damage limitation. And how to stop such an error recurring. I understood it. Overwrought for quite dreadful reasons, I had looked for some comfort. But looked in the wrong place. Bad move. Elizabeth and Mary Strait. Jesus! Dare I ring my answering machine? Yes, forewarned is forearmed. My father's saying. What would his advice be? I don't know. Never had a piece of advice from him in my life. Or his.

For someone quite ascetic, Elizabeth possesses amazing gush.

'Nicholas, dear! What *is* this I *hear*? Love is in the air? Well, she's a very nice girl and I hope this is going to turn out very nicely. She seems quite struck on you. Give me a ring when you get back. I must lunch the two of you. You'll forgive me if I don't say dinner for a bit yet.'

I made the International Squirming Team. Christ, what am I going to DO?! The sign for *St Gilles, église XII siècle* helped. It also brought me to my senses in the greater dilemma.

How should I cope with being targeted by people who didn't know I was no threat? Who, were it possible to tell them so, wouldn't care? I felt like a duck in a barrel looking up at the guns.

Rack the brain again. Did Antony ever tell me anything that might make me a danger to his enemies? Did he ever introduce me to anyone? Did I ever do anything for him that would suggest I knew things I wasn't supposed to know? Did any of his contracts contain anything that might so savagely have impeached me? 'They' can't hate me because I profited handsomely, can they? Normal business.

The countryside looked glorious in a blue-and-yellow light. Over the fields, past two stands of aspens, I saw shining roofs. A little gold cross caught the sun. But suppose the assaults don't stop? Or get worse? Could always come and live in France. Take up restoration architecture here, or in Italy, something I'd often dreamed of. Park the car, Nicholas, and lose these thoughts.

St Gilles proved sweet. Unusually well preserved; they say the stone down here has an extra shale of durability. The little faces on the cornices retain such definition they might have been carved eighty years ago instead of eight hundred.

In this part of France the builders have an old wives' tale: if you encircle your house with a path of sand all around you will never have woodworm. A broad belt of sand ran all round the immediate perimeter. In the door timbers not a trace of worm did I see.

Six columns either side of the nave. Those capitals untouched by any but the masons. Small stone stairs, perfectly curved, led to a kind of half-arcade, just about head-tall. I climbed and saw the purpose of it. The angled window looked directly out on to a lake. Did it reflect the rising sun onto the glass?

I stood and praised the brain of the architect or abbot or whoever had thought of this. Through the window I saw a car on the little road – the same car that had inspected Le Chanticleer Rouge.

Philippe's diligence at work? I should have been warmed by the comfort of it. But, I thought, nothing warms me these days. Or else, I am surprised at his conscientiousness.

As I stood by the altar I heard the door open and they entered. I looked towards them and smiled. The check-shirted one gave a little wave; the other wore a football scarf: nice touch, Philippe. They waited by the tall stone font.

When I closed my notebook they stepped outside. A moment later I heard their engine and they drove away. I put a hundred-franc note in the donation box and lit a candle for Antony Safft. Not that I hold beliefs – but Antony, like me, liked light.

Outside, a curio: there is a short pathway with walls ten feet high, tight as a chute down to the lake. Aha? Was the lake perhaps designed almost as an annexe to the church?

All the stonework's the same age. I wonder if there's a local ritual? A blessing of the waters? A summer rite on the lake shore? Must check St Gilles's liturgy.

Heritage signs on the pathway wall told of a bottomless lake. Naturally. And a great fish. It killed many people until St Gilles blessed it. Thereafter every time St Gilles went out in his boat the fish followed him 'and shepherded unto him' a good catch. Indeed. I like stories about fish; there's one about a fish with a jewel in its belly.

You could launch a lifeboat down that slope. Perhaps that was its purpose. In any case, to see the outside detail of the little arcaded window I needed to look from the water's edge. Only then did I take in that the lake had a high surrounding perimeter wall. Built in the church's limestone, it accentuated the 'perfect circle' of water.

Yes, there's the window. Careful – don't teeter from the step. Perfectly done; no way of telling from here that the window is angled. Now how did he do that? Deep reveals inside and out? Ah, nice! The reveals themselves are also angled downwards. Yess!

I heard a noise behind me, a revving, angry noise at the top of the pathway. Hurtling down the ramp came the car with the two men. And I had nowhere to go. The walls too high. The lake – how deep? Already I stood on the last step. No way out. The car came tearing towards me, barely fitting between the tall walls.

24

Thoughts teemed in a violent rush.

Jump on the bonnet? No! To one side? No room.

I'm dead.

No, I won't let them.

'Associates,' said Philippe.

Some associates.

Can they stop? Doesn't matter. Are my clothes too heavy for the water? My jacket's in the car.

Have they got guns? Don't be dramatic. This *is* dramatic.

Jeez-uss! Turn and jump.

I turned and jumped. Cold, cold, black water. A stagnant history. Now what? A scream of brakes! A clang of metal. I'm under. Shoes, I can't swim in shoes, I need my toes, the evolutionary frog. John Lobb's slip-ons – so I slip them off. Better. Socks too when I surface. Breath, no breath. Three big strokes and surface. Surface and swim. Three more big strokes out towards the middle of the lake – much bigger lake now that I'm in it, everyone knows water's deceptive. Cold. Sport. Pearl had asked me. I told him. Swam for my school, not my university. Now comes my Blue. Blue with the cold I shall be.

The car stopped at the lip of the step. Fantastic brakework – or hadn't it come as fast as I thought? No, I see what he did, he hammered the wing into the wall to slow it. Let the other rear wing hit the far wall, a matter of inches anyway.

The younger man made a waving gesture. That's what I thought peering through the water and the scrap of weed in my eyes and the shock. Why's he waving?

Not waving but drowning. Fuckkkkkkkk! What's that? Something's hit me on the head. And neck. A glancing blow. Not waving but throwing!

He throws again. The driver climbs out of the car. He has a bag. As does the check-shirt. From each bag they fetch and throw.

The missiles hit the water near me. Minuscule plumes. Like little shells in naval battles. Down again – I dive and stroke, change direction, up for air, dive and stroke, one, two, three, four, if I can get up to, say, seven strokes underwater that will begin to take me out of their range, one, two, three. I see or feel a hit. On my shoulder. But the force is gone from it. Up and swim again, then down and one, two, three, four, five . . .

I'm up again, bursting and not cold now, must be fear that's causing my teeth to chatter . . .

I turn, treading water. Maybe they're right, maybe it is bottomless. It feels fantastically deep. I look towards the bank. Still hurling something at me but they're falling well short. I feel like shouting 'Yah-yah, can't hit me for a penny cup of tea.' As we did at school when out of a punch's reach.

Oh, Christ! The men split and ran in opposite directions along the parapet. Wide enough to accept the sure-footed. They meant to prevent me coming ashore. Anywhere. Can I race them to the wall? But those bags? I learned soon enough. The one nearest me began to throw again and almost hit me. A ball-bearing! Bags of shiny, large ball-bearings.

Can I ever be out of range? Of both? I look around. No boat on the water anywhere. They can't get near and stone me. How wide is the lake? Wide enough for crossfire? I don't know. Only I can establish that. So I swim towards the other thug. This also takes me towards what I think to be the exact centre of the lake. But I must swim close enough to him to draw his fire. He waits. I observe that I am tiring.

I draw his fire. Using the kind of measuring I handle a hundred times a day, I turn left. I swim at a distance of five yards from where his best throw landed. I am out of his range.

Check the thug behind? He has run further along the wall. But, by a process of elimination, all I have to do is keep swimming. I slow down. Use the gauge my eye has developed over the years. Soon both of them will reach a point beyond which they will be approaching each other. When they have each reached that halfway point on the wall's circumference, if their missiles cannot reach me – I am out of all throwing range. This is like surveying a site.

I swam steadily. Reached a point where they stopped throwing. At last I bought myself enough time to peel off my socks, an awkward manoeuvre. Toes free. What next?

I saw what next. Each thug sat on the wall. Nonchalantly. They needed only rod and line and a book called *How to Fish*. The picture of relaxation. And I? I have to swim around in circles. All they have to do is sit there and I come into their range. Or after a finite time I tire and drown. That notion almost sinks me.

The water grew colder as I grew wearier. Small circles are more exhausting than large leisurely ones. Psyche them? Swim near enough to tempt a throw. From one and then the other. Establish their limits.

My head and neck hurt like fury. I was bleeding heavily. Curiously this didn't worry me. The head bleeds. Bleeding can be safer than not. But – the fatigue.

My eyes clouded once. That stirred me. Then I started to grow warm and sleepy. That stirred me even more. What good fortune, that boyhood swimming. Memories of cocoa afterwards. Watch that treacherous, sleepy warmth. People who almost die of cold have reported it; people saved from drowning speak of the peace, the light they see.

Vary the strokes. On my back. Reduce the number of

162

strokes. Just enough to stay afloat. No buoyancy whatever. Why couldn't this be the Dead Sea?

I looked across. One of the men walked towards the other. He halted every five yards or so, tested the distance with another steel ball. He did it languidly. The air of a man who knows he has won. Not one landed near me. What did it matter?

I had the thought: should I swim towards them? Let them kill me in the water? Or haul me out and abduct me? No. My instincts refused. I swam on in my circles. A metaphor for my life, was my bitter thought. Cold, repetitive circles. Out of my depth. Terrorized by what walked on terra firma. That's my life.

How long? Five, ten, fifteen minutes? I have no idea.

Suddenly they left. Simply walked along the parapet, back to the car and drove away. Change of plan? Or a new factor in the vicious equation?

Nothing to suggest why. Nothing at all. From my position as a seal or an otter swimming around in the water I saw them reverse up the walled path and I heard them drive away.

25

I'm still breathing. No bullets. Death stayed away. Why? Soaked and barefooted. Shocked through to my lungs – whether at my condition or my torment I couldn't yet distinguish. But the place was truly empty. Except for some birds.

I dropped my head to rest upon the rim of the steering wheel and began to shiver. Thought: In my bag I have a change of clothes, a spare pair of shoes. I turned the car heater on to full blast, found my spare spectacles in the luggage and drove away. Watching. Searching the landscape with my eyes. No grey car. No nobody.

A mile away from St Gilles, down a quiet, wooded lane, I used last night's shirt and tee-shirt to towel myself dry. Then I counted the damage.

Little enough in practical terms – a pair of shoes, a pair of socks, a pair of spectacles: they had fallen off on my first dive. My head hurt. I tried to see it in the rearview mirror, then fetched the mirror from my sponge bag. A large cut oozed blood. My shoulder hurt and I examined it – the ball-bearing had made harder contact than I thought; red contusions surfaced. I dressed.

First the practical thoughts. What do I need? A pharmacy more than a doctor – French pharmacies being one of the wonders of the world. No pharmacy in nearest village, Peyrilhac. Get out of here, get away! Looking for their car everywhere. Too many grey cars in France.

The pharmacist in Nieul sat me down and examined my head, cleaned the wound and sprayed it. Did it need a dressing? Perhaps, but the air is the best dressing. I fell, I said, hit it on a stone. He checked my eyes and my reflexes. Did I fall in water? My hair was still wet. In that case I must have something against infection.

He gave me some *homéopathie*, and a little bottle of the spray he had used and some tablets against infection and some against shock. The latter must not be taken if driving. Sedacollyre drops for my water-reddened eyes. He also advised some food.

Across the road in the Brasserie Limousin I raced frantically through an *omelette aux fines herbes* and some fresh bread. Why didn't they kill me? I ate though I half-gagged on each bite. On the mobile from the table I called Le Chanticleer Rouge, asked for Claude-le-patron. Please give Philippe and the others a message. I have had an accident, have gone home early. Would Philippe be good enough to see that Mlle Strait got to Bordeaux as and when she wished? No, I'm fine, no, just something silly with the car. It has left me shocked. Claude-le-patron said I sounded like a man without breath, a man in a *tragédie*, a man desperate. Yes, of course I will return. Yes, it is a lovely inn and I look forward to coming back.

On the race to the motorway the rough thoughts rode in. Philippe's protectors? I should hate to meet his adversaries. How did they know who I was, know my car? Had they followed us from Oradour? Now for the worst thought. Was Philippe all he seemed? Very frightened, and suspicious as a spy, I drove maniacally to Bordeaux airport.

As I entered the airport two hours later my mobile phone rang, too late for me to switch it off. I didn't answer. It rang again to alert me that a message had been left.

Philippe said, alive with anguish, 'My friend, my friend, what has happened? Are you all right? Please telephone me and let me know. We shall stay at Le Chanticleer until we hear from you.'

He heard from me all right, but not until I was safely in the taxi from Heathrow. 'Oh! We have been so worried! What happened?'

'Your associates. They forced me into the lake and tried to drown me.'

'My associates? Who can you mean?'

'The two men in the car. You said they were protection.'

'But so they are. What were they like?'

'Pretty ordinary.'

'My associates look like soldiers. Which is what they were.'

'These looked like thugs. Which is what they are.'

'You sound so upset, my friend.'

'Yes. Odd, that. I've spent nearly half an hour in a freezing lake trying to avoid being stoned to death. I've got a cut the length of an envelope on the back of my head.'

Could I believe his anguish? Should I believe it? Why did Antony never mention his nephew? Nobody says 'my friend' nowadays. Is this man a rampant liar?

I unplugged the answering machine and let the telephone ring. It rang with several calls. I sat up until three, searching the television for football, finding it here and there. It focused me a little. Eventually I took some of the drowsy tablets and went to bed, but I woke so unrefreshed I'd have been better not sleeping at all.

On Sunday afternoon my buzzer clamoured. I knew who it was and I didn't answer. When it stopped I concealed myself by the window. Mary Strait went away again in a taxi.

In the small, windowless study at the back I listened to hour after hour of Donald Fagen, Grateful Dead, Jefferson Airplane. Then baroque – Albinoni, Galuppi, Manzini. Looking for clues. Looking for clues anywhere. Anywhere I could think of looking. Finding none.

I think of that day now as the day I changed – changed not only my mind, changed my spirit (if it is possible to change the spirit). When I got out of the lake, shocked, bleeding and in utter distress, I felt most of all humiliated. I have heard that is the emotion torturers prey upon – humiliation. What is the first item of clothing they remove from a captive? Spectacles, if he's wearing them. Next item? Shoes and socks. Next? Trousers.

What's the first evidence of fear they look for? That he's wetting himself. I had wet myself in the lake. It didn't matter insofar as no one could see. But I knew that I had wet myself. I had also wet myself when they took me down that side street from the Tube. The thugs had seen it. The police had seen it. The cabbie had seen it.

I can't stand to be humiliated. To be bullied. Worst of all to be bullied and humiliated. Not since school. What was his name? Need I ask? I've never forgotten it, Donnell, coarse, red-faced, tall, fat. He forced my trousers down, I was thirteen. A month later I heard the special crunch of stone on bone. In the dark he never saw my face, saw only the rock in my hand. In the light of the school hallway later I saw his pulped face. A pleasure.

From the bath I reached for the telephone. It rang in an empty house; one can always tell. So much for 'Ring me any time, my friend.'

Naturally, I stayed in; ate from the freezer; ate little. Read, or tried to. Somehow I had to find in myself something resembling my usual working model.

26

The office next morning posed several problems. Such energy as I dredged up came from a mixture of anger and fear. In the lift I told myself, Try not to add up your errors.

Fine, I replied to myself, but I'm about to meet one of them. Bet she'll be in early . . .

A puzzle faced me when the lift opened. A quarter to eight, the office empty – yet all the lights blazed, all the doors stood open. Hal must have altered the cleaning contractor's schedule in some way. Or had somebody come in and gone out briefly for coffee? Or something? My office door stood open too, but nothing had been disturbed. I'm getting truly paranoid.

Lemon's desk held a spare key to my apartment. For emergencies. Is the key still there? Yes, I am paranoid. The key was still there, in the little box with the elephant lid. As I walked back to my office I saw the new draughtsman come in. He nodded respectfully.

Concentrate. How to play the day. 'Head-on,' I decided. I forced two issues to the fore of my thinking – deal with Mary Strait and stop Elizabeth's gush. This way I could take my focus away from the 'Problem', as I called it – and clear my head to address it. I left a note on Hal's voice-mail asking him to see me the moment he arrived.

Hal knew me in this slightly manic state and he became pleasingly wary.

'Can you do something for me?' I asked.

'Sure, Chief.'

That was the advantage of having hand-reared Hal, so to

speak; he knew when the line was drawn – and where.

'If you hear the slightest rumour about me and anyone else in this office – jump on it with both feet. If someone repeats it anywhere – I don't suppose I can make it a sacking offence, can I? Look bloody silly in front of a tribunal?'

I spoke in chopped sentences. He nodded to support the point. To blunt the sharpness a little I added, 'And when she comes in I want to see her.'

Hal's irony is all in his grin. But I felt unclean when he left.

She was late and I wanted to tell her so.

'Trains. I still can't read them.'

I lifted my head. 'Never mind. When you get your own place.'

Slight shift in the eyes: 'Yes.'

'You got back all right?'

'Yes.' She was tentative. 'And you?' Her legs gleamed as though she wore shimmering stockings.

'I'm okay.'

My mind cranked out a speech. Listen. Elizabeth Bentley has gained the impression that you and I have embarked on a steaming love affair that is unquestionably going to lead to marriage. We haven't – and it isn't. I am not going to marry you, no matter how much you launch yourself at me. You're a crafty little gold-digger. I'm sorry I took you to bed and if you feel exploited by that I understand. But that is the end of it. Okay?

I didn't say a word of that: the moment defeated me; nothing I wanted to say came out of my mouth. Instead I shook my head in embarrassment.

'Look, I'm really sorry I ran off like that. I really am. I've had a lousy time. I'll make it up to you. Forgive me.' I blushed as I said it.

She said, 'You must ring Philippe. He thinks you believe he duped you.'

'D'you know what happened to me?'

I told her. She went white. Her concern for me drove me farther down my own scale of self-respect.

'Have you reported it to the police?'

'No. Can't you imagine the bureaucracy? In France?'

I promised her I'd telephone Philippe.

'Do you know you have a hero-worshipper out there?' she said, indicating the drawing office.

'Oh?'

'The new draughtsman. Georgy-Porgy.'

She was bridging some gap between us – she must have sensed something. I've put enough hurt in women's eyes to recognize it when I see it. Yet, wanting, even needing, to be cold, I found I couldn't. Discomfort sunburned me. All I could think of was that she fastens her bra in front where she can see the clasp and then tugs it round her body to line up the cups.

Next – Elizabeth; at least now I'm tackling what I know. It went better. I went on the offensive; it always disconcerts her.

'Now, Elizabeth, what did you mean –' this is me being jovial – 'by that extraordinary message on my machine? You know perfectly well that I have no intention of marrying anyone.'

'Well, I was just being a bit Vatican about it, Nicholas dear.'

'*Vatican?*'

'Well, the Vatican never denies anything unless it is true, and they also say things are so in order to make them happen.'

'Elizabeth!'

'She's a very nice girl, Nicholas. You could do a lot worse. I mean it's a shame she can't have children, as I expect she's told you.'

'Kind of her not to.'

'I told her, dear, that you probably didn't want children.'

'Stop this at once!' Chaffing her sometimes works. 'Or I shall tell everyone you're having an affair with a man who wears a wig.'

She changed tack immediately. 'I don't like this Safft business, though.'

Is there nothing Mary Strait hasn't talked about?

'Antony Safft was very good to me,' I said, knowing this would connect. 'We had become very close friends.'

'But to be made his executor?'

She sounded cheated. I had triumphed. Now came inspiration.

'Elizabeth – another piece of news for you. I'm coming down to have lunch with you tomorrow.'

She objected; 'I've only just seen you.'

But I rode through her; 'I need to see you again.'

There are moments when I bully her quite well.

No time to digest this little victory. Johan Pearl's builder had arrived.

The human capacity for returning to normal astonishes me. A passage of time came when I almost forgot I was under threat. Perhaps there is 'fear overload' just as there is sensory overload. Maybe I'd been through so much terror already it had begun to strengthen me. Admittedly the Problem still hammered at me like a torturer downstairs, not least because I had no sensible answer to the question 'Why me?' Yet I nonetheless found myself calming down.

Tedium helped. Architects measure, argue, account, draw. Mostly it is mundane; mostly we use methods and systems and devices other people have invented. Less than ten per cent of the work is exciting and that is where the adrenaline lies. I have no reason to believe many other professions are much different.

All that day I measured and argued and accounted and drew. I used slide rules with centuries of science behind them, computer programs I could never have dreamed up, systems I took for granted. Mistakes reared their heads; brief moments of excitement turned into false trails; dull telephone conversations took place with clients, planners, suppliers, contractors and subcontractors. Boredom dropped by now and again.

That is my life – except where it hits the public and becomes glamorous, and that is where the two-edged sword of reputation swings. Had I been less prominent would all this be happening to me?

My high social profile caused one edgy moment. A reporter rang from the *Daily Mail*. I know from experience that the *Mail* hires not journalists but hunting dogs. He was working on the Antony Safft story, could he have a word or two? Fine.

You knew him well? Yes, very fond of him, miss him dreadfully. Were you a *special* friend? Depends what you mean by *special*, I breathed a silent 'Ha-ha.' Who d'you think killed him? Wish I knew, I'd be the one arguing to lock 'em up and throw away the key. Sometimes these things fan out a bit – experienced any violence yourself? Only at the hands of planning officers – and clients. Chuckles. You're not, of course, married yourself? No, always the bridesmaid. I believe there's a nephew? Yes, I've met him, charming man. A French lawyer, has he any theories? I don't think so, he's as mystified as anyone. He's a Nazi-hunter? Is he? Oh, how courageous, the French are miles better than us at that sort of thing. Any connection, you think, between the Nazi-hunting and the murder? Gosh, I wouldn't know, I'm just devastated that Mr Safft, Antony, died, he wasn't only a valued client, he was a dear friend, I mean, everyone in my office loved him, in fact, I'm grateful for your call, you've just reminded me I must enquire about the memorial service. I can tell you that it's next month, no venue mentioned yet, I expect the place'll be crawling with cops, they spoken to you? Only to check a few details, you see I was actually waiting to have lunch with him, at the precise time of death, or so the police have told me. Oh, really?!!! In fact I didn't find out for a few days because I went away on the Sunday and didn't get back till the Wednesday, that's when I heard. Musta been a shock for you, were you anywhere interesting? Oh just the usual Euro-round we all do nowadays.

When he rang off I found I was sweating and I mentally thanked Antony; he taught me, 'If a journalist interviews you, no matter how sensitive the topic – give them a little juicy something or other.'

The day travelled on. At five o'clock, six his time, I sank my teeth in the bullet and telephoned Philippe Safft. A secretary said he had left – but, a message. Wherever he was, wherever I was, M'sieu Newman was to telephone him; here are his numbers; he is tonight in Switzerland but he will not be at his hotel yet.

'Can you reach him? If you can – tell him I will call him at midnight British time tonight.'

More calls came in and I was pleased to let the callers have the run of the mill. I signed several letters.

Hal rolled in and said, 'The shareholdings – our new employees – do they get some paper?'

'Yes, the usual procedures. Ask Andy to do it.'

'He's given me the forms. Wanna sign in blank?'

'Yes, of course.'

The usual procedures mean that temporarily I signed over the necessary percentage of my shares until the next AGM when new paper was allocated. It was foolproof. To tamper with it any newcomer would have to start a legal battle lasting years. Elizabeth devised it for morale.

'Shall I tell the "new intake"?'

'Good idea. But – obviously – no details about our individual holdings.' I like Hal better when I'm not with him.

At the end of the day when I went out to the drawing

office, Mary Strait had gone. The new draughtsman, Georgy-Porgy, smiled at me and held up a big card on which he had scribbled *'Shareholder!'* In the *o* he had drawn a face with a big grin.

Cook. A little cooking always helps. On Sloane Street I bought breasts of Barbary duck. Fry them fast, high heat; A little balsamic vinegar, just a drop, at the last moment. Some salad with rye bread. Stewed plums and nectarines, too hard at the moment to be eaten any other way. Stilton and Duchy of Cornwall gingered biscuits.

But I noticed that when I shopped I walked sideways like a crab along the food gondolas, checking behind me at all times, and like a soldier from Ulster I looked underneath my car. Must remind Hal to fix the papers for the new distributions. Get myself back to my fifty-five per cent. Elizabeth must be unnerving me.

My midnight conversation with Philippe lasted no more than a few minutes. He answered the telephone immediately. Play this carefully. I need to establish a number of things, but I must do so in such a way that I seem to remain neutral.

First: could he have had anything to do with the St Gilles attack? His concern – or his performance – knocked that suspicion. He asked me to describe the occurrence in detail; he particularly wished descriptions of the two attackers. Would I help the French police? Identikits, et cetera? I remained noncommittal.

'If you want me to, Philippe. But, you know – I'm trying to get away from all this.'

Second: 'In your opinion, from your experience – I know we talked about this in France – can I remove myself from the target zone?'

He believed so. 'I've thought about it a little more, Nicholas. If you are not an executor any longer . . .'

'But how will they know?'

'If they know you are – I presume they can find out you are not. Let the fact be advertised.'

'But you said – *Le Monde*, *The Times* – it wouldn't necessarily keep them off?'

'Can you think of another way of telling them, my friend?'

Third: assuming the executor role was the 'why' – could he tell me *who* or *what*? He talked about 'this Nazi Antoine had been pursuing. It seems to make a little sense – this person, he may think Antoine told you. And this footballer connection – it is all so confusing, my friend.'

I'll swear if he says 'my friend' again.

'But how could this "Nazi" think such a thing? Did Antony know him? I mean, if Antony got that close, isn't there a trail to follow? How close did he actually get? Because, Philippe, the terror of all this is wearing me down; I could start coming apart.'

I didn't tell him I was dropping things, breaking things, nudging the car against other cars.

Philippe Safft paused, deliberating what, or how much, to tell me.

'My friend. Antoine, the last time I met him, told me this man had attended a dinner party. And in London. And within the previous few months. These were his words. "This year, on the 24th of July, I ate dinner in the same room with this man." That is what he said.'

'And he said no more than that?'

'No.'

'Who was the man? Where was the dinner?'

Philippe anticipated my questions. 'Antoine's diary is missing,' he said. 'He kept it himself, as I am sure you know. Without it we do not know whom he met, when he met them, where he met them. But I do know he put much pressure on the host of that night to lead him to this man.'

'How did Antony know he was the right man?'

'He just knew. You, my friend, you know how he worked.

175

He researched everything and, as he always said, his research was the servant of his instinct.'

It crossed my mind that I was being told some elaborate yarn. We had a few more minutes of conversation. Philippe, sensing that I was about to ring off, tried again to reassure me.

'I am so distressed. It is a matter of pride to me that you know how vairy upset, vairy, vairy upset.' His French accent became sufficiently pronounced to reduce my paranoia a little. A lawyer, however, is always a lawyer and he was unable to end the conversation without seeking information.

'What do you mean to do now?' he asked. 'When will you take your decision?'

'I mean to think very carefully,' I said. 'None of this kind of thing should have anything to do with me. I think I'll have a talk with the lawyers. It makes sense to distance myself from all of this.'

'That will be a pity. But I will understand.'

When I hung up I felt even more trapped and couldn't find an explanation for that feeling. I tried to count out the factors.

So. A war-criminal figure actually existed. Antony had met him. As recently as July. Why should that seem to tighten the cords around me? It must be that this Nazi, or those acting for him, killed Antony. In the process they found some – erroneous – suggestion that Antony had given me crucial information.

This was too much. I am a middle-class professional man deliberately living an undramatic life and I want none of this. Although I now had an exit route I prowled the apartment in a foul mood. It was adding up in fact but not in spirit.

At half past six next morning somebody rang me. I lay in the bath looking at the wallphone. Let the machine take it. Oh, no – I'd never switched the machine back on. Shit! I still didn't answer. The St Gilles cut on my head was sore. The phone rang again. I switched on the machine and walked away.

Before I went to work I pressed 'playback'.

'Nicholas? Are you there? It's Claire. Please pick up the phone. Please ring me when you get this message. Please?'

I rang immediately. No answer.

27

The moment I saw Elizabeth the next day I understood something. I understood it from the cast of her head and face. Why had I not seen it before? Have all my serious errors in life come from self-absorption? Somebody, a girlfriend, howled at me once, 'You can't see because you can't feel.' I saw something now, though, big and clear, the moment I stepped from the car at Faircombe. You idiot, Nicholas.

Nevertheless. Two – or three – can play any game.

'Now, Nicholas, dear, I want to talk to you about your love life.' Very cheerful today.

I answered in merry kind. 'You know, Elizabeth, Mary Strait reminds me of you. She has some of your style.'

Elizabeth deals with the pressure of being found out by not answering, or by asking a tangential question.

'Did you remember my *marrons glacés*?'

I ignored her, sticking to my own agenda. 'Imagine getting another such woman architect. It'll be as though you had never retired.'

This stung. 'Wish I hadn't. I'm so bored.'

No, I'm not letting her off this hook.

'I know it's fanciful – but she even looks a bit like you.'

She caved in, Wagnerian thunder in her voice. 'She's my niece. How d'you think she heard of the job in the first place?' Elizabeth, *in extremis*, got her way by anger.

'I must have known, without knowing I knew.' I unsheathed my knife. 'You might have told me.'

'You always knew I had a niece, who's an architect.'

'No, I didn't.'

'Nicholas, you bloody did, she's Antonia's girl. Jock Strait's daughter.'

'I can't keep track of your legion relatives. Did you know she was applying to Bentley Newman?'

'She wanted to be seen on her own merits. Now take me to lunch.'

She wore the diamond brooch Paul Kale designed for her.

In the car she attacked.

'In any case, what are you doing to Mary? She came home in tears.'

'Out of town' – that was the phrase at Wheeler's. Did Hal know?

'Home? You mean – she's staying with you?'

'Of course she is.'

'I think that's bloody duplicitous.'

'You think everything's duplicitous, that's what's wrong with you. Look – what are you doing with her? You've only just met her, you're in and out of bed with her, in and out of France with her. Are you toying with her? Of course you'll only say it's none of my business, but – to be old-fashioned – are your intentions serious?'

'Intentions? I don't have intentions.'

She tried another tack. 'She'd look after you very well.'

'I don't need looking after. I don't want looking after.'

'You're not listening to me, Nicholas. I'm saying – I really do like her.'

'Time for an old riposte, Elizabeth: then, why don't you marry her?'

She sniffed, always a considerable moment, always followed by silence.

Elizabeth has been eating at Georges Sencor's for years. She is loved there – not least because she introduced her friend Elizabeth David there, who called it 'the only good French restaurant not in France'.

Much reminiscing over lunch; Georges decided to cook the *crêpes* himself. The forgetful Madame Sencor once again ascertained that no, I was not Elizabeth's younger lover. And then, once again, subtly introduced me to her daughter, Danielle, who is in her early thirties.

Lunch went delightfully by. In flashes I began to reach for a forgotten sense of enjoyment. Elizabeth loves an adoring audience. I heard her say to Georges that she had grown tired of retirement.

After lunch we walked down the lane to Barley Hill, at the end of a long, tree-lined enclave. The house, for which Gertrude Jekyll designed the garden, must please those who like Lutyens. His reputation makes itself obvious – that impression of there never having been a problem to solve, as if the house always meant to be where it is. And the way he captured space confidently. His windows have the controlled bohemianism that made Rennie Mackintosh famous.

We strolled through the nearer gardens first, ordered and pure, with a rampart of herbaceous borders. Many shrubs had withdrawn into themselves for the winter.

'I need to talk to you,' I said. 'You keep deflecting me.'

'Look,' Elizabeth said, and pointed to the church in the distance on the cliff's edge. 'That's where the Roman advance party is supposed to have come in.'

'I know. You told me years ago. I need to talk to you.'

She stood and rounded on me, more viciously than I had ever known.

'You are incompetent in your life, Nicholas. And you are ungrateful. I watch you very closely. You think you have it all under control. The minimalist office. The minimalist apartment. Black and white. With just here and there a touch of old mahogany. What was it *Architectural Digest* said? "Carrara marble but as we have never seen it before."

Or was that *Vogue*? But people say you are soulless. I am bitterly disappointed in you.'

I reeled. Tried to recover.

'What have I done?' But it hurt.

'I'm referring to Mary. My niece, by the way. *My* niece. Note the emphasis!'

My turn to let fly. 'Had I known she was your niece I mightn't have hired her. I think you planted her on me.'

'I did no such thing.'

'Then why didn't she say at the interview she was your niece? This was a put-up job.'

'It wasn't! If you weren't so paranoid you'd see she's a bloody good architect.'

'I'm not paranoid!'

We were standing under a huge Karely tree, part of Gertrude Jekyll's imported exotica. Embarrassingly, a young gardener passing made a 'Quieter, please' gesture with his hand.

I said, 'Even the gardeners are disgusted at your shouting.'

'I don't care about the gardeners. I care that you don't know how to behave. You cannot simply heave your body on top of your drawing-office staff, heave yourself off again when you've finished and then discard her.'

'That's not what I have done!'

'That is what she thinks you have done. You are unable to have a relationship with a woman unless you brutalize her or idealize her. Mary is a perfectly all-right girl.'

'This is a conspiracy,' I said.

'Hark at who's not paranoid. No wonder you attract all this violence in your life.'

At that remark my anger needed the most powerful curb. I had evidently been the topic of lengthy conversation. Over and above my immediate reaction, something had gone seriously awry. Elizabeth Bentley and I had never quarrelled bitterly. Harsh arguments over design and policy, yes. Sour complaints from me, especially at the fact that she never praised – yes.

But we had travelled together, built the practice together, fought many good planning campaigns together and had, I knew, deep mutual feelings.

I stopped speaking – in part to cool things, in part to see what she would say next.

She broke the long silence.

'It grieves me to say this. But you are turning out to be a man without honour.'

'Chapter and verse, please,' I said, coldly.

'I remember you refusing to take on a very distinguished Nigerian client I introduced. "Nouveau" you said. Although I knew the real reason – which was the colour of his skin. And look at you now.'

'Look at what?'

'You know bloody well. That footballer. Money changes you, Nicholas. And you'll do anything for fashion. Or publicity.'

'Rubbish!'

'It is not rubbish. And I was absolutely shocked by that piece in the newspapers.'

'What piece?' She had me puzzled.

'The interview you gave – "grieving for your gay friend".'

'In the *Daily Mail*? They rang me. I didn't ring them. Now, Elizabeth, please don't tell me you're homophobic. That's one prejudice I will not accept from you.'

'I'm not. But I didn't like him.'

'You hardly knew him – what *are* you talking about?!'

'Nicholas, I know a great deal about him. He made Paddy Ormeau's life a misery for the last few months. He was unspeakable. All kinds of ridiculous stuff. Trying to rewrite history.'

Blinding flash! I will always remember where she said it.

We stood by a stream. Elizabeth's diamond unicorn brooch.

Paddy Ormeau. Viscount Ormeau. House in Knightsbridge. On the main board of Compton's. Antony a non-exec director there too.

Jesus-Running-Christ! I heard the click-click-click of pieces falling into place.

We walked the gardens slowly. I offered Elizabeth my arm. In the rhythm of this mood she would subside and in half an hour would turn playful and affectionate. At that moment she would expect a gift from me. I would mollify her by offering to take Mary Strait away for a weekend, perhaps for Christmas.

Paddy Ormeau! Christ! Antony had spoken of him. Of course. Paddy Ormeau whose Mosleyite father's memoirs openly embraced Hitler. Of bloody course! May you live in interesting times. But that's a curse, that's what nobody ever remembers. I lost count of how many themed gardens Gertrude Jekyll built in this huge garden. My God! My instinct always tells me the truth.

When we came back to the terrace behind the house, Elizabeth pointed again to the white cliffs in the distance, shining in the low winter sun.

'I was nearly killed there.'

'What?'

'A landing from France nearly went wrong.'

She never let me down. Almost everywhere we went in Europe she mentioned a war exploit. Once, suspicious, I checked a story she told me. She had underplayed it.

I looked at her, the sun in her face, the freckles and brown wrinkles. She looked like a health-seeking German baroness, small, wiry and fine-boned. The bright light showed her age: nothing else did. Did I love this woman? Perhaps.

'Elizabeth?'

'Yes, Nicholas.'

'I promise you this. I will take your niece away for a

weekend somewhere. Perhaps for Christmas. Provided –'

'No deals.'

'Yes, Elizabeth! Yes deals. Provided you do not rubbish my friend Antony Safft again.'

'Yes, Nicholas,' she said, but I loathe that little-girl voice she puts on.

28

On the way back to London, excitement lifted me. It warded off the minute-by-minute fear. And it gave me another bonus – concentration. I became completely absorbed in how to establish that Antony met his quarry at Paddy Ormeau's. I was certain he had. What should I do about it?

The carphone rang.

'I hope you're hands-free. My name's Don Tynan. Acting Superintendent.'

'Ah. Are you investigating the Safft affair?'

'Nope. I do football hooligans.'

'Ah. Good. At last, if I may say so.'

'I'm down Battersea nick. Where are you?'

'I'm on the M2. Coming back from Kent.'

'If you're coming in by Streatham we could meet,' Tynan said, 'You be there by six?'

'Before that, maybe.'

He gave me an address.

'See you at six or before,' I concluded.

'I'll have a bath and a drink ready for you,' he said in a scathing voice.

In a Victorian house, converted (badly) to four apartments, Acting Superintendent Tynan lived on the ground floor and in the basement.

'Come in.'

The smallest policeman I've ever met. Tufts of fair hair in his nostrils. He walked like a rolling barrel. Every movement firm: he closed the door with a crisp slam and then checked that it was locked.

'I'm trying to buy the whole house bit by bit. Hoping that every time a flat comes vacant I'll have enough money put by to get a deposit on it and then I'll rent it out. Police pay is lousy, even though I'm Acting I don't get the pay, that's the Home Office for you.'

He had a disconcerting habit – he shot very quick glances at me and then looked away again fast, as if fearing being caught at it; he did it several times a minute.

The typical double doors connected the front reception room to the rear. Chaos defined his front room, what the first owners of the house would have called the 'parlour'; crazy stacks of books, old newspapers and magazines, clothes, shoes, a bicycle, unfinished meals, broken office furniture, an old television set, a typewriter, and all piled waist-high. The adjoining room, however, seemed to march straight out of a Your Office at Home article in the lifestyle section of a Sunday newspaper.

He saw me looking from one room to the other and made no comment; I had no measure of him yet.

We sat in the neat room. The pencils on the desk lay in a row. I, so anal that I live alone to avoid the rumpus of others, felt almost a stab of envy.

'I saw the first reports. And Geoff Hurst's interview with you. Tell me it all. From the beginning. Sorry to have to ask.' He turned on a little tape recorder.

It must have taken up to ten minutes. I felt pleasure that I remembered more and more; and didn't embellish.

'You're good on detail,' he said. 'That come from your profession?'

'I don't want to waste your time, Superintendent.'

'That the lot?'

'No' – and I added the knife, the flowers, St Gilles.

'Shit. You've been busy.'

He looked at me, very brown eyes and buttery colouring, a tub of a man. And he fidgeted.

'Your friend Antony Soft.'

'Safft. Oh – there is one other thing. In your line of business.' I told him about Johan Pearl, the introduction from Antony, the house in Wiltshire and Pearl's distress at Antony's death.

'Genuinely shattered?'

'Genuinely. He was two hours on the phone.'

Tynan opened a bag of crisps, offered me some and when I declined began to eat them like a hound. He kept coughing as the crumbs went the wrong way. Then he opened a second bag.

'How well d'you need to know your clients?'

I shrugged. 'There's no answer to that. What is it you're after?'

'I don't know. I mean – I don't know yet. Okay. This is one way of looking at it. What happened to you has all happened since old Soft croaked – or was croaked – but it also began since you took on the Pearl. Okay, so you took him on the day your mate was carved.'

I intervened. 'I've never felt the two had any connection –'

'Okay, but I mean, all due respects, like, but you wouldn't fucking know, wouldya?'

'Is that how you intend to look at it? Officially, I mean.'

'"Officially" doesn't exist. Not in this game. Naw, I just want to know if I'm on to something. I mean – if I was I'd sure as fuck hate to miss it.'

'I'm just the architect Pearl hired.'

'He paying you much?'

I said, 'He paid a lot for the site.'

'He has enough to pay ten of you. We ran the checks. He is totally heeled. I mean, serious.'

Was he asking me for information?

'But he's only twenty-three or so,' I protested.

'That's my point. We reckon on him being worth ten to twelve million hard, probably more – there's a wad in liquid funds.'

'Why are you interested in him? Is it him or all footballers? I mean, on account of the violence and so on?'

He was holding something back the way policemen do.

'Your Mr Pearl attracts some odd company.'

'He seems to me – I mean from his family, he seems okay.'

I told him about the house near Noordwijk.

'I know those Dutch barn-houses,' said Don Tynan.

Would this policeman prove a know-all? I raised an eyebrow. He rose and went to the next room, and I heard him rummaging in the shambles. When he came back he handed me two large catalogues.

'Went over for that. Then took a holiday. Cycling. It's a hobby.'

The Paintings, and *The Drawings and Letters of Vincent van Gogh*. Catalogues from the big Rijksmuseum retrospective in 1991. I never got to it and lamented the fact.

'D'you like Van Gogh?' I asked. 'People love him or they hate him. Which are you?' I knew from experience that you can somewhat control the police if you ask them questions.

He had another disconcerting habit – of diving off into irrelevant vehemence.

'Know what I hate? Know what I fucking hate? People who speak to me on the phone when their mouths are full. Or people who phone me when they're eating. Shows where I sit on their priority list.' Who was he like? He was like a sharper Mickey Rooney. Or Charlie Drake.

'How was it?' I pressed my questions, wagging the Van Gogh catalogue, trying to measure Tynan.

'Okay. I went to that exhibition 'cause we get a lot of nutters in this game and I wanted to see whether I'd learn something about the nutcase mentality.'

'And –?'

'Learned nothing. *Nada*. A plate of fat nothings. Why's

Pearl want a house like home? Plus, Wiltshire's a hundred miles from his patch.'

I made an uninterested gesture. 'You know these footballers. Money. And he's living in a neo-something flat.'

'When you meeting him again?'

'Supposed to be next week.'

'Okay. Why'd you take this on?' asked Don Tynan at my elbow, pacing.

'I don't know,' I replied truthfully.

'I thought you didn't. But this-ah, this ain't hay, as the Americans say. I don't want to worry you but there's some nasties in all this somewhere.'

I shivered. 'Did you say "nasties" or "Nazis"?' I asked. Accent? Long-ago Geordie, perhaps. Northern, anyway.

'Same difference. Yeh. Maybe. I-ah, well, you know. No. Look. I'll come clean. I don't know if you getting fucked over on the Tube's tied to Pearl or your old pal, Soft. *I'm* worried 'cause this breaks their pattern.'

'Whose pattern?'

'The scum who did you and that poor old Paki guy. We're all over those swine like fucking ointment, we know when they shit we got 'em so taped, and this one puzzles us. I mean we knew about it before you got back to your flat nearly. And that lanky rat with a port-wine-stain birthmark on his lip?'

'Jemima.'

'Yeah, Jemima. I know that fucker and I hate him, he did one of my best men with a beer glass, bloke lost an eye. But you're-ah, you're okay now? Jesus, you been in it. Ever happen to you before?'

'A bit. Here and there.'

'And, like the old joke, you know this joke, you gotta look at me, it's visual.'

He stood there with his bulging waist and yellow tee-shirt. I looked at him. He made a motion like a rollercoaster in the air with his hand. 'Know what that is?'

189

'No.'

'Neither do I but here it comes again.' He repeated the gesture.

I sighed. This meeting had given me nothing. I said, 'And I thought it had all stopped.'

'Better find out what's causing it. As the widow said to the vicar.'

'But things had been quiet,' I protested.

'Sure-sure. Make you some tea?' he said.

'Any coffee?'

'Bad for you,' he called.

'Are you always undercover?'

'Look at me.' He slapped his paunch. 'Who'd risk a uniform on this? I was hired that way. Never did the usual route.'

'What did you do before?'

He ignored the question, called from the kitchen door; 'Just a thought. D'you have an ex-wife?'

'No. Why?'

'Oh, you know, old rancour, that sort of thing. Or an ex-lover?'

'Lots of ex-lovers. Too many.'

'Male or female?' He shot the question at me so fast I almost didn't pick it up. 'I'm only eliminating the possibilities.'

'Can I eliminate some?'

'Like what?'

'Can I see Antony Safft's diary? If the police have it.' I didn't quite believe Philippe that it had gone missing.

'Nope. No chance.'

'Even if I got from it something that'd give you something you want?'

'Oh, yeah?' I knew his eyes narrowed.

Press him. 'I believe it might.'

'What d'you want me to do?' Quite shirty.

'Get me a look at it. I might remember something.'

'Can't. Different force investigating. That sort of bollocks. I'll try Geoff Hurst.'

'I don't know if he's called "Geoff".'

'That's what we call him. After – you know?'

'You know what?'

'They think it's all over.'

'What?'

He sucked his teeth in exasperation. 'You don't know jack shit, do you? Geoff Hurst won the World Cup for England in 1966, extra time and he slammed in two goals, and the commentator said, "They think it's all over" because – ah, fuck it.' He gave up, like an exasperated teacher. 'Know what they say? "You gotta get out more." I s'pose you never heard that said either.'

I didn't know what in Heaven's name he was on about. Cautiously, I asked a question in my own interests.

'The six who attacked me. I mean – what use could I be to them?'

'They're not the blokes, they're only the frontline. What you need's the ones with the strings in their hands.'

'What are they like?'

'Suits and mobile phones.' Tynan saw that I was baffled. 'You hafta understand what's going on here,' he said.

I looked across at him, spraying his crisps, pouring coffee with the other hand. Yes, a larger (not much) version of Mickey Rooney is the closest I could get to him. A man who didn't sleep well. Something in the past had radically disturbed his life.

'Suits?' I repeated. 'And mobile phones?'

'Okay. From personal experience, and from our mates all over, what we know is – there's organization going on. And there's connections.' He enumerated on his fingers. 'You've got your National Front in this country. There's the neo-Nazis in Germany and Austria. Right-wingers in France, down in the south mostly, some fucking animals

191

there. There's big organizations in this and they're all sucking each other.'

Tynan saw what I was about to ask and pre-empted me.

'No, sister. If there's any Grand Plan we've yet to crack it. I won't go beyond saying there's a fairly organized and reasonably sophisticated bunch of people getting their kicks from giving thugs a way of getting their rocks off.'

He didn't convince me. 'You're talking in riddles,' I challenged.

'I should do. There's a lot of bollocks talked. I mean – the media've all this thing that the bottles and shaven heads are only the pawns. That there's blokes behind them, blokes with suits and money and good jobs and cars and houses and social lives that'd surprise you, that they're the blokes running it all. The mobile-phone guys. They go into a situation and they watch it and they phone their instructions to the blokes on the street. But we don't like talking about any of that 'cause it makes us uncomfortable. We're not able to nail them and until we do we won't say out loud they exist.'

'What kind of jobs do these – these puppeteers – what do they work at?' I asked.

Tynan said, 'Architects?' and laughed.

I did too and asked, 'Seriously?'

'We don't know.'

'What do you know?'

Tynan said, 'We know about a property dealer. That's why we're looking at the Antony Soft thing so closely. We know about a stockbroker, slickest guy you ever saw. Two lawyers. A dentist. Two computer guys. They're a worry. There's a barrister's clerk, but we nailed him.'

I said, 'But there must be some – some big reason.' No answer. I pressed on. 'Nobody does all that without some reason. I mean, have you looked at the people they choose?'

'The foot soldiers? Yeah. They all fit a pattern. Semi-skilled. Unskilled. Hard chaws. Or think they are.'

'But the men behind them – why are they doing it?'

Silence. I said, 'Come on, Superintendent. You're a highly intelligent man.'

'Too intelligent to put forward any theory. Next thing you know some wanker's writing a book about it.'

'But there's a power thing going on,' I said. 'There has to be.'

Tynan asked, 'Have you thought it might only be kicks? I mean if you ever saw a football riot on television? Okay. The thing you'd realize is – if you could market it you'd have the biggest fucking spectator sport of all time. You wouldn't be able to print enough tickets. Or have enough television channels.'

29

I rose to go. The instant coffee turned my stomach. He used milk substitute, some frightful powder thing.

No way forward for my own vital interests. I knew it and Tynan knew it. What he offered me was no more than a chance to understand that there was nothing to understand. In his view, at any rate.

For his own reasons, he chose to see the Tube attack on me as random and mindless. I knew that without asking. Any push to get any deeper would be blocked harder. I tried anyway.

'If I could speak to the ones who attacked me – what'd they say?'

He said, 'They'd spit in your face, call you a fucking ponce and do you all over again.'

'If I asked a reason?'

'Okay. Suppose you met one of them in the street and you said to him, "Hey, I know you, you're that bloke who did me over on the Tube," he'd say, "Don't know what you're talking 'bout, mate," and even if you then called us up and said, "Hey, I've found this bloke and I can identify him," we'd come up against his mum saying he was at home all that day. Or his mates. "Oh, he was with us."'

I said, 'So what's the point in me taking up your time?'

'Point is, bloke don't even know his wire's bein' pulled. All he knows is he's on the Tube with his mates, they're warmin' up for the afternoon and they see this poncy git, no offence meant, and one of the guys says, "Go for it." There's no way you can get in behind that.'

'But yet you say there's an organization –?'

'S'not an *organization* organization. Not like a board of directors an' that.' Tynan stood in his hallway. 'The way I see it is – this is something these guys can make happen. They don't need a reason. Someone gives 'em a reason they take it, and they love it. Yeah, sure, there's big connections, like racism and Nazi stuff an' that, but the web is so wide and the fact that there's no reason – I mean, like, it's not world power or anything they're looking for, so far as we can know.

'In fact,' said Tynan, and it was the most helpful thing he said, 'part of the problem is its reason-less-ness, if I can call it that. If we could get an organized reason we'd have a target, 'cause there'd be a central committee and that.'

'D'you think there's anything like that?' I asked.

He thought – or pretended to. Eventually he said, 'Okay. It's not beyond the power of possibility there's some old bloke somewhere fighting old battles. But if he is – we haven't come across him. And if he was, say, some old Nazi – well, he'd be eighty now, wouldn't he? I mean, I know what I want to be doing when I'm eighty.'

'There are pills, of course,' I said, 'to keep us alive.' Weak joke.

'Naw,' said Tynan. 'This's what I'll be doing, mate. Millwall v. Sheffield United some pissing Saturday afternoon and me there looking and listening and naming names afterwards.'

He made me want to get back at him, so I asked him again, 'What did you do before?'

'Before what? Before my balls dropped?'

'Before you were a policeman?'

He looked at me straight. 'Chewed nuts for sundaes.'

I laughed – but asked one last question.

'The people with the mobile phones? How high up the social scale do they go?'

I had struck something. Something shifted.

'We don't know 'em all.' Tynan controlled himself. 'What you're looking for, and I don't blame you, is some kind of godfather you can get at to see who's giving you all this grief. And nearly more important why they're giving it to you. So's you can stop it. Okay. What I'm saying is – we can't help you. There's nothing in any of our files, our researches or our knowledge that'll get you any closer to what's happening to you. Now, if something comes up we'll be the first to get to you. And if that happened we'd be happier than you'd be, because it'd mean we gained an extra inch. By the same token, if you ever found out something we'd want to know ahead of anyone else.'

'What about your colleagues?' I asked. 'The ordinary police who're investigating the Safft murder? Can they help?'

'The uniforms? Know what the uniforms will say to you?'

'No.'

'Knock-knock.'

Wearily, I said, 'Who's there?'

'Nicholas.'

'Nicholas who?' I couldn't believe this. He grinned; he'd rehearsed it.

'Knickerless girls shouldn't climb trees.' Tynan chuckled. 'Ha-ha, you didn't know that, did you?'

'It's ladders,' I said. 'Shouldn't climb ladders.'

He gave me his mobile number and we parted; he had an unexpectedly pleasant handshake.

Now what? It was nine o'clock and nobody to talk to, just questions to address. I learned several years ago how to fight off loneliness. Do the next thing. So – eat. Don't go without food at a time like this. Eat. Alone? As usual.

I drove from Streatham in light traffic. Snow threatened – 'unseasonably early', they'd say and the bookies would soon shout the odds on a white Christmas. I checked my mirrors. The events of the last weeks made me suspect every shadow.

By Vauxhall a car was staying behind me. It stuck along the Albert Embankment. I crossed Lambeth Bridge, went full circle around the roundabout, recrossed the bridge. The car followed. Or did it? Or was that a different car? Again I crossed the bridge – and lost the car.

No lights in the office. If I hoped Mary Strait might have stayed late I dismissed the thought, not without guilt at my own perverseness. Just as well she'd gone. I didn't think myself strong enough to resist her approaches.

On that front, I hadn't digested my day with Elizabeth. Little details rushed back. I knew why Mary Strait got a mobile phone so quickly. But who else in the office knew she was Elizabeth's niece and hadn't told me? Perhaps they assumed I knew, thought me a nepotist. Irritating thought. And – above all – Paddy Ormeau. That's another day's work.

In the blind alley beside the office sat a car – the same model, certainly, I had seen at Vauxhall Bridge. I turned left, drove round the little square behind the office and came back. The driver's door hung open. This time I turned right, parked and came back on foot to a point where I knew I could see without being seen.

The driver returned from somewhere in front of the office – Tynan! I slipped back to the Saab and drove round the block again, parked in the square. At the office door I saw Tynan's car reverse from the alleyway. He saw me but I pretended not to see him. I gave the impression of trying the door, patting my pockets for my keys, looking at my watch. Then I 'changed my mind' and flagged a cab.

Tynan followed. What the name of Christ is going on? I went to Le Caprice, sat at the bar, told them, No hurry, I'd wait all night to be fed. Through the glass door I could see Tynan's car drift down Arlington Street. By now I had developed a kind of numbness. Well, Tynan could wait. I read the sports pages of all the day's newspapers.

Four mentions of Johan Pearl, only one of them to do with

playing football; the others included a charity appearance and a 'survey' of sporting IQs.

I left Le Caprice at just before midnight. Tynan had moved. He now sat as though parked all night, as close to the apartment block at the bottom as he could get. Must have pulled heavy rank – those concierges are as vigilant as mothers. I never looked directly at him. The cab took me back to my own car, which I then drove home. Tynan followed me all the way until I turned into the underground car park of the block in which I live.

Messages? Two. One – from Elizabeth, asking me to call her. And another.

'Nicholas, it's Claire. Could you give me a ring? I'm at Philippe's; he's away.'

She sounded anxious, but might that be because she feared being misconstrued? After midnight in London, after one o'clock her time, too late. No. Ring.

She answered immediately. 'Oh, thank God. Are you all right?'

'Yes. And you?' So good to hear her voice but I wouldn't say that.

'I need to see you,' she said.

'Oh?'

'Nicholas. Whatever you do – whatever the pressure. Don't relinquish your executorship.'

'What?!'

'Don't. You mustn't. I can't say now. But I will. I have to go.'

And she went – leaving me ratcheted with frustration.

I look out of the window; the car drives by. What is Tynan playing at? Ask him.

He answered his mobile. 'Past your bedtime.'

'What are you playing at?'

'What'dya mean?'

'Come on. I've been watching you. Since Vauxhall Bridge.'

He laughed. 'I stay up late. Insomnia.'

'Tell me the truth.'

'Didja never read any philosophy? There's no such thing as truth.'

I badgered him some more. He refused to budge.

Until I said, 'I've discovered a way to crack all this.'

I felt him stiffen. 'How d'ya mean?'

'*Daily Mail*.'

'Don't-do-that!'

'They're already on to me. I've had one conversation.' I decided to stick with the truth. 'I was suitably evasive – but it might suit me now not to be.'

'Prefer you didn't.'

'Why? You'll have a starring role.'

'Okay, listen. It's twofold. It's keeping an eye on you. And – you want the truth? – maybe you've something up your sleeve.'

'Only my muscled arms,' I said sarcastically. 'Are you going to keep following me? Great waste of taxpayer's money. Unless it makes me feel protected.'

'I do what I have to do.'

'It's not very comfortable being followed. Especially by people you think are on your side.' I switched to the cordless phone and began to walk around the room. 'Did you make that enquiry? Hurst?'

'There's no diary,' said Tynan. 'Or it's gone missing.'

He wheezed.

I asked, 'You an asthmatic?' It made me like him a little more, although I didn't dislike him.

'Yeh. You?'

'Yes. Or I should say, I used to be. It seems to have gone away.'

'A thing that goes away by itself can come back by itself. Didja ever hear that?'

'D'you want some coffee?' I offered.

'Naw, I'm too far away now.' He wheezed again. 'I never asked you how the Pearl job's actually going. There's nothing showing on the site.'

I laughed. 'I might have known you'd have gone there. It's a winter build,' I said. 'I never like them.'

I switched on the bathroom lights, stood at the loo chatting. Siphon lavatories can be more or less silent – if the plumber's any good. My fastidiousness over other people's lavatory habits has one point of rebellion – speaking to them on the phone while I'm in the loo. Otherwise, I hate bathroom sounds.

Especially the one I heard next – a crack like the earth's tectonic plates splitting. My arm felt as if I held some jackhammer gone mad. The lights blew. Outside the bathroom door something flashed and I smelt savage burning. In the dark I was hurled back against the basin behind me. The mirror shattered when my shoulder hit it. My arm felt as though somebody had tried to wrench it from my body. A flash split the air.

The bizarre thing is – I never let go of the phone. Tynan says I shouted into it all the time. That's how he knew what happened – that someone had hot-wired the chrome handle of the stainless-steel cistern. When I flushed the handle the wire hit the water. If I'd been standing naked on a wet floor . . .

My immediate shock didn't direct itself at the fear, or at the attempt on my life. Tynan reached my front door within minutes. I roared at him, 'LIAR!'

While I was chatting to him he had been sitting more or less on my doorstep.

30

The apartment flooded: not much but too much. Tynan had a large torch.

'Halogen,' he said. 'Blinds people.'

Neighbours peered from behind their dressing gowns.

At the fusebox the wall looked like a minuscule Oradour. A fire had started, but the old ceramic insulators, big as prayer books, held. The air hung with burnt smells. I looked at the cistern. Cleverly done – a naked wire to the handle which only touched water when plunged. I had all-stainless-steel sanitary ware which almost got me killed.

Tynan peered at it. 'Newly done,' he said, and pointed to some scratches on the metal.

I rubbed my elbow. Everything jangled.

'What do we do now?'

In blinding rage, I didn't know what to say. Tynan kept me occupied.

'We get outta here. Get some gear first. Got a place you can stay? D'you want to come with me?'

'No. I'll make a call, you can give me a lift, though.'

I walked around like a ranting zombie, gathering clothes and medicaments. My eyes hurt like hell; I remembered the French eyedrops. The skin on the hand that had taken the brunt felt as stretched as parchment. No marks on it but I remembered to take some cream. Elbow still jarring. Disbelief setting in.

'Shine that light over here,' I said to Tynan. I looked at the ruined fuseboard again, if only to remind myself. *Souviens-toi.* In my fury I felt like an unmanageable animal.

At 22 Jermyn Street they checked me in as though it were mid-afternoon instead of the small hours. The world still has a few great small hotels left. They cooked me a truffle omelette and the food allowed me to feel exhaustion. I slept, having closed the bathroom door.

The sun woke me early.

I thought, No front, now, on which I'm not threatened. Suddenly, in a burst, my mind began to work and brought the fear under some control. Maybe the electricity had cleared my brain. Is this why they give shocks to the insane? It certainly decided the decision, so to speak. Yes, yes, go after Them. Him. Whomsoever.

Like all major decisions I made it almost unknown to myself. I don't quite understand the process. Having agonized and shivered in the cold and dark for weeks and weeks, I suddenly reached a sunlit clearing where I had resolve and patience, where I could think and strategize.

In the office I released truncated detail – faulty wiring, ancient fusebox. I called in favours – plumbing, electrical, flooring and decorating, set a meeting with them all for four o'clock. Lemon opened a file; she and I sourced the latest electrical cut-out systems, the safest cisterns. I dealt with the attack by becoming my own client.

At some point during the day I watched myself from afar – bringing a frightening, life-threatening experience onto my playing field and therefore under my control. Good point to me. This local yet sinister disruption could prove a kind of training for the crux I was about to address. I felt up and running.

Keeping up the pressure of normality upon myself, I took ordinary calls, had a row with a supplier of door furniture for the Cleland job, enjoyed an interesting enquiry from the Department of Trade and Industry. And I spent an excellent hour with the modeller on Johan Pearl's house: behind schedule; they usually are.

'He's playing tonight,' said the model maker.

'Where?'

'Stamford Bridge.'

Where my muggers dumped me; I instantly decided to go to the game, too.

'What do you think of it?' I asked the modeller.

'The house? Brilliant.'

I stood back from this laconic man whose highest compliment is 'Not wholly unsightly.'

'Do you mean that? It doesn't sound like the Graham we know and love,' I said to him.

'Warm. That's why I like it. It's warm. All your stuff's cold. Machines could live in them. This one's for a real person.'

'Oh, thanks.'

'Where d'you get the idea?'

I had to tell him. 'It's based on his family home in Holland.'

'You should maybe do more copying.'

Some people can insult without effort.

'I like this,' he continued, lifting the roof and pointing out the relationship between the stables and the kitchen. 'But why don't you do this?' He slipped in two rows of new walls upstairs, with stable doors in them. 'You could have the guest rooms treated as children's rooms and the nippers'd wake up in the morning and see cows and horses looking in at them.'

'How are the cows and horses supposed to have come upstairs?' I asked.

'Up a ladder, of course, how else if you're only four years old?'

He made me smile, the first person to do so all day. All week. All month. It might yet be all year.

'Yes. I like that. I'll put it to the client.'

Graham the model maker looked at me. 'You should have children. It'd soften you.'

He must have touched me somewhere. Oradour surged

into my mind. The dead schoolteacher found with her arms around as many of her pupils as she could reach.

I went back to my office and tried to reach Pearl. 'This cellphone number is no longer in service.'

Odd: that's a new number; he gave it to me a week ago. I rang his mother. She, friendly, asked courteously for my health and gave me a new number. Said nothing about her son.

Pearl answered. 'Oh, hi, man.'

'You've changed your number.'

'Oh, yeah, I forgot to give it to you, I lost your home number, I bet you rang my mother, I thought you would.'

'I have a model of your house to show you.'

'Oh, wow! Is it great?'

'Not bad.'

'Not bad,' he mimicked, 'not bad. If you'da built the Eiffel Tower, man, you'd-a been saying "not bad". Is that what they call "understatement"?'

'English understatement,' I said and realized I was smiling again. He had that rare gift of good teasing – the kind that generates warmth and never offends.

'Where can we meet?' he said.

'Where are you now?'

'Some motorway. The guys, they is all playing cards, we are in London tonight.'

'I know. I've got someone looking for a ticket for me.'

'Hey, no, man, I got comps.'

'Comps?'

'Yeh, you with someone?'

'No. Alone.'

'It'll be at the playing-staff entrance or whatever they call it down there.'

'Thank you, but I wasn't looking for a free ticket.'

'Nicholas, no problems, but I appreciate your manners.' Such self-possession.

'How is the team bus – I don't suppose you can call it "coach", a coach is a human being, isn't he?'

'Not our one. Hey, you know all that big money they give us? This travelling is what they give it to us for. Nicholas, this is the worst thing in all civilization.'

31

At four o'clock that afternoon the night's outrage became flesh. I saw in full the damage to my home, and the danger there had been to me. Difficult to stay calm.

Fortunately Tynan had covered me and squared the Fire Prevention Officer, who ripped out the offending wire. When the insurance inspector arrived all he saw was ancient cabling being scrutinized.

'Miracle it didn't happen before,' murmured everyone.

'Could it have killed me?'

They shrugged. 'The fusebox, who knows . . . You'd have had to make a circuit . . .'

I thought, I'll make a circuit all right, I bloody will!

Four weeks, the contractors said, and I thought, Make that eight. At six o'clock I left. Pearl's model lay in the boot of the Saab. I called Tynan from the car telephone.

He said, 'No trace of a break-in.'

'But I'm the only one with a key.'

'Then check your locksmith.'

'Impossible.'

'Okay. The best guy we have's gone over it with his dick. No lock picked. No prints. No nothing. Want proof? Your chimney's blocked off at first-floor level. We even had a go at that. Is that good enough for you?'

'But who?'

'You tell me, sister. Unless you're some kind of crazy attention-seeker.'

'Don't be ludicrous.'

'Fact is, someone got into your apartment and wired your

bog to the mains. It wouldn't be unusual if you'd forgotten to lock the front door, the pressure you're under. Now stay outta there and don't tell anyone where you're staying. You gonna rent an apartment?'

'I'll have to.'

'Rent it yourself, don't even tell me where you'll be. Where are you now?' I smiled at the inconsistency.

'On my way to Stamford Bridge.'

'I might see you there. What you doin' after?'

'What do you think? Meeting a client.'

Tynan coughed. 'Don't be surprised at a rerun.'

'I don't get you.'

'If you look in your mirror and see a person you know.'

'Why?' I said irritatedly. 'You agreed –'

He cut me off. 'Not you we're after. Him.'

'But –'

'Leave it,' Tynan said.

32

End to end, forward and back, the long diagonal passes I had first loved – the players poured through the evening with skill and heat and cleverness and commitment. Sometimes they bent the ball's trajectory to show off. Delicious.

Different venue, different crowd, same obscene invective. But I had come to the right place; my mind was looking for patterns, wanting to make moves, aiming to overcome.

Pearl dazzled. Three times in five minutes he ran outside defenders, the ball tied to his feet. Once, from the corner flag down to my right, he clipped the ball high across the mouth of the goal, flighting it millimetres from the goalkeeper's fingers. Nobody met it and he looked disgusted.

I applauded. The man beside me said, 'Don't get too enthusiastic.'

'Oh?'

'Look around you.'

I was sitting among rival fans.

I assured him. 'I'm neutral.'

He replied, 'There's no such thing. You get a comp?'

'How did you know?'

'Old trick. Put the opposition comps where they'll be afraid to open their mouths.' He laughed, an affluent man, older than me. 'Whose friend are you?' he asked.

'The Black Pearl,' I said.

He looked at me with new respect.

'Yeah. I watch him a lot. Look at him. See where his arse is? Halfway down his legs. Low centre of gravity. His gluteal muscle's down where he needs the power. You watch any speed merchant, when they move fast the arse drops.'

'How d'you know all this?'

'I'm a sports injury doctor,' he said. 'They break – I fix 'em.'

At half-time he invited me for a drink. By the time we got served the teams had resumed and we rushed back.

'Football's a blood matter,' said my new friend. 'Nobody who's worth anything follows it lightly. You're in or you're out. I mean, I have competitions with my friends to see who can name the Chelsea team that took the field first day the 1974 season. Have you a wife?' he asked suddenly.

'No.'

'Lucky bugger,' he said and then I saw his eyes bite his lip and I said, 'Went close a couple of times.'

He relaxed, not having made the *faux pas* he feared he had. And was further saved by a goal from Johan Pearl – who merely sidefooted a ball passed to him outside a fallen goalkeeper. And then Pearl ran on into the net.

'A simple goal?' I queried.

'No. How'd he get to be there? He thinks. Good brain. Mind you, he's had a bit more education than the usual youth-scheme footballer.'

'I don't know him very well,' I said. 'Friend of a friend.'

'Top of his game, he is, top of the league. But hacked to hell. He'll come off bruised. And every time he hits that far touchline the abuse – pheewwww!'

'Lovely athlete, though,' I said, more to draw him out than to show any knowledge.

'In about four years' time he'll be attending me or someone like me regularly with injuries here, there and everywhere. But most of them'll be in the head, because he'll have had the highest, the peak – and he's asking himself what does he do for an encore?'

I watched the shapes of the action. At its most fluid the

game moved in geometric patterns – long bisecting lines, short connecting ones. These continued as long as one team held possession. Scrambles occurred only when the other fought back.

I thought, Indeed, that's what's been happening to me. From a distance someone's been making moves on me. Unchallenged. And therefore dictating the play. Time to scramble a bit, take possession. Of my own peace of mind.

Pearl at that moment received the ball inside his own half, streaked past where we sat, outstripped all others into a deserted opponents' half and simply set up his colleagues. They one-twoed the ball into the net.

'Nice to meet you,' said my neighbour, leaving early. 'Good luck serving your sentence.'

I looked puzzled; I might have flinched. He waved a hand. 'This – the game – footie. A life sentence.'

When I met Pearl, outside the players' bar where he told me to wait, he showed none of the elation I expected.

'Hi, man. Can we get this over with?'

I'd never seen this side of him – cold and edgy.

'I'm parked a bit away.'

'Can we leave it for tonight, man?'

He avoided my gaze and he fidgeted.

'Yes. But don't you need to see it?'

He looked all around him, mostly at the forecourt behind me.

'I'm not sure – if you say it's okay, it's okay. I have to go.'

Rubbing his palms together, jumpy, aloof – I saw a changed man.

'Shall I give you a call?'

'No, man. Well, yeah, do, I mean, let me call you.'

He went abruptly – just as I was about to ask, 'Is everything all right?'

No smile from him, no enthusiasm, none of the usual

sparky joviality. Should I put it down to anticlimactic blues?

I looked behind me, following the direction Pearl's eyes had taken. A group of five young men had been walking towards us, five purposeful young men, like well-dressed security guards. Next I saw Tynan. From the other side of the yard came a car, whose occupants acknowledged Tynan.

The five purposeful men stood twenty yards from the bus. They deliberated what to do next. A third car appeared; Tynan flagged it in. The five men checked all around. Calmly and by arrangement, they dispersed in five different directions. Tynan and his men let them go.

Moments later, amid laughter and teasing, Pearl's teammates began to arrive in high glee from their win. He walked in the middle of the bunch and ignored me. Head down he boarded the coach and sat on the far side, wrapped up in himself. Tynan left, following the coach.

I went back to Jermyn Street. Tomorrow I would find somewhere to live. On my mobile I picked up a message – Claire again.

'Nicholas, I need to talk to you. I *need* to.'

When I called she said, 'Hello, hello,' as though unable to hear me. I rang again; the phone had been taken off the hook.

33

That night and next day I designed my strategy. First thing – the omnipresent fear. It debilitates me, all heavy anxiety does: therefore, keep it at bay.

I thought, You're the victim of mind games, so play mind games. Put it all into a container you can handle. I made it part of my day's work. As a mental exercise I switched, or tried to, from worry to inquisitiveness. If Pearl came into my mind I turned the thought into an enquiry about him. When Antony Safft's name came up I made a note to check how much in fees we'd earned from him.

Similarly, when I thought of the attacks on me, I attempted to analyse the mind behind them. Sophisticated. Knows how to hide deep. Has a knowledge of terror. My strategy began to work – or at least I could see that it might.

Mary Strait found me in one of my few solitary moments.

'Hi, stranger.'

I hate women – people – who reproach. Not that she did it overtly, but the reproach lurked. She wore bright red-and-black plastic circles in her earlobes.

'Hallo.'

'How've you been?'

'Irritated,' I said. 'My flat's got no water or electricity.'

'So I hear.' She closed the door behind her. 'Was it an attack?'

'No-no,' I said. 'That's all over.' I needed to sell that idea to myself.

She wasn't having any. 'But is it over?'

'Why d'you ask?'

'I spoke to Philippe. He thinks it's happening because you're an executor.'

'He said as much to me,' I said, while my mind yelled, Change this subject! And what were you doing ringing Philippe? So I asked, 'Have you found a place to live?'

'Yes. I found a flat in Richmond and I'm moving in this very night.'

'Pleased?'

'Queen Anne. Lovely, rickety panels. Come to lunch on Sunday.'

'Oh, what a nice idea,' I gushed while thinking, No, no, no, no, no.

She lowered her voice. 'Would you like to hear some gossip?'

'Oh?' She has stubby hands, I thought, not as nice as first impressions.

'New romance.' She pointed towards the drawing office.

'Who?'

'Lemon. And the new boy, Georgy-Porgy.'

'Stepping out?'

'Quite so. He, or so we are informed by Miz Lemon, is a perfect gentleman. Leaves the rest of you standing. Love-birds, apparently. Anna saw them leaving the pub night before last and a sharp breeze couldn't get between them.'

'He'd better sharpen up,' I said. 'Lemon's no slouch. How's Elizabeth?' I should have said Aunt Elizabeth but I couldn't bring myself to the gibe.

'She says she's been looking for you.'

'I'll ring her now.'

Picking up the telephone got me out of the conversation – but not before Mary Strait said, ''Bout twelve, twelve thirty?' I must have looked puzzled because she added, 'Sunday. I'll give you the address another time.'

Elizabeth 'wanted to say something' to me.

'That Paddy Ormeau remark – scrub it.'

'Why, Elizabeth?'

'I was indiscreet.'

'No. Not at all.' Can I get more information from her? 'I didn't understand what you were talking about anyway.'

She spoke dismissively. 'It's just that Paddy's always had German contacts and, you know, the Germans have their war record too. They weren't all death-camp commandants.'

'Didn't the Ormeaus take some flak for all that?'

'Yes, but like sensible people they kept up their connections. You know, Nicholas, a lot of people here – I mean a lot of people – traded with Germany all through the war.'

No comment from me and we parted warmly.

My father, who tossed out into the ether unconnected facts, told me once that in certain African tribes a hunter who has lost his spear will run at the lion facing him, and nine times out of ten the lion will turn tail. I always found that difficult to believe – but now I was going to do it. Do it instead of thinking about it, instead of being slow and feeble.

Being proactive didn't rule out prudence. I didn't rent one apartment; I rented two. By myself, didn't even tell Lemon. From different agencies.

Each night I entered the front door of one and exited the rear door to go to the other, two streets away, where I slept. All I had to do was check I wasn't followed. I put the car in the office garage. 'They' had not attacked me there.

Hour after hour, night after night, day after day, I checked with myself the decision I had taken. I rehearsed the form of words. I worked out the logistics. I prepared the simple routine and refined it until I felt it right.

Then I put it into the hands of Time. Having prepared the What, and researched and decided the How, I would find the Who and let Time decide the When. Time doesn't get things wrong.

34

Christmas loomed. Accompanied by a bad, embarrassing time. I forgot Mary Strait's Sunday lunch. Sleep gave me the ostensible reason; I didn't wake up until one o'clock, the longest sleep I've had for years.

Even then I didn't remember; I knew vaguely I should be somewhere else but I didn't try very hard to recollect. Some time in the afternoon I paged my answering machine, principally to see whether they had restored an electricity supply to Cadogan Gardens.

The machine plays last messages first.

'Nicholas, this is Elizabeth and this isn't funny. It's most inconsiderate of you.'

'Nicholas dear, it's Elizabeth. It's two o'clock and I'm at Mary's. We're worried. Can you ring us?'

'Nicholas, it's Mary. Where are you? I've got a soufflé at risk.'

'Nicholas, it's me. I'm a little anxious. It's five past one, I said twelve.'

'Nicholas, it's Mary. It's occurred to me you may be staying elsewhere while they're fixing your flat. Or you may be on your way to me already. If so, forgive the anxiety.'

Several more callers left no messages.

And Tynan; he hadn't been returning my calls but now his message asked, 'All quiet on the western front?'

I rang him first, to give myself time to sort out the Mary Strait gaffe.

'It's the western front.'

'Glad it's not the eastern one.'

215

'Oh?'

'You been reading your newspapers?'

'Why?'

'Germany, big stuff in Berlin. Düsseldorf. A sea of scum.'

I twinged hard; I had better not put this job off any more.

'You okay, cock?' Tynan asked. 'How's our boy?'

'His house's surging on, haven't seen or spoken to him since Stamford Bridge. Incidentally, you never rang me back. I wanted to ask what all that was about.'

'All what about?'

'Events at Stamford Bridge.'

'Fuck knows,' said Tynan, 'and fuck's not sayin'.'

'Come on.'

'Naw, well, ya know. Okay. Your boy's into some kind of something, something there's not straight.'

'I doubt that.'

'Well, remember where you heard it first. Someone's puttin' an arm on him. Or threatenin' to. You rung him lately?'

'No, no need to.'

'You won't get him. He's changed his mobile again. The club don't know where he's stayin', for which he could get fined. But he turns up for trainin' so nobody minds. His family do, though; they had a little bit of over-the-rainbow a few nights ago.'

I shivered. 'What?'

'Some unscheduled gentleman callers. But the fire didn't catch. Jackanory.'

'*Jackanory?* Speak English.'

'Jackanory end of story.'

That lovely house firebombed. That hit me almost as hard as anything that had happened to me. Oradour's ghosts. The bodies fell apart, Claire said. The swallows lost their homes, too. This is new. Nobody else got attacked. That was the rule, wasn't it? According to the evidence so far, I and only I was It.

What does this mean? Read it, Nicholas. I will if I can. Yes, simple. Pearl and I had Antony in common. Gloom descended. Compounded by Mary Strait. How in hell was I going to get off that hook? Without reopening the relationship? If only I'd gone to lunch! With Elizabeth as chaperone I wouldn't have had to go to bed with Miz Strait. That one lunch could have bought me weeks of ease – could have smoothed my way out of the whole business. Jesus! How irritating!

I rang, told the truth, overslept, pleading exhaustion. This was four o'clock.

'D'you want to come over now? Elizabeth's gone back to Faircombe. Eric brought my things.'

Said I wasn't feeling well. Said let's remake the appointment. Tomorrow I'll send a huge bouquet of flowers. Mary Strait took it on the chin. Or did she? I felt a touch of steel there.

Clear my head. My plans needed some last refinement. Not that I intended a complex action – I merely needed to make sure I had straight lines. Possession of the ball.

After I spoke to Mary Strait I caught a cab to Hampstead. Not quickly recognizable in an enormous Jean-Paul Belmondo cap and a large muffler, I walked the streets. I specifically intended to jog my thoughts of Antony.

Two memories revivified him. A site in east London had run into worse planning difficulty than usual. Every suggestion we made to the council (the problem was industrial access, i.e., suppliers' lorries to a supermarket site) came to a dead end. Unusually, Antony had come to our offices, a reflection of the problem – and the size of his investment.

We talked all day. His brightness was like the sun. He made inventive suggestions – which should have come from us. We selected the four best solutions to offer the planners.

One even included the digging of an underpass to satisfy the council's requirements.

When we had finished, Antony believed we were entitled to a swift response. He said, 'But we will not get it. This is a manufactured problem.'

I and everyone else looked at him.

'There must be a rival,' he said. 'Someone else is in there.'

'But Safft Developments owns the land.'

'Yes, but if I cannot get what I want I will have to sell it. That is what someone is thinking.' He spoke a little thickly, more like an eastern European than a Frenchman.

'So what do we do?'

On his briefed instructions I went to see the council and indicated we were going to withdraw altogether. My client felt very much like selling the property.

'Be despondent, Nicholas, seem defeated. Then sit by your telephone.'

Next morning the helpful planning manager rang me.

'I was just thinking. I know someone who might take that awkward piece of land off your client's hands. If he's thinking of selling.'

When I gave Antony the name he said gleefully, 'Got him! No, Nicholas, I will deal with it. You do not need to know.'

We never had to cut that underpass. Dear Antony. His ageing body sliced into like that. By the melancholy wall of his house I shivered. Lights lit the hallway; a police car stood inside the gate. Shadows fell over the garden, but it was my mind darkening. The second memory came back.

A supper party last July, in the garden; thirty people; a rare fine night in all that inglorious summer. Among the guests was a young architect from another, smaller practice Antony sometimes used, and his very pregnant wife, big and fetchingly blooming. At about the time people might begin to leave, Antony beckoned to me. I followed him into the house.

He whispered, 'I want to give her something, her first child and she is so nervous. What d'you think of this?' From a sheaf of brown paper he unwrapped a most beautiful drawing of a baby's head. 'It's a Gainsborough sketch, what d'you think? D'you think she'll like it?'

I thought of it again as I walked under the garden wall; the child's head, in profile, had a little curl of hair near the ear. Charming. No memorial service so far – and no reason given that I had heard of.

Shall I relinquish the executorship? And pursue my target? A pincer movement. No. Wait until I hear from Claire. My mind cleared by the hour.

I rang Tynan. 'I've been walking in Hampstead.'

'Back to the scene of the crime.'

'That's not funny. Why are there lights on in the house?'

'The newest thing. DNA testing. They take samples of anything from relevant surfaces. If they catch a suspect, Bingo.'

'What's the status of that investigation?'

'On-going.'

'What does that mean?'

'It means they've got zilch.' Tynan sounded sleepy.

'Are you in bed with someone?' I asked. 'In the middle of the afternoon?'

'Talk to you soon,' and he chuckled, a little embarrassed.

35

Sleep. Sleep. Sleep. And then more sleep.

Some dreams; one night I dreamed a neighbour of mine in Knightsbridge said to me, 'I have the most beautiful singing voice, you know.' She opened her mouth and her dress changed colour. The dream switched to Herefordshire. I stood on the hill where I would look down on the house, see the hands of the clock in the courtyard. But in the dream I was an adult, not the boy who knew that view. A man walked towards me, very pleasant and warm to me, even though he seemed a stranger. He mentioned my brother Kim's name. I thought when I woke up, Once again I've had a dream in which Kim has been mentioned but hasn't appeared.

The office closed that week. Sixteen days – that was the holiday period. Bentley Newman takes two weeks every Christmas principally because so many of them have caught the skiing bug. Usually I work some of the time and go to Gleneagles or the Silver Palace in Copenhagen for New Year. Not this year. I had almost three weeks for what I needed – and wanted – to do. Time had begun to stir itself; I gritted my teeth in apprehension.

Mary Strait asked me, 'What you doing for Christmas?'

I forgot I'd asked her – tentatively – to come away for a weekend.

'It's – rather – complicated,' I said deliberately.

'I have a present for you.'

Oh, no! 'Thank you,' I said. 'That's very sweet of you.'

She brought in an enormous box. I looked at it.

'Goodness.'

'Aren't you going to open it?'

'I like to open my gifts on Christmas Eve.'

'Where will you be?'

'Some friends of mine are coming into London,' I lied. 'Will you be . . . ?'

'I'll give you the number I'll be at,' she said and eagerly wrote it on my – up to then – blank blotter. Irritating.

On the morning of Christmas Eve, with the office mostly empty, not really expecting to be let off the hook, I gave my dice one last spin. I telephoned Mr Lewison.

'May one decline the invitation to be an executor of a will?'

'Ah, yes, I half-expected this call.'

'Why?'

'I've had your co-executor on the phone with that same enquiry.'

'Does he want to –'

Mr Lewison interrupted me as I suspect he does everybody. 'No-no, he was enquiring on your behalf. I told him nobody'd ever asked before so I'll have to find out.'

West End lawyer and he can't answer a question like that.

'But supposing both of us wanted out of it?'

'Mr Safft doesn't – he's very keen.'

'Any sign of the papers being freed?'

'Not yet. As I told your co-executor. Indeed I spoke to the police on this very matter yesterday.' Mr Lewison is pompous for such a young man. 'They say late January. I say mid-February. That's just a timescale guess. We're reopening on the eleventh of January. Shall we speak that week, Mr Newman?'

Thus I said goodbye to my last chance of evading the essential course of action. I took a final evening off and in the course of the night I digested that food for thought Mr Lewison had given me.

Philippe wanted me to step down but was himself keen to continue. Was that consideration for me – or for him? I failed once more to get a reply from their number.

Time for action. I considered all options once more. Along the usual lines. Go it alone? Or hand it over to Tynan? Or half and half? Self-respect prevailed. If I won out in all this I would have added cubits to my inner stature. Yes. Time for action. But be prepared for nerves. And fear.

On Christmas morning I telephoned a taxi firm, went back to my own apartment. The cab waited while I packed a case. I wanted any possible observer to think I was going away. The cab took me to an address in Wilton Place and waited. A maid opened the door to a drinks party.

Why did I go there first? A whim. A leap in the dark. Was I crazy? Perhaps, but I reckoned if they're there, fine, and if not, I could judge them by their front door. Now I was in – in the lion's den. I acted like a guest, took a glass of orange juice from a waiter's tray. With the first people I saw, a pleasant man with an anxious wife, I talked about finding 'Traffic, actual traffic, in London on Christmas morning!'

Problem; I didn't know what my 'host' looked like. Am I a good enough student of human nature to guess? The place crawled with servants, some of them fit and thickset. Which could mean the very man I hunted might be there. I had no description of him. Since last night, knowing my own reactions, I had avoided liquids.

I try never to seem aimless at parties; it draws the worst attentions of hosts and other guests. So I tried to look about without looking aimless. Although I didn't know what I was looking for, I felt my instincts would kick in. No candidate crossed my eyeline. Restless guests did, and then a jolly woman – undoubtedly the hostess.

'Lady Ormeau,' I crooned.

'I'm Lilian,' she said, 'and as I don't know you, you must be one of Paddy's. He's here somewhere. And you are . . . ?'

'Indeed, one of Paddy's. As you say. You generate a lovely atmosphere,' I said, looking straight at her bosom and speaking oppressively, not letting her ask again. 'I'm one of Paddy's German connections. Living there but from here,' I improvised.

Spontaneously, she said, 'So you'll be coming again tomorrow night –' and then she froze.

It was nothing she said. It was nothing she did. Her eyes froze. If not for my years of such social cruising I should never have sensed it. But she froze all right, and comprehensively.

'I'll get Paddy.'

'Not at all,' I said, taking her arm. My recent life had made me a little wild. 'I'll find Paddy in due course.'

'No trouble,' she insisted.

I had to let go. It would have been too uncool to restrain her. She cut a swathe through her guests. Seconds later a man whose face I knew from countless somethings or others drove over from her direction.

He chirped, 'How nice to see you.'

So that was the game.

'And you.'

'Ye-es. Ye-es.' He held the pause. 'I see. Yes.' He half-turned from me, then came back. 'Let me – let me – ah –'

'You're Viscount Ormeau.'

'Ye-es. Ye-es.' His voice got more nasal; he was under pressure. Good composure, though. 'Look, I-ah, I'm – why don't we step in here a moment?'

The small study had a perfect George III walnut lowboy, beautifully deckled. I had been looking for one.

'Lovely,' I said, nodding at it.

'Ye-es. Isn't it?' He closed the door awkwardly. 'Now, look, I'm terribly sorry –'

'His name?' I said.

He didn't say, 'Whose name?' or 'I'm afraid I don't know

what you're talking about.' He said, 'This is terribly incon-
venient, I mean it's Christmas morning.'

'Give me his name, please.'

He wore a yellow v-neck cashmere sweater, blue open-
necked shirt, cords, the casual uniform of such a host. Small
eyes like spheres of quartz.

I said nothing. He never took his eyes from mine. This
man knew the game – whatever it was. He sucked his teeth
and said, 'This is – this is –'

'This is serious,' I said. I flattened the word 'serious' into a
metal sheet. My mind coached me like a chess teacher: 'Say
very little. Very little. Make him run.'

I held my silence. He looked at me again; the light in the
eyes had changed. Short, slightly splayed teeth.

'Serious.' A repetition, not a question.

My mind-coach whispered, 'Do not answer, you do not
need to. Take the pressure to him.'

He said again, 'Serious.'

Still I said nothing. Would he seek relief in his own voice?
That is why the tortured confess.

Not a word.

Some people make one babble, or want to impress them.
They create discomfort and one has to assuage it. I've never
known whether they do it consciously for reasons of power,
or unconsciously because of their own discomfort. I know I
make my staff babble. I meant to make Lord Ormeau babble.
No chance.

Dry and cold, he said, 'You must leave.'

I lifted my hand very slowly and placed it near my heart
– a nervous habit. He, though, narrowed his eyes. Did he
think I meant to shoot him? It showed me what worlds
he travelled in the recesses of his mind. Time to speak
again.

'His name. That's what I asked you.'

He merely looked at me.

Moving a fraction of a pace towards him, I said, 'Give me his name. And his address.'

'Go.'

'Very well. I shall make a speech.'

He never moved, never barred the door – and never asked, 'Who are you? Why are you doing this?'

My foot slipped a little on the polished floor.

'I shall ask you one more time. If then you still refuse me his name and address I shall hand the tabloids the scoop of the century. "Peer's Links with Nazi Warlord." Name and address, please.'

An error. If you make a threat stick to it, do not vary it or add another, it weakens you. First I said a speech. But didn't do it. Then I threatened him with the Press. And he called my bluff. He opened the door.

This was a man with a few generations of rough enterprise behind him, protected by a deep survival habit. All that came into play. I had no chance.

'You'll be hearing from me,' I said.

As he ushered me out he said, 'I know who you are.'

36

Sleep renders me wonderful services. I believe in the four-hour principle: if we sleep an exact four or eight hours we always wake refreshed. I would rather sleep four hours than six, or seven, or nine.

The suitcase stood waiting by the door. After my bath and supper – with no wine – I took out the pack of cards and set my mobile phone on recharge.

No pressure, no sweat. I played twenty games of patience, got out two. Need better odds than that. I assessed what plans I needed, and suddenly I knew I needed some help. Told myself, it is no weakness to need help. It is a strength to send for help. It is a wisdom to know who can help. I, too, have read the handbooks on Eastern wisdom.

Philippe? No.

Tynan? No.

No vested interests.

Who else? No, wrong question. What kind of help do I need? Better question.

Answer? In this change of heart I need the kind of help that will get me information and ask no questions. Reach into the shadows of my past.

My nickname for him was Hercule and he even looked a little like Poirot – certainly had the hair for it. He once 'did things' for me, then 'went up in the world, divorce work and that.'

'Sidney, it's Nicholas Newman.'

'I don't believe it. I don't down-the-line believe it. How are you, Mr N?'

'I'm well.' Politeness conquering truth. 'And you?'

'Full of the old spirit, as you can probably hear. I haven't seen you since when? Since that night in St John's Wood. Know what? My mum – she did like you.'

'I liked her.'

'She left us, you know.'

'Oh, I'm sorry.'

'Yeah, gone on ahead. A trump, though. Now what can I do for you?'

'Something odd.'

'The odd we do immediately, the weird tomorrow.'

'How clearly can you monitor a phone inside a house? If you're parked outside?'

'Mr N, I can get you a cassette you can play in the car. Surround-sound. This a lady?'

'No.'

'Hope you're not going pear-shaped on us, Mr N. My lady saw your photo at the hairdressers, were you in *Hello!* or somewhat?'

'Somewhat, I expect. This is the address.'

I briefed him, told him to call me on my mobile and call twice, ring off each time and I would answer on the third. Hercule began to chat.

'What you doin' these days anyway?'

'The usual. And you?'

'More of the same. Everybody needs us. World's in a shockin' state, nobody trusts anybody any more.'

'I might be calling on you over the next few weeks for this and that.'

'I'm all yours, Mr N. Invoice to the usual? What is it, Cadogan Square?'

'Gardens.'

''Course it is.'

'You'll like something about me, Sidney. I've become a football fan.'

227

'Oh?! Which team then?'

'Still making up my mind. But I'm going to Highbury today.'

'Four o'clock kick-off, right? But you don't wanna follow the Arsenal.'

'Who do you like?'

'I like the Cobblers myself. Northampton Town. Tasty little club.'

We parted as warmly as only Sidney can make possible. I played some more patience and made two more calls.

Sebastiaan Pearl said, 'We have to wait for him to call us, some difficulty with the mobile network. How is the house, is it building along?'

I gave him a message for his brother. My instincts had better be right.

One last call; in my hurry to pack at Cadogan Gardens I had forgotten to check the answering machine there.

A raft of messages in the last twenty-four hours. Elizabeth. Mary Strait. Elizabeth. Claire – urgent. Mary Strait. Mary Strait. Mary Strait – she sounded drunk. Elizabeth wishing me Merry Christmas. Hal wishing me Merry Christmas. Hal sounding odd. Hal needing to talk to me. Elizabeth, suggesting I was in hiding, if not why was I not returning calls? Mary Strait. Hal, saying ring him any time, even on Christmas Day, and hoping I was okay. Don Tynan wishing me Merry Christmas. The electrician fixing Cadogan Gardens, wishing me Merry Christmas and saying he had finished but 'the plumber, he seems a bit slow'. Hal again, chirpy and offhand.

I rang Claire; this time I left a message – principally because I didn't wish her worried by unidentified callers.

As I put the mobile down Tynan rang.

'And how are we this morning? Bowels move?'

'Good morning.'

'You active yet?'

'A bit,' I lied. 'Why d'you ask?'

'Your boy's at Highbury.'

'I know. I'm going.'

'Don't.'

'Now that,' I said, 'is a surprise.'

'That's why I asked how active you are.'

'Go on.'

'There's something planned.'

'For Highbury?'

'No. Trafalgar Square. After the game.'

I have a pinball machine in my brain that tells me when I'm on song. It lit up and pinged and rang. That was why the Ormeaus expected a guest!

'Will it be big?'

'Wanna ringside seat?'

He gave me several details – the Northumberland Avenue address; what to say to the policeman and the security staff on the door; the time to get there; where to park, how to get away afterwards. Then he chilled me.

'Don't mean to worry you, but why was the light on in your place last night? Cadogan Gardens, I mean.'

'Shit!'

'Mmm. That's what I thought. There a time-switch?'

'Not that I can think of.'

'Wasn't on this morning. Wanna take a look?'

'No. Can one of your chaps?'

'He'll need keys. Give 'em to the copper who lets you in this p.m.'

37

The last seven hours of Boxing Day gave me enough variety (if that's the word) for seven years. Johan Pearl was subdued in a colourless game; the commentators talked of 'a rock-like back four'. Arsenal scored an early goal from a penalty and fell back upon their resources – something that to my untutored eye they seemed to do rather well. They remained one goal ahead when I left the flat at five. No word from Hercule; I'd instructed him not to call me unless matters seemed extraordinary.

Parked on the Embankment; envelope for 'Superintendent Don Tynan' with Cadogan Gardens spare key; handed it to policeman on door; huge office building, through which I was marched. Corridor after corridor, lit only by the streets outside. We entered a dark corner office. Screens had been erected to make it darker, to kill any interior reflections. Rather like my soul felt.

At each of the three huge windows looking down on Trafalgar Square sat a team of two men. Hunched, with cameras and walkie-talkies, they all looked up as we entered. None spoke.

Tynan, walking around like a wolf, told me where to sit. And not to move. The policeman handed him my envelope with the keys. Tynan then made it clear why he'd asked me.

'Okay. I'm hoping for IDs. See anyone you know – tell us.'

Their walkie-talkies whistled and Dalek-ed. Estimated times of Tube trains from Highbury? Estimated numbers of troublemakers? Winnow out the pure fans? A helicopter's light picked out Admiralty Arch. The beam touched the Zachary building (Bentley Newman's most difficult client – ever).

Someone gave Tynan a countdown of 'About five minutes, boss.' Down in the square a rank of policemen moved from here to nowhere. Another rank faced into the Strand, towards the exit from the Tube. Traffic continued, slow and slack. Passers-by, lit like a French film by the lights on the wet streets, stared curiously at the police. One or two stopped, to be hustled on. Tynan swore at the stupidity of the public.

Our window stood open at the top. Suddenly, we heard the chant – not the words, simply the noise. Twice now I had listened to the victory songs of the terraces. 'You're not singing/You're not singing/You're not singing any more.' And the 'Guantanamera' of 'Score in a minute/We're gonna score in a minute.' This new noise wasn't fun.

They spilled from the Strand, roared into the square. The first few kicked over the metal crush barriers. On the pavement, dozens of them stood together and gave a *Sieg Heil* salute with pointed finger. A missile hit a policeman. Another struck a souvenir-shop window. The police formed up along the pavements to protect the plate glass.

'What are they throwing?' I asked Tynan.

'The fucking usual. Ball-bearings. They can't bring them into the grounds so they have 'em on the streets.'

Ball-bearings. My head flinched at the St Gilles scar. Ball-bearings.

My eye ran to the vulnerabilities. Not much they could do to Nelson or the lions. Passing cars ran a risk, so did pedestrians, especially any rival football supporters. Most doorways along here have withstood war. So why choose this ground? For space, obviously; they could hit and run. Which they began to do.

I counted them. At eighty I stopped, wondering why so

few. More appeared, then more; when they totalled about two hundred, battle lines were drawn. The police had helmets and shields.

It happened so quickly and so slowly and so not-at-all and so neverendingly. A loose ribbon of thugs faced a tight line of police. Abuse, their first weapon, drew no blood. Then a tactic became evident. Two fans detached themselves and raced towards the police. A few feet away they stopped and threw something – liquid, I thought, but no fire was born. It broke the police ranks a little and three of them followed the two fans. Tynan murmured, 'Sill-eee!'

The lines fractured. A dozen thugs closed in. The three policemen saw too late they'd been set up. They tried to get back and made it – at the cost of committing their colleagues. Tynan swore, then tipped me and pointed.

An onlooker in a raincoat stood far from the action. He spoke into a mobile phone. Tynan gave an instruction. I continued watching the man in the raincoat. Within minutes a car drew up near him and the raincoat took off, running. A man from the car followed him, as did the car. They gave up, lost him somewhere near St Martin's Lane. Tynan swore again.

By the haunches of one of the lions a fan made a wide, loping run and threw something. This time flame hit a shield and died. The police held fast, luring the rioters forward. Behind them the last car to be allowed through was caught.

'Jeeeee-suz,' groaned Tynan. 'How in fuck did she get in there?'

A terrified woman fled the car as the thugs rocked it and rocked it and rocked it – and turned it over. Those in front, running at the police, heard the cheer and turned to look. Now they had a totem – and a barricade. All returned to the car, which soon lost its seats, and whose contents became extra missiles.

It grew hot inside the room. Cameras clicked like insects. Tynan took in everything, muttered often, chucked low orders to his walkie-talkie. The car caught fire. Enormous vans hit the square, sealing it. From them police dragged what became huge lights. The helicopter circled. Light, by way of brilliant halogen or flickering fire, became the new protagonist.

Now the running began. In four teams of five the police began to hit the rioters who retreated from the car. Another five-man team moved to put out the fire. The rioters had made two serious errors. They had run out of missiles and they had nowhere to go.

The police attack thickened. Isolated moments and images stay with me. A large young man, 'Fuck You' on his white tee-shirt, standing alone by the edge of his gang shouting and gesturing and swaying. Two rioters trying to tear off a policeman's helmet. Policemen hauling away a kicking rioter. Other figures bending over something – a fallen policeman, it transpired.

My mind altered what I was seeing. No longer did I look down upon a riot for the television news, whose vans were arriving on the periphery. What I saw took on the character of a painting. By whom? Tintoretto? It had the violence but not the splendour. Goya – it had the glare but not the romance. Half-close the eyes and you get Jackson Pollock – slashes and scars of colour that make no sense when first beheld.

I could frame this scene. A chrome inner edge inside a black wide outer case. I could lecture on the detail. The man who had penetrated police lines so far he now rampaged beneath our window might have come from the burning brain of Francis Bacon. Light lit his snarl and threw some of his features into the distortion of shadow.

Let us now look for any autobiographical detail, in the way, say, of a Lavery or a Carpaccio or Schalken who so often put their own faces into their own works. What about that figure over there, running away, his back to us, yet strangely familiar?

I stopped my reverie for a second. Yes, he is familiar. Why? He kicked out at the two policemen who began to apprehend him, and he might have been inviting them to join some mazy old Soho dance. And he got away.

Dance. It mutated from a painting to a ballet. In the background a *corps de ballet* moved back and forward, retreating and advancing. From time to time the line threw something. More frequently they raised their right arms and chanted. Wardrobe mistresses had varied upon a theme – jeans, trainers and tee-shirts with motifs and favours and scarves. Make-up had chosen shaven heads, or flat-top cuts, or crews, with face paint to indicate tribal loyalty.

Finally it changed again and became what it purported to imitate – the war-game of football. Attacks, thrilling raids into enemy territory, dashes across the lines. Territory won, territory lost, territory regained. Penalty areas. Defenders. Attackers. Feats on both sides. Assorted weaponry. Guerrillas versus troops.

This romantic cliché evaporated when I heard Tynan shout and saw him point. All window observers rose from their chairs. One rioter, smuggled forward by the others, waved a machete. He seemed to have cut open a policeman. That caused the general charge that ended the riot.

At that precise moment my mobile phone rang. Made anxious by these 'supporters', I hoped it might be Pearl. Hercule spoke as I turned away for privacy.

'Mr N, trying to ring you but the fuzz closed me down.'

'Where are you?'

'You said tell you if it got weird. It don't get weirder.'

'How?'

'I'm on the bloody Mall, that's where I am, behind Admiralty Arch.'

'Oh?'

'This a good moment?' he asked.

'Go ahead.'

'Well, I got it all on, found my man, got a mate there, the telecoms stuff, put the clips on sharpish. But I got no name and I feel out on that one, I do love a name. I mean – I got Lord Ormrow's name. '

Chagrin – but I said, 'Continue.'

'One call of interest, there was more, but they was all more or less domestics, Ormrow's daughters'n that, but definitely one call of interest to us. You said listen out for a Kraut. We did. Got 'im. From what I and my bloke can make out, he's off to Berlin crack of toot, ten forty-five tomorrow a.m. Call's in German, but I've got the tape.'

'So why are you in Trafalgar Square?'

'That's it. I mean, that's why I rang. Four thirty the Kraut leaves, some exec car picks him up and he comes into town, I'm after him. He's dropped in Trafalgar Square, door of something called Palermo Insurance, big place. Palermo's in Sicily, 'n't it, Mr N? Fuckin' Ada, what kind of insurance they got, offer you can't refuse, eh?' Hercule cackled. 'I can't get in the building on account of it's all closed but I circles the square and what do I see? Our client's sitting at a second-floor window. Just sitting there. There's some other blokes there too, but he's the one with the grandstand seat. I said to myself, yep, this qualifies as weird. Then all hell broke loose, there's a big riot on down here, Mr N. Football hooligans, the scum you see on telly. You'll see it on the news tonight. And your bloke's sitting there watchin' 'em, at least he was when I was moved on by the boys in blue. He's wearing a cap, looks like a Dutchman. Sitting in the window. Gets his kicks a strange way, eh?'

'Well done,' I said.

'Want me to stay on him?'

'Yes.'

He rang off. I rang him back. 'The flight? Which airport tomorrow?'

'Heathrow. Terminal Two. Lufthansa.'

'Thank you.'

Tynan looked at me. Dilemma – to tell him or not?

'Woman trouble,' I said.

He looked disgusted. I looked past him. The square heaved and seethed. Slowly the bright colours of the rioters disappeared beneath a sea of police.

'Borrow those?'

He lent me his Krause binoculars. I first scanned the rioters but only to throw Tynan off any scent. Then I switched and found the building and found the window and found the man.

I saw him in outline only – a figure sitting a little back from a tall office window where no lights shone. He too had binoculars; I could see him clearly enough for that but not enough to discern his features. Light came to him once or twice; he wore a cap of the kind Helmut Schmidt made famous, flat with a broad peak; he sat like a ramrod.

As I watched he moved. My heart surged. Tell Tynan? Bring him in for questioning? Be allowed to meet him? Serve a private prosecution? On what grounds?

My heart sank. No, I had to do this my way. Claw back my sense of freedom. Do it slowly, alone and with care. Yes, Nicholas, do it now! No, Nicholas, to do it alone and without support and in another country is irrational. Yes, but the irrational doesn't have to be unreasonable. Stop this. The see-saw plagues your life.

I said to Tynan, 'Full jails for a few months?'

'No, mate. Full cells. Standing room. One night only. Like a fucking circus. Bow Street Magistrates' tomorrow, all out on bail, suspended sentences at the most. Chum with the machete's going down, though. Even if he's had a childhood worse'n Hitler's.'

236

'Someone you've been after?'

Tynan straightened himself with an aching groan. 'Yep. He's twenty stone of shit in a ten-stone bag. See anyone useful?'

'No,' I lied and eased back from him. He sensed it.

'What you doin' now?' he asked me.

'Well-earned rest,' I said with a chime. 'You know.'

'Cheers, mate,' and he patted me on the arm.

For reasons so far unavailable to me I had begun to feel better.

38

No sleep, no sleep at all. No breakfast, couldn't make it, couldn't face it. Lufthansa has edible food. My last three flights with British Airways should have been impounded by food inspectors from the Authority for Fair Play, that body I long to create.

For once I travel economy class – because he won't. I was right. I never saw his face, only his back, and the Helmut Schmidt Dutch sailor's cap. Too soon to follow him the optimum way – from the front. For now stay behind.

I hate Heathrow Terminal Two. What am I doing here? I should be at a drawing board or on a ski slope. Over a hard little espresso taken at a tall marble table across from the departure gate, I rang Hercule.

'Tell me all.'

After Trafalgar Square, The Man, as Hercule and I had named him, returned to Wilton Place. This time, heavies patrolled the house. Two of them approached Hercule. He told them he was security for Baroness Thatcher down the street; 'They can't be local, Mr N. I mean, they didn't know you can't see the good lady from there.'

People arrived for dinner – the one where Lilian Ormeau 'expected' me.

'I took the usual precautions, Mr N. Got all the reg. numbers. Want me to run 'em through my friends?'

'Please.'

'We got no more phone calls. I mean, there was one, the daughter again, moaning about dosh. So I switches on a little something I have, hoping it'll work, new item, a mate brought it in from Singapore. Tasty, too, gets you a lot of stuff through a solid wall, I mean you can't tell every word, but they was having a reunion or a celebration, drinking toasts 'n' that. Very jolly, they was.'

I told Hercule to keep every tape and thanked him.

Airport lounges ebb and flow. Cool fellows in camel coats wore scarves tied in interesting ways. A family party flying to Rome for the New Year dropped everything on the floor. The girl and boy saying goodbye ate each other's mouths five feet away – and then travelled together.

Another powerful espresso: had the cup been large enough I could have stood on the coffee. The Iranian boy who served it tried to pick me up. Time? Go to the gate. Ten forty: ten-minute delay.

The Man stood there, looking straight ahead. I stayed out of his vision field.

Where's Pearl? He hasn't rung. I checked my mobile's answering machine and electronic address book. Ring Holland. He's there. He can't be. He has a game tomorrow.

Yes, he's there – 'Because he is injured,' said Sebastiaan. 'I will call him for the telephone. My mother wishes to speak first.'

'Good day,' she said. First time I noticed her voice – unusually young on the telephone.

'Hallo.'

She asked, 'May I speak to you privately some time?'

'Of course.' I gave her my mobile number. 'If it's switched off leave a message.'

'Here is Petchi,' she said.

'Petchi?' I asked him.

'Baby name, man.'

'Do the other players know this?'

'This is blackmail, man.'

At least I'd got him laughing. 'Where have you been?'

He whispered, 'I need to talk to you.'

239

I asked, 'Is it true? Your house attacked?'

'That's what I want to talk to you about.'

I said, 'Will you do now exactly as I ask?'

He paused for a moment. 'I'm not really injured.'

'I thought not. Our lunch,' meaning the White Raven.

'Yes?' He sounded wary.

'Go there. Stay there. Tell them it's private. You need two or three clear days. Will they treat it as confidential? Will they hide you?'

'Yeah. But why?'

'I can't tell you. I mean, I don't quite know – but I'll know where to reach you.'

I wanted my field clear of any pressure. If Pearl were part of this I didn't want him available to them.

A man at the next row of seats, a good deal older than me, looked at me very hard and looked away. Not Italian. Possibly American. Wealthy. Alone. Am I a true paranoid after all? The flight boarded.

Am I crazy? Why am I not swimming in Brazil? Or hunting in Oregon? Or fishing in Scotland? I have no protection of any kind and I have been sitting like a duck, simply waiting for the next onslaught – which always might be the final one. What is the matter with me?

Air travel bores me. I daren't sleep. The Man is up there somewhere. I go to the lavatory and ascertain. He's just on the other side of the curtain, in Business Class. I look at the back of his iron-grey head. Kill him now. A hitman would.

We're flying at thirty-five thousand feet and I can have a sleep. I'll follow him down the steps when we land.

In the sun of Berlin airport two hours later, I turn the dial of my mobile this way and that to see if I have received a message. I have and I page it. On it I hear Don Tynan as I have never heard him before.

'Newman. You know who this is. You're out of the country. The phone company says so. Whatever you're thinking of

240

doing, for Jesus' sake don't. This is way above you. Get out of there now. Keep clear. Ring me immediately you get this. Immediately.'

I snapped it shut. Tynan has never been so heavy. He has never called me 'Newman'. Leave it. But he's had me followed. Or knows I'm travelling. Or is fantastically intuitive. I suddenly feel my heart pounding.

The sun half-goes behind a cloud and the light is dark green and grey all at once and it makes the sides of the terminal walls shine like satin. I am all right. I am all right. *The Times* shields my face; this is ridiculous.

But – I must do it by myself. A sane man would ask the police to take over. No. Not that I'm not sane, I have never been saner than now. Call Tynan, Nicholas. No! I can do this alone. This is a good use of my independence. My heart, nevertheless, lurches.

I look up. The Man is still ahead. He walks with a steady and definite tread. Problem, though. His passport queue's faster than mine and there's nothing I can do. Worse than that – my queue now begins to move faster than his and any second now I'll be beside him.

Too soon. Too soon.

I step aside until I 'find' my passport.

39

My phone rings again. In the terminal building. People look at me.

Hal's voice says, 'Happy New Year, Chief.'

'Hal, I can't talk now.'

'I have to have a word.'

'Let me ring you, Hal.'

'It's important, Chief. About the office.'

'Hal –' I shrieked in a whisper. 'Not bloody now!' I lost The Man. Oh, ffffff –!

I didn't think it through. Not enough foresight, nor planning. You fool. You idiot. You self-aggrandising, egotistical idiot. Who do you think you are? Bloody Hal.

There's something reckless in me that I've never acknowledged, something wild and dangerous and I haven't got the honour in me not to let it touch other people. Now what do I do? Stuck at Tegel airport with nowhere to go and nothing to do.

Found him! In conversation with a rich couple, many pleasantries. I still can see only his high, ramrod back and his cap. Soon he moves away, to the taxis. Thank you, God, or whoever You are. What is 'Follow that cab' in German? Don't need it, speaks English. But the cabbie needs an explanation.

'He's having an affair with my wife, I need to find out who he is.'

Cabbie tells me his own wife left him, he found out she'd been 'rattling' his neighbour. Now she and the neighbour've split up and his wife wants to come back and what should he do? We discuss.

From the Tegel slip road our friend goes left and north and so do we, and he turns right and south-east and so do we. A place called 'Wedding' – Mary Strait should come here. At which point we turn right and south-west. The long, wide avenues, they must have suited Marshal Zhukov when he took Berlin. Town planners don't design for defence.

'See,' says the cabbie, and on the horizon rises a forest of cranes. 'Biggest building site in the world. Potsdamer Platz.'

In the unchanging view of an autobahn's straight line I stop counting at fifty-five cranes. Hal always said we should've had a piece of this action but we didn't even get a smell of the Sony contract. Or any other in Berlin. Norman Foster's here, a dome over the Reichstag. The Sony was what I wanted. Helmut bloody Jahn. Traffic thickens and tightens and The Man is a length away. My cabbie contrives to drop back. Soon we have a destination.

'Ah, Wilhelmstrasse. You will find it interesting.'

One hunch was right. My green Loden coat will look part of the furniture. I've seen two so far.

The Man's cab turns into a small area. The cabbie says, 'No, he could get out the other side,' and whisks me round the corner where we see The Man has stopped.

'Kick him in all the sore places,' encourages the cabbie, whom I tip happily.

Now comes the next move and I don't know what that should be.

The day is raw on my face. Cabs drive off. The Man approaches a door as I stride busily past. He never glances in my direction. Street sign – *An der Kolonnade*. Drab, drab claddings; seven floors above ground. This is a small development, probably municipal, drab enough to be Communist. Which side of the Wall was this, where is the bloody Wall anyway? It must have got knocked down utterly to judge by the number of pieces people were showing off across dinner-party London. Shrubs, small trees; no personality in this little square.

The Man's still at the door, facing inwards, waiting for the intercom. Nearby, a shabby woman comes from another door in the same building, wrestling with a carton. The service staircase. Excellent! Directly behind the residential. I've done that too, perfectly acceptable plan.

As the door is answered to The Man I slip into the service area, helping the slattern with the carton. This isn't a high-class block.

Inside I listen. Ringing footsteps. In my mad gumshoe mode I've put on rubber-soled shoes and I trot up quicker than the ringing footsteps from the other stairs until I am keeping pace. He stops on the sixth. I hear the loud exchange through a squawking entryphone, a door and a greeting and a door closes. Hurry.

Sixty-four. It could be number sixty-six. Listen at the door. Wish I had a wineglass to hold against the wall. It is sixty-four. I hear fresh talk. Press the bell. When the squawk box answers I say 'Guten Tag' as gutturally as I can. To the voice I reply in something that sounds German. I hope it's unintelligible enough to make them open the door with safety, because the only intelligible word I enunciate is Bitte.

They repeat the query. I mutter my unintelligible phrase and Bitte. Someone says something irritable, and the door opens, and there The Man stands with his cap in his hand, the mark of its rim clear on his forehead.

The Man – he's not much older than me! This isn't a man who has lived long enough to be a war criminal – he wasn't at Oradour. But he has the face for it. Eyes of pewter. Nevertheless I'm through that door and he can't stop me. It never occurred to me that he might be armed. Or perhaps I'm braver than I thought.

40

He didn't care. With the calm of a nun he closed the door behind me. I spun to face him. If I were he I'd have kept the door open and shouted for help. Unless I lived in a world where this kind of incursion wasn't unexpected. He did live in such a world. Perfectly calm, he looked at me. Powerful face. Steady, cold eyes.

Now I don't know what to say. I'm panicked, so out it bursts from me.

'I'm here because I'm not your enemy.'

Bitte?

'Yes. Please. That is what I mean too. That's the right word. *Bitte*. Please. Please stop harming my life.' This is coming out all wrong. 'I've no quarrel with you. I don't even know who you are or what you represent.' His lethal eyes have the stillness of a flat sea. 'Are you listening to me?' He never moves. 'Look. I don't even want to be an executor.' The Man is well dressed. But not, as my mother would have put it, well bred. Oh, how can I tell? He comes from a radically different society.

'Why are you attacking me? You haven't killed me when you could have done. So what do you want from me?' No reply.

'Executor,' I repeat miserably. 'I don't want to be. I knew nothing about it.'

As I utter the betrayal of my dead friend, Antony, I hear Claire's lovely voice. She won't like this. Can't help that. Claire's eyes darkened when she looked at me at Oradour. Her pupils distended.

245

The Man stood perfectly still. Watching me. Unsurprised – that's what I most observe, he isn't surprised.

Behind me comes a noise. Thinking, Jesus I am dead, I half-turn, I am the death in the sandwich. No, I'm all right. An old man shuffles in, with rheum-red eyes. You that did void your rheum upon my beard. He speaks. He is agitated and he asks a question. They are father and son. It takes not a fool to see the genetic echo. Our friend has come to see his father. Who in salivary German asks the same question again. And again. And again. Oh, the distress of the old man.

'Otto,' he begs. 'Otto.'

Otto calms him, with a flat-handed, peaceful gesture. The old man has a missing forefingernail. He wears a zip-up cardigan.

I say to Otto, the son of his father, 'I'm the man who called to see Paddy Ormeau. Viscount Ormeau. Where you've just been staying. I saw you at the riot yesterday.' I am hyperventilating.

The old man asks his question again and the son calms him, then beckons to me, steps out into the hall, closes the door behind us and I follow him down the stairs.

If I were a bet now I wouldn't take it. My agitation is so great I miss a step and stumble, lurching forward. Otto never flinches below me on the stairs. Broad shoulders. We reach the door and he steps outside and says, 'We walk.'

Zinzee. To my left as we leave the little enclave I see a children's park, all the yellows and reds of Enid Blyton, or should that be *Struwwelpeter*? Or Grimm. Bloody Grimm. Good joke. *Zinzee.* Beneath my feet the ground feels hollow. I fall in beside Otto and begin to get hold of myself. *Endlick.* What was the old boy saying? My head is ringing with the old man's question. It sounded like *Zinzee endlick fur mickey comin.* He meant it. Oh God, he meant it.

Otto is not speaking to me from beneath his Dutch cap. We

leave An der Kolonnade and are on Wilhelmstrasse. Across the way stands a lone brown building, nineteenth century but it is hard to tell, has as many bullet holes as Oradour. I shall put my fingers in those, too. But not now. As we walk along Wilhelmstrasse, to my right, staying in parallel, climb the cranes on the skyline. The cranes are flying.

'I know you speak English,' I begin. Many people walk by and I feel secure. I am a fool to do this. I am a fool. 'Your father. He was upset. Well, I am upset too.'

'Please wait. I am not ready to speak yet.'

His English is almost accentless. My flesh becomes so alert I can feel my eyebrows without touching them. We walk on. Construction work everywhere. And dogshit. Soon we turn right again into Niederkirchnerstrasse. Snappy little name.

What is this I see? I know what it is. A remnant of the Wall. And what is this I see up ahead? Up ahead I see a beautiful, almost Art-Deco building with bullet holes and limbless statues. I recognize it. Oh my God. This is where I come in, this is my temple, or one of them. Is it? Yes? Is this Martin-Gropius-Bau and is it still standing?

It stood, it stood, they never razed it, a relic of the brightest architects, the sweetest designers, the people I love. This is a shrine. Is this for sacrifice? Is this why he's taking me here? Shall I kill him now with my bare hands, I who can scarcely swat a wasp? Am I cracking up?

But all around there is wasteland and he is in command of me. For you, Fritz – or Otto – the war is not over. And there, believe it or not, is The Wall. A strip thereof. White for the soldiers to see figures against it. Graffiti all over it. With a concrete drainpipe forming a domed top. To prevent gripping, I suppose. Get a grip, Nicholas. Get a grip.

I stop; 'I'm not going any further.'

Otto says, 'I am merely taking you to a platform where you can view the constructions on the Potsdamer Platz. I thought you might be interested.'

'Not now. We talk here.'

'Very well. It will be perfect for me.'

His voice, his voice. Voices do not usually frighten me. He is my age, my height, I should not be frightened of this man, I shall not be frightened of this man. *Zinzee*. Ask him what his father was saying. No.

He turned to face me.

'Yes?' he asked. 'What is it you wish to say?'

Disconcerting. But I had been prepared. It was not as bad as it might have been. I had been in training, hadn't I? Had I not since October lived under such fear I could have died? Of fear. Everything has a use. The Uses of Fear. Use my fear to clean my life.

'I have reason to believe that your people – your organization – has been attacking me. I wish it to stop.'

He said nothing.

I continue, 'I have no interest –'

People are coming and going with video cameras, families with children, some of them American. I lean against the wire fence; I am a soft target. So was Oradour.

'– no interest whatsoever in whatever it is you're interested in. Antony Safft was a friend. That is all. I know nothing of his life.'

'Then how did you find me?'

Trapped in my own trap. Tell the truth.

'Through a series of deductions and coincidences and through Viscount Ormeau.'

'Please understand me. I do not believe you.'

I ignored the chilling rejection. Or tried to. This conversation will stay on my agenda, I will not be dragged over onto his.

'Why are you targeting me? Why have you made me a target? I had nothing to do with Antony Safft's preoccupations.'

Betray the dead, Nicholas, betray the dead. Where is your

248

honour? Something's gone horribly wrong. This man is not a Nazi war criminal, he's too young. Too exceptional. He creates space around himself.

'He stole from us.'

'No. You're shielding some war criminal.' The arrow landed – his eyes flickered. 'Your killers tattooed Antony with a Hitler stigma. What was the triangle about? We know these things in England. You forget that.' I tried not to babble.

'The triangle was ironic.'

'Ironic? Some irony.'

'It was ironic.' Quiet, almost amused insistence. 'Your friend wasn't a homosexual. He pretended to be. As he pretended to be a Jew.'

'Pretended?!' His voice is freaking me. Christ! Why didn't I look closer at Antony? Why don't I look closer at life?

'Saaaaft made his money by plundering the bank accounts of French Jews. He made his money from profiteering –'

'His name was Safft, not Saaaaft –'

'He pretended to be a Jew and a gay. He took on those roles to create a false trail.'

'Rubbish. I'm not interested.'

'You should be interested.'

I think, I shriek inside, Safft, not Saaaaft.

'Forget that.' Get away from this man, get away from this voice. 'I'm only interested in keeping you away from me.' My skin is hot and my blood is cold and that is why I can't see through my own sweat. Do I wish to kill him or be killed by him? Victims love their torturers. I reached for as much venom and authority as I had ever known. Safft. Not Saaaaft.

Take the chance, risk it, this is the moment!

'I know who you are. And I know where your father lives. Names. Addresses. Details. Either you leave me alone, or – well, you know the "or", I don't have to spell it out.'

Forget it. He controlled me. He controlled everything, the birds overhead, the sunshine, the pace of the clouds across the Berlin sky. Now he changed tack but he might have done so out of boredom. He even became conversational.

'I may not be able to stop things.'

I fight off the shudder. 'Then you go down too. And your father.' *Zinzee*. Could that be his name, a pet name? *Zinzee*. 'So. Stop them. Whoever they are.'

Those words his father spoke – they were important, I know they were.

'I said I may not be able. It takes time for orders to travel.' But I know by Otto's eyes he is goading me. Or that is what I hope. He patted the fence. 'See where we stand?'

I turn and look. A row of what seem like cellars stretch at basement level under some temporary wooden roofing. Saaaaft? To my right stands a huge mound. In the near foreground I see a row of Portakabins. My eyes strain to see the notice. *The Gestapo Museum*. I turn. Otto is walking away from me, in no hurry. I start after him and then I know. I know!

The voice. On Antony's telephone. The night he died.

'You just rang the number of Mr Saaaaft.'

41

Go, Nicholas, go. And never come back to Berlin. Never come back to this city which damaged so many lives, which oversaw, on this very site, all around you here, some of the worst atrocities of the planet. I slipped and fell on the rough ground, just fell on one hand, jarred my wrist hard. The same arm that took the electric shock. If I chase him he may kill me. His walking away suggests he has released me.

No. I must do this. This is my life. The green Loden coat flaps as I follow him.

'Excuse me,' I called. Such a ridiculous term in the circumstances.

Otto turned.

'You're the one who killed him, aren't you? You fucking bastard. You killed him.' But I felt like a tiny child kicking an adult.

Martin-Gropius-Bau means the house of Martin Gropius. Gropius. The golden name of Bauhaus, the finest, most thought-out movement ever in the world of design and construction. This man is going to kill me here, on the steps. He has led me here, the whole thing is a set-up, including Elizabeth. See, Nicholas, I told you – you're a hysteric. An hysteric. 'A' or 'an'? A hotel. An hotel.

Otto looked at me. He walked towards me. I stood on the lower step of brown stone.

'Why didn't you kill me? You evil bastard, why?! Why?!' Not a word.

'Okay then, fuck you. How did you kill my friend?'

'It wasn't difficult. He was not big or strong.'

'So you admit it. I'll be in the witness box. Yes, I will be. I fucking will be! I'll be there!' Such impotence.

Otto turned away and walked on. Away from my temple. Heading towards his house. His father's house. Bauhaus to our house. I followed him again, yelling.

Otto stopped, turned and looked at me. I went towards him and I halted. The light in his eyes had changed. In the pewter, I swear, came just a hint of red. And his body changed. The shoulders moved. He dropped nearer to the ground. I remembered what that sports-injury doctor told me. 'The arse drops.' The Man dropped a fraction. I'm ashamed to say I took a step back.

Otto said, 'I will tell you how I did it. And then I have advice for you.'

I was about to shout – but I waited.

'The day before, I abducted his manservant and killed him and threw his body in a canal; you can ask your police to check this if you do not believe me. There is a zoo. Next day I called to see Saaaaft, I called to see him at half past twelve o'clock, he thought I was the driver. I made him take off his clothes and lie on the floor of his study. I examined all his papers, he would tell me where nothing was, that is why I cut into his flesh, I enjoyed that. I began to cut him more but he died. I went on cutting. I had to stay there to find things and I found them, which is why you are here. Now, this is the advice I have for you. The advice is – give it back. Give it all back.'

He spoke in the level tones of a neighbour.

From my dry mouth I said, 'If I do – will you leave me alone?'

He walked away again.

I shouted. 'I said – if I do?'

Otto turned and looked at me and his look was so explicitly evil I didn't attempt to speak again. Too stunned. For minutes I didn't, couldn't, move. I followed at a long distance and watched him, back towards his father's apartment, walking slowly and easily. At the bottom of the Niederkirchnerstrasse I stopped, just where the run of the Wall begins.

Go away, Nicholas, go away. This isn't your fight. Go home. Look after yourself. Look after your own business. Most trouble comes when people interfere where they shouldn't. Take care of yourself. Find someone to love. This isn't where you belong. Find someone to love you. It isn't impossible. Whatever you think of yourself.

I watched Otto as he walked onwards, never turning back once. He turned left at the apartments and then turned right into An der Kolonnade and was gone.

Go to the police, Nicholas. This man killed a man I respected and – and – and –

And what? Loved?

Why, even when talking to myself, will I not use the word 'love' with regard to another man? This man, this cold-voiced animal, brutally killed a man I loved and who seemed to love me. Ordinary, human, uncontroversial love. You have just been walking and talking with the killer. It is the law of nature that you bring him to justice. He wandered around Antony's rooms, searching, invading, taking life.

No. It is the law of nature that I look after myself.

These questions! These questions! They razz around the inside of my head like lasers.

Desperate to find an answer I walked. I walked with my head high, ignoring the temporary museum of the Gestapo prison and aiming for what I know – the cranes on the skyline.

But first I walked back to Martin-Gropius-Bau. Oh, they brought everybody together in the house of houses, the Bauhaus – the builders, architects, designers, glass-blowers, carpenters, plumbers! How did a country that produced such a lovely idea of construction also produce Heydrich, Himmler and Hitler?

253

They have closed the Martin-Gropius-Bau for renovations. Martin was the nephew. His uncle Walter the pioneer. Yes, I did put my fingers in the bullet holes. And yes, from its steps I spied a Wall watchtower. And, yes, I saw a huge mound of earth and rubble. From here they planned the destruction of the Jews. This is where they built the tragedies. This is where they took the nests from the swallows of Oradour.

Antony Safft wasn't a Jew! I assumed he was. That's prejudice too. Nor gay? But how do I know Otto is telling the truth? Otto. I wished I'd never heard his name: too much intimacy in that.

The phone gave me a signal immediately I looked for one.

'This is me.'

'Newman, where are you?'

'I won't tell you. Did you know Safft's manservant was missing?'

'Yes. Hurst told me.'

'Why didn't you say?'

Tynan replied, 'None of my business. Or yours.'

'It is now. He's at the bottom of the canal by Regent's Park Zoo.'

'He's *what*? Newman, where the fuck are you?'

'I need to talk to you.'

'I – Jesus – need to talk to you.'

'I'm on my way home.'

For some hours I wandered around the Potsdamer Platz, trying to recover, trying to apply my professional eye to what I saw. We should have tried to get in on this. How ironic had we done so. I recall Antony mentioning it. He mentioned the Norman Foster Reichstag. I, responding to a diffidence I detected in him, said the only thing I hoped I shared with Hitler was a dislike of Berlin. For some reason that I've forgotten I needed to make Antony laugh. He seemed relieved.

But that afternoon Berlin became my haven. I walked in circles around the Potsdamer Platz developments. Tried to work out in my head how much we'd have had to expand had we taken on any of it.

Across the street in the Gemäldegalerie, Carpaccio and Cima and Canaletto might heal me. Oh? Pearl's house. The Pieter what's-his-name painting, Pieter de Hooch. No, can't face it. I fear my soul feels more like Francis Bacon. I think Bacon's *Isabel Rawthorne* is in Berlin. Elizabeth will know.

Elizabeth! Her too! No, she didn't betray me again, not this time, no, she can't have. I know I'm right. Otto was given to me as a gift. Some gift.

'Give it back,' he said. I will, whatever it is. I will. For three months I was beset. Now the stars have changed their courses again. I know my enemy. My enemy knows me. It's coming to an end. I will look for someone who will tell me, who will explain to me, what I have done to deserve all this.

The air got cold and clear, the kind of air that sends fingers down into the lungs, like the cold of Amsterdam and the Zuider Zee. *Zinzee. Zinzee endlick fur mickey comin.*

Berlin had more bullet holes than I expected. Can't put my fingers in them all. So this is where it all began. This is where my father's tragedies with my mother began; the war gave her the taste for infidelity. Every building that stood here gave somebody somewhere a tragedy. In the concentration camps. In Poland forty miles away. All across eastern Europe. The thought gets too big for me. I must personalize it.

The illness that took my father's life began in one of these buildings. On a night of deep snow in Alsace he lost his bearings, broached an enemy line, was shot in the foot. He got away, back to the French who were hiding him. The wound healed, but from it rose the thrombus that eventually killed him when it travelled to his heart in his sixties.

I stood at the corner of Marlene-Dietrich-Platz and looked

up along the huge half-finished Sony building. Hunger came at me like a leopard. Walking along the Herbert-von-Karajan-Strasse I ate a burger. Ahead of me walked an old couple, looking around at everything. They consulted their guidebook; they are Germans and yes, they find the direction for the Gestapo museum site. What did you do in the war, Daddy?

As they walked away I stood and looked after them. Yikes! I saw Otto again. He couldn't have seen me yet, I was in shadow.

This is my moment to find out more about him. He sauntered along. I saw that each movement he took seemed effortless, like a great athlete, like Pearl. Do killers move easily too?

A cab approached and I flagged it. At first I wanted it to follow Otto – but I chickened, and asked it to take me to the airport at Tegel. We drove past Otto and he never glanced my way.

42

London has long been my home; I was only a small boy when we left Herefordshire. Over and above London, however, England is my home, my father's and my grandfather's on both sides. And both my great-grandfathers. And back beyond them, we were all Royalists in the Civil War. England and London welcomed me back.

On the flight I lean back in my seat and order a drink. I believe that I have ended matters. I will inform Philippe and Mr Lawson that I am out of it. Provided I am careful, my dangers have passed. I feel certain that my wish to distance myself from anything that concerned Antony will have conveyed itself. It is over. Another drink. And another.

But from Heathrow I made a call and Mary Strait answered.

I asked, 'I wondered how you spent Christmas.'

'Do you know what time it is? Where are you?'

'It's midnight. Did I wake you up? What was the weather like today? Are you going skiing? Have you heard from Elizabeth?' A manic string of questions – she must have thought me crazy – ended with a fatal one; 'How long does it take to get to Richmond from Heathrow?'

She waited as I asked. I did as I promised. Spreadeagle. The adrenaline. The excitement. The familiar roar in my head, the sounds, the smells, the sucking noises, the creases of flesh, the dark places, most of them in my mind.

Call it reaction to looking upon death in Berlin. That will explain the lewdness. Call it relief at ending my terrors. That will explain why I managed to return her embraces a little more than half-heartedly.

We ate and drank each other, the thrill, the expiation. And I knew she shed tears, the one flash of tenderness I felt.

Call it crassness, call it emotional crime, call it personal injustice of staggering indecency.

Call it what I like, but nothing will forgive my leaving furtively at four in the morning while she slept deeply as a sloth. And nothing on earth will explain why next day I left a message on her answering machine saying, I mustn't do this any more – 'I', note, not 'We' – and I'm sorry but I wouldn't feel able to see her again. What is the difference between what the Nazis did at Oradour and the unacceptably callous sexual usage? No difference.

In those small and despoiled hours I went straight to Cadogan Gardens. It had nagged at me since Tynan's call about a light left on. Had he checked it? I gave him the keys. There was a light and my heart seized – until I remembered; my reading lamp in the front drawing room has a timer on the plug.

The electricity all worked, even in the devastated bathroom. Bloody plumber – he could have finished by now. At least things are not in too appalling a state. Good to be surrounded by what I love. I sat down to pick up the messages from the machine – two; Claire first:

'Nicholas, it's Claire. This is awful, you must ring me, why haven't you? You don't know, you don't begin to know how terrible this is . . . I'm ringing from outside, I'm not ringing from home. Philippe's going to the office tomorrow, could you ring me? Please . . . ? I need to speak to you. It's most important.'

Desperate, no matter how she tried to hide it. I saw her now, in her Burberry jacket, tall and cool and lovely and angry at Oradour.

Secondly, and worse if possible, comes Pearl's voice.

'Man. Can you see me? You gotta come to me, we have a night game at Charlton, can you get to me? This is the twenty-seventh, man, it's three o'clock in the day, the game's tomorrow night and I'm in trouble. You gotta come! You gotta!'

No, Johan Black Pearl, I can't. I'm too tired and I'm not a good Samaritan, I'm a weak and callous man and I wish to be left alone. Knowing it would keep me sleeping, I turned the central heating to 'High'.

The next day, when I finally awoke, flapped with loose ends. I think I shall go to Gleneagles tomorrow and spend the New Year there. Or Venice? Too many people at the Gritti, and the Pregadi's closed. What time is it? Seven thirty. Why am I exhausted? Because it is over. Over.

I rang the Ritz, dinner for one. But I can't wash! Ho-ho, yes, I can, the spare bathroom works. So Antony Safft was a profiteer. How did he do it? Probably introduced to it as a young man. He was a lawyer. Now Barabbas was a lawyer. Put on Fleetwood Mac. There are questions to be answered here. Does Philippe know all this? His problem now. I ring his number again. No reply.

A profiteer? It figures. But, strange, it doesn't alter my affection. Antony had a mysterious reputation. So what? Inspector Hurst asked where the money came from originally. I had been dragged into a war between – between whom? Rival profiteers? The phone rang. I bet that's Tynan. It was. I didn't answer. I intended to enjoy my dinner.

It's dark, so I shall be able to wear my Persian lamb coat, which I can rarely wear in England nowadays. Corelli on the CD player in the car and Sloane Street is empty. I'll not allow anything like this in my life again. Then suddenly I find myself picking up the car telephone and asking the operator for the telephone number of Charlton Football Club and then ringing Charlton and asking for directions.

The match was a sell-out, but they allowed me into the executive suite to watch it on television and wait for my friend. A Persian lamb coat has just as much clout as a camel

259

or alpaca item when you're in among football management and its hangers-on. The blimp overhead gave stunning shots of the Thames Barrier. Now there's one structure I should love to have created. I reasoned that my coming to Charlton gave something back. Whatever Pearl's problems, I will deal with them in order to have done with them. What I love about the Thames Barrier is that it looks as if a race of enchanted aliens might live in it. I have formed a view, evidently, that Pearl is a side issue. But – now I understood my impulse to come here – to tie up the last details. Likewise I will go to France, tomorrow if possible, see Philippe – and bow out.

Pearl played a quiet game and in the sixtieth minute came off.

'May I go and see him?'

'Okay, mate, but you'll have to be outta the dressing room before full-time, the manager won't want anyone to hear their bollocking.'

A boy led me down the concrete stairs – concrete is the leitmotif of football, I decided. Pearl sat on a bench, while a man inspected the calf of his right leg.

'Oh, hi, man.'

This boy had changed in himself. He nodded warily to indicate discretion in front of his minder.

'Thanks for coming.'

'Is it serious?'

The physio looked at me with a mixture of respect and suspicion. I might be a director he hadn't yet met; he said, 'You're not supposed to be in here.'

Pearl pleaded, 'He's my friend.'

The phsyio said, 'I'm going back out to watch real football-ers. Not bloody malingerers.' He looked at me doubtfully as he left; his jagged white hair put him on a war footing with the world.

'What is it?' I said.

Pearl said, 'I'm really glad to see you, Nicholas.'

Trying not to feel irritated with him, I asked, 'What's the problem?'

'Aw, it's just life, man. You know.'

He said no more and I waited, thinking he wished to warm to some theme. A different Pearl, this time; thoughtful and melancholy. Nothing else came, except an anodyne question; 'How you been?'

'You left messages?'

'I did, man. I left messages.'

So puzzling. A few hours ago he had left a message bordering on the frantic. Now – nothing.

'Johan, I came here specially.'

'I appreciate that.' He began to do stretching exercises on the supposedly injured leg.

'I don't want your appreciation. I want to know what the problem is. I broke a dinner appointment.'

'You certainly is all dressed up. I like the shirt.'

'Johan! Listen. Your house in Holland got firebombed – or so I hear. There's some big hassle in your life. So talk to me! I don't need clients with the vapour of crime about them.'

If I've learned anything in my life I've learned that people's reactions don't come from the obvious cause. Especially if they're in the grip of something major.

'The vapour of crime. That is a good phrase.' He didn't look at me.

I had the good sense to get hold of myself. And, while subsiding, think a little. This isn't the reaction I expected. Must be another reason. And if I know that – it must be a reason with which I'm familiar. And the reason for odd behaviour in me recently has been – fear.

I said to him, 'You're seriously afraid.'

'No, man.'

'You should be. Your home attacked. Someone following you. Yes. You're afraid.'

He didn't deny it twice.

'Just tell me one thing.'

'What, man?'

'How much of this has to do with Antony Safft?'

The question distressed him. He flapped his hands. 'I don't know. I don't know.'

'Johan. Black Pearl.' First time I'd called him that; he liked it. 'D'you want to come with me? We can go and eat somewhere. And talk.'

'I gotta go back with the team.'

'Johan, come on! Something's the matter, what is it?'

He looked at me and in his eyes dwelt things he didn't say – terror, need, distress.

'Nicholas, I cannot get out of here now. I cannot speak.'

'What exactly is it?'

'I cannot say.'

'Is somebody after you for something?'

He began to tremble. I moved towards him and he grabbed my arm and put his face down on the back of my hand.

'I'm in trouble, man.'

'Are you in danger?'

He lifted his head a little and nodded. 'But I can do nothing about it.'

I looked at him, this brilliant machine of a young man, at the peak of his powers, blessed with a joyous and original talent, and I stopped regretting that I had come to him when he called.

'I am sure I can help. I know people.'

'Not these kinds of people. No one knows these kinds of people.'

He fidgeted so much I decided to drop the subject. Then I suddenly realized something.

'You speak German?'

'Yes, I do. And Italian. And –'

'Never mind those. In German. What does this mean?'

I said the words. He sat up.

'Say it again.'

He took it piece by piece. '*Zinzee*? Sounds like *Sind Sie* – "Have they". *Endlick*. *Endlich* – "At last" or "In the end". What was next?'

'*Fur. Mickey*,' it sounded like.

'I'd say, *für mich* – means "For me". And, you said, it sounded like "comin" – I think that's *für mich gekommen*. *Sind Sie endlich für mich gekommen*. Does that sound like it?'

'Exactly.' I loved his quickness and his enjoyment of his quickness. This boy shouldn't allow himself to be in trouble. Hark at who's talking.

'It means, "Have they come for me at last?"'

I patted him on the shoulder. 'I will soon thank you fully for that. For now – thank you very, very much.'

'Hey, Nicholas, be careful, I see excitement in your eyes,' and we laughed. That's better.

Some rough noise sounded. Another player clanged in, not injured but substituted. That ended the conversation. I had no choice but to go. The other young man gave me an odd look as I left.

For ten minutes or so I stood on the riverbank looking at the Thames Barrier.

I was right. I was right!

Otto, have they come for me at last?

They will, old man, they will, they will all come for you, all six hundred and forty-two ghosts – and above their heads will fly the swallows of Oradour.

43

Next morning I went to the office. From there I could ring Claire.

I prowled every desk and every drawing board. Found no trace of anything I should know but hadn't been told. The Cadogan Gardens key had gone from Lemon's desk. That gave me a half-turn until I realized: somebody needed access to check the repair works.

On the computer listings, the Pearl job read out as 'Design Completion'. I called it up.

Well – 'Completion more or less.' The builder had been working from the external drawings and didn't need the finalized interiors for another month. He'd have them in ten days; hope I can say the same for his speed; I doubt it.

Made a note on the screen to ask Pearl about the main fireplace and the one in the bathroom. Amelia had generated agreeable computer images of how a Dutch barn would eventually look in the landscape near Stonehenge.

The Alessi in my office hadn't been emptied. Or else somebody'd used it after me. Disgusting. Cleaned it. Made new coffee. My bones shifted inside my skin when I looked at Mary Strait's huge Christmas present to me. It stood on the floor. The wrapping paper had been torn back a little. Someone had tried to peer inside it.

Jesus! Mary Strait – what am I going to do when she comes back to work?! What a stupid thing to do. Which was the more stupid – screwing her or dumping her? Hard to choose.

Time to ring Claire. Eleven o'clock in France.

She answered immediately. She burst into tears. She became frantic and incoherent, this cool, experienced young woman.

My caution reared, my need to be shot of all this. But – in Berlin I'd agreed with myself to take on everything.

I said, 'Call me back when you've had a moment to ease a little. I'm at the office. This is my number.' I repeated it twice.

Fifteen minutes later, fifteen minutes in which I wondered whether this might be an elaborate come-on, I got the call. She seemed a little calmer.

'You must come here,' she said, in a rather straight way. 'Philippe needs to see you.'

'I need to see Philippe, too.'

Then she did a curious thing – she dropped to a whisper while exploding into a wail.

'But you mustn't come here, you mustn't. Things have become very –' and she all but collapsed.

'Easy,' I said. 'Easy, Claire. It's all right. I'm here. I'm still here. What is it?'

She whispered again, trying to control herself, 'You mustn't come here.'

'I don't understand.'

She put the phone down.

I rang again and Philippe answered – different acoustic, he must be in a different room.

'My friend Nicholas, I want us to meet.'

'Philippe, I want to see you. Tomorrow.'

44

So, as the old books used to say, I began the first day of the rest of my life.

I like crossing the Channel – by whatever means. Most of all I now like being associated with such a magnificent design and construction feat as the Tunnel. When the Tunnel first opened the train was quicker than the ferries or the hovercraft. Traffic volume and poor crowd management have made it one of the slowest crossings.

What chance very early in the morning? Every chance. I left Knightsbridge at six o'clock in darkness. Reached the Tunnel check-in at Folkestone at a quarter to eight. Caught a train at seventeen minutes past eight and stepped out at Philippe's door near Jumièges at half past eleven. That's the trick, then – travel very early or very late.

On the train, sitting in my car, I thought, There's that contrast again. The construction was and is beautiful, the travelling convenient but ugly. Paradox. The result being at odds with the beauty of the idea. Like the Bauhaus being of the same race as Hitler. Like football and hooligans.

No traffic at all on the new Rouen *autoroute*. Down along the Seine the trees in the orchards had finally lost all their leaves.

I rang and rang the bell. Nobody answered. No reply. I drove away. But there was someone in the house. I knew it. Edwardian villa, on a curve of the river; large balcony upstairs; in the winter sunlight tugs, lighters and one huge freighter registered in Piraeus passed by more swiftly than seemed possible. The heavy wash slapped the low stone wall below me. Tide's in. I stood by the car, watching the water and then the windows. The house had a curious air.

Nor had I made an error: 'From Rouen,' said Philippe, 'go to the Pont de Brotonne, turn south, follow the Seine, to the signs for Port de Jumièges. Cross on the little car ferry, do not go up into Jumièges, turn right when you come off the ferry, we are the last house on the left to face the river, the one with the statue of an archer in the garden.'

Unmistakable. I drove away and went to Jumièges. Shall I ring them? They may have gone out to do some shopping, not expecting me so early. No signal here on the mobile.

I recognized the tall white arches of Jumièges from books on monastic architecture and from a postcard a lover sent long ago. Rich presence. Distinctive atmosphere. The *abbé* of Jumièges must have been a powerful man. In another mood I would have listened in my head for the music of mediaeval choirs ascending these ruins. But I knew I was almost out of time and out of emotional adrenaline. To recover from all of the recent events I shall need months of rest.

Nobody else came to see Jumièges on that silent, terrible morning. I saw only the woman selling the tickets.

On a knoll of the sward that stretches between the monastery and the residence, my mobile signal rose. Their telephone was answered but nobody spoke. I rang again – same again. Back to the car, but this time I parked several hundred yards from the house and at its rear, reached by a lane among gardens. No sign of life, but an architect always knows when a house is empty. This wasn't. I felt no fear – but I should have done.

Walking softly on the garden path, I reached the back door – open.

No sound inside the house; the kitchen showed no recent activity. A modern French painting dominated the hall; it looked like a turkey crossed with a truck; French modernism has not been good on the hybrid. The large front room downstairs had a television set and ample chairs, a rug on a maple floor and an alabaster bowl the size of a small bath. No sign of life. But I know there is life in this house.

To climb stairs without creaking requires a decision. Either you stick resolutely to the exact middle of each tread, or you walk on the side least used, usually nearest the wall. Four sepia etchings climb with me; they look English, could be Sutherland, heads, a torso. On the landing I pause. There is someone here, I know that.

All doors are open a little – except one. Shall I do as they do in the movies – open each one? Or do I cut to the closed one? It's the nearest.

I open it slowly, without knocking. Claire is standing in the middle of the room. I see her in the mirror before I see her in the flesh. The image makes me start.

Now I look at her. She is wearing an ivory silk petticoat and it stirs me. I have an immediate picture of turning her around, making her kneel and taking her from behind.

But I say softly, 'What are you doing, Claire? Why didn't you answer the door?'

She shakes her head.

'What's the matter?'

It is a known fact that people expecting death sit very still just before the killers come. The greatness of Claire's distress, indexed by her huge calm, required that I speak to her almost as to a child. I helped her to sit on the bed.

'Claire, what is it?'

'You shouldn't have come. I tried to stop you.'

'But you also asked me to come. Mixed messages – which did you most want?'

'I've brought you into – into.' She stopped. 'Look at these,' she said. 'They were delivered some weeks ago. When I first rang you.'

From behind a pillow she produced a red folder. A dozen photographs had been clipped to a sheaf of reports in French.

Claire unclipped the first two, one monochrome, one colour.

'This man was – and still is – an officer in the Israeli Mossad. He was held in great respect.'

The photograph showed a man with curly black hair, a wide mouth, slight cleft in the chin, a little stubble. He wore a white shirt with a stylish tie. In a clean-cut face gaped two black sockets where the eyes had been.

'He went after the people who killed Antony. The report says they captured him. They sedated him. Then, while preserving his life, they cut his eyes out. He was delivered to the Israeli Embassy in London.'

'In London? But the newspapers –?'

'The media receive a fiftieth portion of what happens in this world. Do you wish to see other photographs?'

I hesitated.

'We have here –' she became a little manic, spoke like a stallholder in a market – 'a man with no nose. Another with no scrotum. A man who was injected with more heroin in a month than an addict can take in a year. A man who lost all his fingers and all his toes and his ears and his tongue.'

I took the photographs from her and put them back in their envelope. She tapped her fingernail on another envelope. I opened it.

Claire sunbathed in the garden at Jumièges. Nobody could see her. The garden was secluded. But somebody had photo-graphed her. They had also photographed her through the windows of the house, in various stages of undress – a wonderful body. At the next photographs I had to close my eyes. I still do when I think of them. They had put the nude Claire on a computer scanner and made certain adjustments. To show what they would do to her body.

But a shameful thrill shocked me. How old was my mother when I was born? A body that angered me. The lob of those breasts. Her moans. Her anger at me. My rage. I reached my hand to the nape of Claire's neck and drew her face to me and bruisingly slammed her cheek to mine. I bit at her mouth and she acquiesced.

The fury left me and I asked her, 'Has Philippe traced who sent these?'

She never answered because she began to disintegrate. Then we heard a noise downstairs. Philippe called up the stairs.

'Claire?'

Claire's mettle showed. She rose and strode to the door. Ivory haunches shifted beneath the petticoat.

'Nicholas is here.'

Silence from below, and then I heard his footsteps on the stairs. He seemed awkward with me. Although we had spoken, we hadn't seen each other since the incident at St Gilles.

'Nicholas! You are welcome!'

We shook hands on the landing and walked into a large bright sitting room.

'Of course,' I said, gesturing towards the river, 'We haven't met since my long swim.'

But for his good manners his face would have shown irritation. Claire – such character – attempted a laugh.

'It's Nicholas's English way of saying it's all right about St Gilles.'

'Ah?'

Philippe led us towards the balcony and opened the French windows. What on earth am I going to say to him? Tell him I know his uncle, his family, were profiteers? And that he is a Nazi-hunter because his uncle was overcome with shame? And also his uncle cunningly thought of the best place to hide – by becoming known as a Nazi pursuer? And that he's using money stolen from the people he's avenging? That was how the words formed in my mind.

Philippe dragged wicker chairs into a circle. He then began a series of bizarre manoeuvres. Musical chairs, I thought. He arranged my chair with my back to the open balcony. I can't do that; I have to face the entrance.

'Philippe, d'you mind if I sit over here? I like the view.'

Claire appeared, now in a blue dress.

Philippe said, 'Excuse me, I must do something.'

When he came back he looked agitated. I had forgotten how he churned his hands in circles. Asking me about my journey, he stood on the balcony, staring across the river into the distance. Then he left the room again.

Claire said, 'Shh,' – and listened. 'Philippe's on the phone.' She could scarcely breathe for anxiety.

After several minutes he returned with a folder and sat down.

'Do you know what this is?' he said to me.

I shook my head.

'It is, at last, Antony's will. I received it last week.'

'Last week?'

'Two days before Christmas, I think.'

I said nothing. Mr Lewison's words to me were – 'Late January. Mid-February.'

I asked a foolish question, don't know why I asked it, it made Philippe jump; 'How secure are we here?' Claire seemed to have entered a reverie; gazing out at the river and the crag across the way as I murmured, 'I've been worried about you both.'

He shifted his feet. I had heard a psychologist on a radio programme say the word 'shifty' came from the fact that when people lie or evade the truth, they shift their feet. Philippe shifted his feet.

'I must ring Mr Lewison, he hasn't sent me my copy of the will, but the postal deliveries in London around Christmas – hopeless.' I babbled. Now, I know that when I babble I'm warning myself about something.

Claire didn't move from her reverie, I don't think she heard. Her body is in my mind again. Exorcize. Exorcize.

Her mouth, those eyes, her cheek – I see a faint bruise where I kissed her.

Philippe stood up, walked to the balcony, stood outside, came and sat down again with his back to the world. I thought myself the uneasy one and felt no reason for my reluctance to tell him about Berlin. I looked past him to the high woods above the river. Claire, in something of a daze, rose from her chair – and sat down again. The room became humid with unease.

I began, 'Philippe – there are so many things to say. And to ask.'

He wore a blue, striped business shirt and blue jeans. The sunlight caught the deep blackness and the abundance of his hair. I thought, The French do have olive skin, the old belief is true.

'My friend. One day it will be over. You will be honoured by your Queen, though it might be a king. I will be an old gentleman and I will stand very straight to accept the Légion d'Honneur.'

That was the last word he spoke – 'd'Honneur.'

His hair exploded before I heard the gunshot that did it. The velocity hurled him splaying into my lap and he slid from there to the floor.

I flung myself sideways, clawing at Claire and crashing her to the rug, lay half on top of her – and even then was aware of her body. Glass tinkled and I heard something sizzle or gurgle. Philippe's throat.

His face was inches from mine. I wish I could say that I saw in his eyes a hundred thoughts. But his skin tone changed and the long descent of the blood from the body began. His eyes lost life and they darkened, dark as the clouds that swamped the sky over the Seine, clouds that came in fast from the west, Atlantic clouds.

Grabbing Claire, I made her crawl ahead of me across the floor and through the doorway to the landing. She tried to stop, to touch Philippe's face, but I urged and urged. I heard her voice and she seemed to be praying.

We should have stayed. It was a single shot from across the river. But one doesn't register such things. One registers survival. The explanations, the mournings can come later.

Claire ran like an athlete. In the hall she snatched a bag. Astonishing. Back door. We reached my car parked under the apple trees. My mind remained sufficiently present to know I mustn't be seen running away. I drove as casually as a tourist. On the slip road by the river a small car raced towards us. The driver looked at us, raced past, stopped, tried to turn, changed his mind, raced away.

At the ferry I hesitated and turned to Jumièges once more. Through the village I found a farm lane where, from the crest of the hill, I could see the ruined arches of the abbey. There we sat shaking, drenched with our own urine and without any comprehension of the world. Blood on my shoes; smears, this time, not berries of blood. Oh God, God, God – Who are You and what do You mean by all this?

The arches drifted with the changing light. They had built the abbey on a spur of land just proud enough for the pilasters to reach above the trees. In the shadows the tall, gaunt white heights of the ruin gave me a strange comfort. I could have been that architect; I could have been the one who persuaded the *abbé* and the bishop to build a metre, no, five, no ten, metres higher.

Rain began to spit as we turned to the Seine again and caught the little ferry; ours was the only car.

'*Bon retour*!' said the toothless ticket collector. He and I exchanged a joke based entirely on our facial expressions. But now he, too, seemed sinister. At last the rain burst. It would shield us. Any shield would do.

Claire spoke. It all came out in one breath.

'I wish you had been here two months ago. In the autumn these lands behind us are full of orchards and they all bring their produce to the roadside every Sunday. Philippe and I drive along several small lanes, there are ferry-points up and down the river and we criss-cross, we stay out for hours and travel only about thirty kilometres and come back loaded with apples and pears and the most divine plums.'

Her voice never varied out of a monotone.

45

Calais at nightfall meant mayhem – hectares of private cars, a vast yard of personal freight bound for Britain. Ahead, around, behind, they settled their loads, brown cardboard boxes hefted from boot to interior and back again. Good humour prevailed, with post-Christmas merriment and banter. The women gave the orders and the men hauled the crates.

I stepped out to survey. Saw only families, or couples, or pairs of couples. What was I looking for? Some possible attacker? A sudden, raging menace? I didn't know – but I even checked the sky. The rain had stopped and up near the stars fast west winds blew away clumps of clouds.

Everybody in our queue missed three trains. Claire clasped and unclasped her hands a thousand times. I talked to her some of the time, in a low voice, comforting, comforting. When it felt right I held her hand or stroked her arm. I took her passport from her small bag. At least she had presence of mind.

My fear that we'd been followed was no more than the non-stop music of this horrifying day. I had no consciousness of anything I did. My face felt as if it would explode and my mind refused to think.

We eventually boarded the train departing at 20.47. No mad fiend came running or driving down the ramp to shoot us. Only the little white *Le Shuttle* car stood on the platform as a girl in yellow with a walkie-talkie waved us aboard. Directly ahead of us ran a Mercedes with a couple who never spoke to each other. Immediately behind sat a comfortable Ford

Mondeo – husband, wife, daughter, son-in-law. I hoped we also looked like people who had Christmased in France, not two people whose lives had just been set on fire.

The Mercedes disappeared. I was directed to the upper deck with no car ahead of me. Good! Means we'll be off early. Along the long, long train I drive, the wheels bumping and the car shuddering over the hard metal links between the carriages.

Just short of an empty carriage a sour young man, also in yellow, stops me. I gesture at him irritatedly to ask why we don't continue to the front carriage. He gives me a 'Fuck-you' shrug and closes the door ahead. Next, he walks the length of our empty carriage and then walks the carriage behind. There, he halts the approaching cars. He keeps them in that distant carriage, closes the doors between them and my Saab and we sit alone, a carriage to ourselves, an empty carriage directly ahead, an empty carriage immediately behind. I scarcely notice. All I can think about is Philippe's head. The image stunts my alertness.

The announcements begin, from a throat of steel.

Lavatory? Right beside the car. I check it for anything and everything. It is clean – in all senses. I help Claire from the Saab. Her face is a white colour I have never seen, a flat and pitiable chalk. She goes into the lavatory and I hear her retching. When she comes out I make her lean against me for several minutes and then I lower her gently back into her seat.

When I come out of the lavatory I check in case I've misjudged. No. It's true. One, lone car in the middle of three carriages. No wonder people can't get on the trains if they don't know how to fill the bloody carriages properly. Now unease enters – with force.

I pace up and down. Then I check the doors ahead of me – they open. I check the doors behind me – they won't open. Presumably they open when the train begins to move. The surroundings feel as harsh as the metal they're made of. I lean against the green handrail and send my hands across my face inside this long corrugated tin box where every surface repels.

In the distance I see the Mondeo father and son-in-law trying to open the doors into the empty carriage between us. Presumably they want the lavatory I've just used. I try to open on my side, pressing and pressing again the little green manikin pictogram on the button. It hisses but nothing happens.

I press once more. A hiss, a shudder, but the doors stay locked. The distant people peer at me and shrug and make a gesture of physical failure. I return the compliment. In short we are in a carriage of the Channel Tunnel train with a vacant carriage ahead and a vacant carriage behind and we can't get out. My heart is roaring with fear.

Claire in her seat whispers to herself, still clasping and unclasping her hands. Once more I lean against the green rail waiting to see the lights moving, telling me the train's rolling. We're three or four minutes late departing. Tell me, I ask myself, why I am riven with fear afresh. I look again at my watch.

Directly beneath me I see the possible reason for the delay. The sour-faced young man is speaking to someone. He is speaking to another young man, who has a shaven head. The sour-faced young man accepts something. I can almost hear him say, 'Cheers, mate.'

The skinhead climbs into a large white van. He drives onto the train. In less than a minute the lights of Calais begin to drift by. The fire in my heart spreads to my eyes in disbelief of something awful. I close my eyes.

46

I recognized the skinhead – Juicy. Without question. Without doubt. Might even be the same white van.

Weapons? No weapons. Yes, I have weapons. Toolkit. Standard with the Saab. Am I sure they're coming for us? Yes, I'm sure, yes, I am. I should have killed Otto in Berlin.

But – if we can't get out, how can they get in? They'll get in. That's what the voice inside me says, the voice I must heed. They'll get in. They've bribed Sour-Face. Some central control button pressed somewhere? With a *large* green manikin pictogram? Who knows.

I open the boot of the Saab. The jack-handle's no good. Two screwdrivers, one straight, one cross-headed. Take the straight one. Are they coming for us yet?

I stop and listen. All I can hear is the roll of the train. No, needless to say, signal on the mobile phone. We are under the Channel. Various plays on words splash my brain like spray. In over my head. Up to my neck. Deep water. In it up to here.

Any other weapons. Yes! Walking boots, heavy and thick. Get them on fast!

In the next carriage but one, where the people are, all is silent. In the two empty carriages that bracket us and in our carriage too, the lights dim. Then they rise again, seeming brighter than before. Sweat is trickling down under my arms along the curve of my ribcage. The train hurtles forward with startling soundlessness.

I check a diagram on the wall. They bored three tunnels

– a vehicle tunnel, a service tunnel and an escape route in the middle. No way out.

Can I stand and wait? I know nothing of self-defence. No grilles on the roof through which to escape like Indiana Jones or one of those guys, no false ceiling where we might hide among the wiring conduits.

We can't lie under the Saab. They'll simply drag us out. Or start the car and drive it back and forth over us. Which is what they may do anyway.

Is that an alarm system for the train? But if I activate it, who will get to me? Some youth? Sour-Face himself? If they've bribed all round them, do I have a better chance of waiting until we get to Folkestone? I check the corners of the carriage. Yes, I can stand tight in a corner. I'll wedge Claire behind me in a way no one can get at her. It'll be very tight. The corner is shallow, it's where the doors open back. I'm in a tight corner anyway. Oh, Christ! Then all the lights go out and all I can see is the dimmed lamps of the Tunnel wall flashing by.

The lights go back on. No doubt of it – they're brighter than before. Then darkness again, this time for several minutes.

Behind us, in the carriage where the people are, I hear a sound of breaking glass and I think, 'Good, somebody's doing something,' and this thought is followed by the recriminatory thought, 'But why couldn't it be you, Nicholas? Why didn't you smash the glass and join the people with their cars? And then I reason, 'Because I do not want to involve them, this is my fight.' Ridiculous and pathetic attempt at nobility.

More breaking glass. But then – screams and loud, swearing voices. The lights come on and somehow we know, don't we, when lights have come back on to stay?

A brawl has started. The thugs I have been expecting, four of them, have attacked every car in that carriage with baseball bats. As ordinary men remonstrate with them they crack skulls. One motorist, the father-in-law, is on his knees bleeding. His women are near him; I see the legs of the son splayed on the floor of the carriage, one leg rolling slightly and desperately. Behind them people are pulling frantically on the alarm system – I watch the mechanism come away in their hands. No alarm.

A motorist I haven't seen before darts forward and attacks the biggest thug – who is Jemima. Jemima turns and upper-cuts the handle of his baseball bat into the man's face just under the nose. The man goes down, poleaxed.

I am viewing all this through the tall double rectangles of two glass doors. The door beside me now hisses and I realize that the doors between me and them have somehow come undone. From now on I had better act on instinct. If I am to be attacked, let it be from only one direction. Run back.

'Claire, you must do everything I tell you.' My voice is calm. I am not.

She climbs out of the Saab. We go toward the vacant front carriage and I wedge her in the corner. Checking the floor of the carriage for obstructions, I take up a position in front of her, trying not to crush her with my back. From here I can see their legs coming. The angle's too tight for all four of them to get at us.

Sudden flash of memory: but I did this at school! Stood in a corner, fought them off. Therefore, I press my hands holding the screwdriver behind my back.

'Any loose ends?' Elizabeth used to ask before a client pres-entation. 'One can be strangled by a loose end, Nicholas.'

Whip off my tie. My hair? No, not really long enough to drag me forward by. I tug my shirt tight from the back. Claire is warm and vertical and passive. I feel her breath on my neck and for a moment, like a child, she places a tender hand in the small of my back.

There we stand and the whole moment freezes. Nothing happens. I can no longer see back through all the doors.

Then I hear the noise. They are attacking the Saab as it stands all alone in the middle of its own deserted carriage. I glimpse them from time to time; they attack it with a kind of acid frenzy.

All the windows go – I hear the *crummppp!* of the glass. They slash the tyres; I know that quick *wussh!* A vile rump appears; someone's looking for us beneath the car.

I had made an error. They believed we'd escaped – but I had chosen to defend a point where they could see us, see my legs. I could have taken up a position in the wide spaces between the glass doors on either side.

Cross my fingers. Pray. Wish. They still might not see us. If they believed sufficiently strongly that we'd escaped they might look no further.

Their noise is frightful. They roar and scream. Now they are ransacking the car. The Saab's alarm goes off, to add to the infernalness. I see my overnight clothing strewn about, trampled and urinated on by Jemima. He's the only one I can identify – and I know Juicy's there.

The sound of their hammering on the car became unbearable, like some anvil struck in hell's worst darkness. I saw a spark – how did they do that? The jack-handle – and the jack itself; they swung them along the car's length and breadth.

They finished and walked away from the Saab. I presumed they'd reckoned we'd seen them board and had somehow run from the train. As they passed back along the carriage they had earlier ransacked, I heard their shouted abuse. Once or twice they rang the clang of my jack-handle on some other unfortunate's car.

Then they were gone. But why didn't my body relax? Instinct. My body didn't relax because at the last moment Juicy looked back over his shoulder. In the distance he saw my legs. I heard him whoop with glee.

They didn't run back to us, they walked. Even when they hissed open the doors and came to my long empty carriage where we cowered in the far corner they didn't hurry. Indeed, they stopped and leaned against the door that hissed closed behind them. Four of them. They looked at us and they smiled. Mostly they smiled at each other.

Three of them had been on the Tube; Jemima, Juicy and Noddy. One, crisper and foreign, was new. Ringo wasn't with them. They conferred. The new one dropped to his knees ten feet away. He opened a little leather Gladstone valise, the sort the world knows as a doctor's bag.

From this he took a long black tube and a plastic drum, the kind vitamin C comes in. He next produced a glass funnel, fixed it to the tube and filled it with something from the vitamin drum. I couldn't see what it was.

'For the lady,' called Juicy. 'Somethin' nice for the lady.'

Their work prepared, they faced us. I stood rigid. It must be the case that there comes a moment when Fear has done its work and departs, giving Chance its turn. That's what happened to me.

I thought, 'There's little I can do. But whatever it is I'll do it.'

They advanced. No sign of cowardice from behind me; Claire might have been asleep so still did she stand. Except that she again placed that small hand in the middle of my back.

Two yards away from me they stopped. Juicy – now I learned how he got his nickname – hawked copiously and spat at my face. I ducked and he missed. I remember thinking – hope he hasn't hit Claire; she didn't recoil so he can't have. And I remember thinking – his spittle mustn't hit me because I don't want to bring my hand out from behind my back to wipe my face.

Then I spoke and my voice surprised me with its calm.

'You'll get us. I know that. It's four to two. But I'll get one of you. And I'll mutilate him for ever. Which of you will it be?'

I saw their eyes. Their nerves tingled. They hadn't expected to have to think of their own safety. Bullies never do. They regrouped to form a full semi-circle. That gave me a clue as to their strategy. The one who filled the funnel stood back a shade. Three meant to grab me while the fourth – did what? My worry went to Claire – what would happen to her?

The three took a united step forward. And another. I could smell their breath. What should I do? Wait? Or move?

I moved. Like lightning. Whatever embarrassment I feel, I also glow a little now when I think of it. Juicy was nearest to me and the same height. I raked the screwdriver across his eyes – I felt it hit his eyeballs. Then I swivelled and kicked Jemima, the tallest, on the knee. I retreated again into our metal corner.

They were stunned; they'd probably never been attacked like this. Since the Tube they thought me a soft touch. Oradour was a soft touch. Jemima bent to hold his knee.

But they got Claire. While I attacked Jemima, a third thug, Noddy, reached past me, grabbed her hair and wrenched her screaming out of the corner.

Standoff. I looked at them. They retreated by ten feet. Jemima straightened in the interlude and they all regrouped, with Juicy screaming and holding his eyes. Twisting her arm, they forced Claire to the ground. From behind they splayed her legs. They meant to draw me to her defence and get behind me.

I moved again. Singling out Jemima, I kicked him on the same knee. When he bent in agony I kicked him in the face; bones broke. It all felt as though it took a long time. It lasted shorter than it takes to say, 'How do you do, I'm Nicholas Newman. How nice to meet you.' One and a half down, two and a half to go.

Noddy threw something – a powder that started to burn my face and my eyes. As I recoiled he came towards me. His mistake; he shouldn't have broken ranks. Wildly I swung the screwdriver. I missed and he got my head; I lashed out again and connected with something, heard the scream. But it wasn't Noddy I hit; it was Juicy again, who this time went down.

I, who know nothing of fighting, knew these weren't good fighters.

Noddy stepped back, taking a clutch of my hair in his hand. Barbed-wire agony burned my face, neck and head. My scrotum tingled and I felt the beginnings of an erection. I heard Claire scream.

A quick rub of my shirtsleeve opened one eye. I saw more disarray than a nightmare. My second clumsy stab had hit Juicy in the back of the neck and he spouted blood. He half-knelt at my feet, one hand clutching his eyes, the other his knees. I kicked him again, in the jaw. The other two backed off, uncertain. Gingerly I opened my second eye.

Noddy had taken refuge behind Claire. She was screaming because the stranger was trying to ram not the tube but the funnel into her mouth. Noddy, recovering, knelt to hold her head still. The brutality of his grip on her hair was Neanderthal.

I think I went berserk. On my way to them I kicked Juicy in the face again and again, and tried to kick Jemima's head open. In my ears I heard my voice screaming every obscenity I ever knew. The Funnel dropped Claire's head and backed away. He was the most frightened of them. Noddy rose and stood his ground, and Claire tried to get the funnel out of her mouth. I feared she might bite on the glass.

Going at Noddy so hard I almost endangered Claire, I grappled with him and we rolled on the ground. He got on top of me long enough to call over the Funnel. I saw the legs loom. At which I roared and bit and rolled.

Noddy fell off and I drove the screwdriver so hard into his stomach I must have hit a bone; I broke the two joints on my right-hand ring finger. My ring! My father's ring! I should have taken it off! was my pained and screeching thought. Never thought of not being able to draw. Until later.

Noddy rose to his feet and started to splutter and curse me. I clambered up clumsily, my one thought, Had anything got down Claire's throat? My mind was filled with obscene language and images.

Funnel had backed away. Noddy writhed and sank to one knee in pain. I kicked him so savagely I heard ribs break. Deadly accurate. He screamed, and cursed me, and fell over. I had disabled three of them. Now I went after Funnel. To kill him. I had lost control.

He turned and ran. That eased my mind. The door didn't open fast enough. I had enough wild leisure to look back and check Claire was all right. She had clambered to her feet and was swaying. Funnel got the door wrong. Cornered in the tight space between the doors, he held up his hands like a martial arts man.

'What's in that fucking tube?' I roared.

'*Bitte?*' he answered, but his reply was automatic. He had no room in this tight space. I could hear the ground hurling on beneath us. Funnel's back hit the door. I made a slow-motion gesture that he lie down. He shook his head. I advanced – he had nowhere to go. I roared, 'Down! Lie DOWN!' and stepped back half a pace. He refused and I roared again. He stared at me. I kicked him on the shin and broke the bone, I think. He dropped, then rolled in pain.

With my foot I splayed out each of his arms and hands. I kicked him a flick of my boot on the side of the head. Using my heel, I broke each of his fingers in turn until I heard the bones crack, relishing the crunch. I did the same with his other hand and for good measure jumped on one of his ankles. He lay there screaming, his ankle broken. He will never walk well again.

A crowd gathered in our carriage. Men held open the carriage doors. I had a sensation of people gaping. Claire ran towards the people. Women and men moved to hold her in their arms.

Noddy had risen to his feet.

'You –' I shouted at him, about to swear until I saw the spectators. Some strange prudishness stung me. He backed away, in pain.

Now I rushed to where Jemima and Juicy lay. Jemima was unconscious. I dragged out his hands and jumped on them. Juicy saw what I was doing and dragged himself backwards. Blood poured from his eyes and neck. As he wobbled on his knees I kicked him in the throat. He fell sideways.

Then I turned to Jemima and began to kick him with everything I could muster. Ran to Juicy, crushed his fingers. Ran back to Noddy who had fallen to his haunches, kicked him in the face. All the time I heard this mad voice screaming in my head.

Pairs of hands grabbed me and a calming voice said, 'Don't. Don't. They'll charge you too.'

The screaming voice had been mine. I stopped. Someone said in my ear, 'Easy, big man, easy, easy, you done brilliant, easy, easy. I'm a policeman. Off-duty, but I'm a copper and if you do any more damage they'll charge you too. You done brilliant. We all thank you.'

I shook off his hands, went to the nearest window and began to bang my head against the glass. He followed me and embraced me and I began to weep. The train stopped.

'Where's Claire?' I screamed. 'Where is she?' I called. 'Claire!'

A woman said, 'She's safe, we're all looking after her, she's safe.'

People came forward to me, asking anxiously. Several men designated themselves as custodians of Jemima, Juicy, Noddy and Funnel. Jailers have never been grimmer. The glass funnel lay on the floor of the carriage, watched over by an elderly man with a cut in his head. Somewhere a woman's voice said, 'I think it must be about drugs.'

Another woman's voice said, 'Oh, thank you, Nicholas, thank you, thank you.'

I thought, How does she know my name?

It was Claire.

47

The powder they threw at me had sulphur in it. Most of it hit my shirt, holed the cloth. The few burn marks on my face looked worse than they felt. That vitamin drum held half of Colombia's cocaine. Claire would have died. She didn't; none got down her throat. An ambulance took her away from the train, amid huge confusion. With all those people around her, she passed out. She was taken to a medical centre and sedated.

The police took me too. I spent the night in Folkestone's cells, amid illegal Bosnian immigrants, two violent drunks and an ageing rent boy who had hit someone with a broken glass in the town.

'You can make a call,' the woman sergeant said.

'You make it for me.'

'We're not allowed to do that.'

'You can if it's to another police force.'

That stumped her, but nothing happened until about six o'clock in the morning. Illegal, as I pointed out to them, to hold me like that. They wouldn't even tell me where they'd taken my car. I bumped them further by asking for a doctor. My stroppiness never eased.

The doctor confirmed my heart arrhythmia. He gave me eight beta-blockers. I took none of them. He also explained the soreness in my neck – Noddy's nails had gouged a channel. I had wrenched my shoulder, strained afresh my right wrist, still sore after the electric shock, and without an X-ray he guessed two broken finger joints.

At last I allowed myself the thought, How can I draw?

Concern for my work lifted my spirits. Interestingly, only Pearl's house worried me, and most of what followed on that job would amount to overseeing the construction and choosing/sourcing the interior materials. Anyway, as I knew, the computer held it tight.

The doctor left. I shouted for the policewoman again and I said, 'What about my telephone call?'

No response. She looked at me dully. I doubt she had any of the five senses.

At seven o'clock a detective appeared.

'You've done some damage.'

'Have you seen my car?'

'A car's not human.'

'I want you to put in a call to another police force.'

He shook his head. 'We know you're not one of us.'

'How do you know that?'

'Which police force?'

I said, 'Let me out of here.'

'That's up to the magistrate.'

'Don't be ridiculous.'

'Four men in hospital, one critical, all with extensive injuries. It took three men to restrain you. Attempted murder perhaps. We want to know about you.'

He and another questioned me. I told them only about the attack. My middle-class credentials made them think again. At last they relented about my call. The superintendent wrote down the number.

'Who's this?'

'He'll answer with his name. And if he doesn't answer he's got his name on his message.'

I watched him. Policemen, I assume, learn over the years how not to show reactions – but they don't learn fully enough. From the twist of his jaw I saw that he read the depth of my connection.

When he finished muttering into the phone he said to

me, 'So that's what it's all about. What team d'you support then?'

'I don't.'

After that nothing happened – except that I was locked into an office rather than a cell. A woman cleaner brought bacon and egg, toast and tea. I think I ate them all in one slurp. The morning drifted by. I dozed in the chair, still refusing to think any thoughts. About four o'clock in the afternoon they unlocked the door.

'Look at you,' said Tynan. 'You galoot.'

I almost rushed at him, wishing to hit him. For a few seconds I shrieked every abusive term I could think up. He let me run out of steam, then said, 'You're okay, you are.'

'They're talking about pressing charges. If they do I'm going to go public. I'm going public on what you know and how you've done nothing about it.'

He looked at me, head to one side like a bird.

'Come on!' I said. 'Are they going to press charges? Because I warn you – I'll sing like a fucking canary.'

'First time I've heard you swear,' said Tynan. 'Know whose nickname is the Canaries? For four marks. Gong! Sorry, you're too slow, I can't offer it, it's Norwich City. Poor sods, the seasons they've had lately.'

'Are you deaf? They're pressing charges! Are you fucking deaf?' I didn't know until then that I was still high on my own juice.

'The doc give you tranquillizers? 'Cos I think you're one of them people who's made worse by them. I'd a girlfriend like that once, give her Valium she'd break your face. Chum, cool it.'

'Drop the charges.'

'Cool it, will you?'

This time he barked at me. It quelled me – my first submission to his natural authority. Tea arrived for both of us.

'See your hand?' He looked and clucked. 'See your neck?

Your face? Adam's apple – sore? Jesus-the-Joker, you hammered a job on them.'

'Drop your profanity.' I had calmed down. 'Where's Claire?'

'Recovering. Who is she?'

'A friend.'

'Nice piece of tit there, chum.'

I had to laugh.

He walked around me and looked at my neck, then checked my face again. I was sitting down. He disarmed me by patting my head and then putting an arm around my shoulders and giving me what amounted to a lopsided hug.

I am as water in the hands of any man who shows me tenderness. That was how I got into all this – the kindness of Antony . . .

Swigging his tea, he sat before me and said, 'You done brilliant. The boy done brilliant.'

'What are you talking about?'

'That's what football managers say when they're praising someone. I've just come from the hospital.'

'Can you get me out of here?'

'Those guys are not gonna get out of anywhere for years. We've a list of motorists prepared to swear they tried to kill people. The Kraut's a real prize – nasty little shagger from Frankfurt, Harald something, wanted since last year's European Cup, decked a policeman in Munich. Besides, their injuries'll probably take 'em out of the frame. Maybe for good. They think Jemima's brain-damaged. I told 'em he always was.'

'Tynan, why didn't you arrest them when I asked you to?'

'We did, mate. And at Trafalgar Square. They're out on bail. Took you to put 'em away.'

'But what about me?'

A horror at my own violence began to descend on me.

Whence had it come? I never knew it of myself, I never knew so many things of myself.

'Paperwork. We're doing deals. You're working for us, flushing someone out.'

Now he saw I was shivering. 'I'll go check,' he said. 'You need care. Anyone I can ring?'

'No. No one. I need a blanket.'

Tynan went out; I observed that he still locked the door. Ten minutes later he came back. 'No result yet, I'm just tellin' 'em I'm still on the case,' and he went again. And then I nodded off.

When I woke I had a crick in my neck and a blanket round my shoulders. Tynan had come and gone; an electric heater glowed in the office.

Nothing happened for another half-hour. Then he re-appeared with the young doctor.

'We can go,' said Tynan, 'but I wanted a medical opinion.'

The doctor examined me and said, 'Shock, if he's not careful.'

'What should he do?' as though I were inanimate.

'Let him do what he wants to do,' said the doctor, and left.

'Get me a rented car,' I said.

'Okay, mate.'

'Then tell me how to get to Claire.'

'Okay, mate.'

Outside, I said to Tynan, 'No visits. I'll call you.'

'Look after yourself,' he said. 'The boy done brilliant. But sunshine, do we have to talk!'

48

It was over. At last. I fully believed so. Only the questions remained. Many of the answers would come from Claire, sitting now beside me.

She settled back. No cars followed. The rented BMW had a thousand miles on the clock. We climbed the hill and a moon appeared. Twenty-four hours since we left Calais. I said nothing to Tynan about Philippe; that needed some thought.

Claire had perked up, probably made herself do so in my interests; but I sensed the gathering pain.

'Where are we going?' she asked, as the motorway signs grew less urgent.

'How much do you want to know?'

'Tell me what feels right.'

'I'm going to hide you away.'

'I feel terrible,' she said. 'Poor Philippe,' and the weeping began. 'Terrible. Terrible.'

We fell quiet, driving along the silver ribbons of the broad empty roads. The countryside accepted and concealed us. By the light of the moon my mind became remarkably clear. I could look back on the past three months.

Shock had been building slowly, but adrenaline kept me upright. My life, since Antony Safft's death, was a frightful miasma. Threat, disruption and savagery. For much of the time, as I now saw – allowed myself to see – I had believed I was going to die.

Shock also diluted the satisfaction I should have felt. I had taken a courageous decision to confront those who violated me. No blame to me for being singled out by Antony. By now

I had soothed any injustice I felt at being handed his poisoned chalice. I felt some shame at the injuries I had meted out. A touch of chagrin punished me for the uncontrollable rage found to dwell inside me.

I felt calmer, and I felt intrigued at new things I was learning about myself. They had barely begun to articulate themselves. So tentatively did they rise to the surface of my mind that touching them might shatter something.

In the green glow of the car's interior I looked sidelong at Claire. Then I looked again. A sheet of tears covered her face. Some women weep in Hollywood teardrops; some ooze, or flow in streams. Claire shed sheets.

'Good for you,' I said.

'Oh, God. There's nothing to say.'

I said, 'I feel shame.'

'At what?'

'At being unable to cope. At being singled out. The target of evil. All of that. Philippe. At my own violence.'

She shook her head; I half-expected to see the spray of her tears on the air.

'I'm right in thinking you and Philippe hadn't married?'

She said, 'No.' The way she said it invited, I felt, a question. 'He wouldn't marry me.'

Inside me, massive unravelling begins. I see my mother walking across the courtyard in what my father called her *femme de Résistance* dress, a light, full-skirted shirtwaister with cream flowers on a red background.

'You say that with – with emphasis.'

Claire said, 'I'm not harsh about it.'

Enter my father. He stands at the far side of the courtyard watching my mother. She climbs into the car. My father comes over, almost running. The pairs of doves scatter from the loft beside the clock.

'So what is it? You seemed very happy together. He seemed very solicitous of you.'

'Yes. But –' Claire paused, then made up her mind. 'Difficult living with a man whose life is controlled by the existence of evil. Even if – or I suppose especially if – it's old evil. From a long time back. Philippe wasn't born when the crimes were committed. Nor was I.'

Silence again.

My mother refuses to get out of the car. My father drags her out. My mother shouts at him, claws at him. My father turns her round, twists her arm and begins to beat her. With his hands. On her rump.

She freezes. Then she crumples. Then she turns back into my father's arms and hugs him. He stands there, arms by his sides shouting into her hair and neck.

No traffic. Beside me, Claire suddenly began to laugh. She laughed and laughed, almost to seizure. I had to calm her down. The laughing gives way to more tears. Her dress is different; the blue one must have been destroyed and someone's lent her a dress, it's brown; how kind, but it doesn't suit her. I too feel manic.

My mother doesn't go out in the car that day. She and my father disappear. I see him later upstairs. He is no longer dressed immaculately. His collar's missing, I can see the shirt stud shine above his open waistcoat, and his braces are down off his shoulders, they lie in loops either side of his waist.

Claire found tissues in her handbag and mopped at her face. She turned on the vanity mirror light in the visor over her seat: extensive repairs.

A day before that day I had climbed the back stairs, where Kim said I never should because it's near Mama's and Papa's bedrooms. But it has a door with a ladder off it to the pigeon-loft and I think there are eggs.

I hear moaning and I hear talking and laughing and moaning and Papa is down in the courtyard below talking to Wicked Willie, we call him, the farm manager. I can see into Mama's room from the loft and her legs are swirling in pain, that's all I can see.

Tiptoeing down the stairs I tell Papa something's wrong with Mama, she's talking to herself and has a pain. But he says she's on the telephone and I say she's not.

Papa picks up the telephone in the scullery hall and places his hand over the speaking part and listens. When he looks at me he is very angry.

No clouds blocked the moon. I know the sea is near us, we are driving parallel to it and over there lie the long dark headlands of France. A rush of affection lapped me and became a wave, then a tidal wave. That has never happened in my life. Claire's eyes were closed. We are two shattered people, I know, but it is over. I shall discover what it was but I shall discover it in tranquillity.

Papa did nothing. He replaced the telephone and went out. I went upstairs and into my mother's bedroom. She stood at the window in her slip, her arms wrapped tight about her.

I took Claire's hand and squeezed it and brought it to rest on my knee.

'I will try to take care of you,' I said. 'Let me tell you where we're going. I'm taking you to Rye.'

'A song of sixpence.'

I smiled. 'Sort of. But this is a secret. This is somewhere only I know of.'

I was about to tell her she was the only person in my life ever to know about Rye. Then I recalled that it had been a bone of contention between Madeleine and me. Because I never took Madeleine there. But Madeleine was seven years dead now and her murdered ghost had been paid due honours.

'Several years ago, when I first made a lot of money, I bought an old house in Rye. It is about five hundred yards from where Henry James lived.'

'Shall we gaze upon the portrait of a lady?'

'I did something I later thought foolish. I put a lot of my own ego into it. I suppose I wanted to create an idealized place, I don't know what I wanted. You'll see what it's like. The point is – I got embarrassed about it and could never bring myself to tell anybody about it or even to use it. I've only been there occasionally in the last three years.'

I was talking manically, in an open way I didn't quite understand.

Claire squeezed my hand. 'Stop being so defensive.'

'There's somebody who looks after it. She's a former hotelier. Mrs Lydiard, I told her I hired her because I liked her name. She keeps it beautifully, cooks for me. When I'm there. Have you been to Rye? It's nicely olde-worlde with hilly streets and that. There are inns called The Buccaneer and Sir Francis Drake – or am I thinking of Plymouth?'

Claire relaxed; she laid her head back on her headrest and I said, 'That's better. And that's all you'll have to do. There's plenty to read. Good music. All that.'

We got to Rye at nine. My phone call from Folkestone had been brief. Anyway Mrs Lydiard knew never to ask questions. She'd opened the coach doors and I parked. The lights shone from almost all rooms.

'Oh!' said Claire, like a child seeing a Christmas tree.

We climbed the steps to the door. I couldn't tell her that this was my attempt to give myself the kind of fireside and chintz and roofbeam home I'd always longed for. I couldn't tell her that my longing for such security was the greatest pain lying across my heart. I couldn't tell her the true reason I rarely came here. The reason – my own failure to find a relationship that would make this empty house a home.

And I couldn't tell her that Mary Strait was yet another in the long list of such errors – all made in the search for The Wife of Rye. I'd thought I'd given up the search, conquered my need for it.

Mrs Lydiard, aged sixty going on a thoughtful forty-five, is a woman completely without crassness. She calls me 'sir' in a way that is never cloying – and only in front of others.

'This is Claire.'

'How d'you do, madam.'

'Mrs Lydiard, let me tell you straight away. We've had an accident. We need to rest.'

No reaction: a hotelier's tact.

Claire looked around. 'I love this house.'

Mrs Lydiard said, 'This is a lovely house. Mr Newman has a woman's touch, I've always told him that's a great compliment. Now, there's a fire blazing, and the drinks tray. How about dinner by the fire? Heavy frost is forecast, sir, and, madam, we almost never get it here, the sea, you know.'

She led us into the Long Drawing Room. I'd forgotten how lovely it was – although most probably I'd refused to allow myself to remember. The Square Drawing Room stayed more clearly in my memory, probably because I kept my jigsaw puzzles there.

'Do you know, we'd a squirrel come down that chimney last summer,' said Mrs Lydiard. 'You were quick, sir, to remedy that. Other people here've had their furniture torn by them. I've told them all and they're all putting up little grilles now. Now, madam, would you like to see your bathroom?'

When Mrs Lydiard came back she said to me, 'You look tired.'

'We had a problem,' I said.

'This is a nice place to rest.'

I gestured around. 'Looks lovely, doesn't it?'

'May we hope to see a little more of you here?'

'Who knows? Would be nice, though.'

'Oh, it would.'

Claire returned, wrapped in one of the guest robes I had provided and which had never been used. The fatigue of fear creased her face. Nobody knows how tiring fear is; it still creased mine.

'Dinner, I'm afraid, will take about another forty minutes,' said Mrs Lydiard.

That was her way of saying that she believed we should sit and drink and feel the warmth of the fire.

There we sat, as mourners, as victims, as two citizens of a planet that is sometimes glorious and sometimes vile. And sometimes, if we remain alert, it gives us the privilege of doing something vital for somebody else.

49

If life is full of surprises, one of its best tricks must be the speed of recovery. The nearest GP helped, an ex-navy doctor. His wife, also a GP, attended Claire.

The major immediate problem hanging over us had no physiological cure. We'd been there when a man was killed. The lover of this woman opposite me.

Physician, heal that.

I didn't know what to do about it and could ask no one's advice. My best possibility lay in Tynan.

'Where are you?'

'Can't tell you.'

'I can trace you, you know that.'

'Don't, please, Tynan. Just listen to me. Something I didn't tell you in Folkestone. Because I wanted to get away.'

He listened to the Jumièges horrors. 'Okay. This is murder we're talking. You shouldn't have run. You should have reported it. Jesus, Newman!'

'I know, I know. I don't want a lecture.'

'This isn't a lecture, this is a serious offence.'

'Do a deal?'

'This isn't the movies.' He had become worryingly official.

'If I give you the man who orchestrated Trafalgar Square and who killed Antony Safft – he told me he did and told me how he did it and told me about the manservant.'

Silence – the silence of Tynan thinking.

I was thinking quickly. 'His DNA – it'll be in the house, won't it? He went through all the papers.'

Tynan came back with a question.

'You say nobody knew you were there?'

'Yes.'

'I can't do a deal. But I can support your story.'

'So long as we're off the hook. I'll give you your information then.'

He toughened. 'I could arrest you. Accessory after the fact. Get my info that way.'

'I could play rough, too.'

That eased him. 'Okay. I hear what you're saying. But you'll be needed. I gotta report that now, you know that.'

'I know. Special pleading?' My uppermost impulse was for Claire. 'Please?'

'Yeh, sure. But you better play ball.'

'So – we get some peace?'

'Yeh. For a few days. I'll get this one moving. The French guys owe us. This one'll be a big story, though, and they'll all think it was the guy's war-crime stuff that got him killed.'

I said, 'Shall we do it in a civilized way?'

'Like?'

'Bring them over. We won't go there. I'll find a good hotel, I'll hire a suite and we'll do it over a long lunch.'

He agreed. 'Frogs'll love it.'

After dinner that first night in Rye, Claire and I continued to sit by the fire but spoke little. I kept falling asleep; so did she. We could scarcely speak. Once, when Claire went to the bathroom, Mrs Lydiard came to see me and offered to stay the night should Claire need her.

'I don't know what's the right thing to do,' I said. 'The man she lives with has just died violently.'

Mrs Lydiard adjusted her spectacles and said, 'On second thoughts, I think you'll look after her best. I'll personally come in first thing in the morning but I'll not draw attention to myself. Are Doctor and Mrs Doctor coming back?'

When, by the fire later, Claire began to close her eyes again, I said, 'I think you must sleep.'

I led her along the corridor – she could just about walk – to a room already made up, the Bay Room, on account of the window and the view.

'I shall be next door,' I said, 'if you need anything. Mrs Lydiard will be in first thing in the morning. Use the sleeping tablets.'

Claire said, 'I don't want to sleep alone.'

I never questioned her. She came to my room, where the fire still burned high. Leaving some lights on in the hallways and the long corridor, I went and bathed. When eventually I climbed into bed she seemed asleep.

We lay side by side, our bodies touching laterally.

Desperation is at its highest when it is passing. That night all the desperation I have ever known suffused my body like a slowly exploding bomb – and then departed. Shame lingered, at my own capacity for savage violence.

Some time during the night or dark morning I woke. Claire lay on her side now, facing away from me. I fell asleep again. The next sound I heard was a clock chiming and in bright blinking sunlight I counted with it up to twelve.

The doctors arrived again as requested. My hand gave cause for alarm; Claire had contusions and cuts; I was described as 'wounded'. When they had examined us and gone, all ointments and antibiotics prescribed afresh, Mrs Lydiard and I had what she liked to call 'a conference'.

'Will madam be staying? Because the house is, it's really for a man, and I'd need to get some things –'

'She'll be staying for as long as I can persuade her to,' I said with some fervour.

After that, smiling at Mrs Lydiard's surprise and pleasure, I walked back to the bedroom. Claire sat back against the pillows, her face that ghastly white colour again.

'How are you?'

'I don't know,' she said. 'I can't find anything to say.'

I agreed.

'Nicholas?'

'Yes.'

'D'you think he died instantly?'

'How much do you want to talk about it all?'

'Let me talk when I can. If you can – don't ask me questions. I'm sorry, I know you must be anxious . . .'

She took my hand and kissed it. I found I was in tears and didn't trouble to hide them.

'Is there any reason you're crying?' she asked. 'Or is it just everything?'

I wanted to say, I think it's you, but couldn't squeeze out the words.

She patted the sheets. I climbed in beside her and lay in her arms until the shadows gathered.

50

So much to do. So little to do. I did nothing.

Mrs Lydiard and I had another conference, sorted out some extra costs. I bathed again and attended the various injuries. The wrist worried me and the fingers hurt like hell. My face might have a small permanent scar under my right eye. Sorest of all were my clawed neck and my feet, where I had kicked so hard.

I thought hard about checking my answering machine – and then I remembered that I had only been gone forty-eight hours; I would do no telephoning.

In dressing gown and slippers I revisited my own house room by room and took pleasure in how much I liked it.

The Long Drawing Room looks out to sea, with a deep window seat. All my old books, the overflow from Cadogan Gardens, lined the shelves. I took down Frank Lloyd Wright's autobiography and sat to read. Half an hour later Mrs Lydiard brought me tea and two of her éclairs. My reading stopped.

What was left to do? Nothing much.

My mind had begun to race, a sign I was recovering. I thought about writing down the teeming questions. Claire held many of the answers. Some things might for ever remain a puzzle – such as the break-in at my flat for that lethal wiring, the randomness of the attack on the Tube. And Pearl.

Yes, Pearl. No, Pearl. Pearl must take care of himself. If he couldn't bring himself to tell me what bothered him I couldn't help. I'd done enough, suffered enough. His house would be finished in time for him to move in at Easter.

As for Mary Strait – I winced. Prepare for a backlash, I thought, but nothing I can't contain. With any luck she'll move on. I hadn't covered myself in glory across that encounter. Not a clue how to deal with it, so leave it alone. No doubt Elizabeth will read the Riot Act . . .

And Elizabeth herself? Never did find out what game she was playing. Wasn't as simple as matchmaking me with her niece, was it? Maybe she still has a game going on . . . Curious how trivial all those machinations feel now. Evil and violent death, when seen in the face, see off everything else.

I looked out of the window at the gathering fog and I thought, It's over. I have a new chapter in my life. I had better write it – and write it well.

An excitement gripped my heart, an excitement I had never known and had only read about. I knew what it was but dared not call it by its name. Leave it alone, leave it all severely alone. Whatever happens happens. But when I thought of Claire perhaps going back to Jumièges and perhaps taking up the threads of her old life there, I began to feel panic and I had to fight it off with real effort.

I fell asleep in my chair by the window, the fire crackling behind me in the room and its reflection glowing in the leaded panes. Something woke me – a soft hand on my cheek and a voice whispering, 'I came to see if you're all right.'

She sat.

'What has happened to me?' she said. 'I have caused so much distress to the men in my life.'

'Distress?'

'They said I was aloof, that I withheld, that I was remote.'

'That's what I am accused of,' I replied.

'Maybe we're both just lonely.'

'Maybe.'

'You won't die, will you?' she said to me.

'No,' I said. 'The gods don't love me enough.'

That night we found some clothes for Claire, principally my shirts. Mrs Lydiard had nervously bought her some underwear during the day at Marks & Spencer.

'Where I always shop,' Claire assured her.

51

New Year's Eve. I thought of venturing out but it rained and rained. We woke late and ate well. Mrs Lydiard's cuisine escalated.

In the early afternoon Claire asked me for a notebook: she wanted to write everything down. I read by the fire while she sat across from me. From time to time I stopped reading. I could hear the scratch of her pen on the page and the sound of her breathing. We might have been living in a past century.

Meal times varied. I told Mrs Lydiard we'd eat when hungry. She loved that and provided the most delicious snacks – leek soup with hot oatmeal bread, or a *tarte provençale*, or a feathery Stilton soufflé; she insisted Claire downed a few gallons of stewed fruit.

My manners returned. I found myself able to behave to Claire as I had always longed to behave to a woman. She would want for nothing, I told myself.

The doctors returned and after their examinations accepted a sherry. They left at six.

Claire said, 'Which would you rather do? Talk – or read what I've written?'

'Talk first,' I said. 'Then perhaps I might read it.'

'I've written it as a statement,' she said. 'In case I'm asked.'

I said, 'Perhaps tomorrow?'

She nodded. 'Good idea. New Year.'

I poured another drink. Heat from the fire stung my shins. The peace of the house comforted us like goosedown.

I looked at her over and over, her face lit by the fire. Not a sound could be heard. No outside world existed; everyone had gone away. The depth of the rooms and the age of the house and the stone of the fireplace took us and held us in a safety neither of us had ever known. Time moved forward an inch at a time. Time was away and somewhere else. No. Time was away and she was here.

I remember the single chime of the mantel clock at half past eight that evening. As the hand moved towards the half-hour and inside the glass the hammer of the brass mechanism lifted slowly and fell with a stutter to the bell, I was overcome with tender excitement. All day I had been fighting it off.

The word 'extraordinary' always has to be qualified; it has no global significance, not even a commercial dimension. Yet in terms of the change one man may make in himself in a lifetime, in terms of how he may say, 'Formerly I was like that, now I am to be like this,' the word 'extraordinary' had a profundity that night.

And here we sat, Claire and I, tired but no longer danger-ously so, opposite each other across the hearth for our third consecutive night. Soon Mrs Lydiard would bring dinner. She would leave us after that, to see the New Year in with her son and his family.

The clock chimed that half-past-eight chime and we both glanced at it. I looked around this big room that glowed with warm shadows – the lovely furniture I'd chosen so hopefully, the miniature grand piano I wanted to learn on, my favourite paintings on the walls, that exquisite rug I saw in Tunis. Elizabeth often asked me where I hid everything, accused me of keeping my possessions in a bank vault. My work, my money, my tunnel-vision commitment to my own infrastructure, planning regulations, services – they had, whatever their shortcomings, brought me all this.

Now they enabled me, I hoped, to give a prodigious depth

of comfort and safety to the woman opposite me. I remember looking at Claire and thinking, If only for this, if only for this moment and this woman – it has all been worth it; all the loneliness I never admitted to; all the pain over the failures no one else saw; the abstinence, the silent evenings, the dinner parties, the social events, the hollowness when the time came to leave. If they had all combined to help me recognize what had now arrived in my life they had all been worth it.

I decided, a clean and clear decision, that I would hide nothing of myself from this woman. No more deception through aloofness, no more verbal footwork, no more sleekness, no more smokescreen of sophistication.

Whatever happened, I would make myself open as I had never done in my life to another human being, not since I was eight, the last time I recalled feeling the warm cyclone of my mother's affection. The fact that I didn't know how to open my heart to anyone seemed not to halt me.

Claire picked up some change in the room's atmosphere. She looked at me in a question mark. The gentle chime died away. She stroked her throat again.

And I straightened up in my chair and said to her, 'I will only say this once, because it may not come out the right way again – *I would do anything in the world for you.*'

No need to say more. No more to say.

She went on looking at me for what must have been several seconds and then she looked into the fire. Her fingers stroked up and down to her chin.

Then she spoke. 'I've always known that when it came along – I would recognize it.'

We said nothing else. How could we? I had changed more in a moment than I had ever envisaged. My entire inner being felt as though encased in glass; a loud noise would shatter it.

I like to think it all happened in that chime of time. It

didn't: it had been happening. I believe Oradour triggered it. Something about those black, forlorn ruins made me think that there must be one force in life capable of stopping such a thing ever happening again, the force people call 'love'. Every summer the vine grows again on the corner where those men died; I had stroked its tendrils and on the opposite wall put my finger in the bullet holes . . .

When Mrs Lydiard brought in the beginnings of dinner she never said a word, merely looked from one to the other of us.

And then, when she had set out the plates of oyster mousse, she left the room and came back with a jug of white flowers. Where she got them at that time of year I do not know; I didn't recollect her leaving the house all afternoon.

Claire said only one more thing during dinner. 'I must telephone my father later. I want to make sure he's had a flu injection.'

I said nothing. Not a word. Some time during dinner I put on Alfred Brendel's Schubert Impromptus and marvelled at how complete and simple everything seemed.

No need to stay up for the New Year: we had our own emotion. Before we went to bed we stood at the window and looked up at the moon. I could see half a fog over Romney Marsh. We didn't touch actively; she leaned her shoulder on mine.

'I remember how frightened I was when I read *Great Expectations* the first time,' Claire said. 'D'you think Magwitch is still out there?'

A sense of responsibility I had never before felt coursed through me. My simple words 'I would do anything for you' had, I now realized, said all I could want to say. No great statements of passionate love, or undying devotion came to me; I couldn't, it seemed, speak flowers and roses. Indeed, I had no idea how to express love. Whatever my successes and failures, I could only say what I knew. That sense of responsibility and willingness seemed to be, for me at any rate, what is generally called 'love'.

'Did you know?' I asked her. 'Did you know I felt like this for you?'

'Nicholas, how could I? I can only speak for me. And I knew something about me. I knew it within five minutes of meeting you at Oradour.' She caught my hand. 'You don't have to say anything. You don't have to feel anything. Whatever you feel is all right by me. I want nothing and I expect nothing.'

52

The next day and the next and the next and the next, we slept and sat and sat and slept. I developed a streaming cold, Claire a sore throat. One of the bruises on her shoulder swelled alarmingly and she needed an antibiotic injection. We postponed the long debriefing talk.

On the night of the fourth of January, Tynan rang me on the mobile.

'So?'

'So what?'

'How's it going, how's the totty?'

'Still out of it. She's very shaken.'

He expressed sympathy, this emotional chameleon.

'Look after her. Toast and tea. Slice o' Wonderloaf does the biz. When's too soon to bring in the Frogs? They're hoppin' up and down.' He wheezed a laugh.

'Good question,' I said. 'I'm trying to split the difference – between getting it over with and when she's fit enough.'

'I'll buy that,' he said. 'It'll be a strain.'

He had obviously abandoned all officiousness.

I said to him, 'Let me try. I'll call you back.'

Claire opted for the soonest possible date.

Tynan always surprises me. He chose the hotel – in Eastbourne; he booked the room and he laid on a car for the French detectives. I still had the rental car and meant to hold it as long as necessary.

The room, ancient and Victorian, had been a large parlour. Tynan stood by the fireplace, drawing his height up to lean an elbow on the mantel; he failed. I had never seen him in a suit.

'See,' he said proudly, pointing to the fire, the table set for five, the ambience. 'I got 'em to do all this.'

He greeted Claire with warmth and regard. 'How old're you?' he said.

The Frenchmen laughed.

'I won't answer that even if you're a superintendent.'

'Bli-mee, remind me never to arrest you!'

I loved the way he was smitten with Claire.

We sat down and began immediately. Claire and I agreed we would focus only on the events of that day. I, in an aside to Tynan, kept the Antony Safft business and Berlin separate. I pleaded exhaustion, told him I'd give him a full statement.

'Extradition's going to be a bugger from Germany,' he said.

'But aren't we all in Europe together?'

'Fuck Europe. Every time I see those football thugs I hear the sound of jackboots. Why'dja think I'm doing this job?'

Cool without being cold, businesslike and pleased with Claire's almost native command of French, the police asked her question after question. They had clearly decided to take the line Tynan expected – and I presume he led them along that way. Most of their questions related to Philippe's war-criminal hunts: they wanted to know details of threats.

Our stickiest moment came when we described Philippe's death. To the inevitable question 'Why did you run, why did you not report this murder?' I never expected to have a good answer – at least not one better than the truth.

Which was – 'I wanted to get the hell out of there and bring this woman to safety. This man's uncle, my friend, had been savagely killed a few months before, I myself had been attacked simply because I was to be the man's executor and I wanted out of there.'

The one with the hardest face said, 'What you have done is a serious crime in France.'

I played a trump card. 'My need was to get the protection of my own police.'

Tynan rode shotgun for me on that. 'You'd know nothing about this if Mr Newman hadn't told me. Anyway, he was helping us on something else.'

The questioning went on. One of the detectives asked Claire if she had heard of 'the Lumière bank'.

She said, 'No.' I knew she lied.

'Never heard the name?'

Non.

Absolument pas?

Absolument pas, she said.

Tynan hit me with another surprise – a burst of French that made the detectives laugh. One of them, with a massive nose, looked like a pugilist. Claire laughed and I diverted.

'I never knew you spoke French.'

Tynan said, 'I have a beautiful mind.'

Claire said to the detectives, 'I think M'sieu Tynan learned his French on the quayside in Marseilles.'

Everybody laughed again and the ice we'd been skating on thickened under our feet.

We left them at about five o'clock; we would never hear from them again. I had no doubt of that.

In the car Claire asked, 'D'you think that's it?'

'Yes,' I said.

'Then why don't you and I talk now, so that we get it all said?'

'Are you not too tired?'

'I'd rather do it now.'

We began at the beginning – her relationship with Antony. I reminded her of her discomfort at Oradour, how she skated over the question of how she and Philippe met. Antony met her at a Foreign Office dinner when she was eighteen, her father's escort for the evening. He offered her a job, not in his office but in his home. She became a kind of personal assistant.

'In practice I was a concubine,' she said.

'A concubine?'

'He kept me for himself at first and then he lent me to what he called his "classier" friends. I knew your name but he kept me away from you.'

'Why did you go along with this?'

'Two reasons. He kept me supplied.'

'Ah,' I said.

'It's okay. I'm over that now. That's a long story.'

'And the second reason?'

'The second reason,' she said, drawing a deep breath, 'is that I found out how he made his money.'

'The profiteering?' I asked.

She was astonished. 'How did you know?'

'That, too, is a long story, and it's just about to end,' I said. 'M'sieu Tynan, as you call him, is about to settle it.'

Claire's father had first voiced a suspicion about Antony's money. 'The City is a gossip factory,' she said. 'No secrets there.'

One day, distressed at Antony's use of her and unable to break his hold, she went looking.

'I found it,' she said. 'In fact he didn't hide it very well.'

'The Lumière bank, I presume.'

'You are quick, Nicholas. Antony knew I knew. When I came off drugs he had a problem. He told me about it very calmly. He might have to kill me. The compromise we worked out was that I would be taken over by Philippe.'

'But you loved Philippe?'

'And I loved Antony, too. Not the way they wanted and not the way they expected. I don't believe they could be loved in an ordinary way. The money, the taint they felt from it and the way it clashed with their greed for it – and their need to hide its source. It was all too much. So they coped with their own incapacities by telling me I didn't love them. It's a thing men do.'

I shivered a little at her accuracy.

'I couldn't survive unless I kept some distance. First from Antony and then from Philippe. For years I thought I was only alive because they couldn't bring themselves to kill me. Then slowly I realized they weren't killers. Deceivers, yes, killers – no, they couldn't kill anyone. About four or five years ago I relaxed and by then I couldn't leave them. I was still attached to Antony and had grown towards Philippe.'

'How did the profiteering happen?'

It seemed that in 1941 Antony and two other young lawyers had intercepted the transfer of confiscated Jewish bank accounts to Reich accounts in Paris and London and diverted the funds. Unknown to them a firm of German businessmen with affiliations to the Reich had the same idea. The Germans got some funds, but learned in time that they never got all that they had been promised.

'Not all accounts had been transferred and they missed out heavily. Antony covered the trail so effectively the Germans never got to him. Eventually, when the Wall came down, those businessmen, who had hidden in East Germany, felt free to investigate.'

I asked, 'But how did Philippe get involved?'

In heavy rain we entered the town of Rye.

According to Claire, Antony experienced a profound conflict of emotions after the war. It hit him when he heard of the death camps and when he visited Oradour. But the money he had intercepted made him fabulously wealthy and he couldn't give it up – not simply because of the wealth but because of the crime. He decided to hide where he would never be found – in a welter of attempted retribution against the Nazis. For half a century Antony had hidden behind his alleged sympathies.

'Is that why he allowed the impression he was Jewish?'
I asked. 'I watched you and Philippe field my question the
night we were at Le Chanticleer.'

'Obviously, if he were Jewish he would never be suspected
of having stolen Jewish money.'

'Why did he pretend to be gay?'

'He didn't,' said Claire. 'Where'd you get that idea?'

'The police.'

'No. He wasn't gay. He wasn't very highly sexed, but he
wasn't gay. He liked men – but he was homoerotic, not
homosexual.'

'What's the difference?' I asked.

'You mean you don't know?' She waited while I drove the
car through the gateway. 'Many men – in fact all the men
I like – are homoerotic. They like the company of men, but
it's not sexual. I expect you're homoerotic.'

'Don't know,' I said gloomily. But my gloom was connected to the fact that one day, and I didn't know when,
I was going to have to tell her I'd met Antony's killer. Not
now; she'd had enough for now – but what came next blew
that apart.

'You kept on leaving messages for me. And I couldn't get
hold of you. Then you said, "Come over to Jumièges," and
then you said at the same time, "Don't come over." What
was all that about?'

This distressed her. 'I need to be indoors to tell you.'

Mrs Lydiard brought us drinks and promised us dinner in
an hour.

'Have a bath,' I urged Claire.

'Only if you'll come and talk to me.'

She'd fallen dreadfully morose. I brought her drink to the
bathroom. The sight of her body stunned me, as did her ease
in my presence. I also saw that she carried many more bruises
from the Chunnel than she'd admitted. She lay back, quiet
and distant; her breasts floated a little.

'I will answer your question, Nicholas. I promise.' Then she thought and said, 'No, I'll answer it now.' I watched as she gathered courage.

'Philippe knew all of Antony's business. He also knew that Antony had been found at last by these East Germans.'

'Hang on,' I said. 'The irony is, while Antony was looking for Nazis –'

Claire interrupted: 'They were looking for him.'

We both smiled ruefully.

'Philippe was a fine negotiator and he believed he could negotiate them away. He couldn't. The only offer they made him was his life – and mine –'

I squeaked, 'Your life?'

'My life – in return for all of Antony's estate. Every part of it.'

'When was this offer made?'

'Oh, last year some time.'

'Estate? But Antony was still alive.'

'Yes, but they knew they were going to kill him. They told Philippe.'

'Why didn't Philippe tell Antony?'

'He didn't need to. *They* told Antony.'

She raised herself in the bath. It really was the most extraordinary business – hearing these revelations while gazing at that wondrously desirable body and my heart was on fire with the whole thought of her and our future.

'Now,' she said, 'the bad part. Philippe was shocked beyond belief that Antony had named you as an executor. He didn't know you but he couldn't bear the thought of an innocent and talented man being drawn into this fire. He knew they would kill you. But of course he had mixed emotions. He wanted to hold on to some of the wealth. He also thought the Germans shouldn't get it – that it should be repatriated. But he thought he could buy them off. Above all, he didn't want anyone killed. He thought you'd help him in all that.'

'Hence his need to see me in Jumièges?'

'Yes.' She told her story coolly but the weight of what she felt was coming across. Her maturity astonished me.

'Philippe pressed me to ask you to Jumièges to negotiate. I went along with it, then, as you know, tried to refuse. I had mixed feelings, too. When he saw that you wouldn't step down as an executor he was very distressed. But, in his mixed motives, very elated – he thought he might make a stand with you. Then the mood changed. Those photographs arrived. Philippe changed. He became very depressed, told me that he had been instructed to get you to Jumièges. He was going to try one last pressure on you.'

'I knew something was up,' I said. 'He didn't get the will from the lawyers. Meaning Antony's killers had a copy which they gave to Philippe.'

'They meant to kill you,' Claire said. She had a small mole on the underside of her left breast. 'But I didn't know that until after you'd agreed to come. That's why I was so upset when you got there. That's really why I said, "Come, don't come".'

I said, 'Why did they kill Philippe?'

'An error,' she said. 'That was meant to have been your head. You saw how he rearranged the chairs. With you dead he controlled Antony's will.'

My recent experiences had steeled my palate and I was able to carry on looking for explanations.

'But at the Chanticleer,' I said, 'he seemed to be asking my help to find the Oradour Nazi. And yet you're saying he wanted me out for my own safety.'

'As I say – he had mixed motives. Philippe didn't decide his final position towards you – "They" did. He even had mixed feelings where I was concerned. What bothers me is that he might have given them me. To save his own life.'

I had to tell her. 'I met them. In Berlin. Told them I had no quarrel with them.'

She took the shock well. 'Did they believe you?'

'Yes. They said it might take some time "for the order to reach the troops". I suppose that's why we were attacked on the train. The "foot soldiers" didn't know I had suddenly become valuable.'

'And the shooting at Jumièges?'

'Same reason.'

'That's more or less it,' she agreed.

'I still don't know how they did some of the things. I mean, the Tube attack?'

'Oh, I know about that. They followed you.'

I mused on the questions that had racked me for so long. 'The knife, the flowers, they were easy. The attack at St Gilles?'

'Don't,' she said. 'That was my worst moment until the end. I think I knew that was going to happen. If you ever want to know anything about guilt – just ask me.'

'How did they get into my flat – to do that wiring?'

'I don't know. They are the most terrifying people. I showed you those photographs.'

I reached for her hand. 'It's okay, it's over. I know it is.'

'I'm worried, Nicholas. Berlin is only the façade.'

'Where's the rest?'

'They hide. Albania, perhaps. Somewhere across the Adriatic. They use Venice as a port of entry. So much shipping. Philippe used to say, "I live in terror of the Dalmatian coast." It took me some time to understand.'

'Did they get involved in all those Yugoslavian wars?'

'Once a profiteer always a profiteer? I don't know. They're headquartered over there somewhere. Antony tried to meet them in Venice several times. So did Philippe. And in Munich. Their tentacles are everywhere. Those football hooligans, for instance – they finance them, they run them at times like a militia. Munich and Venice are the two control centres. And

I think, largely for the buzz. Or to do a job of work, such as –'
she winced – 'you.'

'So this is an elaborate business,' I said.

'Very.'

'Then we're well out of it.'

Claire said, 'Yes – but there's still the matter of the will.'

I replied, 'I know what to do with the will. I'll give the
lawyer power of attorney. I'll write to him tomorrow. The
money has to go back to where it came from. I will be giving
all the details of the Berlin connection to M'sieu Tynan.'

'You clever man,' she said. She hesitated. 'You will do
that?'

The question meant more than it seemed.

'What do you mean?'

'Nicholas, I would rather die than let those evil people
have a penny. It must go back – to the families it was
stolen from.'

She spoke with an unusual passion.

I said, 'Is there a reason – I mean, that I don't know about
– a factual reason, why you feel so strongly?'

'Haven't you guessed?'

'No.'

She climbed out of the bath. 'At the risk of being clichéed,
my lovely Nicholas . . .' She stood naked before me. 'If I were
a man you'd know my reason by now.'

'What do you mean?'

'You don't get it, do you?' She kissed me on the top of
the head. 'I'm the one who's Jewish.'

I said, 'Hang on. Jewish kids don't take drugs.'

'That's a prejudiced remark. And anyway, I did.'

Dinner that night proved the best yet, peaceful and easier
to talk. When Claire needed more wine I didn't reach across
the table – I rose and stood beside her to pour. That way I
could touch her hair.

Already we were healing. She spoke of Philippe a great

deal, of how driven he was. He had suspected since a student that his uncle had been in 'some great something'. When he discovered – that was why he became a Nazi-hunter.

Then Antony transfixed Philippe with the same mixed motive – by giving him unlimited funds to pursue them. She described how the mixedness of the motive eventually took over until it corrupted Philippe's original motive of expiating the family's crime.

I went to bed, exhausted. During the night I sensed Claire awake beside me. We held hands but never spoke. The feeling of security was something I had never felt as an adult. Not much as a child, either; I could remember Mother's warmth, but then it all seemed to go away and never come back.

Next afternoon I said to Mrs Lydiard, 'You haven't had an hour free since we got here.'

She accepted, leaving us food. I spent the first domestic evening and night of my life as an adult male-female couple – being ordinary, fixing the fire, preparing food; we even washed dishes. Every time I found myself near Claire, I touched her or hugged her or kissed her softly; at supper, I attended her like a butler or a footman. If I had seen a film of it I would not have believed it was me. Not the old me. At ten o'clock I telephoned Mrs Lydiard from the kitchen with Claire listening and gave her the weekend off.

It became the most lovely three days of lazy hours and small domestic chores. I had to find the woodshed and we had to order milk; I had to light the fires and Claire hoovered the rooms we used. A kind of happiness came over me that I'd never believed in. If I came across it in a novel I skipped the pages; if I saw it in the cinema I dismissed it as saccharine. Sometimes we just stood in the middle of a room, our arms around each other. I never let her lift anything, I ran to her side.

For Sunday lunch we had cheese, biscuits, fruits, crêpes and sweet wine. I needed to sleep and went to bed, Claire sat reading and looking out to sea. Dozing, I felt her slip into bed beside me. She rose on an elbow and kissed me and fell back.

Then we devoured each other. I clawed at her without direction; she slammed her fists into the bedding out of rage and need. Within minutes I was inside her and we both burst into tears and held and held and held as if tomorrow would never come. She didn't call me 'Philippe', although I expected it. No name came from her, and no sound except the screaming and then the whimpering as she buried her face in my shoulder. My mind went completely clear and free. She seemed unable to stop sobbing and I just held her inside my arms. How could I dry her tears when I was unable to stop my own?

That evening she asked, 'Were we horrid to Philippe's memory?'

'I don't know. I don't think so. I hope not.'

'Neither do I. But I should be the one who answers it.'

Oh, but again, again, again. This time she climbed on my knees by the fire and the feelings in us were more bitter and more sweet, and it seemed to me that if we were to go on making love it would be different every time . . .

Afterwards, she said, 'If Mrs Lydiard were here would she have heard us?'

I stroked her hair. 'She would be delighted,' I said. 'She's a true romantic.'

Claire stood to retrieve her robe and the fire flickered on her, on all the hollows and shadows and whiteness.

53

On Monday the world at large returned to its desks after the holiday. Time to apply a gentle normality.

I telephoned the office. Lemon told me that Hal, in a meeting, couldn't come to the phone. She sounded odd.

I said to her, 'You'll need to know, so keep the address to yourself and use only the mobile number.'

Strangely, she never asked how I was. I told her to tell Hal I called but that I didn't wish to be disturbed. We arranged for the delivery of the final Pearl drawings. I intended to complete the job in Rye with full instructions by phone and by courier.

Next I telephoned Elizabeth. Della told me, 'Miss Bentley has gone to town.' She made it sound like a movie title. 'For a meeting,' she added. I gave Della the mobile number, told her to have Elizabeth call me.

The answering machine at Cadogan Gardens had been a matter of some dread. Finally I checked it. Not a word. Astonishing. Not a message. Not a sausage. No Mary Strait. No Elizabeth. Who's in the doghouse?

Mid-morning I finished my telephoning and reviewed my time. If I wanted to stretch it I had no cause to be in the office until the end of the month. Lemon's rundown of my diary-listed meetings I could easily miss. Three uninterrupted weeks stretched ahead in which I only had the logistics of Pearl's house to bother me; my car, the rented car, insurance, Tynan, all these would work out. Recuperation could be total. Peace descended.

I had lunch with Claire and we stood for ten minutes

on the balcony – her first look at the sky since Philippe's death. She didn't want clothes; she had no desire to shop; she 'might' get her hair cut in a few days.

On Wednesday drama broke out and I discovered Elizabeth's long game. I rang Lemon to confirm that I had received Pearl's drawings. Again she felt awkward.

'Hal wants to talk to you.'

'Chief, howya doing?'

'Fine. You? The boys and Pam have a good holiday? Did you ski?'

'Yah, yah. Forgotten by now.'

He behaved differently towards me; he was chippy and disrespectful. Not in what he said – more in the tone.

Coldly I asked, 'Hal, is everything all right?'

'Sure, Chief. Not a bother. Something eating you?'

I felt uneasy. Later I rang Lemon.

'Transfer this call into my office,' I said, 'and speak to me from there.'

'I can't.'

'Why not?'

'Because there's somebody in there.'

'Lemon, there's not supposed to be anybody in there.'

'But there is.'

I sensed it would not take long to draw tears.

'Right, Lemon. When can you speak to me? What is all this?'

'I'll ring you back.'

Five minutes later she called from a payphone.

'Where are you?'

'Round the corner. Something's hap-pened.' When Lemon exaggerates her accent I know she's under pressure.

'What?'

On Monday morning, the office's first day back, Hal had called an Emergency General Meeting, saying he'd been 'unable to get hold of' me. He took the chance I wouldn't turn up; it would transpire that he'd got everybody in at half past eight. The purpose? To reappoint Elizabeth as a partner. Even if I'd been there I'd have been in a minority, because of the temporary surrender of paper to accommodate Mary Strait and Georgy-Porgy. The meeting voted to reappoint. New 'paper' was issued: my shareholding, temporarily below fifty per cent, was cut to below forty.

Lemon said, 'I didn't know where to ring you, I didn't know until Monday.'

She talked freely. Hal had organized it all. She believed he had cut short his holiday, had meetings with Elizabeth and Mary Strait.

'Where, Lemon?'

'I think down at Faircombe.'

So Hal had found a way to feel liked by Elizabeth. The treacherous bastard. Not exactly far-seeing, either.

My anger, buried since the Tunnel, flared. Mary Strait's revenge. Elizabeth's tricks. The 'interest' in the company had always been notional but it had legal standing. It would take a horrendous battle to get things back to where they had been.

I felt impotent all across the problem. If I rang and asked I would reveal that I knew and in my absence they'd sack Lemon. If I didn't ring – what changes would have been made when I got back? Over lunch I brooded. Then I decided to sit it out, wait to see who would have the courage to tell me first. Elizabeth had played her usual long game and played it brilliantly. Was that what Hal had tried to tell me when he rang me in Berlin? I had completely forgotten his call. But he could have done more. Never trust a man who picks between his teeth with a little piece of cardboard . . .

On and on my thoughts seethed. No wonder Elizabeth never rang.

I told Claire. Should I tell her the whole story – Mary Strait and all of that?

Claire said, 'Mary Strait told me in Le Chanticleer that she meant to marry you. Whether you wanted it or not.'

'Hell hath no fury,' I said, bitter at my own stupidity. 'What do I do now?'

'Nothing, I suggest. You'll not be able to win this quickly. But you will win it.'

'How? I don't see a way?'

'The moral authority. And you're brighter than any of them.'

'You don't know that.'

'Yes, I do.'

I felt soothed and optimistic. Then I began to see-saw between comfortableness and bitterness about Hal. About myself. Mary Strait had nailed me. Jesus, that's hard to take.

For the rest of the week I never let Claire out of my sight except when she went to the lavatory. Claire was as possessive of me. I believed the relationship had begun as it meant to continue. Unquestionably, given my configuration, storms lay ahead. If and when they happened, I would do all in my power to quell them.

On Friday, I unwittingly left my mobile phone on. It rang, late.

'Answer it,' she said.

'D'you mind if I do?' This was our first uninvited incursion.

Pearl's voice came at me like a banshee.

'They tell me, Nicholas, they tell me. It's tomorrow, they gonna get me tomorrow.'

I froze. 'Where are you?'

'In London. They gonna get me.'

'Give me your number. Now calm down, Johan. Calm down.'

Bit by bit I got from him the fact that he had been hiding, disappearing, because of violent threats. He would not say whom he suspected; he would not say why he was being threatened.

'They all gonna be there, Nicholas, I know it.'

'I'll keep in touch. I'll keep calling you. Keep your phone on. You can always switch it off if a call comes through that you don't want to take. Now I'll call you in an hour, I'm just finishing dinner.'

Claire said, 'What's he like? Philippe mentioned him.'

I told her, in as much detail as I could.

'But we must help him.'

I said, 'No, Claire. He doesn't want to be helped.'

'Those are the very people who most want help.'

'I saw him, Claire. The night before Jumièges. He wouldn't say. There's nothing I can do.'

Something in my tone struck her.

'There must be. You're resourceful.'

I shook my head. 'This is a police matter. I'll ring Tynan.'

'It's you Pearl wants help from.'

'No. Not my job.'

She put down her glass. 'Is it because he's black, Nicholas?'

I reddened, I know it. 'You're beginning to sound like Elizabeth Bentley.'

'You have too large a spirit to harbour any prejudice,' she said. 'Prejudice is one of those convenient feelings. You don't need those.'

'I'm still not going.'

'The boy is scared. I could hear his voice across the room.'

'Claire, haven't I been through enough?'

'But this is connected to Antony too.'

That was the argument I feared she would use.

'I will do one thing,' I promised. 'I will ring his mother.'

Sebastiaan Pearl answered. 'Oh, hi. No, she's not here, she's gone to London with my father, something about Johan, he rang.'

'Is everything all right?'

'No, not really, but I don't know anything about it, Petchi's always getting himself into trouble.'

Sebastiaan Pearl replaced the telephone and I knew in my gut Claire had won.

Tynan already knew. 'Yeh. Something's up. Lotta guys here who shouldn't be here. Scum from abroad. Nasty. Why do I love my job? 'Cos I hate that vermin.'

Claire asked me what I was going to do. I said I thought I'd try and meet Pearl.

'Tell him.'

'No.'

'Do. Tell him.'

I rang his hotel. He answered his room number immediately.

'It's all right, it's Nicholas.' He sounded tearful. 'I'll come to the game. Would you like to meet me afterwards?'

'No. Before. I'm going to Holland after.'

I relayed the arrangements to Tynan, all done in Claire's earshot.

'Happy now?'

She nodded. 'I think this really will be the end of it all,' she said.

In the morning Mrs Lydiard gave Claire the number of a hairdresser in Rye; she made her appointment and we kissed goodbye. I said I might bring Pearl back with me, if that proved appropriate.

Pearl had asked me to meet him at the Hilton in St John's Wood, where the team were staying. He wanted me to follow the team coach to the ground. He said he needed to see me there when he looked out of the coach window.

I waited where he said. Exactly on time he arrived. As he walked towards me two team-mates intercepted him in a friendly way but he indicated me and kept walking. They followed him and just as we shook hands they said to me, 'Get out of it, mate.'

I said, 'I beg your pardon.'

'Ooooo, "I beg your parding",' and wagged their heads like drag queens. 'C'mon, Pearly,' they urged, 'you don't wanna be –'

'I'm okay, fellas,' and he brushed them away.

The bigger of the two arched an eyebrow at me.

'What's all that about?'

'Pay no attention, man, they just fooling around. You here afterwards?'

'How much time have you got off?'

'I'm so scared I can't walk. Here, man. Keep this for me.' He handed me a small leather briefcase.

'Johan, are you going to tell me why you're scared?'

'I promise I will after the game. I got you a ticket.' He handed it to me. 'It's down near the touchline. If you see something bad beginning, man, will you be there for me?'

I couldn't bear to point out to him the ill-placed logistics of trying to help him in a crowd of fifty thousand people – of trying to get to him, even.

What he wanted of me I couldn't quite ascertain – comfort, moral support; these seemed more possible than crowd protection or an escape route. But he wanted me there and that is what I undertook. I decided not to mention Tynan to him.

I locked his briefcase in the car boot. When the coach left the hotel I slotted in behind it. At the first set of traffic lights someone threw a missile which clanged off the side. Pearl came to the rear window and checked that I was where I'd said I would be.

At the ground the coach discharged the players in full view of the arriving fans – another mistake. Pearl walked to the car, rapped it briefly and gave me a raised thumb. Someone else rapped – much harder; it had to be Tynan.

'Got you a permit, Christ knows how.'

He waited while I parked.

'Show me your comp,' he snapped. 'Quick.' He examined the ticket. 'Stay here.'

I waited inside the precincts. Through the gate I could see a much heavier police presence than I had so far observed in my small football experience.

The home team arrived. Fans swarmed to the coach. I felt the excitement and relished it. I thought, Isn't it ironic? Antony didn't manage to convert me to football when he was alive – and has done so since he died.

My thoughts ranged over Antony. He hadn't changed in my mind. The story of his life altered no opinion I held. Were he alive, and were the subject up for discussion, I would make my disapproval plain. Had I been assured by him that his 'cover' had a sincere and not a cynical intent I should find the atonement somewhat acceptable. Until I thought of the people robbed.

We had a discussion once, Antony and I, about the war. He disliked my distance from it; I disliked his involvement. We did agree on a scale of values – that the Holocaust must remain untouched in its position as the greatest single crime of that or almost any other war. But I remember that he became uncomfortable when I raised a favourite topic – the property.

I said how difficult I found it to imagine being a Jew in, say, Berlin and one day being told to vacate the home I had carefully built up and nurtured and protected for my family. And then to meet on the staircase the local German family to whom my home was being allocated free.

It surprised me that he didn't agree with me. It surprised me more that he was shifty about it. When I pressed the point he said, 'Well, you know, I wonder if all that wasn't exaggerated.'

'Antony,' I said, it was on one of our post-lunch walks by the Thames, 'it was on a scale so large it has never been measured and the people who got those apartments, probably because of their Nazi party sympathies – they are still living in them. And so are their children. Surely that's a cause to take up. You're a property man.'

He changed the subject.

A more devastating thought now began to afflict me. I had taken part as an investor – at his invitation – in at least three of his big property deals. My profits proved handsome; from the biggest of them, my take eventually amounted to four million. Tainted money? Haven't I participated in a war crime? Just as that pleasant little thought hit me Tynan returned.

'What's happening? Should I be sitting down?'

'There was a burglary here last night.'

'Significant.'

'No. Nothing taken. Normally they go for the bar – the fags 'n' booze. Nothing. *Nada*. We've got the sniffer dogs in. Hey, you could help.'

I followed him. Security melted before us. He walked me through the stewards.

'Stand here.' We had reached the halfway line. 'If you designed this place where would you put the fast exits, meaning also the fast access?'

I looked. The widest possibilities lay behind each goal.

'What do you want to know for?' I had never seen Tynan tense; I had heard him urgent, as when he tried to recall me from Berlin. But now his face tightened like a drum.

'If these scum stage something, they're gonna have a stunt they're gonna pull. One of my lads thought they might block exits. Then start a fuss.'

I sucked in my breath.

'Right. Amen,' said Tynan.

'Give me a moment,' I said.

'Can't mate, gotta go, I'll touch base.' For a man so small and so plump, and with such specific gravity, he could almost evaporate.

A steward took me to my seat. I stood and inspected the exits. A mob blocking them would cause havoc. Something about the goal arrested my eye. Bizarrely, Cadogan Gardens flashed into my mind. But the image remained undefined.

A voice called me – I turned; Lemon and her boyfriend, our new draughtsman. Their presence bothered me too – I wanted to talk to her and I bloody wanted to find out how he'd voted. But we'd exchanged no more than a word when Georgy-Porgy dragged her away. I watched them go. Lemon has superb legs.

A sense of disturbance returned to me. I had tried not to think of the office débâcle – but I couldn't put it out of my head. What brooder, such as I am, could? Yes, I'll win it back but I felt savagely hurt. Who voted against me? Who? Who?

The excitement I felt at the prospect of the game took on the red tinge of fear again. I thought of Claire and looked at my watch – perhaps at her hair appointment about now? I missed her – but she wasn't up to facing a crowd.

My seat placed me the closest yet to the field of play. I would be able to see the expressions on Black Pearl's face.

Like those lights that flash in pairs, giving alternating signals, my mind went back and forth between the goal and Lemon, Lemon and the goalposts. Cadogan Gardens. The bursting bathroom.

No, can't get it, it's like a sneeze that won't come.

The players came out. Fields of praise. The theatre when the lights go down. The orchestra tuning up. I don't appreciate my life enough. I have become blasé but this is good for me, the real world. My God, look at what I have survived!

In the preliminaries, Pearl ferreted along the touchline and I knew he was looking for me. He had evidently checked the seating and assessed where to find me.

'Look behind you,' he called to me.

Two rows back sat his mother, Elma, and a man who from

333

his appearance could only have been Johan's father. Elma saw me and we acknowledged. The crowd had all but filled. A vacant seat remained behind me. I should have known – reserved for Tynan. He arrived.

'Come up and see me some time.'

We were in for a day of Brewer's *Phrase and Fable*, I could tell.

'Where's the problem?' I asked quietly.

Staring straight ahead, he said, 'To your left, down in the corner, and to your right, down in the corner. That's why I asked you. They're concentrated near the goals.'

'Most vulnerable points,' I agreed.

'Ever architected a football stadium?'

'No, I'd love to.'

'Talk to us if you do; nobody ever asks us.'

Tynan rubbed his hands back and forth, back and forth.

I said to him, 'Are you worried?'

'I'm always worried.'

His breath could thin paint.

Whistle. Kick-off. In the opening minute the Black Pearl laid it on, I presume, for his parents and, I hoped, for me. Right in front of us he simply outwitted his opponents by sheer skill and broke out of a group tackle and crossed the ball, where nothing much came of it. Such a vivid green, the grass.

'Pinpoint,' said Tynan approvingly. 'Why's he need all the stuff he's into?'

'Do we know what it is?'

'Can't be sure. But it's causing pressure.'

'I think he's an innocent,' I said.

'His boss thinks so too. But he sure gets the scum round him.'

Pearl again, in front of our faces, flicking and feinting. He had such grace and such good humour; he looked like someone enjoying himself to the full. This time he fell and

334

an opponent fell with him, and when I saw Johan help him up I saw his kindness to the other player.

For long periods they kept Pearl out. The home side retained possession, that nonchalant stroking back and forth across the breadth of the pitch. It's more than movement or skill, I thought. It's more than winning, or outwitting, or breaching their defences to plant something deep in their citadel. It is a series of controlled and uncontrolled movements within a space – that is what makes it like architecture. Lovely thought – but I can hear what Tynan would say: 'Oh, yeah? Tell it to that cokehead with number eight on his shirt, or that piece of shit up there in the stand defiling the England shirt he's wearing. Fuck that, chum.'

A new thought blazed at me, an unfinished thought, too extraordinary to give voice to, but I had already said, 'Tynan!' and he turned.

'Nothing,' I said. 'Something's trying to tell me something.' Cadogan Gardens. Trafalgar Square. No.

I said, 'Sorry. Can't reach it.'

'Keep trying. That's how we get there sometimes.'

He grew more and more tense, chewing gum, jaws circling like a concrete mixer.

A break. Goalkeeper throws a long ball to Pearl a few yards from us and like lightning he covers the ground. Defenders race back as he arrows inwards to go it alone.

'Tynan,' I screamed, 'Tynan, I have it, it's the net! My flat! Cadogan Gardens. The net!' How did I know? I don't yet understand.

He didn't waste a second. As he knew the way, I raced after him.

I could see Pearl pounding through and hoped the defender who tackled would, for once, beat him. He didn't. Pearl rounded him with the grace of a yacht. We weren't going to get there. I recall registering that the fans in the corner as we passed didn't cheer. They started to rumble forward. Tynan

335

turned two uniformed officers and a steward around and we all ran in the same direction. I think I was shouting.

The crowd told me what had happened – they jumped to their feet and my line of vision was blocked. I could see Pearl's legs crossing the goal line and I screamed his name – it seemed to echo. Then everything froze. Tynan was on the pitch with the linesman and they were running flat-out towards the goal.

I can see Pearl now. He does that strut of his on the line. Next he'll turn, there he goes. The goalkeeper is standing looking on. Pearl lashes the ball again into the net.

'Go on doing that,' I beg at the top of my useless voice. 'Don't do anything else, no jokes, kick the ball again, don't touch the net.'

I have the good sense not to run onto the pitch but I head for the rear of the goal. My mind is yelling, 'I hope I'm right and I hope I'm wrong.' I'm right but where is the source? Oh, shittttt! The small lights along the perimeter of the field. They took a feed off that. The break-in last night. Central control or individual switch. Doesn't matter – everything is happening so fast.

The crowd section behind me bursts open and at the same time into the ground pour the reserves of policemen and still the linesman hasn't reached Pearl – who looks up, he seems to have heard me.

He lashes the ball one more time and then he reaches for the net and he sees me waving frantically and then I see him being pitched backwards, he's rubbing his arm but he's still on his feet and I see the blue flash and I hear the cracks and sparks and a few feet away from my knee a small lamp standard spits smoke.

I'm by Tynan's side now and he's screaming at the goal-keeper, 'Outoutoutoutout!' The linesman's uncertain until Tynan hauls him back, screaming, 'The net's wired! The net's wired,' and fifty thousand people can't believe what they're

336

seeing and fifty million people watching it on television can. At that instant I know everything.

Tynan gets to Pearl first. Behind us the police are going at the rioters. I get to Pearl and he sees me and says, 'What was that?'

'Can you walk?' I ask.

'Fucking run!' screams Tynan.

Pearl doesn't seem to know what's happening. Do I understand this! The shock displaced him, slowed his reactions. No more than a signal, no more voltage than fairylights, not enough to kill him. But he's shaken. He sees the fracas. I see the fright in his eyes.

'Gogogogogo!' yells Tynan. We get there, to the touchline on the other side of the field. Then to a space under the stand. Pandemonium. A steward grabs us. A plainclothes policeman intervenes.

'I'm with Tynan! Car park, car park!' I snap.

Tynan's man runs ahead of us. In seconds we're away. Even though I feel we've over-reacted, I don't stop, not even at the next traffic lights which are just snapping from orange to red.

54

Pearl didn't say a word. Nor did I. Not until I hit the M25. He spoke first, very low voice.

'What happened the Saab, man, this is a BMW?'

'You must be all right,' I say.

'I got no clothes.'

'We're not stopping now.'

'Thanks, Nicholas.'

'I could get used to this,' I said sarcastically. 'Jesus!'

'What happened? My arm is empty.'

'They threaded a white electric wire through the goal. Invisible in the cords. Fixed it so that someone shaking the net, you're famous for it, would hit the bare wires together.'

'Why didn't the keeper see it?'

'He didn't.'

'Was it meant to kill me?'

'No. A signal. Did you score in your last game?'

'No, man, I been injured.'

'Did the world know that in advance?'

'Not till the teams took the field.'

I told him, 'The nets at your last ground are probably still wired.'

This is a child sitting beside me. He has been lethally targeted and his next remark is, 'I gotta go back for my clothes.'

'Absolutely not.' And to remind myself of Claire I added, '*Absolument pas*.'

'Nicholas, I can't go round like this, man! I got my name on my back.'

'Johan, you're going nowhere. What's the story?'

Pearl clammed up.

'Tell me.'

Not a word. I waited for a few minutes, handling traffic. Then I asked again.

'Come on. What is it?'

No reply. I said, 'Fine.' I pulled over into a layby. 'We're going to sit here until you tell me. All weekend if we have to. D'you realize the police are trying to find a reason to arrest you? What is going on?'

Not a word. Then I yelled, 'Johan – TELL ME!!!'

He jumped. 'Okayokayokay.'

'I'm trying to help you – so tell me. What has all this been about?'

'It is about blackmail.'

'Who's blackmailing you? What for?'

He became extremely uncomfortable, a discomfort I could identify with; it had an emotional root. I waited for him. Then he looked away from me, almost turned the back of his head to me. Sitting there in his football strip, he looked like a child who refuses to wear anything else.

I repeated my question. 'Who's blackmailing you?'

'I'm being blackmailed – because. Because –' Words not coming out.

'Because what?'

'I'm – gay.'

My jaw dropped. 'I see. But millions of people –'

'If the fans know I'm gay – I can't play to the noise they'd make. Nobody could.'

'Oh, come on.'

'I mean it. Imagine the dressing room.'

It clicked and flashed like a pinball machine. The glances. The suspicions. The physio. The other players. The mock-prissy 'beg your parding'.

'But people, your team-mates – I mean, people guess.'

339

'Doesn't matter. They leave me alone because I win their matches for them. No, man, I'd have to leave the game. It'd be the worse thing. The jeers. The songs.'

'Haven't there been gay footballers?'

'Name them, Nicholas. Justin Fashanu, yeah. Anyone else?'

'I'm the wrong person to ask.'

'And look what happened to Fashanu.'

'I don't know and I don't want to know.'

We sat in silence. Then I asked, 'Is there more to tell?'

He hesitated. 'They know something else about me, about my family. Our money's wrong. Our history's wrong.'

It's coming together. Chunk by clunking chunk it's coming together. Be careful. Ask the right questions.

'Is all this – is it tied in to – Antony? It is, isn't it?'

'There's a connection.'

'What kind of connection?'

'I was sent to see him when my transfer came through to England. He was important to us.'

'In what way?'

'It is very complicated. And very secret. I do not know it all, the story. But since Antony died somebody found it out and that was another thing to put pressure on me. But it was much more serious. To judge from the things they said to me. Bad people, man.'

'Don't I know,' I said with a twist. I paused. 'Did you ever meet a man wearing a Dutchman's cap, blue, you know the kind of thing – well you should know?'

'I did, man. I met him. He scared me.'

'Where did you meet him?'

'First time I saw him was in the White Raven, he was having lunch when you and I was there. He came looking for me. He went to his room and phoned me. I said to you it was a journalist.'

My turn to shiver. 'You mean – the day you and I were

340

lunching, that first day I went to see your family home?'

'Yes, Nicholas.'

Poor Pearl – he had become extremely meek.

'Have you seen him since?'

'Yes, man. He was at the hotel last night.'

The return of Otto! He must have left Berlin immediately after me.

I said, 'I still can't get what's going on here. First you say you're being blackmailed. Then you say there's an Antony Safft connection.'

'They is looking for money, man. The gay thing, they want money from me.'

'Who?'

'The same people.'

'What do they want the blackmail money for?'

'To pay for their travels, to pay for these guys goes around disrupting football.'

Tynan had said someone was 'putting the arm on Pearl'.

'And the Antony Safft connection?'

'My family was given a lot of money by him, my father knew him or something about him. And I was given money by him.'

I got it. 'And the man in the cap – he wants it all back?'

'Yes.'

'And he also runs these thugs.'

'Yes.'

I thought and thought. It all fitted. No matter which way I turned. I didn't need to know why he and his family got money from Antony. It went back to the war and I had to get away from that.

'Nicholas, can I ask you a question?'

'That is a question.' I wanted to make him smile and I succeeded. Then he put on a very serious face.

'Will you not like me now? Because I'm –'

'Because you're gay? No.'

341

But I saw that I couldn't put out a hand to reassure him. Instead, I started the car.

In a moment Pearl said, 'Look, Nicholas, that's a big shopping complex, please buy me some clothes. Please!'

Nobody seemed to have followed us; I checked. I bought him two of everything. The mobile rang. Tynan. 'Newman! You okay?'

'Yes.' We got cut off.

In the car park Pearl changed into black shirt, black trousers, black shoes.

'I like your colour sense,' he said.

I heard the dryness in his voice. Then I handed him the parcel I'd kept hidden.

He opened it. 'An anorak! A grey anorak! Man, you want to destroy me! An anorak!'

His genuine dismay tickled me and lifted my spirits.

The mobile rang again. 'Newman, I need Pearl.'

I switched off the phone.

For the rest of the journey I quizzed Pearl. He could tell me nothing except that when he was twenty-one his father settled on him the equivalent of five million pounds with strict instructions that it was to be hidden in a Swiss account. He had since been given a further two and a half million. Add his own football earnings and Pearl had become wealthy before his time.

Last August, as the football season began, he went to see Antony Safft on his father's instructions. Antony dealt him into properties – specifically Green Park and Amsterdam. The trouble began the following day. He had since been hounded by all sorts of people. Football thugs trashed his car. Nameless men jostled him.

'Why the house in Wiltshire?'

'I wanted to hide.'

'But you told me there would be prestige in it, publicity.'

'I didn't think it through, man. I'm disgusted with myself.'

342

'It's going to be a lovely house,' I said. 'And now, for the next few days – you can hide.' We drove down the hill into Rye. 'Because this is going to take some time to sort out.'

He said with the pessimism of the young, 'It'll never be sorted out.'

The lights blazed their welcome and Pearl whooped at the sight of the house.

'I've got someone for you to meet,' I said and called out, 'Anybody home?'

Mrs Lydiard appeared. I introduced Pearl. She took him in her stride.

I said, 'Where's Claire?' As the words left my mouth I felt the chill on my neck. I knew what Mrs Lydiard was going to say.

'She hasn't come home. I'm a little worried. There isn't all that much to do in Rye and the mist comes down over the marshes very quickly if she's gone for a walk. I personally never go for a walk if I've just been to the hairdresser.'

'What time was her appointment?' – but I knew.

'Three o'clock.'

'It's six now, what time should she have been here?'

'If she had a beauty treatment – but she didn't. I've rung.'

'And?'

'They didn't answer.'

'Will they still be there? At the salon?'

This time they answered and the voice of doom cracked in my ear. 'The gentleman collected her at about four fifteen.'

'Gentleman?' Is that my own voice?

'Yes. And another in the car.'

'What kind of gentleman?'

'A tall gentleman. He was waiting outside the salon for her.'

'Was he wearing anything distinctive?'

'Yes.' She didn't have to say. She didn't need to describe.

343

I replaced the receiver and went crazy. Out of my mind. Shrieking.

'Is this drugs?' Mrs Lydiard kept asking. 'Is this drugs?' And I kept saying, 'No, it's worse than drugs, it's money.'

Pearl stood back from the force of my reaction.

'This is my fault, man. My fault. If you had not come to help me –'

I stopped dead. '*Your* fault?'

'Yeah, Nicholas. I'm sorry. They forced me to call you.'

'You mean – the game. You were the bait.'

'Yeah, man. I'm so sorry.'

'But why'd they bother with the electrics?'

'They're double-crossers, man.'

I had no coherence, no sense. They'd got her. I remembered the photographs, the computer mock-ups.

Pearl, again; 'Do something, man. Call someone, go somewhere.'

'Come with me.'

I ran to the car, nothing else to do.

'Do it like football, Nicholas,' said Pearl. 'Do it automatic. That's how you'll know the right thing.'

Automatic. Automatic. Shut out all thoughts. Automatic. I gave orders. He worked the telephone, handed it to me.

'Hallo, Mrs Welsh.'

'Who's this?'

'Nicholas Newman, Lemon's boss.'

'Oooooh! I tink I know you better than I know myself. Lemon speaks of you always. How are you?'

Same wonderful Jamaican accent.

'Could I have a word with Lemon?'

'No, yar gonna have to wait. Lemon is in love.'

'So I gather. Where is she?'

'She went to the football and then she's going to the airport, she's seeing him off, and Lemon's comin' home. Will you cawwll her layater?'

'Is he going anywhere nice?'

'He's going to look at some building in Berlin. He's a very ambitious boy.'

I was right. I was RIGHT! The sky burst in a shower of fire. The familiar face. That was him! The stride, the run. I saw him heading for the white van. I saw him lope onto the Tube. I saw his walk this afternoon. The key in Lemon's desk drawer. Tynan said it – 'architects', oh Jesus-Jesus-Jesus! Georgy-Porgy was Afro. Afro/Ringo. Ringwald. George Ringwald. Georgy-Porgy. With open access to me. Christ! They had infiltrated every part of my life. That was how they found Rye.

Check every airport. Can reach all three from M25. Gatwick. Heathrow. Stansted. Information. Gatwick-Berlin seven fifty. Or Heathrow ten minutes past ten. More likely. Fuck – no! She's at Gatwick, that's where they've taken her. How will they do it, she'll kick and scream? How do they do it with spies? There was something on television, Cold War stuff, they pretend they're invalids, drugs and wheelchairs, oh, fuckkkkkkkkk!

Ring Tynan? Risk it. He answered.

'I want you. And Pearl. Now!'

His force shook me, but I resisted.

'Where are you, Newman?'

'In a minute. Listen. If you were smuggling someone out of the country by air, how would you do it?'

Tynan snapped, 'Wheelchair. Drugged. Don't you watch spy movies? Now, where the fuck are you –'

I cut him off.

I up the speed, take the exit and we race into Gatwick. The desk! The desk! Flight to Berlin. Boarded, sir, and left the gate, I'm sorry, did you have a ticket? Was there a woman in a wheelchair? Don't know, sir, my colleague's gone home. Where's the flight? Where? Oh, it will have started taxiing by now, sir.

I hear the roar and I see the bright shape in the night and I know in my heart she's on it . . .

On a green metal bench I collapse, lost.

Pearl stands over me. 'Gimme your hand.'

He takes my hand. People look at us.

'Nicholas. Listen to me. I know more about pressure than you do. The reason football and me is very good – I know how to be calm when I get the ball. You have the ball. Be calm. Otherwise you run everywhere at the same time. Now. Tell me what you think. Because what you think is what you know.'

'They've abducted her.'

He said, 'Think some more. The manager tells me where to apply the pressure, man. He says, "Their number four's slow on his left foot." He says, "Their keeper's bad on low balls to his right." She is your pressure point. Where is their pressure point? Come on, Nicholas, where d'you hit a house to knock it?'

'They've taken her to Berlin. She was on that flight, I know it.'

'Then we go to Berlin.'

We drive to Heathrow. My head feels like ice. Johan keeps asking me questions. I can't answer. I won't answer. Think it through. Think it through. I can't. This woman is my heart. This woman is my new life. This woman is – is me! I lay inside her last night and she is home for my body and my soul. Never give all the heart.

Having found her, I never let her out of my sight. I bathed her. I poured wine from my mouth into hers. I stayed awake until she went to sleep. I woke her up in the mornings. I fed her. Call Tynan, Nicholas. No! I will find her! I will be invincible for her! You fool!

Running from the car park, I stop dead.

'You can't come, Johan.'

'I must, man. You gotta let me.'

'You have no passport.'

He hits his face and groans. Then yells, 'Yes, I have! Where's my briefcase?'

We run back to my car.

We board for Berlin. Pearl eats his meal – and mine. A stewardess asks for his autograph and he gives it. The captain announces a delay of one hour and then fog in Berlin. We are rerouted to Frankfurt. My heart moans in agony.

Passengers are asked if they want to forward messages. Yes, I do, and I know to whom, and I know each short word of the short message. But I don't know where she is. The stewardess fixes a car at Frankfurt. We land at Frankfurt at five to two in the morning and there is no car, no envelope, nothing at the information desk, the car hire bureaux are all closed and we have missed the coach transportation they have laid on and no cab-driver will take us to Berlin on account of the fog.

55

I remember a hotel. Just about. I remember a room. Just about. I remember chiding myself for sleeping and I remember a thumping on the door in the morning and the telephone ringing and it's Pearl and he's saying, 'Up, man, come on, why you sleeping like this?'

Outside the windows the fog is thick, thick. Fear death, to feel the fog in my throat, the mist in my face. Everyone misquotes that, don't they, they say 'the mist on my face', but that would ruin the line. I must be firing on some cylinders because under pressure my mind always fills with all the things I have ever known, songs I have attempted to write, other songs, advertising jingles, school poems.

Pearl is saying something. 'I've ordered breakfast. The fog's bad, man. They not flying to Berlin.'

'We'll drive.'

'I will chase last night's car.'

He picked up the telephone and barked at someone. I looked at him in amazement.

'We always give the Germans orders.'

'How many languages do you have, Black Pearl?'

'Seven if you call Frisian a language. Is more a dialect.'

'Seven?!'

'Dutch and English. German and Italian. French, but not the best. Spanish and Frisian. And a little Albanian.'

'Albanian?'

'We had a worker, he was called Rotu, he was Albanian, he never learns any other language.'

'Black Pearl?'

'Yes, Nicholas.'

'*Zinzee endlick fur mickey comin.*'

'That is a bad German accent. So, who said that to you?'

'That,' I said, 'is the pressure point.'

He didn't know what I was talking about.

Breakfast came. 'I don't want to eat,' I said.

'More for me.'

Which made me eat. But the knot in my stomach tightened and I might as well not have eaten because I threw it all up in the airport concourse lavatories.

We got the car. With a telephone. We got cash from cashpoints.

'You really splashing out,' said Pearl. He took my hand again. 'She's okay. I know in here.' He tapped his chest.

I wanted to scream, How could you know in there? Jesus, you haven't even begun to live your life yet. You're *gay*! What do you *know* –?!

The nightmare drive began. Visibility down to between ten and twenty yards. Metres, we are on the Continent. I can see nothing of anything. Two hours later we are still in the conurbation of Frankfurt. Why is the fog soothing me when it should be driving me wild? I feel hidden by it and therefore invulnerable and therefore competent to find Claire.

'Black Pearl, why didn't the goalkeeper see the wires?'

'Goalkeepers is stupid, man. The wires was probably white, like the net.'

As long as I don't think of Claire. As long as I am not reminded of those long horsewoman's legs and their capacity to twine around me. As long as I don't remember the way her thighs don't quite close at the top.

I want to weep. All the time I want to weep. Just as I had found her I lost her. Is this revenge on me? For all the hurt I've spread?

Pearl says little. He fiddles with the CD player but we have no CDs. Sensitively he doesn't turn on the radio. Then I ask him, 'Get us a weather forecast.'

He reports after myriad tunings; 'It lifts in the country areas.'

But not by much. Is it a foggy day in London town? Had me low, had me down. I'm running out of fog references. The brown fog of a winter something. Is that Eliot? Fog isn't brown. Claire, you must live, Claire. *Live!* Now that I've found you – no don't go down that road, no way out of that lane of thought ... The signs say Dortmund and Kassel. Which one? Kassel. Christ, these are terrible driving conditions.

'What time is it, Johan?'

I know what time it is but I just need to be told something true.

'Nearly noon, man.'

Nearly destroyed, man, nearly coming apart. Nearly there with Claire. After all the years of searching. Now I know why I never clinched it with anyone – too much to lose. That's why I never wanted children. That has changed too. There's a real barometer. I know about children and losing, I had a brother and I lost him and I had a father and I had a mother, and after I lost my brother I lost them too, or they lost me, but it was never the same again, loss after loss after loss. Not win-win but lose-lose, stop this, Nicholas, this is maudlin, this is self-defeating.

'Black Pearl, why didn't the linesman see the wires? He checks the nets, doesn't he?'

'Man, touch judges is *really* stupid.'

The fog lifts a little. My depression doesn't.

This was planned. A touch of the old paranoia returned. Did they set up Pearl to lure me away? Look at the arrangements. They lift her the only moment I'm gone. And the timing gives them a flight from the airport nearest to Rye. The fog lifts a little more, and some sunlight tries to get through.

'What are you doing?'

He has to be doing something, can't be still. Doesn't answer; he is speaking in German. Now he has been given some information because he once again lapses into chat. He terminates the call.

Snapping the phone back into its bracket he says, 'Nicholas, they took Claire into Berlin last night. She was on the flight from Gatwick, last flight to get into Tegel before the fog came down.'

'How did you do that?'

I looked across at him and he winked. 'Automatic, like I said. People's not automatic enough, the Boss says.'

It is two o'clock. The sign says *Berlin 190km*, and that is 115 miles and that is two hours to the perimeter of the city. I go as fast as possible but the fog won't go away. Just like my spirit. Time after time thoughts of Claire force their way into my head and time after time I force them out. Luckily I have never sat beside such a packet of energy as Johan Pearl.

In the glove compartment he finds a square grey box with a lead attached and he squeals with delight.

'Man! Nicholas! A traffic computer!'

He plugs it in and inside half an hour, quietened by his absorption with this toy, he has cracked it.

'Where are we?' I tell him and he feeds it in. 'I gotta route for us. Where we going?'

'Potsdamer Platz. Wilhelmstrasse.' Unhesitatingly he keys these in. 'Got it.'

'Get me to Tegel,' I said. 'I know the route from there.'

'And I can check it.'

At least one of us was happy. Pearl guided me in until I parked on the Volkstrasse yards from An der Kolonnade. Back in the old routine.

There is no reply. I press the doorbell again and there is no reply. A neighbour arrives. Johan Pearl charms her and we enter the building. Yellow daylight filters onto the quiet staircase.

Johan grimaces at me. 'This is nervous stuff. Worse'n Arsenal at Highbury.' He jigs from foot to foot, looks down at his anorak, tugs it, says to me, 'How could you do it to me, man? An anorak?'

Extraordinary irrepressibility. Or else he doesn't know danger. But that can't be true. Sixty-four? Sixty-six? Could I have got it wrong? Sixty-four. No reply. I press. Johan presses. A neighbour appears on the staircase and Johan translates. 'He's out.'

'Ask her. Is he out? Or has he gone out? There's a difference.'

'What difference?'

'He may go out every day. Or he might have gone out to go away.'

No greater illumination comes forth. She goes back in. We are stuck.

'What do we do? Wait?'

'Go to the car. Wait in it. I'll wait here. Ring my mobile if someone comes in.'

Half an hour passes. Johan rings. 'A lady entering. You okay?'

'Yes.'

'Nicholas, d'you know where we are? It's really interesting – but spooky.'

'I have to conserve the phone batteries.'

Another forty minutes. The shadows are falling across the stairs. Telephone in my hand.

'Elderly man.'

'Alone?'

'Yes. Very slow.'

'Head very bowed?'

'Bowed, Nicholas?'

'Bent down?'

'Like an old tree, man.'

'Come in with him. I need you here.'

I hear the door and I slip around the corner. Slowly he comes up the stairs, slowly, slowly. Here you come, old man, while your son is out killing people. What did you do in the war, Daddy? I think I know. Pearl tiptoes behind him.

He has his keys ready but it takes him an age to find the lock and open it – one, two, three tumblers, is this man security-conscious or what? The hinge creaks. Johan and I get there together. We are in behind him and we close the door.

He doesn't hear us. He actually doesn't hear us. But I say, *Guten Tag*, just behind him and he turns serenely as though we are the people he has been waiting for all his life and perhaps we are.

56

From that moment on, he controls us. When I think of it now I remain astounded.

First he takes off his coat and he hands it to Johan who is about to hang it across a chair. But the old man points imperiously to a closet. Then he hands Johan the gloves and scarf. Then he points to his own genitals and shuffles off and we hear a lavatory flushing. He comes back. We are still standing in the hall. He speaks and it sounds not unlike my *Zinzee* mantra.

'He says, "Ah, so. You have come for me",' Johan translates. 'He wants us to sit down.'

We sit around a table in a living room. On the mantel is something that can only be the Iron Cross. He sees me looking at it. When I look back at him I realize that it isn't the weather that has affected him. This man is in tears. Tears of what? Fear? Relief?

I say, 'Tell him wait a minute.' To Pearl I flash, 'Keep him here.'

I jump up, go to the hall, open the door, check where the services are coming in, find them in the kitchen, unclick the incoming telephone line. No warnings, I want no warnings. On incoming or outgoing calls.

'Ask him where his son is.'

Such a dilemma. His age and fragility make me wish to be kind, even tender, to him. But I see in my mind Oradour. I think of the baker, naked to the waist and covered in flour and anxious only to bake for his customers.

Pearl asks the question. The old man shakes his head.

'He says he doesn't know but he has something to tell us.'

'What is it?'

For a moment I am frozen still by the event in which I have found myself. This man was there on that sunny afternoon. I know he was. I shake my head and sit at the table again. This is not moving at the pace I want.

A statement follows. I am tapping the table. Johan says, 'He cannot sleep. All the time he hears screams, sees faces, sees fire. But he was only a soldier.'

I have to ask the obvious question. That is what I am like. 'Was he at Oradour-sur-Glane?'

The man does not look at me at all, not once. He keeps his eyes fixed on Johan. His eyes are red and raw, probably with decades of insufficient tears shed. Another long speech follows which Johan breaks up as he speaks.

'He was at Oradour . . . with General von Lammerding . . . they were very frightened . . . they had orders to wipe out the Resistance . . . he was told to do certain things, to cut off the village . . . Major Dickmann . . . he believes matters got out of hand . . . no, he has changed his mind, he believes they did not behave as soldiers . . . they were like the barbarians of old . . . he thinks he is a Visigoth . . . never a day has passed that he has not thought of the sunny afternoon and the fields looking so beautiful . . . he remembers the tram station . . . he remembers the smell from the bakery . . . the fresh coffee smell from the café beside the church . . .'

'Ask him if he remembers the post office. It had two Art-Deco scrolls.'

My voice sounded so lame. Soon my chest will be unable to contain my fibrillating heart. I want to reach out to this man and make him more restful, to take his poor old gnarled hand, I want to offer him kindness. Then I remember the schoolteacher who tried to get her arms around as many of her little pupils as she could.

'No . . . he doesn't remember the post office . . . he remembers the division of the men from the women and children . . . he was responsible for that . . . he asks if we want to kill him . . . he believes he is ready to die for what he did.'

'No. We do not want to kill him. Ask him if he remembers the church.'

I look at the old man and I wish to tell him how beautiful Claire is, how she looks at me as if in pain when I enter her and how I cannot stop my hands from stroking her cheeks, her hair.

'He was not at the church . . . but he was very near it . . . those are the screams he hears . . . those are the flames he sees in his mind every night and every morning . . . he remembers marching a group of men to a wine store . . . he remembers giving the order for the machine-gunners . . . he remembers it was very sunny and one of the soldiers was laughing and he told him to stop . . . he says they had casualties too . . .'

'How many? Ask him how many.'

'He says . . . he lost a lieutenant . . . he thinks his name was Kung or Knug . . .'

'How did that man die?'

'He says he was killed when part of the church fell on him . . .'

'A bit different from being roasted alive or shot in the head.'

My eyes went red inside. I wanted to rise and kick this old man to death. I wanted to run to him and hold him and say, Sleep, old man, rest, I pity you the past fifty years of your inner life. I wanted to reach out and rip my nails down his pocketed cheeks. My skin tightened on my face again, in that way that makes me think I can feel the shape of my own skull.

'Ask him what else he did.'

'He says . . . he played the radio very loudly . . . he says he made the soldiers set fire to the barns . . . he says he was one of the ones who commandeered a house that night so that he could feed his troops . . .'

'Ask him if he knows that he killed six hundred and forty-two people, every man, woman and child in Oradour.'

Pearl's aplomb had long slipped, but his high intelligence drove him along. I rose and turned on the lights.

'He says . . . not everyone died . . . he says he didn't kill them all, there were other soldiers . . .'

'Soldiers? They call themselves soldiers?! Ask him how many does he think escaped.'

Silence from the old man. Pearl asks again. The old man shakes his head.

'Tell him seven – seven people escaped. Ask him if he ever saw von Lammerding again.'

The old man became cautiously enthusiastic.

'He says he saw him every year, every two years, there were reunions of the Panzers . . . but he says he himself is haunted . . . he would prefer to be punished.'

And still the old man controls us; he does so with his body language, his face, his very being.

'Ask him if von Lammerding regretted Oradour.'

My body feels weary. My brain feels burned out. I sag. The old man gave Pearl a curt answer.

'He says he doesn't think so, that von Lammerding was an officer of the Reich.'

Pearl looks at me. Change of tempo. 'Nicholas, may I ask him a question?'

I flap a hand. But the question produces an animated response and just a hint of military fire. This old man is still controlling us. Johan turns to me. I know by his face that he would laugh if he felt it all right to do so.

'Aw, man, that is something.'

'What did you ask him?'

'I asked him why he chose to live in a block of apartments built right on the site of Hitler's bunker.'

'Wha-at?!'

'That's what I tried to tell you. From the car. There's a tourist notice outside, this is where Hitler died, underneath us. These apartments were built on the site of Hitler's bunker. He says his Führer died here – he wants to die here. He says Herr Hitler was his commander-in-chief and he was a good soldier.'

I don't know what to do. The feeling of disgust makes it impossible to stay. Glaring at the old man, I say to Pearl, 'Ask him if he knows that beneath where he lives, in his Führer's bunker, Magda Goebbels put her six children into their white nightshirts and gave them each a cup of hot poisoned drinking chocolate and killed them.'

When I'd said it I grew weary. Keep your eyes on the prize, Nicholas. This won't find Claire. I held up my hand; I had taken control.

'Ask him again – does he know where his son is?'

The old man looks at me for the first time, truly worried.

'He says he does not know but he is very proud of his son, who lives in a good tradition . . .'

Now I see it all. The son was hired because the father had been at Oradour. A vile continuity. 'Vile' is an anagram of 'evil'. I am about to walk out. Johan rises to follow me.

'Ask him one more question. Has he ever been back to Oradour?'

The old man nods and speaks.

'He says, yes, once, when he and his late wife were on holidays in France . . . he wanted to show her where he had been a soldier . . .'

Tourists. I wish I were not so often right about the wrong things.

All my ideas are now working overtime. But they are not good ideas. I race down the stairs and Johan follows me.

I bark at him, 'The notice, the notice!'

He leads me to it; I stand and read; I look around. Over there, by the children's playground, where I made my Grimm joke to myself. That must be it. Grimmer joke. A kids' playground over Hitler's bunker. This is East German thinking. This is East German architecture, too. We walk across fast. On the pavement there is a large manhole cover. I pound. Some mad thought in my head. Who was that killer? Kidsgrove. Kept a girl underground. I should have been a Gothic architect, I have a Gothic imagination. I tear at the manhole cover. Pearl helps me. We prise it up. No, too shallow. I look around. There – over there! A huge vent, coming from below. Together we wrench the cover off. No, it emerges from concrete.

'That woman, over there, grab her, ask her, ask her where the entrance is.'

Pearl trots back. 'She thinks we're crazy, man. The Communists, they filled in the bunker.'

I drop back into place the metal flange securing the vent cover. It clangs in the night and I scream. We've lost her.

I echo it to Pearl. 'We've lost her.'

He peered at me anxiously under the street light. 'Why do you say that?'

Hastings Banda. 'Don't ask me that question.' On being interviewed when he came to London. The cutglass interviewer says, 'Dr Banda, why are you in London?' 'Don't ask me that question. I won't tell you that. Don't ask me that question.'

'We've lost her.'

Johan Pearl doesn't know what to do any more than I, Nicholas Newman, know what to do. We stand in this nondescript suburb which was once the locus of unsurpassable evil and the fingers of that evil have reached down and choked the valves of my heart. I begin to feel ill and all I can do is lean against the board that tells the world Hitler's bunker once stretched beneath our feet and not a word about Magda Goebbels and her children.

'I'm freezing, man,' said Johan Pearl.

He gets back inside the car and there I stand alone, under the yellow light, by a little patch of garden at the entrance to a parade of shops above which climb these apartments.

I've never found a manual that tells you what to do when you reach a dead end. Turn back, perhaps. Climb over. Find a way around. Were I a Zen Buddhist I might say, wait and the end you have come to will tell you what to do. I am not a Zen Buddhist.

Slowly I walked to the car. Inside, Pearl asked me, 'What will happen now?'

I almost bit him. 'How should I know?'

'You don't understand my question, Nicholas. Who will do what now? Will the old man warn his son?'

'He can't. I've cut off his telephone.'

Pearl said, 'That was a good move. Then we stay here.'

'What the fuck are you talking about?'

He put his hand on my arm. 'The son will ring the father. He will not get a reply. He will come to see what has happened. Like playing. I get the ball. I look up. I look what to do next.'

I thought, Don't be so fucking simplistic. But – I had no other thought. And therefore no other choice.

Pearl asked, 'What's this Oradour – is that what you call it – what's that stuff?'

I told him. Everything I could remember. He had different triggers. The cut telephone wires. The football team. Not the swallows, not the bakery, not the face of Christ. He shook his head slowly.

'If you weren't black,' I asked him, 'would you be pale now?' Crass of me, but he laughed.

'Man, I *am* pale now.'

How long did we wait? An hour? Perhaps not. Pearl, with

his quick wits, saw him first. He hissed at me and we dropped low in the car seats. My eyes did not believe it. Otto emerged from an old house on the other side of Wilhelmstrasse. He walked in his stiff way towards An der Kolonnade. Should I follow him? For what? Kill him? Then what about Claire?

I made no move, as much through paralysis as through expediency. He didn't look towards us – the car was partly concealed by the kiosk at the entrance to the parking facility for shops.

Shall I follow him?

Pearl hissed at me, 'I knew we hadn't lost her.'

I followed. Saw Otto enter his father's door. I ran back to the car. Trying to do what Pearl said. Trying to figure what happens next.

It happened quickly. Otto returned from his father's apartment walking very fast. We sank again in the seats but could observe him. Did I imagine he looked closely towards us? He looked all around. What now?

'Now' became dramatic. He re-entered the house he had first left. Minutes later a car arrived, drawing up with speed. The driver spoke on the telephone.

A door in the house opened and a man appeared, conferred with the driver, who reversed round the corner; what's round the corner?

I started the engine. If ever I needed luck. Their rear door nearest the kerb stood open. I pulled in beyond them, a good way down the clear street.

'Fix your wing mirror, double-check what's happening.'

Pearl confirmed what I also saw. 'Another door. They taking someone out in a wheelchair.'

Bloody Tynan. Right again. Why hadn't I given all this over to him?

57

My heart dropped like a plumb. What had they done to her? Those long, lovely legs.

'Can you see the wheelchair?' I couldn't.

'No. Yes. No. Being lifted. Into the car now.' He softened his voice. 'D'you think that's her?' I knew he was scared too.

How had I got myself and him and everybody into this? What have I not put back into life? It demands such cruel things of me now.

Aloud, I trace events. 'The old man told his son of us. The son is moving her now, in case we ask around, or call police. We have a night of driving,' I said.

The thought oppressed me, horrified me. And wrongfooted me. All around me on these grounds stood the buildings of terror: the Gestapo, the SS, Hitler's Chancellery. Here now is their legacy persisting down to this very night. This is appalling.

We nearly lost them – because they drove a very short distance. I thought at first they had begun to move her to another apartment. My gut knew it was Claire. I overtook them. Follow them from the front, like the movies. They had wrapped her in something.

I could see a scarf and a touch of her hair.

I could see a piece of her face, a hint of the broken-looking nose I teased her about.

Any passer-by would assume this was an unwell woman being taken somewhere in the back of a car. Traffic roughed up our line of contact. They spun off behind me and Pearl

362

shouted, 'They going to the train station.'

'Out,' I yelled. 'Get platform number. Destination. Everything. I have to park this in case we need it again.'

I dropped the car down a side street opposite the entrance to the Zoo, never checked for parking restrictions. Pearl, brightly, waited under the destination boards at the foot of the steps.

'They gone up to the trains, man, but it's okay, they no train leaving for another seven minutes, yet.' He had cocooned himself in his anorak hood. Underneath the grey plastic you could still tell he was a star.

'Where are they going?'

'Don't know yet.'

I looked. They stood between platforms. No trains in yet. No destinations flagged up here. They're confident. They risk keeping an abductee, no matter how well packaged, on a platform for this long. How are they going to hide, given their fears at being followed?

'Is he with them?'

'Yah. Wearing his cap.'

'Did he see you?'

'No, man.'

'Black Pearl, what will we do?'

He heard the pathetic desperation in my voice. He looked at the board. He turned to me.

'If they come to the station they is taking a long journey. Where's a good place to hide someone, Nicholas? On a night train. They is putting her on a sleeper.'

Who said footballers are stupid? He heard my thought.

'Man, everyone'll tell you footballers have no brains.'

'How many sleepers are there?'

This boy knew everything. 'One in twelve minutes, to Munich.'

I ran to the ticket desk. No queue at first class. Two sleepers to Munich. Pearl transacted. I kept watch. He talked nineteen to the dozen at the ticket girl. His credit card failed to go through. She hadn't swiped it fast enough. He swiped it for her, pointing out the platinum. More chat.

'Ask her,' I said, 'where you can get trains to from Munich.'

I saw the girl smile. Pearl chatted and chatted. She named a list on her fingers. I jigged about like rabies. He got the tickets, spun away from the desk, beckoned me and ran like the wind down the hall, away from the trains.

We stopped at a kind of baggage store. Pearl grabbed a big cap and scarf. He chose for me a hat and walking stick.

'We gonna do this right, man.'

Then we raced to the trains, slowing on the stairs to the platform.

'They there!' he whispered back at me. 'They is beside us or near us, I bet.'

'How d'you make that out?'

'They bought tickets before us.'

My blood turned to iced water. I could see the blue cap of The Man. Four of them in all, and Claire. At least they had propped cushions at the back of the wheelchair.

'That person, they is asleep,' said Pearl.

'Drugged.'

He nodded. We waited.

I whispered pathetically, 'Could we move on them?'

'No-no. Better chance on the train.'

'What did the girl say to you about Munich?'

'I asked her where she'd like to go to if she came to Munich with me. She said all kinds of places. Innsbruck, Monaco, Venice.'

'Christ!'

'They is on, man.'

'What do we do?'

'We gotta go. Now, limp, Nicholas, put on your hat and limp.'

'This is ridiculous.' But I did it.

The fat conductor had exquisite manners. I counted – five cabins to a carriage; I had not been on a *wagon-lit* since the Verona festival five years ago.

Pearl led the way, after the conductor. I kept my face half-down and limped like an old man. Not difficult, the way I felt. This was ridiculous. I should be facing them.

We had one cabin at the end and a cabin intervened between us and the nearest of them. Into which one had they wheeled Claire? Perhaps the middle one – four of them and her. One with her, one in a cabin by himself, two sharing, taking turns, I presumed. Take them out one by one? With what?

I heard a moan and almost spun. I heard it again and my heart twisted. But it was the conductress in a mock argument with the fat conductor. We reached the cabin and I almost fell through the door.

Pearl's energy kept up. He disappeared. I closed the door. Along the corridor I heard the voice I knew with the elongated *a* address the conductor. It made me frantic that I couldn't know what they were saying. The conversation continued.

Pearl, where are you?

Here he is.

'I heard all that. He was saying his wife's very ill. They may have to take her off the train during the night. They is only one stop, in Nürnberg. He asks him how many people is in this carriage. Does it look like they will all be sleepers? Or is they men who might drink and make noise? The guy tells him they is only another husband-and-wife, that is them here next to us, and an old man and his friend, that is us. An old man!' Pearl's smile turned into a silent joy. 'Now I go get the food.'

He brought back a pantryful, most of which he ate. When he finished I said, 'We take turns to sleep. But at Nürnberg we both get out and stretch.'

What could we do in the small hours of the morning? Against four of them, who were almost certainly armed? I had no idea.

I went to bed. Pearl read some densely printed, thick German newspaper that had been complimentarily placed in our carriage. His huge feet hung over the edge of the bunk. He flexed his toes all the time.

I settled down. Not an idea did I have of what to do in such circumstances. Some years ago a diplomat friend went on a course to tell him what to do when kidnapped. He said they mostly told him how to pretend fainting. No good to me. To my later amazement, I slept a deep sleep.

A shuddering sensation woke me. Pearl was on his feet and trying to peer out of the window.

'I think we are stopping, man.'

He dressed and put on his cap and scarf and went to the door.

'Nürnberg,' he whispered.

The doors along from us slammed one way and another as the train finally came to a halt. Pearl came back and held open the door of our compartment so that we could both look out. Two of the men jumped down to the platform. They walked to and fro for several minutes. The conductor approached them. Back on board the train a conference then took place. Pearl eavesdropped.

'They not getting off,' he whispered. 'What does that mean?'

'I think it might mean they feel safe, they don't feel they're being followed.'

'Man, they looked at me so close in the bar.'

'Did they hear you speak?' I asked, appalled.

'*Italiano*,' he said. '*Perfetto*.'

All doors closed. Pearl checked again. Members of the travelling party stood in the corridor. The train moved off.

'Now your turn to sleep.'

'Thanks, man.'

I dreaded this. The night, and the silence, and the solitude. Nothing to read. Nothing to do. Too simple for my imagination to run riot. I tried and tried to break it down to straight lines.

One straight line. Claire is two doors away. She is in mortal danger and I am powerless.

Second straight line. Why not call the police? Call Tynan and ask him to coordinate something. Because I fear what will happen to her. And I fear that I will be the one arrested.

The straight lines led nowhere. I was not in possession of the ball, so to speak. No support and no ideas. Just like my emotional life. My style, my fashionable life. They are no good to me now. Do I have to return to that world? How can I survive this? I cannot help someone who is important to me. That is why I cannot embark upon relationships. I have no guarantees to give of security or freedom or any of the things that people can bestow upon each other through love.

My imagination fights back. I could go there and do as I did in the Chunnel. I did well in that fight. But my instincts rail against it. A voice comes through, a sensible voice, telling me that the best resolution will be the simplest. And the simplest resolution will be the best. Just like my work. Lines again. Straight lines where possible. But what is the simplest resolution here? The simplest resolution here is to numb my mind.

I did what I always do; I designed a building in my head. And then I recalled, floor by floor, stage by stage, something from the portfolios of my past.

A nightlight burns in the tiny *wagon-lit*. It shines on the dark wood and the bunks and the curtains and the fruit and the bottles of water. The noise of the train begins to find a groove in my mind. I begin to rock with it, rock slowly, rock from side to side. And somewhere in my body the swaying must have released some chemical because I am becoming more at ease with myself.

Or it could be the thought that I have just had. Which is, I don't care if I die now, I know something about myself. I know that I have the capacity to surrender everything for someone else. That someone else may die. I may die and she may live. It doesn't matter . . . It doesn't matter . . .

It does matter. Now I know why I am going it alone, why I'm not alerting the international police. Previously, I went though my life alone because I never needed anyone else. To face Otto in Berlin I had to go it alone – an extreme counterbalance to my huge inertia.

Now I do so because only I know the power of going alone. I know that I never want to know that power again, the power of caring about nobody because with that power – and perhaps with all power – comes desolation.

At twenty minutes past seven, although I am wide awake, I start when someone knocks hard upon the door.

'*Bitte?*' and even though I understand not a word of the conductress's reply, I hear the jangle of the tray. Opening the door the barely necessary width, I take it in – two huge breakfasts. By now I am so paranoid that I have to wake Pearl immediately.

'Did you order breakfast?'

'No, man. Oh, yes, I did. Where are we?' He climbed down from the bunk. Half asleep and he still moves with the grace of a cat. 'Shower, man,' he mumbled, but tried to open the cabin door. I steered him in the opposite direction.

He bounded out in a towel five minutes later.

'I hope we can buy some clothes in Munich, man.'

I smiled. 'Who knows?'

We ate in silence; I ate fully, unthinking of the consequences. A risk: my stomach doesn't like such pressures.

'What do we do now, Nicholas?' whispered Pearl.

'I don't know.'

'Man,' he said, 'you never tell lies, do you?'

'Oh, I do, I have done. Too often and too many.'

'Not to me you don't.'

'Thank you.'

'Nicholas, you are so English.'

But I am thinking about Claire and I am falling apart inside because whatever my brave thoughts in the night it is now the cold light of day or will be soon and this is so far above my head and I am so deep out of my depth.

I try to plan. They leave the train at Munich. What then? Do we follow? And when they reach a destination – what do we do then? Take it simply, the good voice inside me keeps saying, take it simply. The goal will open, as Pearl might say. Ask him.

'Black Pearl. When you're about to score a goal – is the goal wide or narrow?'

He loved the question. 'You should be a Buddhist, Nicholas.' After a moment's thought he said, 'When I'm playing well, it's like I open the goal wider for myself. Yes, sometimes you squeeze through a gap – but the best goals – wide.' He opened his arms.

'Do you like it when you score?'

'I was embarrassed in the beginning. Now I sometimes like it very much.'

We finished breakfast. We opened the door. We took the chance. Nothing. Nothing from the corridor. In a moment the door next to us opened and the husband and wife emerged, fresh and showered and silent. The train slowed down at a sign, *München*.

'What is he saying?' I ask Pearl because the conductor is braying.

'He's saying the train terminates here.'

'When is your next game?' I asked with sudden irrelevance.

For some reason this doubled him with laughter.

The couple beside us got off and so did many, many other people. But nobody came from the compartments we were watching.

'Jesus, have they gone?' I asked Pearl.

He put his head out. 'No. They talking to the conductor, he's telling them it's all right to wait until everyone's gone.'

'We'd better get off.'

I went first and instead of leaving the platform walked to the far side and pulled the mobile phone from my pocket. Pearl followed and lounged about in his cap and scarf. People streamed past us; we found a kiosk which took us from view.

Outside, snow had begun to fall. I will, I swore, walk with Claire in the snow and teach her how to look up and have her eyes and face fill with flakes.

58

No one went and no one came on the bare platform. Who's that? Edward Thomas. Adlestrop. Ring Tynan, Nicholas, and do it calmly. I rang Tynan.

'D'you know what fucking time it is?'

'I'm in Munich.'

'What's up?'

'They got her.'

'I thought something happened. Suppose I'd better not call you a stupid git.'

'I need help.'

'Is Pearl with you?'

'Yes. He's safe and he's in the clear. I'll tell you all.'

'I know some. We did some rounding up. What you up to now? I mean – Newman, do you know how fucking crazy this is? You're like some chimp who thinks he's in a movie.'

'I asked you not to lecture me.'

'I shouldn't even be talking to you.'

'Can I ring you? Any time?'

'I should have arrested you, Newman. Protective custody. I may oblige you to tell me where you're going.' He calmed down a little. 'Want me to be anywhere?'

'Maybe. Let me think about it. Anywhere?'

'That I can get to in a day. If it's any help to you – we've set up a big make on the bloke you're likely following. The Berliner.'

'I only know him as Otto.'

'I can tell you the headache pills he uses. He's gonna need 'em.'

'I'm looking at him right now.'

'What? Jesus, Newman, I should –'

I cut him off. Pearl beckoned me. They left the train. A hydraulic platform lowered the wheelchair. I saw her – Claire all right, unconscious, deathly pale, dressed to look like an invalid.

The bastards. BASTARDS! I must have rushed forward because Pearl grabbed me and said, 'No, man, no, no. No!'

'Oh, shitttttt! We're gone, Johan, we're gone. We have no car, we can't follow them.'

'No, man, look, they not leaving the station, look!'

'Check the boards.'

'They going to platform what, eight?'

He checked the boards but I got there first.

I said, 'It'll say Venice.'

Pearl came back. 'How d'you know that?'

I shook my head. Tynan had brought me into the real world. Yes, it's Venice. Then to Albania or Yugoslavia or Oblivion. Claire knows about that silent Dalmatian coast. But she only hinted. Why, oh why, hadn't she told me more?!

Pearl said, 'We have no tickets.'

'How long to go?'

'There's time. Sixteen minutes.'

He and I walk steadily and slowly down the platform. I do something foolish, I try to walk so that I can see Claire's face. Pearl sees what I'm doing and drags me to one side. One of the men looks at us and I cannot see Otto anywhere. But I see him in a moment. He is in the ticket queue.

Pearl sees him at the same moment and I know he wants to run and I say very quietly, 'We are not the Keystone Cops, this is how we do this.'

This switching of roles between us. Keep it simple.

So I walked up the queues, and luckily there was some-body queuing at every window and I took advantage of that

372

and stood us both directly behind Otto, gambling that he would be so involved that he wouldn't look behind him, people rarely do.

I didn't wet myself. I directed Pearl to listen to Otto's transaction and then place our order. Otto walked away without a glance, the tickets in his hand.

Pearl placed our order and the girl said to him, as he reported to me, 'Everybody's taking the train to Venice today.'

We watched them settle in a carriage. I led Pearl in the opposite direction. Board the train far away from them. Work our way back to be near them. At the last minute one of the suits jumped off. I thought they meant to cut and run.

I waited. The suit boarded. So did I.

Snow was falling in light, tiny whirls. No great feathers of flakes, just a swirl of snowdust. Outside Munich, the sun banished the snow. We ran through delicate farm country, with wide pastures and little level crossings where women with dogs walking in the early morning waited and watched the passing train.

Pearl slumped and slept. He swung between maturity beyond his age and childhood.

There is something wrong here. Otto's minders looked at everybody. Except us. Nicholas, put that terrible thought away.

Soon the mountains came to meet us, huge clean clefts white with snow, and mighty enough for eagles. Several times I saw a house by a track and I longed for it to be mine and live there with Claire – but I choked the thought before it reached any kind of apogee. Somewhere near Sterzing, Pearl pointed out a frozen lake, with tyre tracks to half way and we both laughed silently at the awful possibility. The pink sky was as sweet as a baby. I thought about succession. Antony 'fathered' me. Shall I 'father' Pearl? Grandfather. Father.

Son. Sweet fancy. I turned such thoughts to Claire. And shall we have children? And if they do shall we tell them all this? I think not. The war must end some time. Or must it? If we don't tell them how will they know what to do when we're dead and the next dictator comes along? Oh, my God, I miss her!

Italy made its presence felt long before it should have done, by adding its own names to the Austrian nameboards at the train stations. At Chiusa/Klausen a man roamed the platform ringing a bell and offering biscuits and cheese and fruit and bottles of water. I tried to behave in my mind as though Claire were just another passenger on the train. We kept the curtains to our compartment closed and only the ticket collector disturbed us. Apart from our thoughts – or mine anyway.

Somewhere near Bronzolo/Branzoll my phone rang.

Tynan said, 'Whatcha want me to do?'

'I don't know.'

'Newman. I can have them picked up. You say where.'

'No.'

'Don't be stupid.'

'Tynan. If you do and it goes wrong – I'll kill you.'

The blow landed.

'Okay.' He snapped off. He rang again immediately. 'What about – if I do it myself?'

My decision-taking process had changed. Changed with feeling responsible for another person. 'Can you get to Venice? There's a Heathrow flight at half-past ten. I know it well.'

'I'll stay for the opera.'

Pearl had fixed himself where he could peek through a chink of curtain. We were one carriage away. They were at the end of their carriage and we at the beginning of ours. The gap between the carriages was, I reckoned, our psychological defence.

'Hey, man,' gasped Pearl. 'They coming to us.'

The door swung open and two suits stood there.

'You.' They pointed to me.

Thought about resisting. Followed them. No choice. Is the train going fast? Pearl rose from his seat. One of them pushed him right on his shiny dome, back down in the seat. They left him alone.

Otto sat in the corner of the compartment. Beside him facing away from the door, stood the wheelchair with Claire. I stood in the doorway. Otto spun the chair around and I looked at her white face, half-conscious now.

'You may speak to your little Jew. Who is also our little Jew.'

'Claire.'

'No, do not move. She cannot speak.'

Her eyes have glazed. More of this and she won't be recognizable. An unhygienic smell filled the compartment.

'Why don't you have a woman looking after her?'

'The boys do it rather well. They enjoy it.'

I lunged, then realized I was held from behind. Otto smiled.

'Are you trying to repeat your heroics? Do you specialize in train fights? We owe you for that. And we owe your friend Pearl for – shall we say, other things.'

I was unable to think. But with enough sense left to say nothing. We thought we were shadowing them. They knew they were luring us. Story of my life. Claire's eyes lolled.

Otto spoke again, in that level voice like deadly gas. 'This is the situation. She will be ours until you return everything you find in the Saaaaft will. If you do not we will kill her. You know that.'

'Claire, can you hear me?'

No answer. I glared at Otto. 'Why haven't you killed me?'

'We need you. To fulfil our demands. You have control of Saaft's will.' I shivered again at the drawn-out 'a'.

Did she flicker? I hope so.

'Mr Newman. Go back to your compartment and to your friend, Pearl. Do not attempt to follow us. You may if you wish but it will get you nothing. You have heard my offer.'

'One question. If I hadn't followed you to Berlin?'

'We'd have come for you. As we did for her.' Otto indicated Claire, then nodded to his heavies.

Two pairs of unbelievably strong hands lifted me a little from the ground, turned me around and pushed me back along the corridor, opened the door and shoved me into the compartment. They slammed the door and went.

Pearl looked at me. I couldn't divine what he felt. Fear? Rage?

His voice shook. 'So they knew all along.'

I nodded.

'D'you think they set us up?'

'I think so. They softened me up. Attack after attack. Four months now. So that I would crumple.'

'Nicholas, this is for the police, man!'

Tynan's answering machine said he was 'travelling'. I calculated. His flight landed in Venice at two local time; our train got in at three. I hope the flight isn't delayed.

Pearl suddenly slammed his fist into the seats.

'Shit, man. I hate this.'

'So do I.'

'No, man. What I hate is being a fool. I thought we were fooling them.'

Suddenly a deep depression came over me. I counted the cost of the situation. Presumably they drugged Claire at Rye. Then, in a half-conscious state, they took her to Berlin. But would an airline let her on board? Yes, if one of the others posed as her doctor. It, too, happened a lot in the Cold War. But – her passport? She carried it in her handbag: I remembered from the Chunnel. I groaned.

'Black Pearl.'

'Yes, man.'

The sun lit the Tyrol and a train shattered past us in the opposite direction.

'We've left your lovely watch behind, haven't we? Will it be safe in your kit?'

He shifted. 'No, I lost it, man.'

'Oh, what a shame.'

Pearl stretched his legs. 'Not like you think, man.'

'Then how?'

Making myself articulate to keep at bay these dreadful apprehensions about Claire. Knew they might lead to an outburst of violence from me. Someone could die. I would have done macramé to keep those feelings subdued.

'It didn't fall off my wrist.'

I looked puzzled. He looked uncomfortable.

'Blackmail, man. Another player.'

'How much of this has been going on?'

'A lot, Nicholas. I must be paying already thousands. I pay chaps' gambling debts.' He played with the word 'chaps' like a toy.

'Are those people pressuring you?'

Pearl shrugged. 'Mostly, man. They have friends.'

'When this is over – we fix all that. Agreed?'

I put out my hand and he shook it. 'Agreed.'

But the thoughts coursed on.

Trento. It is mid-morning and snow lies on the ground at the high snowline. What am I to do? If I can be objective – nobody else in my milieu has ever been involved in such violence outside of war. Serravalle. Touch of Greek Orthodox in the church architecture.

We had a client whose managing director was kidnapped by the IRA and held to ransom. He came home safely – but his life was ruined. All my life has been constructed towards the avoidance of violence, of tragedy. I doze, then I wake.

'Black Pearl, how well did you know Antony?'

377

'Not now, man. I'll get upset.'

The train comes down from the mountains to reach the Adriatic coast. It crosses wide valleys where the roads run alongside the tracks and motorists fall behind, no matter how fast they drive. I dozed, knowing only a handful of stops remained between now and Venice: Verona, Vicenza, Padova, Mestre. Mestre is Venice's very own hell, every beautiful city has to have its Mestre, isn't that the central dogma of town planning . . . ?

At Verona Pearl became excited. He heard chanting and left the compartment. We had evolved a rule that if leaving we would always go in the direction opposite. Luckily for him, the restaurant car lay in the same direction. And the bar, and that is where the chanting crowds went. He followed them and came back.

'Verona is playing Venezia in *Serie A*.'

'But it's Monday.'

'We play Mondays too, sometime.'

'Did you learn much?'

'Only that they is a huge police force going to Venezia today.'

'Jesus, Pearl, did they recognize you?'

'Sort of, man, I told them I was Dino Pegatti, who played for Venezia two seasons ago and got injured.'

'Did they believe you?'

'They must done, they said *Venezia merda* and they kept saying it, it was fun. I told them we was going there, too.'

'Can we use them?' I had the wild thought of getting the fans to overwhelm the compartment and take Claire out. Pearl understood. He shook his head.

'Only two can get in there. They pick us off one at a time.'

The train rocked on, in the shadow of a malt-brown foothill higher than most British mountains.

'Pearl, you asked me once if I liked you.'

He laughed. 'Oh, man – did you squirm!'

'Ask me again.'

And now he squirmed and I didn't let him off the hook.

The scenario began to clarify. Otto's planning stunned me. Never made a move that didn't have a future. What is the next move and will I be able to gain from it?

59

In Belmont there is a lady richly left. Did Shakespeare come here? Portia's land. I played Jessica in the school play. I can see the tower in Padova, slim and Florentine – or Venetian, it matters not which since we have lost for ever the capacity to do that kind of work.

The colours have changed. There's no snow here, only sunlight and the echoes of summer's brown terrain and some vines and cottage gardens, not that the Italians call them cottages. I see goats and a tractor and the white tops of the Dolomites. I live in terror of the Dalmatian coast. Antony's words. A hundred and one Dalmatians. St George was a Dalmatian. Carpaccio. Wonderful St George and the Dragon in San Giorgio, where else? The architecture has changed completely. Soon we are running along beside the road, the pathway by which American armies got to Venice in both world wars, or so I seem to remember from Hemingway.

'We nearly there, man.'

'I know, Black Pearl.' And I think, I know you're going to ask me 'What do we do now?' and I will have to tell you I don't know.

'What do we do now?'

'I don't know.'

We had both been stunned by the knowledge that the murderous people two compartments away, whom we saw walking up and down, knew who we were and always had known.

Which was worse? The fact that they knew – when we

thought we were so clever? Or the fact that they breathed menace? Neither. Worst of all was the fact that they held Claire. I had another battle to keep her images out of my mind. Her long back, the way she lifted her hair.

The rolling stock in the sidings at Venezia Santa Lucia come alive with graffiti – except on the Swiss and German trains. Pearl calls me.

'Look at this, man.'

Down the corridor, Otto is talking to two football supporters who defer to him as to the Pope.

Pearl says, 'Nicholas, I am going into politics one day, to stop that crime in my beautiful game.'

'Black Pearl, I will come and run your campaign. I will pay for it.' And then I think, If I'm alive. If I have a profession, a practice. If I have any belief left.

I stand and face the door, and I realize that I am no longer afraid, I am neutral, I am numb and I feel genuinely that anything that happens now can have nothing to do with me. This has all gone so far beyond me I am helpless.

A long, smooth, ice-blue train draws up alongside us, the Alpine Express en route from Geneva to Trieste, and one day I will be on that train with –

No. I have to sit down again.

An obscenity hits my eye – they have draped Claire in the Verona colours and then I understand why; a large boat, called *Aquilae*, awaits by a rear dock at Santa Lucia, to transport all the fans. Claire is wheeled aboard. We lose ourselves in the throng. Otto doesn't even look around to see if we follow.

No Tynan. I had hoped for him at the station. I ring Tynan. Still the machine. I should be planning something – but what? The best I can hope for is, in Pearl's word, 'automatic'.

The *Aquilae* moves away and takes us out into the north of the lagoon, in the water between Venice and the airport.

In the distance I can see the leaning tower on Burano and the reassuring square campanile of Torcello. I look at Pearl. He has, I think, detached himself.

'We have a problem.'

'What, Nicholas?'

'We have no Italian money.'

Pearl shrugs. 'D'you think they gonna ask football supporters to pay for tickets?'

Now we are out in Canaletto territory and I can't remember where the stadium is in Venice. If nothing else, I can enjoy the view – because I know that in the next half-hour or so it might be that somebody will die. It might be Pearl or it might be Claire – or it might be me. I have no plan whatsoever, I, the most planned person I have ever known, I who know when I am going to shop for groceries ten days before I do it, I who can tell you where my next three years of holidays will be taken, venue by venue.

The boat swings us around to give us a view of – what is that? Murano? No – there is no Campari sign on Murano, it must be the Lido. Death in Venice, thank you, boatman, when I die there'll be a coin in my mouth to pay your fare.

Pearl stood beside me, watching everything. I knew this must have been his first freedom among fans since he became famous. If they knew he would be mobbed. I saw one or two look closely at him but his cap and scarf were so outrageous he got away with it. Now our destination appeared – the stadium; but it looked so small.

'Twenty thousand here,' said Pearl. 'We know all these things on account of what it's supposed to be like to play here. Players like it here, the crowd is far back from the pitch.'

The *Aquilae* docked and we waited, watching. They took Claire off slowly and she seemed to have awakened; her head was no longer supported by a pillow. Dozens of police stood

382

with guns trained on the crowd – which now included us. Pearl eyed them.

'No,' I said. 'I've thought of it.'

He shook his head and gritted his teeth. 'This is it, isn't it?'

'I reckon so.'

'Do it,' he said. 'Whatever it is.'

We all proceeded. According to the police, the crowd was to be divided two ways – those with tickets, and those without.

For us it split into three. Otto and his band slipped away and I watched them. They headed to another dock, where a boat waited, not much smaller than the *Aquilae*, but more powerful and slicker. It stood about a hundred metres away. To get there they had to get through difficult ground. Crowds pushed towards them. An unutterable sadness poured over me. Fear the Dalmatian coast.

Otto rearranged his group. Two hung back, two went in front. Otto pushed the wheelchair himself. Nobody would ever guess. I looked closer; Otto had his hand tight in Claire's hair. She must be conscious – and terrified. The hair I had stroked in the first loving I had ever known or accomplished.

'Tickets,' I said to Pearl. 'Help me.'

'Nicholas, what you doing?'

'Making it up as I go along, that's all I can do. Ask for three tickets with wheelchair access.'

We bought the tickets and I began to move very fast. They had fifty yards to their boat but on ever rougher ground. Pearl trotted behind me. When he had room on the path he came alongside.

'How good's your tackling?'

'A foul to tackle from behind,' but he looked scared.

It happened so fast. Almost all the fans had gone. The path curved around a tank and we were on them. The two ahead had reached the ship and were busy with the gangplank.

Nobody saw us. I was back in school, a rock in my hand. I think I broke his skull. Pearl took the other man's legs and I heard the soft splash as he hit the dock's deep mud. Otto spun and looked. He stood facing me and drew a knife. Two down, how many more to go? We didn't know what the boat held. The two gesture from the gangplank.

A pain spread across my chest. Claire had been given something anew. Her head was roaming, she was beginning to drift. Otto held the knife to her throat. His pair of thugs now stood beside him.

Otto said, 'You will stand back, please.'

His thugs, thinking the situation stalemate, began to help their companion from the canal; the man I hit rose groggily from the path. It was all so calm. A boat chugged to the dock. Nobody looked. From around the corner marched some uniformed police. Intent on the stadium, they never looked at us across the rough ground.

I flapped my hands by my sides like a useless duck.

'Drop the stone,' said Otto.

'Drop the knife,' said Tynan behind him.

He stood on the pathway, had come up out of the newly arrived boat. The uniformed, armed police simply did a fast right angle and trained their guns on everyone. Me included. And believe it or not, Claire. They came forward. Gun muzzle one foot from my right temple.

Everything and Time itself stood still. Claire moaned and her head fell. The sedation kicked in fully. Involuntarily, as her head fell towards the blade, Otto withdrew his knife. Tynan was at him, took the knife.

I ran forward and all but smothered Claire. They tried to haul me off her but Pearl stopped them. One of the policemen, in the farcical tempo of all such occasions, recognized Pearl and gave a little cheer. An animated exchange broke out and I hugged and hugged and hugged my frail and dearly beloved woman.

60

It is now Whit Monday and the sun is dancing on the waters of Rye harbour. I am sitting in the window of the Long Drawing Room putting the last touches to this long account of one year in the life of Nicholas Newman. Well, eight months, to be precise. Claire is reading the Sunday newspapers. She holds up the sports pages. The Black Pearl is the star of the show. The football season is over and he has been taken up by the Gay Rights movement and seems to be thriving. In a while I shall read and enjoy.

This morning I had to help Claire dress. I enjoyed it again – but, as I tell her, not as much as when I help her to undress. I say that every morning and she laughs every morning. Her coordination has not yet returned. The specialist says it will take about another four months and in a year or so she will be back to normal. She keeps saying she wants to make love but she can't until all her faculties have returned.

The drugs they used on her reacted badly. She was never meant to recover anyway. They intended to kill her. She told me that when they first abducted her she spent some time conscious until they increased her dosage. Otto made clear to her his pleasure that she was Jewish. Hitler's hatred, as she put it, had never died. My rage at this triggered my arrhythmia; I have to be a little careful for the time being.

It is at least good to understand that some of one's judgements are true. She said the most virulent anti-Semitism poured from Otto. In spirit as well as breeding he was the son of an officer who had been at Oradour.

The old man wasn't arrested. I advised against it. Now the

old man is in hospital with pneumonia. Reports filter back that even with sedation he finds it hard to sleep. It is thought he won't live long.

His son will never get out of jail. The German police co-operated. DNA from the Wilhelmstrasse apartment matched Antony's house. Extradition proceedings are under way. They will take a year – and more. Claire gave Scotland Yard, the French police – and Tynan – five hours of tapes. Then she asked to see them again and gave them another two. She had observed a great deal. Lemon's tears poured. They caught her Georgy in Berlin. Tynan told me all. Elizabeth and I have yet to speak. I have not returned to Bentley Newman – yet.

Last Sunday we went to Wiltshire for Pearl's housewarming. On the journey Claire and I talked – for the first time in detail – of the ending of it all. The will is being admitted to probate and I have informed the French authorities and those organizations who represent Jewish families deprived of their wealth during the war. Nobody knows the full figure yet because all the Safft properties have to be realized. There are twenty-nine of them, all worth many millions.

Next month we go back to Venice to say thank-you in person to Giacomo Ciorelli who opened the scaffolded doors of the Pregadi to us, and to thank the ambulancemen who were our taxi drivers. The Pregadi's rooms weren't all being refurbished. We stayed that dreadful night. We would have stayed the year if that was what it needed to bring Claire back to consciousness.

From Venice we flew privately at my expense to Heathrow, with Tynan clearing everything, emigration, immigration, customs. He left us briefly at Marco Polo airport and came back five minutes later with a bunch of tulips for Claire.

'Sainsbury's best,' he said. 'If they've got Sainsbury's here. I s'pose they haven't on account of the flooded streets.'

She was too drowsy, but on proper medication, to do more than smile.

'You, young man,' said Tynan to Pearl, 'have to report for training.'

Pearl, as he always did, just laughed.

The debriefing didn't happen for several days. I wouldn't put Claire into hospital; I wouldn't let her out of my sight; I've not done since then, not been back to the office. That battle has yet to be fought. It will be long and it will be bloody. If I still care.

I may not. She told me about all her past and I told her some of mine. The rest, she said, can unfold. She fought to recover like a prizefighter. Pearl looks as if he will go to Inter Milan after all.

But last Sunday we went to Wiltshire. We talked about Antony's will. I said how guilty I felt at having benefited from his investments and that I didn't know what to do, didn't know how much to give back. I left the A303 before we hit Stonehenge and cut across country.

Claire said nothing and I hoped I hadn't offended her. We passed some children on skateboards, slowed for some girls on ponies. Approaching Pearl's house from the south, we had an excellent view. The house looked glorious, even if I say so myself. I still find it extraordinary that our computer modelling can produce something that is so like the eventual product.

Several cars were parked outside, some with foreign registrations, all glitzy – Porsche, Jaguar, a Ferrari. Behind the house on the open sward a mini-fair had been set up and fit-looking young men in sharp casual wear shied coconuts, tried the rifle range. Three marquees teemed with people holding glasses and plates.

I said to Claire, 'This is costing a fortune.'

Pearl saw us and ran over. He hugged Claire and kissed her face again and again and then hugged me so hard he nearly knocked me over. I had never seen him so excited. His mother came up behind him; only at that moment did

387

I remember that I had never met Pearl's 'girlfriend' – what did he say she was called? 'Nicola,' I think. I may tease him about that soon.

Elma Pearl looked at me directly and said, 'Thank you for all you have done. I know about it.' Then she said softly, 'I was right about you. I was right to ask you for help.' I introduced her to Claire immediately.

Pearl led us indoors and even I gasped at how accurately we'd reproduced the house in Noordwijk. That journey came back to me vividly. The hall with its peaceful elm floor had golden light. I showed Claire the bathroom and she asked Pearl, 'May I have a bath? Now?' and everybody laughed.

All around, young people chattered and music played louder than noise. It felt incongruous yet delightful that these glitzy kids were wandering around a house that seemed to come from a painting of a Dutch interior – as, I suppose, it did.

Commotion at the door. A policeman appeared.

'A Mr Newman here?'

Pearl looked shocked. 'Oh, no, man, not again.'

I laughed, said, 'It's all right,' and went out, warning Pearl to stay indoors.

The gentleman I'd been expecting waited with his transport. I led him to the side of the house where no one was looking and opened the barn; the gentleman did his unloading, with a bit of coaxing.

From inside the barn I knocked hard on the top of the door. I had briefed Claire and she was waiting with Pearl. She made him open the barn door into the kitchen and the first thing he saw was the head of a large black and white cow looking him in the eye.

'Black Pearl,' I said. 'This is Sonja.'

Pearl laughed, as he always does. 'You remembered!'

At the end of the afternoon, Pearl and I stood chatting.

'Sometimes I find it hard to think it is all over,' he said.

'I've always meant to ask you, Johan. The money that came to you and your family from Antony. How d'you feel about it?'

Pearl looked at me, knowing full well that I meant, Are you going to repatriate it?

He said, 'I think about it. I didn't steal it, Nicholas. The war has to end some time. What are you going to do?'

I shrugged. 'I'm working it out. But I will certainly repatriate some of mine. It'll be hard to work out the exact figure.'

He said to me, 'I have a present for Claire. For those lovely hands.' I called her. She stood beside me, arm through mine. 'Come. I need that hand,' said Pearl.

He took a box from his pocket and, concealing it with his hand, slipped a ring on Claire's finger. He took her hand from him and looked at it – a ring with one perfect black pearl. She burst into tears, hugged me and Pearl and walked away.

We all said goodbye. We will all stay friends. I have 'adopted' football with the zeal of a convert, never miss a game on television. We will go to see Pearl play as often as possible, even when he goes to Italy.

In the car on the way home we talked about the day. Claire was still tiring easily. She held her ring up again and admired it. Then she put on a tense voice that I now can recognize.

'There is something you should know, Nicholas. Nobody knows this.'

I looked at her. She had on her strange, straight-ahead expression.

'You already know, because I've told you – I'm Jewish. Are you prepared for a great irony?'

I think I knew what was coming.

'This is the irony. The biggest losers in Antony's "interception" of those wartime bank accounts were my grandparents. It is all documented and provable. They died in the camps.

Only my mother survived. And, as I told you, I am an only child.'

All I could do was reach for her hand. I will go on doing so.